BULLETS AND OTHER HURTING THINGS

BOOKS BY RICK OLLERMAN

Non-Fiction

*Hardboiled, Noir and Gold Medals: Essays on
Crime Fiction Writers from the 50s through the 90s*

Fiction

Turnabout
Shallow Secrets
Truth Always Kills
Mad Dog Barked

As Editor

Blood Work
*Denim, Diamonds and Death:
2019 Bouchercon Anthology*
*Bullets and Other Hurting Things:
A Tribute to Bill Crider*

RICK OLLERMAN, EDITOR

BULLETS AND OTHER HURTING THINGS

A TRIBUTE TO BILL CRIDER

Down & Out Books
3959 Van Dyke Road, Suite 265
Lutz, FL 33558
DownAndOutBooks.com

Cover design by Zach McCain

ISBN: 1-64396-178-0
ISBN-13: 978-1-64396-178-1

TABLE OF CONTENTS

To Bill—
Wish you were here to read these stories yourself.
You are missed...

Editor's Note

Bill Crider was a wonderful writer and an even better human. His wit, knowledge and charm were only some of his attributes and when he passed away in 2018 he left a gap that will never be filled. His blog, also known as *Bill Crider's Pop Culture Magazine,* was filled with book reviews, news of his own writing, and numerous bits of reportage that let us know the latest happenings of various creatures such as alligators, wealthy socialites and the residents of a certain southern state. I invited the contributors here to write about small-town crime, hard-boiled PIs, or really just anything they thought Bill might have gotten a kick out of. Some of the biggest names in crime fiction responded and here is the result. If you're a fan of Bill's work you'll see connections in some of the stories, and if you haven't sampled any of Bill's many novels and stories, what's stopping you? Sheriff Rhodes is waiting down there in Blacklin County, Sally Good is hanging out in the English department of Hughes Community College, and PI Truman Smith is prowling the streets of Galveston...

Introduction:
Bill Crider, Man of Mystery

Angela Crider Neary

When Rick Ollerman asked me to write this introduction, suggesting that I might include anecdotes about my father, Bill Crider, his writing career, and a personality that was enamored of both gritty crime noir and the antics of socialite Paris Hilton, I was honored and excited yet perplexed at the same time. Why perplexed? Because Bill Crider was a man of mystery. Not just in the sense that he was the author of dozens and dozens of mystery novels and short stories, but by virtue of the fact that he was often a quiet and private person—even around his own family.

So, even though I'm his daughter, I'll confess that I know less about him than I wish I did. As he was coming into his own as a writer and expert in the area of crime and mystery fiction, he didn't share a lot of insights into who he was with me. I was the kid and he was the dad, a dynamic that hung on even into my adulthood. I find out something new about him every time I read an article or a work of fiction he wrote. A lot of us take for granted so many things about our loved ones while they are alive only to find ourselves piecing together the memories of who they were when they are no longer with us.

Dad wrote of himself that he was socially awkward and the

very picture of an introvert. You might not believe this if you knew him through mystery or sci-fi conventions or the many writing forums he participated in online (or in print before the internet—think DAPA-Em, the first and only amateur press association devoted to crime and mystery fiction), but I'll get to that later. He once told me that he was much more comfortable speaking in front of a large audience than being in an intimate setting with a few people he didn't know well. Invariably I had to warn boyfriends who met him, "He's very quiet. Don't take it personally," while on the other hand, pleading with him to be friendly to these poor guys. Maybe that's a bad example since he may have tactically assumed an intimidating posture around his daughter's romantic interests.

He said in the Acknowledgements for his last Sheriff Dan Rhodes book that his daughter and son "had to put up with a father who often sat behind closed doors in the evening instead of watching TV or playing board games with the family. They never complained. Maybe they were just glad to get rid of me for a while, but I like to think they understood what I was doing and forgave my absence."

I don't know if his recollection was completely accurate. I'm sure we complained. He did spend a lot of time in his office, surrounded by his comforting and overflowing shelves of books and writing about the characters who'd become our friends. But he also managed to spend time with his family, for whom he would have done anything, and do the things he enjoyed. Although I'm missing some of the pieces in the Bill Crider puzzle, I'll tell you some of my favorite remembrances of him.

He did watch TV with his family—my mother Judy, my brother Allen, and me. *Wonder Woman* was a favorite. His lecherous "Ohhhhhh yeah!" every time Lynda Carter did a spin that converted her into a super hero always had us in stitches. We were exposed at an early age to Doc Savage and the campy neon green wigglies in *Doc Savage: The Man of Bronze*. We never missed the yearly broadcast of *The Wizard of Oz*. We piled onto the couch together to watch the Mary Tyler Moore and Bob Newhart shows. Dad got a kick out of Larry, his brother Darryl, and his other brother Darryl in the later Newhart show.

He played games with his family and friends. I particularly remember many a game of Triominos and Scrabble—he never lost a round of Scrabble. I still have a score card demonstrating how soundly he thrashed us all. He and my mother played dominoes with my grandparents around a small table in their kitchen. They belonged to a bridge club in Brownwood, Texas, made up of their close friends, many of whom taught with Dad at Howard Payne University.

It's no secret that Dad loved music. He was an amateur musician, himself. Over the years, he was a member of a folk music group (The Fabulous G-Strings) and a barbershop chorus (The Next Edition). You can find his charming renditions of "The Banana Boat Song" and "Darkness on the Delta," among others, on YouTube.

If I had to pick one, I'd say the Kingston Trio was his favorite band. He was invited backstage at a Kingston Trio concert where he gave each of the band members a copy of his book that he had dedicated to them. Some of my favorite memories of him when I was growing up are of him sitting on the floor playing the guitar and singing "La Bamba" or "What Shall We Do with a Drunken Sailor," not to mention original compositions like "Angela Crider's Got Sand in Her Shoes," or "Allen Crider's Got Sand in His Shoes," depending on who had been playing in the dirt that day and was complaining about it.

When my brother and I had saved up enough of our allow-ance money (it probably took months since I can't imagine that we got more than fifty cents a week) Dad took us to the local record store. He recommended my first ABBA album to me, and encouraged me to buy the Beatles version of the *Sgt. Pepper's Lonely Hearts Club Band* album rather than the 1978 movie soundtrack. I figured out later that he was so keen on the ABBA album because he wanted to listen to it himself, and of course I now understand why the Beatles were the better choice.

But it wasn't all hearts and rainbows—he could get grumpy. He once ironically dubbed himself "Mr. Jolly" and posted a sign on his office door that read "Mr. Jolly—Fun follows me around," after an old David Letterman bit.

Dad was a lifetime cat aficionado, like his father before him. We always had cats growing up—strays that would show up at the house and choose to stick around. One of Dad's dearest was Speedo, named for the Cadillacs song (or lead singer, it was never clear). Speedo became an animal character in Dad's Sheriff Rhodes series, reincarnated there as a border collie. Just when he thought he had reached the end of his cat wrangling days, Dad rescued three tiny kittens from a ditch in 2016. They became famous on his social media as the VBKs (Very Bad Kitties). He named them Keanu, Gilligan and Ginger, after the pop culture figures. Many speculated that they had been sent by my mother to keep Dad company after her death.

Not one to shun technology (before cell phones, he and his friends had CB radios where they used 'handles' to communicate—his was "The White Rabbit" after his white Pontiac), Dad started a blog on his sixty-first birthday. He was a month away from retirement, and I think he started the blog in anticipation of needing something to keep him occupied (more than he was already). But it became so much more—a place where mystery and pop culture fandom communicated every day, sharing their fascination with the subjects. He initially used the blog as a diary where you can find scintillating tidbits about his daily runs, his lawn mowing adventures, and going out for TexMex.

Eventually, the blog morphed into Bill Crider's Pop Culture Magazine, addressing issues of global concern, such as the media's persecution of Paris Hilton, gator and croc updates, and items demonstrating how Texas Leads the Way, be it through scientific breakthroughs or less commendable acts like instituting a "pole tax" on strip clubs. Dad always had an interest in pop culture. For a mild-mannered guy, he was drawn to things that were unusual or absurd. A hint of where the blog was headed came in one of his early diary posts where he discussed what he thought of Anna Nicole Smith's reality show—spoiler alert, he didn't like it but he had a soft spot for Smith. She was from the same small town as Dad, Mexia, Texas, where Dad's brother taught her in high school and she once worked at the Jim's Krispy Fried Chicken. (Smith was also persecuted, to hear Dad tell it.)

The blog also included a plethora of other things like book and movie reviews, a song of the day, stories about my father's and mother's travels, experiences at book conventions and festivals, and more. Something for everyone. He kept up the blog with daily posts until his death at age seventy-six.

And of course, there's his writing. Dad wrote over one hundred books and short stories, including mysteries, westerns, sci-fi, horror, and children's books. Some of his first children's stories were never published but were told to me and my brother to keep us entertained on long road trips. These involved the adventures of Reddy Fox and Cubby Bear, who played among the hay bales we would see in the fields from the highway.

Then there were the cons—AggieCon Science Fiction Convention, ArmadilloCon Science Fiction Convention, and Bouchercon World Mystery Convention, to name a few—physical places where the blogosphere and writing coalesced—venues where he could mix and mingle with fellow bloggers, writers, friends and fans. Dad came alive at these events. My mother, his constant companion, described the book-conference Bill Crider as a person transformed, an extrovert who stayed up into the wee hours of the morning, holding court with some of his favorite people about books and writing. If you knew him through book conventions, you experienced the finest and most contented side of him, when he was in his element and his most true self.

Dad would sometimes take the family along when he attended and I was able to soak in the excitement in the atmosphere and the camaraderie of the participants. I was fortunate to attend

Dad's last three Bouchercons with him. It was heartwarming to be introduced to Dad's lifelong friends and witness the love and admiration they shared.

In writing this, I realize and appreciate the memories I have to cherish. But to me, Bill Crider was still inscrutable in a lot of ways. There were clues to his personality that he kept to himself, or imparted only to others with whom he shared a specific interest or bond—like the contributors to this anthology. I never found out much about his creative processes, his tricks of the trade. If I asked, he was vague, as if it all somehow came naturally. And perhaps it did—if you love something so much, it seems to come with ease even if it involves a lot of hard work. He encouraged me in my own writing, always willing to assist with editing in his generous hands-off approach. I'm grateful for all that he did share with me, and that he left a part of himself in his writing through which I can walk into his office any time and continue to unravel the mystery of who he was.

Rick told me his intent with this anthology was to organize a collection that would put a solid smile on my dad's face. He's more than accomplished this goal, assembling stories in Dad's most-loved genre by some of his esteemed and adored friends and colleagues. A perfect tribute, this compilation would have put a smile on Dad's face and in his heart as well. I can see him now, sitting in his recliner, a cat (or three) sprawled in his lap, shaking his head and saying in his humble manner, "I'm not deserving of this." But, of course, he is. You have a criminally entertaining time in store for you in the pages of this anthology.

Award-winning and bestselling author Kent Krueger is never afraid to stretch his writing and surprise us with his genuine inventiveness and skill. With this story he takes us along with Nick and Pet as they search for...something. With "Innocence" Kent tugs at all the right strings and hits all the right notes. Then, in the end, he pulls a few more...

Innocence

William Kent Krueger

"Do you like it, Pet?" Nick asked.

His daughter looked around the room and, with the dirty finger of a four-year-old, probed her right nostril. "Where are we?"

"Minnesota. Do you like it?"

"I'm hungry."

"So am I. I got us a room with a kitchenette, see? I could cook us something."

"I want a hamburger and a milkshake."

Nick stroked his chin and considered. "I saw a diner down the road. It looked like just the place for a good hamburger and milkshake. Let me get the suitcases in first, okay?"

Nick went outside, lifted the back door of his station wagon, and stood for a moment looking at the lake on the other side of the highway. The sun was going down and the water was like mercury, vast and silver. Pet came out and stood with him.

"How long are we going to stay, Daddy?"

"That depends."

"I want to go home," she said.

Nick looked away from her at the lake.

"Can we go back to Aunt Ida's then?"

"You liked her?" Nick said.

Pet shrugged. "She had a swimming pool."

"I don't know, Pet. We'll see."

"That's what you always say."

He looked at the silver lake, where a boat moved lazily, black ripples in its wake.

"Maybe we could fish tomorrow. Would you like to fish, Pet?"

"I don't know." She scratched at a mosquito bite on her leg.

Nick took the suitcases inside. Pet sat in a white metal rocker under an oak tree in the middle of the courtyard and held Buster, her rag doll clown, in her arms. She was singing to him when Nick came back out.

"Let's go eat, Pet."

"Buster's hungry, too."

"Then Buster can eat with us, how's that? He can eat anything he wants."

"He wants a hamburger and a milkshake."

"Then a hamburger and a milkshake he shall have."

They arrived during the dinner rush. The place was busy. Even so, Nick found a small table for two next to a front window. They could see the lake from there. The color of the water had changed, amber now, like the sky, and there were more boats, moving as majestic as swans. It all looked so peaceful, like the most peaceful thing imaginable.

Nick said, "I always wanted to fish."

Pet said, "Buster wants a chocolate milkshake."

"Then Buster will get a chocolate milkshake."

The waitress came, a pretty woman, tall, with honey-colored hair piled up in a way that made her taller. Her face was flushed. She seemed out of breath but was smiling. Nick liked the way she smiled.

"Sorry about the wait. It's always busy like this on Fridays. Are you here for the fish fry?"

Nick looked at his menu. "I think we'd both like a hamburger and milkshake. Chocolate."

"Don't forget french fries," Pet said.

"And french fries," Nick said.

"Don't forget Buster," Pet said.

"I'm not really very hungry. How 'bout if Buster shares mine?"

The waitress smiled at Pet. "Your doll's name is Buster?"

"Yes," Pet said.

"I have a doll named Bonnie," the waitress said. "She sleeps with me every night."

"Buster sleeps with me," Pet said.

"Everything but onions on the burgers," Nick said.

"You want the California burger, then."

"The what?"

"A burger with the works we call a California burger. See, there it is on your menu." She leaned over his arm and pointed with her pencil. She was wearing a nice perfume.

"Okay. Two California burgers, no onions. And could you bring us some water when you have a chance?"

"Sure. Water for Buster?" she asked Pet.

"No, thank you. It makes him wet the bed," Pet replied.

The waitress didn't laugh. She said seriously, "That could be a problem. No water for Buster, then. Be right back."

Nick leaned on his elbows and stared out the window. He imagined what it would be like fishing on the lake for a living. Catching fish for the fish fry every Friday night at the diner. He thought it would be a nice quiet way to live, give a man lots of time to think, to put things together. A good life for Pet, too. She would come with him on the boat. They would sit all day in their boat out in the middle of the lake, just the two of them, gathering fish for the fish fry.

"I have to go potty," Pet said.

"Okay." Nick stood up just as the waitress came back with water. "Could you tell us where the little girl's room is?"

She looked down at Pet. "You have to go, honey?"

"Uh-huh." Pet nodded.

"Here, I'll take you, sweetheart." She glanced at Nick. "Mind?"

Nick smiled. "Thanks a lot."

"No problem. You come with Jessie, honey." She took Pet's hand and led her across the room.

Nick watched them go. He thought Jessie had nice legs. He sat down and looked out at the lake some more. When they came back, Pet seemed happy. "They have clean bathrooms."

Nick smiled at Jessie. "They say you can always tell a good place by the restrooms."

Jessie smiled back. "I'd say the food comes in there somewhere."

"Jessie!" someone shouted from the kitchen.

"Gotta run." She moved off quickly.

"She's nice," Pet said.

"Yes," Nick agreed. "She certainly is."

By the time Nick and Pet finished eating, the dinner rush was over. The lake was dark. The boats had come in. Jessie returned to clear the dishes.

"Can I get you anything else?"

"No, thanks. We're stuffed. Say, Jessie, do you know of a place that rents boats and fishing gear? Pet and I might try our luck on the lake tomorrow."

"Sure. Lots of places. What do you want to catch?"

"Are there trout in that lake?"

Jessie gave her head a hopeless shake. "You don't fish much, do you? That lake's the kind for pan fish. Sunnies, bluegill, crappies. Or bass. Some pretty good bass. All good eating, but no trout." She looked at Pet. "You ever fish, honey?"

"No."

"It's lots of fun."

"You fish?" Nick asked.

"I used to all the time. I don't much anymore."

Nick looked at Pet, then back at Jessie. "I don't suppose you'd consider going fishing with us tomorrow. Be nice if we had someone along who knew what they were doing."

Jessie scratched her cheek with the eraser end of her pencil. "Are you staying in town?"

"We've got a room at the Northview Motor Court. We're staying a few days."

"Vacation?"

"No. Hard to explain."

"Just the two of you?" She looked down at little Pet. "You want me to come fishing with you, honey?"

Pet said, "Yes, please."

Jessie stuck out her hand. "I'm Jessica McDonald."

"Nicholas Lynch," Nick said taking her hand. "Most folks call me Nick. And this is Petula. Pet to her friends and family."

She shook Pet's hand.

Pet said, "And Buster."

Jessie shook Buster's rag-doll hand.

"How old are you, honey?" Jessie asked.

Pet held up five fingers, then crooked her index finger in half.

"Four and a half? I think that's a perfect age to start fishing."

"What time's good for tomorrow?" Nick asked.

"I work breakfast and lunch, so I'm not off till two. What if I came around five? We can rent a boat and head out for an hour or so before sunset. Fish should be biting about then."

"Great." Nick looked at her eyes, shiny and blue. They made him think of a satin nightgown. "And thanks. Pet likes to have someone female to talk to. You know."

"Sure, I understand."

"We're in number twelve at the motor court. See you tomorrow."

"I'm looking forward to it." She smiled at Pet.

In the car, Nick said, "A nice lady, don't you think?"

"Yes." Pet leaned against him and yawned. "I'm sleepy, Daddy."

"Me, too, Pet. It's been a long day."

In the room, they brushed their teeth, then Nick read

"Rapunzel" from a big book of illustrated fairy tales he'd checked out from the library in Rapid City and had never returned. She was asleep before he finished. He stepped outside. Moths and other summer bugs buzzed and fluttered about the yellow light above the door. He looked at the cars parked around the courtyard, checked the license plates. Minnesota mostly, but a couple from Iowa, one of them a brand new '65 Thunderbird convertible Nick would have loved to own. But it was way too conspicuous. His Rambler station wagon was dull as dirt but just fine for Pet and him. He crossed the road, stood at the edge of the lake looking out over the black water. Tomorrow he'd see what was biting.

She met them at the motor court. She'd let her hair down and was dressed in shorts and a blue work shirt. She'd tied the shirttail in front in a way that showed her flat belly and her belly button. She wore makeup and the perfume Nick had noticed the night before. Her nails were polished a bright red. She had on open-toed sandals and Nick saw that she'd painted her toenails, too. She brought three poles when she came. She said she'd borrowed a friend's boat, which was tied up to a dock at the marina in town. Nick drove.

On the lake, Jessie sat at the back of the small boat, handling the outboard, guiding them across the water. She let Pet help her. Nick took the bow, peering over the edge at the water sliding past. The sun was low in the sky, and the light glanced off the lake into his eyes and made him squint. Whenever he looked back, he caught Jessie smiling at Pet. To Nick, it seemed like they went a long way, which was fine. He liked the feel of the boat gliding along so easily. After a while, he sat with his back to the bow, watching the wind blow Jessie's gold hair. She watched him, too. Pet let her hand dangle in the water.

They stopped in a small inlet where reeds grew near the bank. Jessie put a worm on Pet's hook and cast the line.

"Watch the bobber, Pet honey. Soon as you see it start to jiggle, you know a fish is nibbling. Let him nibble a little, that's okay. I'll help you set the hook in him." She turned to Nick. "Need any help?"

"I can handle my own worm, thanks."

She grinned and shrugged. "Suit yourself."

The afternoon was still and warm. They were the only boat in the little inlet. Nick thought about how it would be to do this every day. To get away from everything. To let it all go, like dropping a big anchor into deep water and watching it sink out of sight. He looked at Jessie. She was studying Pet with those eyes like blue satin.

After a while, Jessie said, "Your plates say Utah. That where you're coming from?"

"Not directly," Nick said. "Been on the road a while now."

"My bobber's jumping," Pet squealed.

Jessie swung around, but the bobber was still. "He'll be back, Pet. Just you wait."

"What about you?" Nick asked. "You a native here?"

"Lived in Indigo Lake all my life."

"Seems like a nice, quiet place."

"Quiet's the key word. Not much goes on here. Next week, kids in Minnesota have to be back in school. All the tourists'll vanish. Then there's just the waiting for the snow to come. It's like that every year."

"I've heard about Minnesota winters," Nick said. "Sounds like something to avoid."

"Your bobber's moving," she said.

Nick laughed. "I'll try to control myself."

They ended up with ten good-sized crappies, which Jessie threaded through their gills onto a stringer she'd hung over the boat in the water. Pet caught one of the fish. Nick caught one. Jessie caught the rest.

The sun was setting when Jessie said, "Whyn't we take these back to my place and cook 'em up?"

Nick said, "We couldn't intrude."

"Mostly my fish. And I can't eat them all alone. What do you say, Pet? Want to see my house?"

Pet said, "I want a hot dog."

"Don't you want to eat the fish we caught?" Nick asked.

"I don't like fish. I like hot dogs."

"That's okay, Pet," Jessie said. "Hot dogs I've got."

The house, old but beautifully kept, sat on a huge corner lot. It had a couple of fat cupolas, a long front porch with a swing, a widow's walk, and lots of gingerbread lattice. A white picket fence enclosed it all and made it look safe. Nick pulled around to the garage in back, a building that had once been a carriage house.

"This place is yours?" Nick said.

"I inherited it when my folks died. It's too big for me. I know I should sell it, get something smaller. But I can't quite bring myself to do it."

"Do you have a television?" Pet asked.

"I sure do, honey."

"Aunt Ida had a swimming pool."

"Aunt Ida?"

"Family," Nick said.

"Sorry, Pet. No pool, but a very nice television. Come on."

In the kitchen, Jessie offered Nick a can of Grain Belt beer.

"I don't drink," he told her.

She smiled. "I kind of like that in a man."

She opened two cans of Pepsi instead and set to work preparing the fish on a cutting board. In the living room, Pet sat on the sofa. The television was tuned to a summer rerun of *Flipper*, but mostly Pet was playing with Bonnie, the doll that Jessie had brought down from her bedroom.

"Know how to peel potatoes?" Jessie asked.

"I can handle that."

"Drop the peels in here." She bent to lift the lid from the kitchen garbage can, and Nick had a pretty good look down the top of her loose shirt at her breasts. She wore no bra.

"How many?" he asked.

"One apiece should be plenty. Potato peeler's in there." She bumped her hip lightly against the drawer next to the sink.

Nick stood beside her, peeling while she worked on the fish.

"Mind if I ask you a question?" she said.

"Go ahead."

"Where's Pet's mother?"

"Dead."

"Oh, Nick. I'm sorry."

"Two years ago." Nick slowed in his peeling. "Rachel woke up with a headache in the middle of the night. I gave her aspirin. In the morning she could barely stand up the pain was so bad. I took her to the hospital. She was dead before the afternoon was out. Aneurysm, they said. They said there was nothing they could do." Nick watched the peelings drop into the trash.

"I'm so sorry."

"It's not so bad most times. But sometimes in the middle of the night I wake up and realize how empty everything is and it's like my heart's gone and Pet's the only thing keeping me alive."

Jessie set her knife down and put her arms around Nick. The fish smell was on her hands, but the perfume at the nape of her neck blotted it out nicely.

"The worst part is that I haven't told Pet."

She was sleeping, curled on the sofa, her arms cradling Bonnie. The television was on, turned low, a late-night news show broadcast out of Fargo. A weather map showed clouds swirling through Montana. Nick and Jessie sat on the floor next to each other.

"I just couldn't bring myself to do it. Everything was so hard then. I was pretty shook. Not thinking straight. When I left Rachel there, dead on that hospital bed, I left for good. I gathered Pet up from the neighbors, went back to the trailer, collected what clothes would fit in a suitcase and left. Everything. My job, the trailer home, the furniture, everything. I told Pet her mother was lost and we had to find her. We drove away from Salt Lake City and we've been on the go ever since."

"Oh, Nick." Jessie laid her head on his shoulder. "It sounds awful."

"Pet used to ask when we were going to find her mommy. She doesn't ask anymore."

"What are you going to do?"

"I don't know. Something soon. She starts school next year. I'd like to be settled somewhere then." Nick took a swallow of his Pepsi and studied Pet on the sofa. "Will you look at her? So innocent. I should have told her, but God as my witness, I just couldn't. Christ, I'd do anything if I could keep her this innocent forever. I'd tell her any lie." He checked the small brass clock on top of the television. "Late. I gotta get Pet back to the motor court and into bed. Thanks, Jessie. You've been great to talk to."

"I just listened."

"Been a long time since I had someone to do even that." He kissed her forehead. "I better go."

He gathered Pet into his arms.

Jessie smoothed Pet's hair. "I have to go with you, remember? My car's parked at the motor court."

"Good. You can open doors for me."

Pet slept laid out across the back seat. The night was warm, the town quiet, the sky full of stars. The lake was a huge black emptiness at their side.

"Jessie, are you involved with anyone?" Nick said. "I mean, you know."

"In a town like Indigo Lake, all the good men go early. The rest aren't worth the time you'd waste." She turned her head and stared out at the night. "I was married once. Down in Saint Paul. Didn't last long. I came back when my folks died. I figured I'd just grow old here, like them, and die. God, that sounds so hopeless, doesn't it? I didn't think of it that way then. After the hell of my marriage, it sounded pretty good."

"There must be someone here."

"Nick, there's no one. Believe me, I ought to know."

Only half a dozen cars were in the gravel lot of the motor court. Nick saw that they were all the same ones that had been there before. Jessie's car was parked out of the light under the boughs of the big oak in the center of the courtyard. Jessie took the room key from Nick, opened the door, switched a lamp on low, and turned back the covers. Nick carried Pet in from the car.

"Help me get her undressed," he said.

They pulled off her shorts and T-shirt, which smelled of fish. They left her in her underwear and slipped her under the covers. She barely opened her eyes through it all. Nick got Buster from the chair where she'd left him and put the clown doll into her arms. He walked Jessie to the door.

"You've been great. Thanks for everything."

She stood looking at him, then she kissed him. They kissed a while, their hands pushing at one another's clothing.

"No," Nick whispered. "Pet."

"Come on."

Jessie took his hand. They stepped outside, walked to where her car was parked under the shadowy oak. They got in the back seat.

"Jesus, it feels like it's been forever," Nick said.

Jessie laid herself down on top of him. "For me, too."

"I think you have to tell her," Jessie said.

They lay in the bed she'd told him was her parents', a big four-post affair of dark, heavy wood. It was in good shape. The springs made almost no noise at all. Pet was asleep in Jessie's bedroom, with Buster and Bonnie on either side of her. Nick had put her down, had read "The Twelve Dancing Princesses" from the fairy tale book, and had stayed with her until she went to sleep.

"I know," he said. "I've gone over it a hundred times in my mind. It tears me up every time."

"Would you like me to help?" she asked.

"No!" He sat up. "No."

"I'm sorry. I shouldn't interfere."

"It's not that. It's just—shoot, Jessie, life's too hard. I'd give anything to keep her from having to find out how the world really is. I know that's not healthy. But I think about the terrible things that can happen in life and all I want to do is keep her four years old forever."

"Nick, you're so sweet. I don't think I've ever known a sweeter guy." She sat up, too, and kissed his shoulder.

"There's something else, Jessie."

"What?"

"Our time's almost up at the motor court."

"What then?"

"I don't know. I honestly don't know. I didn't plan on staying in Indigo Lake this long."

"Why not?"

"It was just supposed to be a stopover, a place to get some rest and give me a chance to think where next."

"Why does there have to be a next, Nick? Why can't you just stay here? You said yourself Pet's got to be in school pretty soon."

"I've been thinking about the Twin Cities. I've been thinking it would be a good place to get a job. I don't have much money left and I need a place where there are lots of jobs."

"There are jobs here. What kind of work?"

"I'll do anything. I live for Pet now. All I want is what's best for her."

"You can't do everything for her, Nick. You can't be everything."

"I've done okay up to now."

"It's been tough on you. And Pet could use someone else sometimes."

Nick rubbed his face with his hands. "It's so hard to know

what to do. Once you start running, Christ, you can't figure where to stop."

"You could stop here for a while. See how things go. You wouldn't have to stay forever necessarily. I could help make it a good place."

Nick turned to her, drew her down, laid himself out against her with his head on her breast. "You already have."

They picnicked in the town park on a point that jutted into the lake. They pushed Pet on the swings, on the merry-go-round, chased her up and down the slide. There were other people with children. Jessie waved to some of them and called them by name.

"This is Truman Park," Jessie told Nick.

"Named after Harry S.?"

"Oscar. He was mayor here forever."

They sat on a tablecloth in the grass. Nick flicked away a big black ant that was crawling toward his paper plate. "We should fish again," he said.

"It was fun, wasn't it? Did you like fishing, Pet?"

Pet was busy with Bonnie and Buster, feeding them with a plastic spoon. She looked up. "No, Aunt Jessie."

"No?" Nick and Jessie said together.

"Why not, honey?" Jessie asked.

"The fish got killed."

Jessie looked at Nick. Nick looked up at the sky.

"Clouds rolling in," he said. "Looks like rain."

A wind came up that lifted the edges of the plates. The lake turned choppy. As soon as the clouds overtook the sun, the water became gray and cold looking. The other people in the park began to pack up their things.

"Time to call it," Nick said.

"Can we go back to Aunt Jessie's?" Pet asked.

"Sure, honey," Jessie said. "Okay, Nick?"

"Sure."

"I want to play with the dollhouse."

Jessie had taken down an old dollhouse from the attic. She'd said it was hers when she was a girl. Nick had bought two Barbie dolls to go with it. Jessie had bought some clothes.

"I picked up pork chops from the market last night," Jessie said. "Want to help me with dinner?"

Nick said, "I'd help you with anything."

They put the picnic things in the back of Nick's station wagon. It started to rain, big drops that felt cool and refreshing in the summer heat. Nick and Jessie jumped in the car, but Pet stayed out a moment, dancing in the downpour.

"Will you look at her?" Nick beamed. "God, she's beautiful."

"You like women in the rain?" Jessie opened her door and leapt out. She chased Pet around, both of them drenched and laughing. Finally, they came back to the car.

"That was fun," Pet said from the back seat.

"You'll need a bath," Nick said.

"Will I need bath?" Jessie asked. "And will you wash me, Daddy?"

She wore a thin, yellow blouse. The wet material clung to her, and her braless breasts were faintly visible beneath.

Nick said, "You might be due for a spanking."

"Sounds kinky." She smiled wickedly.

The rain came down so fast and heavy the wipers barely kept the windshield clear. Nick drove slowly through town, down the main street. As he approached the only traffic light in Indigo Lake, he swung the car hard into an alley, turning so quickly that Pet and Jessie were thrown against their doors.

"Nick, what are you doing?"

Nick sped up the alley, fishtailed onto the wet pavement of the next street, made another turn toward the edge of town, and drove a short distance. When he finally pulled over to the curb, his fingers were tight and bloodless on the steering wheel.

"For Christ sake, Nick, what was all that about?"

Nick looked back at Pet, then through the rear window at

the street behind them.

"Nothing," he said. "It was nothing." He drove slowly to Jessie's house. "Mind if I park in the garage?"

Jessie opened the door of the old carriage house and Nick pulled in. Without a word, they gathered the picnic things and made a dash for the house.

Jessie ran a bath for Pet and put her in with a bar of Ivory soap that floated. Pet played with it as if it were a boat. Nick followed Jessie to her bedroom and watched as she pulled off her wet things and put on dry clothes.

"Are you going to tell me what was going on?" she said.

Nick walked to the window and placed a hand against the pane. On the other side, the rain flowed down the glass like a river.

"What do the neighbors say when Pet and I stay all night?" he asked.

"I don't care about the neighbors."

"You should, Jessie. They're good people. They have only your best interests at heart. I talked with Mrs. Olson next door yesterday. She likes Pet."

"Nick—"

"I also went to the school district office yesterday. I applied for a job as a janitor. I think I have a good chance."

"Nick, that's wonderful. But I don't see—"

"I lied to you."

"About what?"

"Something important." He turned, sat on the window sill, and looked at her. "I didn't just up and leave Salt Lake City. Well, I did, but not right after Rachel died. I stayed for a while."

"Go on."

"See, Rachel's parents are wealthy. Rich Mormons. They didn't approve when Rachel married me. Cut her off from the family money. That was fine. We didn't care. We made enough with my job. Christ, we were happy." Nick laid his head back against the pane. "I loved her so much."

"Oh, Nick." She came and sat beside him on the sill.

"I fell apart after she died. For a while, I fell apart completely. I started drinking. I lost my job. I stayed in the trailer with Pet all day. Everything was a mess. I know it. I knew it then. I just couldn't bring myself to do anything. That's when Rachel's parents stepped in. They used their money on good lawyers. They wanted to take Pet away from me. They claimed I was unfit. And they were right. I was unfit. But when I saw how things were going, what was going to happen, I pulled myself together. Only it was too late. Those lawyers were too good. I could see I was going to lose Pet. So I left. Grabbed Pet and just up and left."

"Nick, you're so good with her."

"It doesn't matter. The court had awarded them custody. If they ever find us, Pet has to go back with them. I'd die if that happened, Jessie. God, I know I'd just die."

"How could they find you?"

"They have money. They hired someone. I don't know who. I just know he drives a black Cadillac. He was in Billings. That's where I took Pet first. I don't know how he found us. One of the neighbors in the trailer park tipped me off, said he came asking questions, said he was driving a black Cadillac, Utah plates. We left without even getting our clothes. Then in Rapid City he caught up with us again. I saw the Cadillac parked outside the apartment building. The guy inside it had a little moustache, wore black driving gloves. I watched him through the blinds for an hour. For an hour, he just sat there staring at our building. I don't know what he was waiting for. Maybe the cops. Maybe he'd tipped off Rachel's folks and they were coming. I don't know. I took Pet out the back way. We were on the run when I stopped in Indigo Lake."

"Maybe it's not what you think, Nick. Maybe—"

"Maybe what?"

"You don't know for sure it was the same car or the same man. Maybe it was just some terrible coincidence."

"Coincidence? Would you take the chance?" He balled his fist, hit the window sill lightly. "Look, I saw a black Cadillac stopped at the light this afternoon. I panicked."

"Nicky." She came and put her arms around him and held him. "I'm sure no one could find you here. You don't have to be afraid."

"I have to be afraid everywhere. Jessie, I have nightmares about them breaking down the door, taking Pet away and I can't stop them."

"It's okay, Nick." She rocked him. "It's okay."

"Daddy! Aunt Jessie!" Pet cried.

Nick said, "Pet doesn't know any of this. I don't want her to know."

"I won't say a word, Nick. And, Nick honey, we'll figure out something together, okay?"

Nick held her tightly. "I wish I could believe you," he said. "I wish to God I didn't know the things I do."

He felt her leave him and he opened his eyes. The storm was over, the room full of moonlight. The window was open to a breeze coming out of the Dakotas, fresh and clean.

"Where'd you go?" he asked when she slipped back into bed.

"To look at Pet. I do sometimes at night. She looks so peaceful. You know what it makes me think of?"

"What?"

"The way my parents probably looked at me in that bed. It makes me think about them differently. It makes me think how I broke their hearts." She was turned away from him, looking where the moonlight was like a long silver carpet rolled down from the sky. "What were your parents like, Nick?"

He lay on his back, staring up at the ceiling. A crack ran across the plaster, a thin, black line through the darkness above him where the moonlight didn't reach. He wondered if he ought to offer to fix it.

"My mother was always on the move, dragging my brother George and me around, chasing one fool after another. Losers, con men. We never lived any place very long. She loved us, I guess, but I never had the feeling we were all that important to her. George and me, we were kind of like big, cumbersome pets. She'd hold us when she was lonely."

"What about your father?"

"I never knew him. He deserted us when I was three. My mother didn't keep any pictures. Sometimes, though, I think I almost remember his face."

She turned to him, lay her arm across his chest. "My folks were nice people. I thought they were too ordinary. Too satisfied, I guess. Their life here was exactly what they wanted. They loved each other. I never realized how lucky they were in that." Her fingers thoughtlessly traced his ribs, one after another.

"When you were married, Jess, why didn't you have any kids?"

"I didn't want any. Not with him."

"What was he like?"

"Awful. Full of himself. I didn't really love him."

"Why'd you marry him, then?"

"Everyone kind of expected I would. He was handsome. The high school quarterback. I was a cheerleader."

He put his hand on her belly. "You still have a cheerleader's body."

"We got married right after high school. Neither of our parents wanted us to. But we did it. Out of spite, I think. We went down to the Twin Cities so he could work for the railroad. It wasn't long before I found out he was cheating on me with everything that wore a skirt. He swore he'd stop. He didn't."

"I'm sorry, Jessie. You deserve better."

"What's done is done." She was quiet. He stroked her hair. "While I was down there, my folks were killed in a car accident, hit by a train at a crossing. Kind of ironic, I suppose. Anyway, I never had a chance to tell them I was sorry."

"It's like that sometimes," Nick said. He didn't know what he meant by it exactly, but it was something to say and it sounded soothing.

"What was she like, Nick?"

"Wonderful. Pet looks just like her." He waited a moment. "Would you be hurt if I told you something?"

"I don't know."

"Sometimes in these last few days, when I wake up at night with you beside me, I'm disoriented and I think—for just a moment—it's Rachel. I'm sorry."

"I understand."

"But you know, when I realize what's what, I'm so happy I almost cry." He put his arms around her and held her long into the night.

He said, "You stay here with Pet. I'll gather up the things at the motor court and check out."

Jessie said to Pet, "We'll fix my old bedroom up while he's gone. We'll fix it up just for you."

Pet said, "Can I keep the dollhouse there?"

"Of course you can, sweetheart. It's yours. I gave it to you. And Bonnie. She's yours now, too."

Nick kissed Jessie at the door, then looked out at the day. "This is the nicest Wednesday I've ever seen. I think this is the nicest Wednesday since the beginning of time."

Jessie said, "Hurry back."

"I will."

The lake was a huge promising pool of sunlight. As he drove, Nick smiled thinking of the day they'd fished. It seemed like a long time ago, although in truth it was only ten days. He pulled into the gravel lot of the motor court. There were just two cars now. A red Crown Victoria from Michigan and a white Plymouth

Valiant with Minnesota plates. Nick gathered their things, packed the suitcases, double checked under the bed for anything Pet might have kicked there. He wasn't sorry at all to leave the room behind. He hated motels as much as Pet did.

"What can I do you for?" the desk clerk asked pleasantly when Nick stepped into the office.

"Checking out," Nick said.

"Where you off to?"

"Ever heard of Eldorado?"

"No, sir, can't say that I have. That in Minnesota?"

"Looks like it might be. Looks real possible."

"Well, good luck to you. And your kid."

"Thanks," he said. "Thanks a lot."

In the car, Nick turned the dial of the radio to a weather report. Sunny, was the forecast, with a high in the mid-seventies. Perfect day, Nick thought happily.

He hit the brakes and pulled to the curb when he saw Jessie waving him down in front of the Rexall drug store. Pet was with her.

"There's a black Cadillac parked across the street from my house," Jessie said as they jumped in. "Utah plates. The man at the wheel has a moustache, and he's wearing black driving gloves."

"Christ," Nick said. "Let me think."

"We went out the back way so he wouldn't see us."

"What's happening, Daddy? Are we leaving again?"

"I don't know, Pet," Nick said. "I don't know."

"You have to," Jessie said.

Nick looked at her. "I can't, Jessie. I can't go anywhere. I've just about used up all my money. I can't run anymore."

Jessie said, "Go back to the motor court with Pet. Wait for me there."

"What are you going to do?"

"Just go back and wait."

"If he knows about your house, Jessie, he probably knows

about the motor court," Nick said.

"All right. All right." Jessie folded her hands and put them to her lips as if she were praying. "The park, then," she said suddenly. "Truman Park where we had the picnic. Wait for me there."

"What are you going to do?"

"You'll see. Go on now." She got out of the car and waved them away.

Nick parked out of sight behind the small pavilion. There were a few other people in the park, who smiled at Nick and Pet in a friendly way. Nick pushed Pet on the swings. They walked to the lake and threw rocks at a stick. They played hide and seek. Nick was beginning to worry. Jessie had been gone a long time. He began to think something had gone wrong.

Then he saw her crossing the road to the park on foot. She carried a big brown paper bag. Pet ran to her.

"I was worried about you," Nick said.

"I'm not the one you should worry about. Here," she said to Pet. She brought out Buster and Bonnie from the paper bag. "I knew you'd want these."

Pet hugged her dolls. She looked at Nick. "Daddy, are we leaving again?"

Nick didn't answer. He looked at Jessie. "What's all this about?"

Jessie reached into the bag and pulled out a big envelope. "Here."

Nick took the envelope and opened it. There was money inside. A lot of it. "Where'd you get this?"

"The insurance settlement when that train killed my folks. I got over a million dollars, Nick."

"But you waitress," Nick said.

"To pass the time. I don't have to."

"I can't take this." Nick thrust the money back at her.

"It's not for you. It's for Pet. I want her to stay with you."

"Jessie—"

"Go on before he finds you."

Nick looked at the money. "I don't know what to say." He put his arms around her and drew her close. "I'll find us a place somewhere safe. I'll find it and I'll let you know. Will you come?"

"I'll come, Nick." She was crying. She knelt down and hugged Pet to her. "Take care of your daddy."

"I will, Aunt Jessie. And I'll take care of Bonnie, too."

"Good for you. You'll be a good mommy, I know you will."

She walked them to the car. Nick had his arm around her waist. He opened the back door for Pet, and she scooted inside with her dolls.

"Do you know where you'll go?" Jessie asked.

"The Twin Cities is a big place. It would be hard to find us there."

"Let me know," Jessie said. Then she added, "I love you, Nick."

"I love you, too." He kissed her a long time.

She was standing alone in the park when he left, her hand lifted in goodbye. In silhouette, with the sun off the lake behind her, she looked like a small, leafless tree with only one branch.

He drove out of town, slowly following a back road that wove among cornfields. The warm sun through the car windows and the gentle rocking made Pet drowsy. She lay across the back seat and went to sleep. He watched his rearview mirror. As he came to a crossroads, a black Cadillac appeared behind him, swinging fast around a blind curve. He turned quickly to the right. The Cadillac followed. He pulled to the side of the deserted road, stepped out but left the car running so Pet wouldn't wake.

The man with the moustache got out of the Cadillac.

"Where's Pet?" he asked as he approached.

Nick nodded toward his car. "Napping in back. Let her sleep. She doesn't have to see."

"All right." The man looked at the envelope in Nick's hand. "How much?"

"I haven't counted it, George."

His brother reached out and Nick handed over the envelope. George did the math.

"Twenty-five grand," he said. "Even better than Aunt Ida in Rapid City."

"What's next?" Nick asked.

George lit a cigarette and blew smoke into a soft wind that came across the fields. "I checked the papers in the Twin Cities for the last year or so. Best lead I've run across so far is a kindergarten teacher in LaCrosse, Wisconsin. Husband drowned ten months ago. Owned a construction business. Left her pretty well off. I drove past her house. Looks like it would run five, six hundred thousand easy. She's not much for socializing. Not too old. No children of her own. I figure we could work an angle with Pet in her classroom." George held the cigarette and studied the smoke drifting from the tip. "I got a look at her, Nick. She's not nearly as good looking as this one was. Sorry."

Nick said, "They have names George. Her name is Jessie. And she's more than just good looking."

George studied his brother's face. "You okay?"

"I just get tired of the lies."

"I know what you mean, Nicky, I really do. But think of it this way. You leave them with something extraordinary, something they curl up with on a lonely night and remember in a good way. You're like something out of a fairy tale, you and Pet."

Nick sat on the back bumper of his Rambler. The metal was hot through his pants, but he didn't care. "Remember when we were kids, how we'd tell ourselves stories about what it would be like when Mom finally settled down somewhere?"

"I remember."

A quarter mile away, a tractor crossed the empty road and disappeared into the high corn. George said, "We'd better be moving before somebody spots us and gets nosy."

"Where do we stay tonight?"

George crushed his cigarette on the asphalt. "Booked us into the Holiday Inn in St. Cloud. Tomorrow we'll head down to

LaCrosse."

"You go on ahead. Pet and me'll meet you in St. Cloud."

After George had gone, Nick stood for a while leaning against his station wagon. He stared across the cornfields. The afternoon light coated the tall plants in soft yellow and the wind made the tassels on top move together in waves. A smell came off the fields, a sweet smell. Nick began to imagine how it would be to farm here. To plant the corn in the spring, riding the big tractor with Pet up there beside him. They'd watch it grow all summer as it took strength from somewhere deep in the earth, from a place they couldn't see. But they'd feel it, too, something flowing up into them, filling them with what it was that made the simple things grow tall and strong. And something would go out from them, something like roots, which he'd never had, nor Pet. And all summer they would smell the sweet smell off the fields, and in the fall they'd harvest together on the big tractor and fill their silos with grain, and all winter they'd be together in their warm farmhouse with their work behind them and nothing to do but keep one another company. Just Pet and him. Safe and warm and full of sweet, sweet dreams. It seemed like a good life, a peaceful life, the best life a man could imagine.

Bill is one of our most prolific and versatile writers, penning series featuring the likes of the "Nameless Detective" and the historical duo of "Carpenter and Quincannon." He's written across all crime genres, as well as westerns, hundreds of short stories, and several volumes of award-winning criticism and commentary. With "Night Games" he gives us a suspenseful cinematic adventure story perfect for reading on a dark, moonless night...

Night Games

Bill Pronzini

When Brennan was within two hundred yards of the island's wooded leeward shore, he cut off the skiff's dashboard and running lights and throttled the 40-horsepower outboard down to crawling speed. There was no moon, but a broad canopy of coldly winking stars provided enough light so that he could make out the slender strip of pebble beach—the only spot other than the inlet on the north shore where a boat could be landed safely. He shut off the engine as he neared the beach; swung out as soon as the skiff scraped onto pebbles, then dragged it halfway out of the water.

He ungloved his right hand and drew the silenced Beretta from the pouch at his belt, listening for the dogs. Nothing to hear other than the thin late-summer wind rustling branches in the pines, but that didn't have to mean they weren't somewhere nearby. The dogs were Dobermans, a breed that if properly trained could attack silently and swiftly under the cover of darkness. These two weren't reputed to be vicious, but you could never be sure about watchdogs.

The layout of the island was fixed in his memory. A topographical map he'd bought in Seattle had provided the contours, and the answers to a few discreet questions of area locals in Doe Bay had told him the rest of what he needed to know.

A quarter-mile wide and half-mile long, it was one of the smallest in a series of islands between the coast of Washington state and the southern tip of Vancouver Island. Volcanic in origin, some were large—Orcas Island had seven small communities on it—while others were unnamed vacation spots only big enough for a handful of buildings, the exclusive retreats of the well-to-do of Seattle and Bellingham. The waters surrounding them, frigid and treacherous in bad weather, were reachable only by private boat or ferry.

This one had been bought by a wealthy Seattle businessman in the early seventies as a summer retreat. He was dead now, and his surviving relatives had no interest in the property except as a source of rental income. One of those relatives had been a college acquaintance of Lukash's. A perfect place for Lukash to arrange to hole up for a while, or so he'd stupidly believed.

Brennan set off on a well-worn path that led north along the shoreline, one of five footpaths crisscrossing the island. Dressed in black clothing and a black woolen cap, he was a moving shadow etched against the still waters of Rosario Strait. Now and then he had to use the shielded beam of his LED penlight to guide him, but it wasn't far around to the east shore inlet. Not much more than a ten-minute walk, even in the midnight dark and at a retarded pace.

Where the path emerged from the woods he paused to reconnoiter. A squat boathouse bulked on the cove's near side, sided by a short wooden float. On the high ground above, the rest of the buildings were visible—main house, caretaker's cottage, utility shed where the generator that was the island's only source of power was housed. Diffused light showed at the cottage, but from this vantage point Brennan couldn't tell if it came from inside or an outside fixture. The main house, set at an angle overlooking the inlet and the open water beyond, appeared dark. If Lukash was in bed asleep, taking him would be that much easier.

Brennan made his way to the boathouse. Inside, with the door shut, he felt along the inshore wall; the structure was solidly built, with no large chinks between the boards that would leak flashes of light. The penlight showed him the two small craft anchored there. One, a fourteen-foot skiff similar to the one he'd rented in Doe Bay, belonged to the caretaker, a man named Denbow. The other was Lukash's inboard.

Brennan disabled the inboard first by removing the engine's rotor and sinking it into the dark water. Then he unbolted the outboard from the skiff's transom and sank that, removed the oars and pushed them out through the open end into the strait, where the currents would carry them away.

He still had the night to himself when he stepped back outside. No movement, no sounds except for the wind-rustle, the cry of a nightbird, the faint lapping of water against the float. All right, but where were the dogs? Penned up for some reason? A break, if so. Then he wouldn't have to shoot them.

Another path, this one of crushed oyster shells and wooden steps in a couple of places where the ground humped, led from the boathouse upslope a hundred yards or so to a terrace fronting the main house. Good-size place, built of pine logs and redwood, with a porch that wrapped around on three sides. The smaller, plainer caretaker's cottage stood at a distance to the south, the utility shed at an oblique angle between them.

Bent low, Brennan started up the incline to one side of the path so as to avoid making noise on the shells. He'd covered a third of the distance when he heard the muffled report.

No mistaking what it was—the gutty eruption of a shotgun. He couldn't tell where it had come from, only that it had been somewhere above. Whatever the reason for the shot, it hadn't been directed at him or he'd have seen the muzzle flash.

There was no second report. And the first hadn't set the dogs to barking.

Brennan ran up the rest of the way to the terrace, dodged across it past the shapes of wrought iron outdoor furniture. He crouched in the cover of shrubbery growing alongside the porch, watching, listening. Nothing to see, nothing to hear. The night was cloaked in silence again.

He waited another minute before moving again. He climbed half a dozen steps onto the porch, padded to a sliding glass door. Locked, curtains drawn behind it inside. Same with an adjacent window. He followed the porch around to the front, found the door and windows there equally secure, and went on around to the far side.

Another sliding glass door, this one with a dim yellow glow showing through a narrow gap between the closed curtains. Brennan laid an eye close to the glass. The gap was wide enough to allow him a partial view of what looked to be a study—desk, leather chairs, Indian rugs, native stone fireplace. A gooseneck desk lamp was the source of the light.

The other thing he saw, extended outward on the floor behind the desk, was a man's bent leg.

This door was unlocked. He slid it open with his gloved free hand, eased himself inside with the Beretta upraised. The room was empty except for the man on the floor. The silence here and in the rest of the house was acute.

He crossed to the desk, leaned over to look down. Sightless eyes stared up at him out of a middle-aged, bearded face. Anthony Lukash had been clean-shaven in the photo Brennan had been given but there was no mistaking that mole on the left cheek. Lukash hadn't been dead very long; the blood was bright crimson around the hole between his eyes. Shot at close range with a small caliber handgun.

Nothing much surprised Brennan anymore, but this did. What the hell?

He straightened, scanned the room. A picture had been pulled away from the pine paneling next to the fireplace. The door to the wall safe behind it was wide open. Even at a distance he could tell that it was empty.

The desktop was bare except for the lamp; the drawers were full of nothing.

Nothing on the body, either.

Everything important gone, taken away. Laptop, cell phone; Lukash would have brought both, even though there was no internet service out here and cell service was sporadic. Flash disk. Hard copy of the design specs, if he'd printed one. And the $75,000 in cash.

The inner study door opened into a short hallway. With the aid of the penlight, Brennan looked into the rest of the rooms. Waste of a couple of minutes, but he had to be sure the house was empty.

He went out through the study door, down off the porch. From the south corner he had a clear look at the caretaker's cottage. The light still burned over there. An inside light, its glow brighter now because the front door stood half open.

The wind had picked up, its faint disturbance of the trees and shrubbery all there was to hear. Shapes and shadows all stationary within the range of vision. Brennan ran across to the near side of the cottage, away from the lighted doorway. Paused there long enough to listen to the silence, then climbed a side set of steps and edged along a narrow porch to the door.

He went in fast, fanning left and right with the Beretta. Small, cluttered living room, the odor of cheap whiskey strong in the air. And another dead man on the floor.

This one was tall, thin, sprawled belly-up in front of the hearth, his head and face a bloody red ruin. The fireplace stones and mantel behind him were peppered with buckshot, spattered with gore.

An open wallet lay beside the body. Brennan picked it up with his gloved hand, saw that it was empty of everything except for Arthur Denbow's Washington state driver's license, and dropped it. He didn't touch the body. He detoured around it, took a cursory look into the living room and the other three rooms.

None of the missing items were here, either.

He quit the cottage through a door off the kitchen. At the rear was a wire-fenced kennel, and on a bed of pine needles and leaf mold near it he found the two Doberman watchdogs. A quick look with the penlight was all he needed to tell that each had been shot once in the head.

Lukash and the dogs killed with a handgun, the caretaker with a shotgun. Why the use of two different weapons? One thing seemed certain: the shooter had been known to the dogs; no stranger could get close enough to a pair of trained Dobermans to put bullets in their heads without being torn to pieces.

So who the hell was responsible for all this carnage? Somebody Lukash had contacted about disposal of the design specs? An acquaintance of Denbow's? It didn't figure to be anyone complicit in the original theft. All indications were that Lukash had acted alone. Used his position as a research engineer with the large industrial outfit known privately as the Company to embezzle the $75,000, then found a way to bypass security measures and steal the specs, and disappeared with both. Bright, crafty, gutsy, but with a couple of screws loose to have expected to get away clean.

As soon as the theft was discovered, the Company had called in the investigation firm Brennan worked for, specialists in cases of industrial espionage. He was their best field man, a loner whose methods were unorthodox and who now and then crossed the line. There were some who thought he had a screw loose himself, but he didn't care. Results, whatever it took to get them, was what he was paid for.

It had taken eight days to track Lukash and uncover the link to the old college acquaintance, the son of the island's deceased owner. The fact that he was still holed up here meant that he still had the goods in his possession. He hadn't tried to ransom them back to the Company so he must have intended on selling them to the highest bidder, domestic or foreign. Brennan didn't know what the specs were for, just that it was some sort of electronic device; he didn't want to know. All he needed to know was that the device was valuable and the Company wanted the specs and the money back—and Lukash taken out of commission, one way or another.

Well, that part of it had already been done by somebody else. The damn fool must have been careless in concealing his hideout, his hoard, or both. $75,000 in cash was more than enough to tempt the commission of a double murder; the specs even more so if the shooter had found out or guessed how much they were worth.

The crazy goddamn coincidence of Brennan's arrival and the slaughter was galling. His timing couldn't have been much worse. If he'd come out here this afternoon, or made the crossing just a couple of hours earlier tonight, he could have prevented all this from happening.

But it wasn't too late. The shooter and the plunder were still somewhere on the island. The boathouse had to be where he'd gone when he finished up here, and when he found both boats disabled he'd have known there was someone else on the island, someone alive and with a purpose.

What would he do then? Two options: stay put and try to repair one of the boats, or go hunting for the intruder or the craft he'd come in. He had to have a piece of luggage with him to hold the plunder, if nothing else; he wouldn't let go of it for long, or lug it on a hunt in the dark. And he had no way of knowing if the intruder was armed.

It hadn't been long since the shotgun blast. Chances were he was still in the boathouse.

From this vantage point Brennan could see only part of the structure. That portion was swathed in darkness, but that didn't have to mean anything. The shooter would have a flashlight and be careful how he used it.

Beyond the kennel was another stretch of pine woods. Brennan took a zigzag route to them, then headed downslope inside their outer edge. Thick-dark in there even so; he went slowly so as not to trip over something, stumble into one of the trees.

The stand of pines thinned as he neared the inlet. He halted at a point opposite the boathouse, separated from it by thirty yards of open ground coated with ferns. The only audible sounds were those made by the wind.

He stepped out of the tree cover and started over there, skirting a rotting moss-covered log—

Bright flash from the thick shadows at the inland corner, sudden explosive noise, stinging pain along his left side and enough impact to knock him off his feet.

He didn't stay where he fell; if he had, the second shotgun blast would have cut him in half. He rolled sideways, scrambled behind the rotting log in time to avoid being pinned by a flashlight beam.

Ambush. The son of a bitch had spotted him moving around up above.

Pain radiated along his right arm, his right side, but the charge of buckshot had been a glancing hit and missed a vital spot. He could still use his arm, but he'd lost the Beretta in the fall or the scramble.

For a few seconds the flash beam probed for him over and around the log, then winked out. Sharp clicking sound...a fresh shell being jacked into the chamber of a pump-action shotgun.

Brennan's hand was slick with blood from the arm wound. He sat up and wiped it off on his pant leg, sliding the hand downward to the cuff.

Slithery movement on the other side of the log.

Brennan yanked the cuff up, drew the backup .32 automatic holstered on his calf. At the same time he fumbled the penlight out with his left hand.

The dark shapes of man and upraised shotgun appeared not more than ten feet away, silhouetted against the starlit sky.

Brennan stabbed him with the penlight beam, freezing him just long enough to make him a clear target, and then fired five rounds as fast as he could squeeze the automatic's trigger. Killshots, one or more of them. The man grunted, jerked, went down fast and hard on top of the shotgun and stayed that way.

Brennan held the light on him while he sucked in air to get his breathing under control, then used the log as a fulcrum to shove onto his feet. He felt steady enough, the pain from the buckshot wounds ebbing now. When he turned the light on his arm and side he found the damage to be superficial, more blood than torn flesh and not too much of that. He wouldn't bleed to death before he got back to Doe Bay, and he could patch himself up in his motel room.

He found the Beretta easily enough, pocketed it. Then, with the toe of his shoe, he pushed the dead man over onto his back. Same age and size as the corpse in the caretaker's cottage: mid-forties, tall and gangly thin in a bullet-torn wool shirt and Levi's. The only items of interest in the pockets were a .32 caliber Ruger revolver and a California driver's license issued to a Thomas Kinsey. The face in the license photograph might have been the dead man's, but Brennan didn't think so.

No, Thomas Kinsey was the one in cottage with his head blown apart. This one was the caretaker, Denbow.

Substitution switch—that had been Denbow's game. He must have found out about Lukash's stash a few days ago, made contact with Kinsey—a man he knew, or a stranger he latched onto because of the resemblance—and lured him out to the island on some pretext or other. Maybe got him drunk enough to pass out, then went to shoot Lukash and claim the valuables. The dogs had been next, Kinsey the last to be disposed of with the shotgun.

Clever enough plan, a better one than Lukash's. Denbow would have left the island in Lukash's rented boat, abandoned the boat in Seattle or Bellingham, then gone anywhere he chose using Kinsey's ID. The bodies might not have been found for weeks. Two inhabitants of a lonely island murdered, with no apparent motive or suspects—a case to baffle the authorities for years.

Brennan, through blind luck, had spoiled the game and created an even more puzzling mystery—three human corpses, each shot with a different weapon. Not that it mattered to him. All that did matter was finishing what he'd been hired to do.

He found Lukash's computer and cell phone, the flash disk and bundles of cash, in a suitcase inside the boathouse where Denbow had stashed it before setting up his ambush. He carried the suitcase around to the gravel beach, taking his time, resting now and then to conserve his strength. Stowed it in the skiff's stern and wrestled the craft off the pebbles into the water.

The buckshot wounds were giving him hell again by the time he shoved off in the direction of Doe Bay. He ought to get a bonus from the Company, if not his employers, for what he'd been through tonight, but he probably wouldn't. They'd say it was all just part of the job.

Joe's work can cut you open and make you bleed, make you cry, or have you rolling on the floor, and sometimes all at once. His standalone novels as well as his series, including the Hap and Leonard books, offer some of the best writing we have in multiple genres. And his short stories are often brilliant. Here we have a pair of hit men going about their jobs, dealing with a man who "sort of lost his cornbread" and did something he shouldn't have...

Promise Me

Joe R. Lansdale

Me and Griffin were driving down 59, on our way to collect some money.

It was our job. Seems a fellow we knew a little because he worked for the company had stolen a half million dollars. His name was Ravel, and he was an accountant. A chubby, balding man that had a way with numbers. It was thought he had siphoned off a lot of money over the years, and then he sort of lost his cornbread and opened the safe and took out a half a mill in large bills and went home.

Least that was the word, that he was home. That seemed silly. Steal a half-million dollars then head to the house. We knew too he was divorced as of recent and had two near-grown kids, daughters. We knew he was a mousy man of regular habits.

On through the night we drove, stopping at a filling station just outside of Livingston, Texas. We got gas and bought some doughnuts and some really bad coffee, then we drove on.

Me and Griffin didn't talk much, but we talked a little on our way down 59.

"Guy like that doing a thing like that, then going to the house," Griffin said, "he must have a screw loose."

"Not what I hear."

"Why would anyone bother to steal five-hundred thousand dollars then go home, especially knowing he works for people that like things tidied up and don't take things like that lightly."

"We only heard he's at the house. Wouldn't surprise me if he isn't."

Griffin grunted and on we rode. We turned off on Highway 7, took another turn off a country road.

The house was down a long drive and the drive was bordered with trees. We stopped at the front of the drive, turned out the lights and walked. We pulled on our gloves as we went.

The house was a two-story job. Not overly fancy, but nice enough. We came to it and went left and right. I took a side door and Griffin went around to find a back way in. There were lights on in the house and I could see through one of the broad windows that our man was at the sink doing something or another. I reached for the side door knob, sure I'd end up having to break it down, but it was open and I went in.

Ravel turned at the sink and looked at me. He was drying his hands on a dish towel.

"Hello," he said. "I was expecting you."

I had my gun in my hand when I came in. I said, "Yeah?"

He nodded, and turned his back and carefully arranged the dish towel on a rod next to the dishwasher.

"Sure. I knew they'd send someone. Be okay if we have a drink first?" he said.

About that time Griffin came in through the same door I had used. He said, "The back was locked, but this is nice and easy."

"I left it open for you," Ravel said.

"Yeah, well, that makes it all right," Griffin said. "Thoughtful of you."

Griffin had his automatic in his fist and he lifted it.

I said, "Hold it. He wants to have a drink first."

"A what?"

A drink.

Griffin looked at Ravel. Ravel wasn't even sweating. He looked as calm as a deacon on his way to heaven.

"All right," Griffin said. "I can do that. I like a drink just fine. Maybe when you're gone, fat boy, we'll finish the bottle."

"There are other bottles in the cabinet," Ravel said. "You can help yourself."

"Sure can," Griffin said.

Ravel went to the cabinet.

I said, "Make sure what you pull out of there is liquor and not a pistol."

"I don't even own a firearm," he said. "Truth is, I deplore them."

"Do you now?" Griffin said.

It wasn't really a question.

Ravel brought the bottle out and then he got three glasses, using his fingers to hold all three clutched together like grapes.

"You got your fingers in the glass," Griffin said.

"After I pour, you can drink from the bottle," Ravel said.

"No," Griffin said. "I like a glass. Little more class to a glass."

I thought that was funny. I didn't think Griffin could spell class.

"Can we sit at the table?" Ravel said.

We all sat at the table and sipped our drinks. The bottle of whiskey was brought over too, and when we'd had one drink, Griffin poured himself a second, then looked at me, holding up the bottle.

I shook my head.

Griffin looked at Ravel. "What will the dead man have?"

"If it's okay with you," Ravel said, "you can pour me another."

"I can pour him another," Griffin said, looking at me, grinning.

Griffin poured Ravel a drink. He sat back in his chair with

his gun in his lap and the glass to his lips. His eyes floated up to a photograph on the wall near the table. It was of a plump woman and a young girl, maybe thirteen.

"Well," Griffin said, "that young one looks pretty good, but you're lucky you got rid of that fat woman."

"I love her," Ravel said.

"Do you now?" Griffin said.

"I do," Ravel said, and it was the only time he had seemed anxious, talking about her.

"Well now," Griffin said, "we've had our drink, and you've had your drink, two drinks, so shall we get this over with? It's a long drive back to Houston."

"Of course," Ravel said, as if he had just been asked to step off an elevator to allow a wheelchair in.

"Would it be okay with you gentlemen if you did it with me sitting in my big chair? I've always liked that chair. Very comfortable."

"It's not like you're going to be comfortable long," Griffin said.

"It's all right," I said. "Sit in the chair."

"Yeah?" Griffin said. "What you going to do then, make him a little snack, bring milk and cookies?"

"It's all right," I said. "Go on and sit in your chair."

Ravel got up and slowly moved to the chair and sat down in it. It was a big, padded chair and Ravel rested his head back with a sigh.

We had walked over with him and there was a bar nearby with stools under it and Griffin pulled one out and sat on it. I leaned my butt into the bar.

"Gentlemen," Ravel said, "you've been very gracious. May I ask you not shoot me in the head? In case my wife or daughter comes in, it won't be so messy."

"Ex-wife," Griffin said.

"On paper," Ravel said.

"You'll be dead, so what's it matter?" Griffin said.

"No, that's all right," I said. "We'll shoot you in the chest. It'll still be bloody, messy."

"I know. I just don't want my head blown apart, if you'll give me that courtesy. Promise me that, at least."

"Sure," I said. I turned to Griffin. "You're okay with that, right?"

"What the hell?" Griffin said. "Sure. Let's not shoot him in the head. We can give him a little bit of a pedicure after he's dead, maybe change his socks and underwear while we're at it, wipe his ass."

"Going to give me a pedicure," Ravel said, "you might as well change my socks and underwear. That would be a nice touch."

"You think this is a joke?" Griffin said. "That we're going to go away?"

"No," Ravel said. "I don't think it's a joke, and I hope you don't go away."

"That's enough," Griffin said and stood up off his stool, pointed his gun at Ravel.

"Hold it," I said.

Griffin looked at me as if I had just brought an elephant into the room.

I said to Ravel, "Guy like you, what you done, knowing we're coming, what gives?"

"Does it matter?" Ravel said.

"In the long run, probably not, but I won't kid you, I'm curious."

"I'm not," Griffin said. "I want to get back on the road."

"What you want is to stop at that burger place near Livingston, that's what you want."

Griffin looked at his watch. "Yeah, well, it closes at nine. I was thinking we left pretty soon, we could make it."

"Forget the burger," I said. "I want to hear what's really going on."

"Ain't you the curious cat?" Griffin said.

"I stole some money," Ravel said. "You're going to shoot

me, and that's the end of the story."

"I like that story," Griffin said. He was itching to get it over with.

"By the way," I said to Griffin. "Might be nice we got the money before we shot him."

"That is indeed a worthy point," Griffin said. "But I bet he's already spent it, put it in the bank. So now we're just giving him payback for being a goddamn thief."

"It's actually in a desk drawer in my office." Ravel pointed to the door.

"Go look," I said to Griffin.

"Why don't you go look?" Griffin said.

"Because I told you to, and you're a little too gun happy."

"It's not like we're spending the night watching old movies and drinking fruit juice. He's going to get popped."

"Go see if the money is in the drawer."

Griffin saw something in my face that made him go do what I asked.

It took about a minute. He came back with the money. It was in two enormous rolls of bills clamped down with rubber bands.

"He's got some big denominations here," Griffin said.

"It was easier to carry that way," Ravel said. "I waited until I could change small bills for big bills, packed them away in the safe, same as usual, and then I waited for a while, and then I took them."

"And then you went home to do the dishes," I said.

"It was day before yesterday," Ravel said. "I didn't do dishes. I went to the movies, had a good dinner and came home. I left the door unlocked then, but you didn't show up. I stayed home all day yesterday."

"They had to figure some things before they sent us," I said. "We heard you were out here. You know your neighbor works for the company?"

"Sure. He helped me find this house. We used to play cards at his place, sometimes here. Me and his wife, and my wife,

Dorothy, were friends. Well, as much friends as you have in this business."

"I give a damn about friends," Griffin said.

Griffin was back on the stool and was beginning to look frustrated. He had placed the two rolls of bills on the bar, and now and again he glanced at them.

"Okay," I said to Griffin. "Say it. I know you're thinking it."

"I'm thinking we split the dough, say he spent it all. It's not the money they're worried about—"

"I think it might be something that concerns them a little."

"Yeah, a little, but to them it's pocket change. They just don't want him to get away with stealing, all about payback, sending a message to others, but the money, for all they know, it's gone."

"You get that money, first thing you'll do is go out and spend it on a new car, new clothes, no telling what all."

"Women would be in that what all," he said.

"They'd know you stole it in a week, and then that would bleed back on me. You're too stupid to get away with it. You'd need to lay low for a while, maybe go somewhere else. You're too stupid for that."

"You're going to talk smart-ass to me one too many times," Griffin said.

"Am I?" I said.

I looked right at Griffin then. He looked away.

"Ravel," I said, "tell us what you're doing here. You know you're going to die, so spill it. I got to know what it is you're dying for. Why this way?"

"I'm already sick," Ravel said. "Doctor gives me a year, maybe two I take all the right medicine, but that's expensive. It would bleed me dry, and I'd still be dead in a couple of years, at best, and I'd be seriously sick the whole time. Why I divorced Dot. I didn't want to be a burden. But the thing is, she's still in the will, her and my daughter. I got some insurance. It's worth a lot."

"Oh," I said.

"I still don't get it," Griffin said.

"The insurance," I said. "He wants his family to have it. He kills himself, suicide, he doesn't get it. His family doesn't get it. But if he's murdered…"

"That's right," Ravel said.

"Okay," Griffin said, "but with that money you could have got the medicine, hid out somewhere, even sick you'd have had another year or two."

"I don't want another year or two," Ravel said. "I'm ready to be done with it. I want to make sure my family is covered. And the money I've handled, how it was earned, bothers me. Used to not think like that. I thought, I'm not the one doing what's done to make this money. I just count it. Oh, I skimmed a little cream off the top now and then. One day, my daughter, she told me, 'Dad, I want to be an accountant like you. I want to work with numbers.' So, I think, hell, she wants to be like me, but she doesn't know what I'm like. What I'm doing. What the company I work for does, the things it does."

"No one is making a whore be a whore," Griffin said. "No one is making folks stick those needles in their arms."

"That's the way you see it," Ravel said. "That's the way I saw it too, because I didn't want to see how it really was."

"Now that's a thing I haven't heard," Griffin said. "I'll give you that, a guy turning down a half a million so he can be killed and have his family get insurance, that's up there with some big time crazy."

"I get it," I said.

"One more thing," Ravel said. "A reminder. About the head."

"It's all right," I said. "We'll do it your way."

"I appreciate that," Ravel said.

That's when Griffin shot him in the head.

We had the money and were heading back when I finally said it. "We promised not to shoot him in the head."

"Made sure he was dead that way. What is wrong with you? You getting soft?"

"We promised."

"A promise don't mean nothing unless you mean it," Griffin said.

"I meant it."

"Yeah, but I didn't."

"I keep my word."

"For Christ sakes. You're a hired killer, just like me. What's your word matter?"

We rode along in silence until we got to that burger joint Griffin was worried would be closed.

"I'm going to go in and eat," he said. When I didn't get out of the car, he said, "You coming?"

"I don't think so," I said.

"Suit yourself."

He went inside and I sat in the car.

I thought about Ravel. I thought about him and his family. I thought about me and Griffin. I thought about all that money. That was a lot of money. Griffin had put the rolls in the glove box. I opened it and looked at the money. Those were big wads. I closed up the glove box and sat and thought about it all the while Griffin was inside, and when he came out and got in the car, I said, "Okay."

"Okay what?" Griffin said.

"We split the money, take off."

"All right, then," he said. "Now you're being smart. I'm getting too old to be chasing down people and shooting them, you want the truth. I want to enjoy the high life while I'm still young enough to enjoy it. Money can buy a lot of things that you can't get through charm."

I was thinking in Griffin's case this was absolutely true.

"We should separate," I said.

"Yeah, we should. But we got the one car."

"I have an answer to that."

"What kind of answer?"

"I'll steal one and ditch it and buy another. You're smart, you'll get rid of this one and do the same. They'll be coming for us, you know?"

"Yeah, that makes sense," he said, and kept driving.

"Pull off somewhere near some houses. Not too close. Close enough I can get out and walk down to a house and hot wire a car."

"What then?"

"That's not your problem."

I got one of the rolls out of the glove box and put it in my coat. "Now we're split up."

"Let me see the other roll," he said.

I opened the glove box, took it out, showed it to him, and put it back in.

"All right then," he said.

Griffin pulled down a well-lit cutoff, and then down a less well-lit road with some houses in the distance. He stopped, cut the lights and killed the engine. We got out and stood in front of the car.

"I see a lot of cars in drives," Griffin said. "You ought to do all right, fast as you can hot wire one."

"I'll be fine," I said. "Before I go, I wanted to tell you something."

"What's that?"

I lifted up my gun and pointed it at him. "Us splitting the money. I didn't really mean it."

"Damn," he said, and I shot him in the head.

I think you make a promise you ought to keep it.

Next morning, I found Ravel's wife's house. It was easy to locate. I put Griffin's share in a cardboard box and wrote "Mrs. Ravel" on the box in big black letters, taped it up and placed it on her porch. I kept the other roll for myself.

On the way out of town I took a back road, stopped by the river and threw my gun into the water.

I took a deep breath. The air tasted like freedom.

I climbed in my car, turned on the radio, and drove away fast to somewhere.

Patti excels at writing short stories that take ordinary people and cut their lives to the bone. Here she gives us a mystery featuring a murder and a small-town police department with a strong connection to family. There's a dark side to the citizens of West Lebanon, Michigan, and when things go wrong at the local department store, it's up to the town's chief to show the big city cops how to get the job done...

Pretty Girl from Michigan
Patricia Abbott

"Doesn't look like you've got much choice, Chief."

I looked up from the never diminishing stack of paperwork on my desk to find Sam Hunter standing over me, his thick fingers thrumming rhythmically. It was always the same tune, but one I could never place. I wondered if he could. From the twinkle in his eye and slight curve of his lip, I knew my so-called "choice" stemmed from some incident he found humorous, and the list of what made him laugh was considerable. Lately, most of the joking at the station came at my expense. This situation dated from last March when my mother moved from Berkley, Michigan, outside Detroit, to West Lebanon. My dignity began its slide when it was discovered she brought along six beat-up footlockers filled with memorabilia from my childhood. Sure there were baseball cards and Batman comics, but there were also pet rocks, Stretch Armstrong and a skateboard. That's what I got for drafting Sam to help me unload the rental truck.

"I give. A choice about what?"

"What to do with *yo* mama," he said. I could hear Ed Stuyvesant chortling in the back room. Or, more correctly, at the back of our only real room. We were a small police force. There were two cells, an office area, a tiny break alcove, a john, and that was pretty much it. The second cell doubled as a spot for naps, a sick bay, a place for storage. Right now, Christmas decorations, recently removed, weighed down the cot. Is there anything sadder than Christmas paraphernalia on January 10th?

"You're gonna do *yo mama* jokes again? Really?" I placed my elbow firmly on his fingers, bringing whatever tune it was to a halt.

He winced. "Only jokes about *your* mama. Looks like she got herself some pretty snazzy binoculars, nothing she could get at Walmart anyway. There she was, 'round six a.m., out on her deck, scoping the lay of the land when I took a skimmer to my ice hole. Colder than a witch's—well, you know. When she spotted me, she hightailed it inside. Anyone else—I would've been suspicious, looked around for a courier, or maybe a boat easing in." He chuckled. "Guess all she wanted was to keep her penchant for snooping a secret. Good luck with secrets standing out there in plain sight."

"Penchant? Ten-dollar words so early in the day? Okay, so what's my choice?"

"Arrest her as a peeping tom or put her on the force."

"Just 'cause of the glasses? The cells would be stacked up with birders if using binoculars was a crime."

"Hers were pointed at a cottage. No way she was looking for a black-bellied plover," Sam said, winding his way out the door.

Where's the harm, I thought to myself. How much was there for an elderly woman to do in West Lebanon in January? Still, at the end of the day, I drove over to Mom's.

"You're turning into the town eccentric," I said when she opened the door. "People on Monarch Lake are used to their privacy. They pay plenty for it. And they don't want to see someone peering into their house at sunrise. Weren't you freezing out there? Seems like the temp was about six degrees. Sam said you were coasting around in houseslippers."

Holding the storm door open, she said, "Nobody's business where I point my eyes. I hadda listen to the citizens of Monarch Lake partying away on their docks last summer, waiting for the night one of the boats sliced through my dock 'cause they were hopped up on something. I paid plenty for this place and if I want to look, I will. Coffee, tea or something stronger?"

"Have any decent beer?" None of what she had just said explained her early morning spying.

"Blue Moon do?"

I nodded. "Okay, do me and yourself a favor, Mom, and put those glasses away. We've got plenty of birding trails for you to try them out on."

She went into the kitchen and pulled a bottle from the fridge. "You're just worried I'll train them on your place. Maybe catch you with a woman."

"We're not going to get into this again."

"It's been twenty-five years, Chet Plummer. Once you had Billy as an excuse but not the last five years."

I shrugged. "Women don't seem to stick around." This was true. I was the king of first dates.

"You have to display evidence of pheromones for a woman to latch on."

Apparently this was going to be the morning for big words. "Whatever you say," I said, looking at my cell.

Mom shook her head disgustedly. "Anyway, did you know Barbara Joyce has a piece of art by Lotti Van der Gaag sitting on her sofa table? Just begging to be stolen."

"It's Barbara Joss. And you know this artist's work because...?"

"Remember Nomads?"

It took me a minute. "The travel group?"

She nodded. "Doesn't exist anymore, but I went to Amsterdam with the Nomads in the late nineties and saw Van der Gaag's work at the Cobra Museum. Other places, too. It's pretty distinctive." She got out her iPad and google-imaged Van der Gaag.

Primitive looking creatures as well as abstract paintings filled the screen.

"Ain't technology a marvel? I don't even think of pulling out the photos anymore. I must have taken fifty rolls of film on that trip. Don't even know where the albums are up here." I peered over her shoulder. "People tell me to scan them into the cloud, whatever that means. Only pictures worth saving are ones with people in 'em anyway."

"Probably just a copy of a Van der Gaag," I said, looking up. "She doesn't seem like someone who could afford original art by an artist with work in museums." Although I really couldn't say because Barbara Joss and I had never exchanged so much as a hello. That was unusual in a town of fifty-five hundred, especially where one of us was a cop. "So who else you been spying on?"

"Nobody much. People would go and hang drapery." Her mouth puckered with distaste. "Pay big bucks to live on a lake and then never look at it."

I knew I'd be digging those old red and white checkered curtains out of my attic when I got home. I wasn't on the lake, but Mom liked to take walks too. "Stick to the birds, Mom." After turning over a variety of issues, I finished the beer and headed out. I hadn't put my key in the ignition when I heard a voice come over the radio.

"Chief?" It was Ed. "Chief, we got a situation here at Grueber's."

"Shoplifter?"

"Wish that was it. Looks like the pet department girl was attacked."

"Attacked and okay?"

"Not hardly. I'm expecting to find Dorothy and Toto somewhere in this mess. A real melee."

"Be there in ten. Don't touch anything." I had to remind Ed even if his feelings got hurt. We didn't run into chaotic crime scenes often. Five years ago, my boy, Billy had been murdered, and we'd fucked that one up pretty good by wading through the evidence.

The pet department girl was Lena Lefkowski. No one could figure out why a pretty girl like Lena was working in the dark and dank basement of Grueber's Department Store for twelve dollars an hour. The topic was discussed by the men in town regularly. She'd been there for better than six years, wearing an orange lab coat, her hair pulled back in a tight ponytail as if an errant hair might sully her kingdom. In the town's biggest event of 2018, she'd married Righty Lefkowski, whose nickname dated from his prowess as a high school pitcher ten years earlier. Funny how many of us in West Lebanon still carried nicknames from our school days. Lena had been crowned Miss Cherry Blossom every year since high school. Probably would have won again, but someone had put an end to that aspiration. Was this the work of a rival for the title? As ridiculous as that sounded, titles and trophies carried prestige in towns the size of ours. The town's number one realtor called his agency MVP Properties, dating from his days as a third baseman.

When I looked at Lena Lefkowsi's body ten minutes later, it was hard to remember her wearing that crown. From the grill marks on her face, head, and neck, it looked like she'd been beaten to death with the birdcage lying nearby on its side. The birds, set free by the scuffle, were perched on various light fixtures and shelving units. An iguana presided over a pyramid of cat toys. Trays of plants, Lena's secondary job assignment, were toppled. She'd probably just watered them because mud coated the tops of some display tables as well as liberally smearing the floor. Looked like a newly planted field with so much seed and dirt. Ed was perched on a counter shooting photos.

"So you know we're going to have to call in Traverse City?" I said, helping him down.

"Makes us look like Andy and Barney whenever you do that," Ed said, frowning. The topic of *The Andy Griffith Show* came up at least once a week at the station, and it usually wasn't to make a flattering comparison. I made the call, and after forty minutes two freshly washed cop cars pulled up. How did they pull off such a pristine arrival with grimy snow piled everywhere? TC must have had a personal car wash at headquarters. The citizens of Traverse City were probably only too happy to pony up cash for their cops. Just one more thing to remind us of our lowly status.

"I cordoned off the entire block," I told them.

"Expecting a terrorist attack?" a pasty-faced guy said, hiking up his trousers. After that I kept my mouth shut. From what I could see, they didn't do anything fancier or more clever than we would've done. No special equipment or clever theories were bandied about. The next morning, I took a look myself.

Tom Eshu, the store manager, had enough to say to fill two pages in my notebook. "Nice girl. Pretty. Never missed a day. Got married about eight months ago to her high school sweetheart. Loved animals, had a green thumb, was talking about having kids soon. Everybody liked her." Eshu obviously had a crush on Lena despite the thirty-year age difference.

"If she loved animals, why not work in a kennel?" I asked him. "Why spend her days in a moldy basement?" And most importantly, why not get paid a decent wage? I kept that to myself, figuring his pay was low too.

"She didn't love *every* animal," he said. "Mostly it was the birds. That iguana, for instance, they didn't get along at all. Sounds funny, but he used to try and scare her. Jumped out at her whenever he had the chance. Maybe he was jealous of the parakeets." Tom thought a minute, running his fingers through his wiry, black hair. "Look, Lena wasn't the brightest girl. Took her a while to learn how to use the computer, even the phone system. She was always fooling around with her PC, trying to master the software. I had to give her a hand more than once. But anything to do with caring for her birds or the plants came quickly. The birds lined up to get their feathers stroked. She found a wild one on the sidewalk outside and nursed it back to health. Took weeks. And I have to confess, having her work in this department sold us a lot of animal accessories, gardening tools, dog food. Folks could have gone to Ace Hardware for most of it. Saturdays, more than one male customer roamed the floor down here." He scratched his head. "It's a small town, right, Chief? We don't get many Lenas. Pretty girl," he repeated.

And I bet Tom Eshu was her number one visitor. Helping her with more than her laptop. I could picture him perched on a counter amidst the pet toys, wiling away the day, explaining the intricacies of Excel. Could he have made a move and been rejected? Easy enough for him, or anyone for that matter, to slip down to the basement. There was a freight elevator, two sets of stairs, and several windows that were unlocked despite it being January. Grueber's got by with a staff of ten or so. Unless a sale was underway, there were rarely more than a dozen customers inside, and few of them were in Lena's empire in the basement, no matter what Eshu claimed. It was the sort of store that'd disappear after a bad Christmas season. Or when Walmart decided to put a store on the highway into town.

Because Ed had taken some photos before the Traverse City contingent arrived, I got a good look at Lena's wounds. Aside from the ones made by bashing her head and face with a metal birdcage, there were claw marks, and it looked like an attempt had been made to strangle her. Had a bird or two attacked? Her tunic was splattered with blood, dirt, and seeds, and the floor under her head pooled red. The store basement was so packed with inventory, cleaning supplies, and surplus stock for the departments upstairs, it was hard to know where to look for clues to her assailant. Under the counter, sat an extra smock, also orange, that Ed had managed to capture on film. Her purse was there too, seemingly untouched. Nothing was missing from the store's cash per their bookkeeper.

It was difficult to eliminate anyone as a suspect because of the many points of entry. The only thing of note, another employee told me, was that the girl who manned the cosmetics counter upstairs had dated Lena's husband a few years earlier.

"But I'm pretty sure *Colleen* ditched *him*," the electronics clerk said. "He wasn't la-di-da enough for Colleen. She took up with our cosmetic supplier next. Never heard about any hard feelings between the girls. They ate lunch together most days."

"I dated Righty just after graduation," Colleen told me next, windexing the mirrors on her counter as we talked. I couldn't help but notice how often she took a peek at herself as she worked. If Lena was naturally pretty, Colleen's beauty came from the products she sold. Her face had the painted perfection of forties movie stars. "Once I saw his ambition only ran to coaching high school teams, I found someone else." She shrugged. "I tried to clue Lena in, but she was giddy over him. Positively infatuated."

"So what's the deal with that smock?" I asked Tom Eshu later. "No one else wears a smock."

"No one else's clothes get dirty. We ordered three so she didn't have to rush home and wash it every night."

"Why orange?" I asked.

Tom shrugged. "She picked the color herself. Something about a canary she had once."

"So no one heard anything? I mean, look at this place. There must have been significant noise: birds squawking, Lena screaming, things falling off shelves."

"These old buildings are insulated pretty well. Plus, we play music over the intercom."

"It must've been a marching band yesterday," I said.

Tom laughed. "And then there's the heat going off and on. That old boiler can make a helluva racket."

Back at the station, I looked at the photos again, getting Ed to blow up the computer version on his Mac. "Looks like nail marks on her face," Sam noticed, peering over my shoulder.

"Could be from the cages falling. Could be bird claws too."

"If the birds were in a state of hysteria, I guess." Both Sam and Ed hovered over the photographs. As I've said, it wasn't often something like this happened in West Lebanon.

I gathered the pictures up and put them back in the envelope. "We'll have to see what the medical examiner says."

"By the way, your mother called. She said you should stop by when you can."

I stifled my sigh and then tried calling to put her off, but she didn't answer either the landline or cell. This was one of her tactics to get me out there. I had to admit though, Mom and I got along pretty well. She raised me by herself after my father died, and I was pleased when she'd decided to move north. Having her nearby saved me miles on my old Fusion, gas, and a lot of worry. Plus it'd been awfully lonely since Billy's death. And a home cooked meal once or twice a week had put a few welcome pounds on me.

"So what did you spot this time," I asked, pushing open the door with some difficulty. The weather stripping was coming loose. I'd have to fix that before Mom tripped and broke a wrist or a hip. She was grilling salmon and corn on her stovetop.

"Why don't you do that out on the porch? I got you that nice big Weber."

She gave a start. "It's winter out there, son. More winter than I want to deal with."

"Everyone up here grills outside if the temperature's over 20. Hard to get the smoke out of a cabin this size. Hey, you don't seem to mind the cold when you're snooping before dawn."

"Staying for supper?"

"That looks like too much food for one. So, sure. Do you want to hear about my case?"

"I think I've heard most of it," she said, sliding the salmon onto a plate. "Never will get used to the way a topic can ricochet through this town like a pinball. Now with that town gossip thread online, I don't even need to leave the house. Do you want some soy sauce? Or maybe ginger and scallions. Salmon doesn't have much taste without something extra."

"I don't remember you being a gourmet cook forty years ago." For that matter, I didn't remember eating fish except as prepared by Mrs. Paul.

"Was anyone? Our idea of a fancy meal was a T-bone, a baked potato and an iceberg lettuce salad. You might throw in some croutons on a holiday. Maybe blue cheese once in a moon. Anyway, what else do I have to do now?"

"Join the book club. Volunteer at a hospital. Work on Harry Schreiber's state senate campaign. So what've you heard anyway? About my case."

"I heard that that girl in Grueber's basement was murdered."

I nodded. Mom asked a good question then. "Didn't they have a camera down there? To catch shoplifters."

"Yeah, they did. But apparently no one ever bothered to turn it on. Who wants to steal plants and birds, I guess? And it looks like it's been busted long enough to acquire rust. The women's room, right above it, had a leak."

"Lovely." Mom snapped her fingers. "It's a wonder she didn't die from the air down there. One idea shot. But I got another."

"I'm listening."

"What time do you figure she died?"

"Shortly after lunch. That's the last time anyone saw her." I pulled out my notebook to check on it, then nodded. "Her lunch pal, Colleen, returned to cosmetics around one-thirty."

"Well, not long after that, maybe two-thirty or so, I saw Barbara Joss walk into her living room wearing an orange smock. I thought it was Lena visiting until I heard the news. That smock is all you need to see to assume it's Lena. But it wasn't, it seems."

"So why would Barbara be wearing Lena's smock?"

"I have some ideas about that, but you're the detective."

Too much time had passed without me interviewing Lena's husband, Righty Lefkowski, so I decided to stop by his place. Vehicles, mostly pickups, were parked helter-skelter on the shoulder. Piles of blackened snow, pushed to the side of the road by the town plow, took up most of the space. Righty's family was, no doubt, providing him succor. I hoped it wouldn't be imposing on their grief too much to pay a quick visit. Righty had been ruled out as a suspect when the school where he worked placed him in the gym at the time of Lena's attack.

A woman in jeans and a heavy sweater answered the door. Though it was January now, Santa's elves hightailed it across her front. "Marge Lefkowski," she said. "Her husband's sister." She saw me eyeing her sweater and added, "Highly inappropriate of me to be wearing this instead of mourning clothes, but I didn't bring anything suitable along. Thought it would just be an Epiphany service. Not a funeral."

I asked if I could talk to her brother. "Just for a few minutes," I assured her when she looked dubious. He came into the room looking sleep deprived and mournful. A big guy, boasting significant musculature, he wouldn't have had to kill her with a birdcage or his fingernails. Unless he wanted me to think that.

"I already talked to those two guys from Traverse City," he said, his voice barely audible above the noise coming from what must have been the kitchen. It was a queer thing that no matter how sad an occasion, if you put a bunch of people together there will likely be more laughter than tears. Especially if there's food and drink involved.

"I know, Mr. Lefkowski. I read their report. Got a couple of follow-up questions." He nodded tiredly, waving me into a side room where he sunk onto the sofa.

After some words of condolence and small talk, I asked, "Did Lena have any sort of relationship with Barbara Joss?"

"Who?"

I repeated the name. "She's the manager of a fitness center in Traverse City, but she lives here—out on Monarch Lake."

He shrugged. "Name's familiar, but I can't place it." After a few seconds, he snapped his fingers. "The cat lady. She went into the store now and then. Lena talked about it."

"I didn't know Grueber's sold cats."

"They don't," he said, sitting up a little straighter. "Mrs. Joss came in to buy cat collars. Lena said she must be an honest-to-goodness cat lady because she bought them all the time. We thought she must run a rescue operation. Once I even delivered one to her home. A rush order for a cat. Ha!" The lighthearted exclamation reminded him of why I was here again, and he sank even lower on the couch. "Sorry. Every few minutes, I forget she's gone...and then I remember."

I cleared my throat. "I lost my wife when I was about your age, son. It takes a long time before that sort of thing stops happening. The forgetting, then remembering." He nodded.

"Anyway, did she ever get into a dispute with Barbara Joss? Or have some sort of trouble with her?"

Righty looked mystified. "Not that she ever mentioned. You don't think she's the..."

"No, probably not. Something brought her name onto my radar, and I thought I'd better check it out. One other thing, did Lena keep her smocks at home?"

"Smocks?"

"You know—those orange jackets she wore to work."

"She brought them home to wash."

"Sorry to ask this, but are there any around now?"

Silently, he got up and left the room, coming back a few minutes later. "None in our bedroom or the laundry room." A look of horror crossed his face. "The one she was wearing...that day...is probably with the TC cops." He caught his breath. "Should be two more at the store. Not sure where they were kept. She had three at least."

I nodded. "Again, I am sorry for what you're going through, Mr. Lefkowski."

"I still can't believe it," he said at the door. "Everyone loved Lena. I was so lucky she married me and now..." His color drained. We shook hands, his sister quickly returning when she heard the door opening. I was glad Righty had a close family, and especially that he had Marge to buck him up. We didn't get homicides much, but I'd done my share of breaking bad news. Sometimes I had trouble coming up with a friend or family member to sit with the bereaved. As I walked toward the car, it sounded like people were praying in unison. Maybe The Lord's Prayer. I wasn't much of a churchgoing man myself but could testify to its healing power in times like this. If I remembered right, Epiphany was the season after Christmas. Maybe I would be the recipient of an epiphany of my own.

I checked with Traverse City, and they'd come up empty-handed so far. "We're knee-deep in interviewing everyone in the store that day. Seems like they were running an after-Christmas sale on snow boots and winter accessories. The place was supposedly a mob scene. I'd like to evacuate the place, but some guy pleaded with me. Said they paid for a full-page ad in the *Record-Eagle.*" I hung up the phone, still thinking.

"Sam," I said a few minutes later. "Find out everything you can about Barbara Joss." If I was going to stop by her cottage, I might as well be prepared.

According to what Sam dug up, she'd led a blameless life. Fifty-four, never married, no kids, worked at the Fitness Center three days a week and designed websites to supplement. No church affiliation, no criminal record, not even a recent traffic ticket. Could someone who made their living fooling around with links and social media sites online live so far under the radar? Maybe what she knew about having an online presence led her to avoid one. The only interesting piece of information I found was that Barbara Joss seemed to buy a lot of cat and dog collars. Righty had been right. Grueber's kept pretty good records. "Mostly for reordering purposes," the bookkeeper told me. I went down to the basement and looked at their stock, then I decided it was time to meet Ms. Joss. I dragged Sam along.

A tall, thin woman with frosted chin-length hair, Barbara Joss answered the door promptly, as if we'd been expected. It was a pleasant cottage. Similar to the mushroom houses down the road in Charlevoix. Stone house were somewhat uncommon in Michigan, and Barbara's looked like a domicile for hobbits. I had to duck under the head jamb and I'm by no means tall. I looked around the place, noticing that the Dutch sculpture Mom had spotted wasn't the only interesting work of art. I'd expected to see cats and dogs, given her interest in Lena's basement kingdom...not an animal in sight. And as someone with allergies to cats, my nose usually told the truth.

There was no sense making small talk with a woman I'd never spoken to before. "I understand you are a frequent purchaser of animal collars," I began. "You bought," I looked at the figures the store gave me, "seven in the last six months." I looked up. "Do you have a kennel out back?"

She shook her head and crossed the room to get her iPad. She typed something into it and passed it to me. *Etsy dog collars*, the heading said. "I thought I could sell them. So I bought one now and then, but I gave up on the idea fairly quickly."

"The ones Grueber's sells are like this?" I asked, stabbing a collar that said *Lucky* with my index finger. It was basically a woven collar with the name stitched in. It bore no resemblance to the collars I'd seen in the store.

"No, that was the trouble. The ones Grueber's sell mostly have jewels in them. Well, fake jewels, that is." Did she really think I was buying this? But nonetheless she'd been prepared for the question.

"Let's forget about animal collars for now. You were seen wearing an orange jacket like the one Lena Lefkowski wears about the time she was murdered. Did you admire it enough to want one of your own?"

Now she was fumbling even more. "I have an orange sweater," she said haltingly. "Well, really it's more red than orange." She made as if to go get it but I shook my head.

"Sam can take care of it." He inched toward her bedroom as she watched warily.

"You must've gotten to know Lena pretty well, buying so much of her inventory." I started roaming around the room, looking at what I would normally call knickknacks. I picked up a piece that looked like pre-Columbian art. She noticeably flinched. Not a souvenir apparently.

"Not really," she said. "I'm usually in a hurry. I grab what I want and take off."

"Your number's in her contacts." That was a lie. There were no calls between the women. We'd checked that already. "You must be one of her best customers."

She fell for it. "You could hardly call me a customer." Her voice was sullen now.

"We'd like you to come down to the station, Ms. Joss. We found a few decent prints on the bottom of the birdcage Lena was pounded with. We've eliminated half the town, but not you as yet."

"I don't see how there could be a fingerprint on a wire birdcage."

"Well, let's just rule it out," I said, taking her arm.

"We didn't get the story exactly right," I told Mom a few hours later. "In fact, we missed some of the more interesting details."

"I'm all ears." She settled into her lazy boy with a cup of cocoa. Only in our family was a murder the stuff for a cozy evening.

"Getting the obvious part out of the way first, Barbara Joss killed Lena Lefkowsi. Perhaps accidentally when a piece of metal from the broken cage severed her carotid artery. Perhaps not. Anyway, Barbara put on that third orange jacket to make it look like it was Lena leaving the store if anyone spotted her. Quick thinking on her part. We found remnants of it in her fire pit."

"So you don't think she went to Grueber's with the purpose of killing her?"

I shook my head. "Don't think so. The unexpected part of the story, the fact that makes it interesting, is that Barbara Joss was working for our Miss Cherry Blossom."

Mom gave a start. "Well, that is surprising. Working for her how?"

"As a jewel mule, I guess. Stolen emeralds came into the store on those ubiquitous dog collars. Barbara'd get a text from Lena with some innocuous message and know the stones were there. She'd go in, buy the collars, remove the stones, and take them to a fence in Traverse City."

"How long did this go on?"

"For several years from the looks of Barbara's bank statement. You don't make money like that at a Fitness Center."

When confronted, Barbara Joss had looked me straight in the eye at the station and said, "Then she decided to pull the plug, the little bitch." She spat the word out. "After I took all the chances for more than three years. Digging the stones out, taking them to that sniveling little man in a back room in TC. Letting him paw me to keep things running smoothly. Waiting for my cut."

"What changed?" I asked. "Why did she want out?"

"Her marriage," she spit out. "Claimed she got saved. Wanted to live a clean life for Jesus." Barbara made a scoffing sound. "Like I was supposed to lay down and go along with that. Not do anything about it." She winced. Then her eyes lit up. "Anyone tell her husband what his little canary was up to?"

I had indeed. Wasn't sure he believed me but his sister, Marge, did. I guess the Lefkowski family was used to sinners.

Strangely it was Tom Eshu who seemed the most upset. "Girls like her come along once in a lifetime." He looked at me sheepishly. "I may have even abetted her operation without knowing it, fooling around on that computer all the time. I guess she was smarter than she let on."

Or she thought she was smarter, I thought. *At least until she crossed Barbara Joss and her giddy infatuation with collecting art.*

Ben took over Bill Crider's short story column at Mystery Scene magazine. He's another cross-genre writer, penning several westerns to along with his crime fiction. With "Asia Divine" we are treated to a dark tale with sex, betrayal, and an alligator, Mr. Crider's favorite reptile.

Asia Divine

Ben Boulden

Detective Mike Giles gagged on the stink as the Maglite's glare bobbed across the dim and ragged interior of the bus. He leaned against the pock-marked pole next to the torn-out driver's seat, a hand cupped over his mouth and nose.

From the back of the bus a disembodied voice said, "It gets worse."

A bright white light exploded and retreated, fireworks popping in Giles' eyes.

The simulated whir and click of a digital camera saturated the confined area, and the dull ache in his head blossomed into a roar.

As his vision recovered, another flash bounced. The camera clicked.

"Jesus, Danny." Giles stroked his throbbing head. "Hold off on the photos until I have a look, huh?"

Danny Hanlon, lead crime scene technician for the Tooele County Sheriff's Office, grunted. Giles raked the aisleway with his light. Dirt and rocks and broken glass littered the worn-out carpet. The overhead luggage racks had pulled away from the ceiling and walls. The windows were plastered with old newspapers.

"You got your booties on?" Danny sounded aggrieved.

Giles flashed his light at his covered feet and held out his hands. "I'm gloved, too."

"Come on back, if you can stand the smell." Danny focused on the camera's large viewscreen, its glow contouring his face in ethereal blues and whites.

Giles stumbled down the aisle, illuminating the surface of each seat with the flashlight. Plastic bottles, used condoms, a shoe, a greasy sweatshirt, and dirt-covered socks littered the benches. Nothing Giles saw would help now, but he knew Hanlon would bag everything for analysis. It would take weeks or even months for the report to hit his desk. But the victim's body was a different sort of evidence. It would tell a tale about what happened and with luck, provide the clues that would identify the killer.

When Giles reached Hanlon, he said, "Good morning, Danny."

The crime scene tech made a pinched face and nodded at the corpse. "Not for her."

Giles studied the woman. Her hair was long and black, twisted and disheveled. It hung in waves across her face. Her head jutted against the bus frame, the neck at an uncomfortable angle. Her chest broken with gunshots. She wore a slinky black cocktail dress caked with dried blood. Her legs were uncovered and her feet were bare. The area around the body was bloodless and almost clean.

He said to Hanlon, "Is this the murder scene?"

Danny's attention shifted from the camera to Giles. His wispy mustache gave him a shabby teenager look. "She was dumped here."

The smell told Giles the victim had been dead more than 24 hours and the way her body had sunk into the seats made it clear she'd spent most of her afterlife here.

"Did you count the bullet wounds, Danny?"

Hanlon sucked his teeth, a habit that annoyed Giles. "At

least six. Doctor Keith's autopsy will tell you for sure."

"He been here yet?"

Hanlon snickered. "It's Saturday and I imagine the man has more important things to do."

Shit. Dr. Keith Johnson was Tooele County's Medical Examiner. A sanctimonious prick and he would give Giles hell for disturbing the scene.

"He tell you to start working?"

Hanlon nodded.

Giles pointed at the woman's battered chest. "An angry killer."

"Her tongue's been cut out, too."

Giles eyes widened in surprise as he glanced at Hanlon. "Her tongue?"

A grim nod. Danny said, "She talked too much, I guess."

"I guess," Giles said as he kneeled on the seats to the front of the woman's body. He looked at Hanlon. "You done photographing the body?"

"I would be—"

Giles cut him off. "You document her position?"

"Yeah."

Giles smoothed the woman's hair away from her face. The pale, almost blue flesh was clean of blood and makeup. Her eyes were open and clouded with death. "Why would the killer clean her face?"

Giles could feel Hanlon's smirk. "Do I look like the FBI?"

"Maybe if you shaved?"

"Okay, I read a book once." Hanlon sounded interested, and Giles knew he enjoyed pop-culture criminal profiling. "The killer knew her, maybe he loved her. He needed to see her like she was. When she was alive."

Giles peered at Danny across the body. "Not bad."

"But?"

"But nothing. Keep going."

Danny's mouth puckered with distaste. "No way. I'm the crime scene guy, not an analyst. I take the photos and vacuum the floor. Last time—"

The last time Danny Hanlon had speculated about a corpse, Dr. Keith Johnson had complained to the sheriff and anyone else who would listen to him.

Giles rubbed a palm across his thundering forehead. "You find the tongue?"

"Nope."

Giles leaned over the seatbacks, steadying himself with his right hand on the window sill. He looked over his shoulder at Hanlon. "You sure the body's been moved?"

Hanlon sucked his teeth. "Absolutely."

"You check for rigor?" The muscles in the human body stiffened in the first three hours after death and relaxed again after twenty-four.

"She's loose as a goose. I moved her arm to see the tattoo."

"The tattoo?"

Hanlon grinned. "Yeah. A weird one, too."

"And?"

"There's an alligator on her left triceps."

Giles reached for the woman's left arm and turned it over. A dime-sized image, almost like an advertising icon, was etched there in black ink.

Giles hadn't seen the tattoo in years, but it was the same one a pimp named Harvey Skinner—Skinny to his friends, which was most people—had marked his girls with before he'd gotten religion after a few years at the state pen. When he'd been released, Skinny had moved his business into Nevada's legal brothels but, Giles thought, maybe he was expanding east into Utah.

Without looking away from the ink, Giles said, "You photo'd this, right?"

Hanlon grunted.

Giles replaced the arm where he'd found it and then pushed his hand between the corpse and the seat cushion. He ran his fingers along her spine until he felt a flat and rigid spot at her lower back. With a delicate touch, Giles opened the dress's zipper far enough to remove a thin aluminum wallet.

"We need to document that."

"Sure."

Hanlon snatched the wallet from Giles' hand.

A blinding blue-white flash.

"Damn it, Danny!"

"Sorry, just shooting the wallet."

Giles let the body drop back into place and moved into the aisle. "You got her face?"

"Yeah, but let me get a couple more since you messed with her hair."

Hanlon kneeled in the seat well and leaned towards the woman. The camera whirred and clicked. The strobe light blossomed white then retreated to black.

"Send them to me." Giles clicked his tongue a few times, thinking. "Along with the tattoo."

"You're the boss."

"You see any other marks? More ink, scars?"

Hanlon shrugged. "Nah."

Giles held out his hand. "Wallet?"

Hanlon handed it over.

As Giles turned to the front of the bus, he said, "Let me know if you find anything else, Danny."

"Sure, but I still need to document the contents of the wallet."

Giles waved a couple fingers at Danny.

On his way out, Giles noticed a special fuel user's license taped to the right of the steering wheel. It had been issued to a company with a familiar name: Newberry & Skinner Gold Mining. He pulled his phone out and snapped a picture.

In Giles' experience, homicides were solved in the first several hours of the investigation, and so far, this one pointed at a pimp named Skinny.

The blistering morning sun welcomed Giles as he stepped from the bus down to the hard-packed sandy soil. The desert heat was a welcome relief from the stink of decomposing flesh. Sweat beaded on his brow and trickled from beneath his arms. Trooper Ashley Bingham was at the back end of the bus talking to the scrawny kid who found the body. One hand was on her gun belt, the other was holding the chocolate-colored campaign hat worn by the Utah Highway Patrol.

Bingham caught Giles staring. She winked and he walked to his sedan.

Sitting behind the wheel with the driver's door open, Giles studied the wallet he had taken from the victim. Elegant, narrowing at the center, its aluminum exterior was dappled pink. In the top right corner the letters *H* and *L* were engraved into a monogram. When he released the clasp, the wallet opened on concealed hinges to reveal its contents: fifteen one-hundred-dollar bills, an *American Express* card, and a Nevada driver's license.

The name on the card and license was *Hye Lee.*

The woman smiling for the DMV's camera was a stranger to Giles, but her name jangled familiar.

The detective gazed at the scene through the windshield of his unmarked prowler. Hanlon's silver and black Tooele County Sheriff's crime scene van was parked next to the bus's door. A dozen feet away Ashley's Utah Highway Patrol cruiser was idling, the driver's door open. *Mother should I trust the Government?* was written with an unsteady hand across the bus in red paint.

Giles shook his head at the graffiti. He felt his age this morning and wondered who still listened to Pink Floyd. He popped the top from an ibuprofen bottle, chasing four pills with a gulp of Dr Pepper. The soda's sweet taste came as a relief. He almost smiled, but then he remembered the woman in the bus.

Hye Lee.

Giles opened the laptop attached to the dashboard between the seats. He clicked the email icon and with two fingers punched the woman's name into the search box. A week-old telephone message from the dispatcher popped up.

Hye Lee—775-555-3281; call ASAP, re: Harvey Skinner.

Mike Giles had added a note, "lft msg—7/18/19, 09.50." But Hye Lee had never returned his call.

Giles stared at the computer screen. "Shit."

"What's wrong, you find a dead girl or something?"

Giles flinched and then laughed when he saw Bingham standing a few feet away.

She said, "What's up?"

The scrawny kid who had found and reported the body drove past in a dilapidated Ford Ranger, its muffler as loud as the truck was ratty. When it was past, Giles said, "I have an ID on the victim."

"Yeah?"

"Hye Lee. She has an Elko address." Giles pointed at his computer. "She left a message for me last week."

"No shit?" Bingham stepped into the gap between the car and the door, her left hand on the frame. "No wonder you look like you've seen a ghost. You talk to her?"

"Never connected."

Bingham took the driver's license from Giles and studied the photograph. "She's pretty." She flipped the card over and scowled. With a fingernail she pried a business card-sized paper off the back. She looked at Giles. "*Asia Divine* mean anything to you?"

He shook his head. "Anything else there?"

"No." A dimple appeared on Ashley's left cheek as she frowned. Giles' heart was thumping in his chest. The memory of Ashley naked and panting above him sparkled through his aching head. His hands began trembling, sweat beading on his upper lip. Giles hated and loved that this woman, half his age, made him feel like a flustered teenager. He reached out and pulled Ashley closer, bringing her soft lips to his. She surprised him and slid her tongue into his mouth. The pounding headache evaporated with her soft touch.

Ashley pulled away, her smile impure. "Later." A whisper

and a promise. "I was thinking, if the victim called you about Harvey Skinner, that gives him motive, right? I mean, maybe…" She didn't finish her thought and cocked her head to the side. "I thought you had today off, it being Saturday and everything?"

"Nobody else in the department's qualified for a murder investigation."

"You must feel pretty important about that." A twinkle flashed in her eyes. "But Skinner—Seems like he's our guy, right?"

"Maybe." Mike turned to the computer and opened the internet browser. He searched for "Hye Lee AND Elko Nevada." The first hit was a pay site for personal information. He went back to the search box and typed "Asia Divine AND Elko Nevada." A legal brothel called "The Damp Thistle" came up. Giles was greeted with an image of a nude Hye Lee.

Bingham leaned into the car for a better look. A beguiling mixture of soap and vanilla and sweat came with her. Giles tried hard to ignore her scent, but failed. When she swiveled her face to Giles, their noses a few inches apart, he wanted to taste her again. Ashley said, "I bet she was an expensive appetite."

Giles grunted, not trusting his voice.

"You see that dress she was wearing?"

Giles arched an eyebrow, his interest shifting back to the investigation. "What about it?"

"Extravagant." Ashley pointed at the image of Hye Lee on the computer screen. "More than an Elko whore could afford, I bet."

Giles motioned for Bingham to keep talking.

"When I got here, Hanlon told me the dress is a Saint Laurent." She laughed at Giles' obvious confusion. "It's a Hollywood brand for rich people and celebrities."

He gestured expansively at the surrounding desert junkyard. "Not something we'd expect to see around here, then?"

Her blue eyes sparkled in the buttery morning light. "You could say that."

The dress made Giles wonder. "You see the tattoo?"

Bingham shook her head and he told her about Skinny.

"You think he owns this place, The Damp Thistle?"

Bingham shrugged. "I ticket speeders and look for dope, but I like the name."

"Yeah, it sounds prick-ish and wet." Giles clicked back to the search page and scrolled through the listings. Hye Lee was on two adult dating sites with the tagline: "Looking for Adult Play, Sugar Daddies Only." A Facebook page with Hye Lee posing on a pristine beach in a barely-there pink bikini. "Looking for love," and a telephone number. The 801 area code made Giles think Lee had been working Salt Lake City.

Ashley said, "You think Asia Divine"—a mocking sexuality plain in her voice—"had a falling out with Skinner?"

"We need to talk to Skinny, for sure." Giles tapped the steering wheel. "But we can't jump to conclusions. Skinny's a pro and it's hard to believe he'd dump a body at a junkyard where a curious walker might find it when he could bury it somewhere in the desert."

With his phone on speaker, Giles dialed the office. He said to Ashley, "I have a feeling—"

He was interrupted by the phone. "This is Adams."

The detective looked from Ashley to the phone. "Hank, this is Mike Giles. You busy?"

The uniformed deputy was on desk duty with a broken leg. "I'm reading the funnies."

Bingham smirked. Giles said, "I didn't know that was still a thing."

"What do you want, Giles? If I want a ball-busting I can call home."

"Do you have time to run down a few leads on the homicide I'm working?"

A clattering noise—"One sec." The phone thumped on the desk. A drawer opened and closed. "This official detective work?"

"You bet." Everybody wants to be a detective.

Adams said, "I'm ready."

"I need you to review Harvey Skinner's sheet. His nickname's

Skinny. Look for any violent crimes—rape, assault." Adams grunted. "Find a home address and telephone number; find out if he owns The Damp Thistle in Elko Nevada and if he's connected with Newberry & Skinner Gold Mining in Carlin, Nevada."

"Okay."

"Also, find out who owns the property here."

"Anything else?"

Bingham shook her head when Giles' looked to see if she had anything.

"Get back to me soon."

Giles disconnected the call.

In the distance, Giles recognized Keith Johnson's flashy Mercedes SUV hurtling down Stansbury's main dirt road. He said, pointing at the bulldozer working the gravel pit across the road, "I need to ask the driver if he saw anything." He looked at Bingham. "If you're coming, get in before Johnson gets here. I don't want him bawling me out for touching his corpse until tomorrow."

Bingham smirked. "I better take mine."

Giles closed his door and backed away from the scene.

The gravel pit operator, an overweight man in desperate need of a belt and a laundry day had seen nothing, heard nothing, and knew nothing. Giles figured all three limitations dogged the entirety of the man's life, but he stayed polite and asked as few questions as possible. Ashley Bingham listened intently but the line of her mouth told Giles she was doing her best to keep from laughing. Walking back down the steep incline to their cars, Giles' telephone buzzed. He hit speaker so Bingham could listen.

"Adams?"

"Newberry & Skinner owns 200 acres on Stansbury, the junkyard included."

"Any relation to Skinny?"

"Skinny inherited the Skinner half from his father in 2006.

He purchased the Newberry half in 2010. The gold mine's closed and from what I've found the corporate entity is a holding company now. It has businesses and properties in both Utah and Nevada, including something listed as The Damp Thistle."

"Okay. What about Skinner's sheet?"

Adams cleared his throat. "Pimping and pandering going back to the '90s, but he's been clean since he was released from prison five years ago."

Giles shook his head. Ashley smiled and winked. A tingly feeling started in Giles' stomach and threatened to move southward. He looked back at his phone. "Did you find a home address?"

"He lives in Utah, west of the Salt Flats near Wendover." Adams paused to clear his throat. "I found something else, too."

"Yeah?"

"Skinner has an exotic animal permit for an alligator."

"No shit," Ashley said as Giles caressed her thigh with a gentle stroke. She slapped his hand away and said, "That explains the tattoo."

Adams said, "I got nothing on that, ma'am. Mike, would you tell the sheriff I was helpful?"

"Sure thing, Hank."

Giles clicked off.

Ashley leaned in close. Giles' heart was beating drums. She kissed him with an open mouth, sliding a hand down his stomach, two fingers sliding beneath his belt.

Giles tried to step away, but his feet wouldn't move. "Someone's going to see us."

Ashley tipped a shoulder, smiled. "I don't think I care."

Giles looked at his scuffed boots, coughed into his hand. "You have anything going today?"

"Patrol. I-80 between Wendover and Tooele."

"I'm headed to Skinny's place. I need back up, if you can get permission."

"Saturdays are always boring as hell." With a devil's grin, she said, "On the way, I know a place."

Giles didn't know where the place was, but he knew what Ashley's intentions were and that tingle turned into something else entirely. "Thinking about lunch already, Ash?"

"Mm-hmm."

Giles wanted to say something clever, but instead he simply admired Ashley's creamy white skin and her golden hair. The cop stance, her feet wide, the right thumb hooked on her tactical belt, the other hand on her hip...

Ashley was a vision wrapped in coffee and beige polyester. And Giles felt like a sixteen-year-old worshipping at a centerfold's altar.

Giles turned off Leppy Pass Road and onto a well-maintained gravel drive. Ashley Bingham's Charger bounced in his rearview mirror. Her smell and taste were still vivid and distracting. When he pulled onto the wide concrete drive in front of Skinner's log-style house, a window blind next to the door lifted and fell back into place.

The motion pulled Giles all the way into the present. An electric anxiety constricted his chest as he shut the engine off. He grimaced at his reflection in the rearview mirror.

"I'm too old for this." Giles wasn't sure if he was too old for cop work or Ashley Bingham. He closed his eyes, clearing his mind for what was coming. He wasn't here to make an arrest. This was a routine interview. Get an alibi, look for deception and gather facts. At the end, Skinny's name would either be crossed off as a suspect, or it wouldn't. But that feeling...The same feeling he'd had all day was nagging at him.

I'm missing something.

Giles opened his eyes, wiped his damp palms on his jeans and pulled the key from the ignition. He opened the car door and stepped into the sharp desert heat.

Bingham's cruiser rolled to a stop on his left. Its air conditioner clicked and groaned when the engine shut off. Giles palmed his gun in the belt holster, its grips reassuring and cool.

With a tense face, Ashley adjusted her campaign hat and unfastened the thumb break on her holster.

Giles pointed at the window next to the front door. "We've been seen."

Bingham swept an arm at the desolation. "It's hard keeping a secret around here."

Giles' laugh felt good and eased his tension. "I guess you're right." Then: "I'll take the left side of the door. When I knock"— he pointed at the five wooden steps to the front porch—"you stay on the top step. If anyone shoots, shoot back."

Ashley nodded.

Giles' boots clacked on the wooden stair runners. He crossed the wide porch to the front door, looked over his shoulder at Ashley. Her right hand was curled around her holstered Glock's rubber grip. He rapped the door three times with his knuckles and stepped backwards and to his left.

Inside the house, light steps approached the door.

After several seconds, a man's voice said, "Yeah?"

"Tooele County Sheriff's Office. Please open your door so we can talk."

Giles watched the doorknob.

After three beats, the voice from inside said, "Talk about what?"

Giles glanced at Bingham. Her face was tight, she was leaning forward with bent knees.

"You have an employee named Hye Lee?" Giles' heart thundered, his ears buzzed.

The doorknob turned. Giles muscles strained with anticipation. The hinges squeaked, a gap appeared between door and jamb. A plump little man appeared, his face pinched and anxious. His hands were empty.

"What about Hye?"

"You're Harvey Skinner?"

The little man cleared his throat. "Yeah."

"May we come in?"

Skinner's eyes shifted from Giles to Bingham and he drew a ragged and surprised breath. Giles noticed his trembling hands. "Why is she here?"

"Helping," Giles said. "That a problem?"

Skinny's gaze swung back to Giles. His eyes were wide, pupils dilating. "No. No. It's okay." He backed into the house. "Come in." He shrugged. "I don't get many visitors."

Giles followed him inside, the entryway ceiling towering more than twenty feet high. A warm hardwood covered the floor with a lighter wood adorning the walls. "Is anyone else in the house?"

"No." Skinner looked around as if he thought someone might stumble down the hall. "I'm here alone."

"You're sure?"

"Of course I'm sure. Come in, please." He motioned for Giles to follow him into a large room at the back. A television was attached to the wall above the fireplace, a large sectional couch hugging two of the room's walls.

Skinner dropped onto the sofa, keeping his legs spread wide. He seemed calmer here than he had at the door. He gestured at the couch. "Sit anywhere you like."

Giles looked over his shoulder at Bingham.

She moved to Giles' left, her eyes never leaving Skinner. She said, "I'll keep my feet."

Giles sat on the couch's corner, a few feet from Skinner's perch.

Skinner stared at Ashley like she was an apparition. "What about Hye Lee?"

Giles stamped his foot. When he saw Skinny's eyes, he said, "You're talking to me."

Skinner gulped, his Adam's apple bobbing. In a quieter voice he said, "What about Hye Lee?"

Giles cleared his throat, watching Skinner intently. "She's dead."

Skinner blinked. His face paled to chalky-white. The tremor

in his hands started again. "She's—dead?"

Skinner's surprise seemed genuine to Giles. "When was the last time you saw Ms. Lee?"

Skinner's eyes slipped to a framed photograph next to the television. Skinner and Hye Lee were smiling in front of a tropical waterfall.

"Was she more than an employee, Mr. Skinner?"

Skinny gulped and rubbed his forehead with a shaky hand. "Yeah. She was."

"Did she live here with you?"

"No. Only sometimes."

"Sometimes?"

"She stays here when she's not working." A silver tear ran down Skinner's cheek as he studied the photograph.

Skinner wiped his face with the back of a soft hand and then looked at Giles. "Where is she?"

Giles ignored the question. "When's the last time you saw her?"

Skinner drew a trembling breath. "Three days ago. Thursday. She had a..."

After a few seconds, Giles said, "We know she was a prostitute."

"She had a date in Salt Lake."

"With whom?"

"Shit, man. I don't know. Some guy referred by some other guy willing to pay fifteen hundred bucks for a happy ending."

"Can you find out?"

"Yeah, I can find out. I keep records like everybody else. But where's Hye?"

Ashley said, "What was your relationship with Ms. Lee?"

"She. We."

"You were fucking?"

Skinner's eyes bounced, his fear packed the room.

Giles was confused and angered by the question. He raised his hand. "Hold on, Trooper." He patted Skinner on the shoulder and walked to Ashley. Her right hand was still tight on the Glock at her hip. He jerked his head for her to follow.

When they were in the entryway, Skinner still visible at the back of the house, Giles put his hands on either side of Ashley's shoulders. He leaned close and whispered, "What's happening?"

Ashley glanced at Skinner on the couch, and back to Giles. "I don't like him, Mike."

"What are you seeing?"

She shook her head. "A feeling."

Giles squeezed her shoulder. "I've had a feeling all day, but he's cooperating. We need to keep things light, do everything right. If he's our killer we want him to be comfortable enough so he'll make a mistake."

Bingham looked over Giles' shoulder at the family room. With a trembling smile she said, "I can do that."

"Okay. Good." Giles winked. "I want a private tour of the house. When the time's right, I'm going to ask for a bathroom. You'll be alone with him for a few minutes. You can do that?"

Bingham's eyes were alive, vibrant. She flashed a mischievous smile. "Of course."

The earth moved under Giles; he was awed by this woman's power. He cleared his throat. "Take your hand off your Glock and sit next to me on the sofa." He touched her elbow with a finger. "And try to act sympathetic."

"Got it."

Ashley ran her hand across Giles' jaw as he turned back to the family room. Her steps echoed down the empty hallway.

When they were on the sofa, Bingham's hands on her thighs, Giles said, "Before we go any further, we need to tell you Hye Lee's body was found this morning. She was shot to death."

Skinny blinked, tears streaming down his face.

Giles let him cry. After a few minutes, he said, "We need to know who she was meeting in Salt Lake."

Skinny's eyes were unfocused and lost.

"Can you get that information for us?"

Skinny's head trembled. "I probably don't have a name, but I should have the client's contact information, how the date was set up."

"Can you get that here, or do you need to call someone?"

The pimp raised his eyes at Giles. "I have an office here, everything's on the computer. You think the client killed her?"

"We won't know until we check it out."

"I didn't kill her," Skinny said.

Giles raised an eyebrow at Ashley. To Skinny he said, "We're looking at everyone at this point in the investigation, Mr. Skinner."

"Let's get what you have about Ms. Lee's *date*, Harvey." Giles heard sarcasm in Ashley's words, but he didn't say anything.

Instead, he adjusted his belt, and said, "I hate to ask, but I need to visit the bathroom."

Skinner pointed back towards the entryway. "There's a bathroom around the corner and to the left." He took a step past Giles. "I'll show you."

Giles waved a hand and smiled. "No need, I'm a regular wilderness scout when it comes to finding restrooms." With embarrassment plain on his face, Giles continued, "I'll be a few minutes."

Fear sparked in Skinner's eyes.

"You'll be okay without me?" Giles said.

Bingham said, "Of course we will, won't we, Mr. Skinner?"

Skinner nodded, the same cold fear from earlier obvious on his face. "Sure." He pointed to a wide hallway at the room's far end, in the opposite direction from where the bathroom was, next to the fireplace. "My office is down there."

When Giles rounded the corner, he paused, listening to Skinner and Ashley walk in the other direction. He heard a few quiet words and when the footfalls and voices went silent, he moved further into the hallway. He passed a kitchen, white and silver everywhere, a bathroom—shiny and clean—a room piled high with cardboard filing boxes. A locked steel door on the back wall.

Moving back toward the entryway, Giles noticed a sliding glass door on the kitchen's far wall. On his toes, Giles crossed the cold floor.

Water shimmered on the door's far side. A kidney-shaped pool surrounded by exotic trees, large-leafed and spiny, green as a jungle. The door slid open without a sound. The unexpected heat and humidity made it hard for Giles to breathe.

He said, "Hello?"

A flash of green, a splash of water. The movement smooth and unhurried. Two prehistoric eyes studied Giles. An ancient fear fluttered in his belly. The alligator sized him up, moving without care across the calm water, a languid wake rising at its tail.

Giles backed up, never losing the alligator's progress across the pool, until he bumped into the glass door.

He gasped, startled by the contact. He chuckled at his fear before finding the door's handle and pulling it open.

A low boom roared, and sudden pressure thrummed in Giles' ears.

The detective jumped, adrenaline and anxiety rushing him.

He knew it was gunfire and the implications were bad. Either Ashley was shooting, or someone was shooting at her.

Trying to get back into the house, Giles stumbled, fell to his knees. In his peripheral vision, he saw the alligator stepping onto the concrete, its short legs fluid on the solid ground. He flung open the door, its metal frame slamming against his shoulder. Pain crackled down his right side. Giles tumbled ahead into the kitchen. He reached back and pulled the door closed behind him with a thud.

The alligator lazily watched from the other side, its black eyes dead of anything recognizable to Giles.

The detective pulled the gun from beneath his jacket. On bent knees he passed through the kitchen, the Browning's muzzle aimed at the ground a few yards ahead.

In the hallway he stopped, listening. His heart banging in his ears.

"Trooper Bingham!"

Silence.

"Ashley!"

Giles rushed into the entryway. Ears buzzing, white heat in his head, he scanned the empty family room and the quiet stairway leading to the second floor.

He shouted again and crossed into the family room, slowing as he approached the hallway leading into Skinner's office.

"Ashley?"

From inside the office: "I'm here!"

Giles darted into the hallway, stopping at the door of a large windowless room. Its walls were littered with lurid posters—dancing women, promising magic and happiness. Bingham was on her knees at the edge of an opulent desk, leaning over a supine Harvey Skinner. Her left hand was pushing into her back pocket. With her right hand she was checking Skinner's pulse.

Giles stepped into the room, his Browning steady. He said, "Ashley?"

She looked over her shoulder. He could see blood smears on her uniform shirt.

"Shit. Shit, Mike." Anxiety shadowing her words. "Skinner pulled a gun from inside the top drawer. He was going to—to—"

Giles said, "Are you shot?"

Ashley shook her head. When she noticed Giles staring at the blued automatic on the floor next to Skinner's right hand, she picked it up.

Giles holstered his gun, not noticing the blue latex gloves Ashley wore.

"Harvey—" Bingham's chest shuddered, her head and neck trembling.

Giles shifted to where Bingham stood. He placed a hand on her shoulder. "It's okay, Ash, but you need to tell me what happened."

"Shit." Out came a timid smile and it broke Giles' heart. "He said wanted a cigarette"—she pointed at the desk—"and he pulled a gun." Ashley held the slim automatic out, showing it to Giles. "He pulled it from inside the drawer and—"

"You shot him?"

She giggled. Giles knew it was her body's way of releasing fear and adrenaline. "My gun was in my hand and—I shot him."

Giles walked to the desk. The drawers were closed tightly one on top of the other. His instincts were shouting at him, but he wasn't thinking straight, wasn't understanding what they were telling him.

He turned to Ashley. "Where was the gun?"

Ashley didn't move, not answering, the blued automatic she'd taken off the floor still in her hand at her side.

Giles looked at Skinny's crumpled and lifeless body on the floor, and then at the desk. "The drawer, did you close it?"

"Ah, Mike. I fucked up."

When he looked at Ashley, all Giles saw was the gaping chasm of the automatic's barrel.

The trooper shook her head, her ponytail bouncing. Her mouth was pulled into a hard and angry line. "You sure picked a good time to become a detective, Mike."

Giles blinked with confusion.

"You don't see it yet, do you? I forgot to open the fucking drawer."

Giles was iced with fear. Nausea fluttered low in his belly as he understood. "You?"

"You're as stupid as everyone else, Mike. Yeah. Me. I killed the whore. She—"

Giles shifted, his hand moving to his holstered gun.

"Don't, Mike. I'll kill you."

"Why?"

"He—" Ashley pursed her mouth and the dimple appeared on her cheek. Mike wanted to cry.

"Why, Ash? Help me understand. It's not too late—"

Ashley smiled. It was hard and unforgiving. "I didn't know who he was at first, just a nice guy with a fat wallet. I fell in love, Mike. You understand that, right?"

"Sure, I understand it, Ash."

"But then he wanted to know about work, where we patrolled. When we patrolled. It seemed so unimportant, Mike. I mean, some guy who lives in the middle of nowhere. I thought he was just being nice. But then"—Ashley's face paled, and red splotches crept up her throat and splashed her face. "That whore. She poisoned him against me."

Giles whispered, "Hye Lee?"

"That bitch!" Her gun hand wavered, the muzzle rolling in small circles.

Giles' gripped the Browning and waited for an opening.

"Mike," Ashley's voice soft, "I don't want to kill you. You know that, don't you?"

Mike nodded, his mouth a desert.

"Harvey didn't want me anymore, but he still wanted our schedule. When and where, everything. I told him to get lost, but he threatened to send photos—Photos of me, Mike. You know how hard it is for a woman. For me. I should have made corporal last year..."

Mike knew they'd given the stripes to a trooper with less experience and a lower job performance. He knew Ashley had deserved the promotion.

"I know, Ash. It's not fair, but we can work this out. Skinny pulled a gun on you, you shot him in self-defense. I'll back your story. I will."

Ashley shook her head, the gun steady again.

"I love you, Ash. I really do."

"It's too late for that, Mike. You would have worried on those closed desk drawers until you figured it out."

"What about us?"

"Us?" Ashley sounded sorry. "Me and you? There's no me and you."

Mike saw everything then. She'd worked their brief relationship, fanned into his lust at the crime scene, fogging his head with impulse and desire as she scuttled the murder investigation from the start. He pulled his hand away from his gun.

"I'm the sucker."

"You're the sucker, Mike, but I didn't want this."

Bingham's gun flashed, pain flamed in Mike's shoulder. He smashed into the wall and tumbled to the floor. Blood gushed from the wound. A metallic taste to his mouth, and a darkness formed at his vision's edge. He watched as Ashley pulled the trigger again, fire leaping from the gun's barrel. Its impact was flat and hard. He coughed, a hot sticky fluid bubbling in his mouth and oozing across his lips.

Ashley said something Mike couldn't hear. She walked behind the desk and pulled open a drawer. She knelt by Skinner.

A fog drifted past Giles. A muted boom fell into his cold world.

He opened his eyes, Ashley had a phone in her hands, at her ear.

Her words were far away, but almost recognizable. "Off...n...ee.s...as...tance."

And Mike Giles drifted into nothing.

Michael Bracken is something of a short story specialist, publishing well over thirteen hundred stories during his career—so far. His tally increases with "The Ladies of Wednesday Tea," the story of a group of Texas ladies that know how to stand their ground. There's mention of an alligator as well as a trio of very bad kittens as we see that a flower shop can sometimes be more than it seems...

The Ladies of Wednesday Tea

Michael Bracken

Wednesday evening, after Florence Quigly closed Flo's Flowers & More—her nursery in Theodore, Texas—she sent her middle-aged grandson home. When she was finally alone, she stood at one of the counters in the back room preparing her special sachets for that evening's meeting of the Ladies of Wednesday Tea. Veronica, Betty, and Kevin—three tailless Manx cats she'd rescued from a drainpipe when they were just-weaned kittens—lay in various locations around the room watching her. She thought she had locked the front door several minutes earlier when she'd flipped the sign from *Open* to *Closed,* so she was surprised when she heard the tinkle of the brass bell affixed to the door.

Flo stopped what she was doing and stepped from the back room onto the dimly lit sales floor, where she found a stocky man staring at a display of seed packets. Broad shoulders and thick chest tapered down to a narrow waist. Muscled arms strained the short sleeves of his navy-blue polo shirt, and tight-fitting jeans hugged his hips and thighs. Dark hair stood up straight in a butch-waxed flattop above a weathered face, and the Confederate

93

flag tattooed on his left forearm caught her attention. She said, "May I help you?"

He turned with a start, and his eyes narrowed as he took her in.

Though weathered by decades of working in the sun, Flo stood ramrod-straight. Wavy gray hair framed her narrow face and her ice-blue eyes tracked his every move. "We're closed, but I would be happy to assist you."

He poked a finger at one of the seed packets. "The petunias," he said, his voice deep and low. "How much?"

"Two-seventy-nine."

Kevin had followed Flo from the back room, and he took an interest in the stranger.

"You have a nice place here," the man said. "Surprised I hadn't noticed it before."

"You from around here?"

"I pass through now and then."

"So would you like me to ring up one of those seed packets?"

"Another time," the stranger said as Kevin rubbed against his leg. He kicked the cat aside as he turned to leave. "Another time."

Dee, Charlene, and Twiz were well into their second glasses of wine when Flo finally bustled into Dee's dining room. As she handed each of them one of her special sachets, she told them about the customer who had delayed her arrival. She described his appearance and repeated everything he said, ending with, "He kicked Kevin."

"He kicked Kevin?" Charlene asked. "Why would anyone kick Kevin? Kevin's the sweetest cat ever!"

"I had locked the door but had not set the deadbolt," Flo said. "When I finally locked up for the night, I double-checked. There were marks around the strike plate. I think he jimmied the lock."

"Why would he do that? What do you think he wanted?" Twiz asked.

"To steal something, obviously."

"But what? A rake? A sack of compost? You don't have anything of value to a non-gardener," Charlene said. Flo's Flowers & More sold everything a gardener might need—bags of compost and fertilizer, various forms of pest control, drip irrigation systems, gardening tools such as trowels, cultivators, rakes, shovels and pitchforks. In the greenhouse behind the concrete block building housing the sales floor, checkout counter, and office, were all manner of potted plants suitable for East Texas.

"Cash," suggested Twiz.

"What cash? Most everybody pays by credit card these days."

They stared at one another and fingered their sachets, small muslin bags filled with dried herbs that would ease Dee's glaucoma, Twiz's arthritis, and Charlene's anxiety.

"You don't think...?"

Flo shook her head. "How would he know?"

After a moment of silence, Dee said, "Well, he's gone now, and nothing happened." Then she handed Flo a glass of the red she and the other ladies were drinking. "You have some catching up to do."

The oldest by only a few months, Flo had been a surprise gift her father gave her mother upon his return from serving in the European theater during WWII, and the other members of the group had likewise been post-war babies. Friends since childhood, they had aged into their seventies with various amounts of grace.

Flo began Flo's Flowers & More when she was a young mother, supporting her family after her alcoholic husband disappeared. Growing flowers and vegetables to sell at weekend farmers markets slowly developed into a full-time business, and several decades after selling her first pansies, she owned the nursery on the edge of town, where she still worked five or more days each week.

Dee Goldstein, the first female criminal court judge in East Texas, nicknamed "Gallows Goldstein" by defense attorneys for her harsh punishments, had faced criminals of all stripes across the bench. She had received so many threats that she took to carrying a snub-nosed .38 beneath her judicial robes.

Charlene Whit followed the path of her father, working for him in the only compounding pharmacy in a hundred-mile radius. He berated her almost daily until he died in a hunting accident, and she ran the pharmacy alone until it became obvious she could no longer compete with the chain retailers.

Red-headed Twiz Hanson, the youngest of the four and the only one who still dyed her hair, had married well, never worked a day in her life, and had the misfortune of being exceedingly clumsy, having fallen down stairs and run into open doors throughout the seventeen years of her marriage. When her husband died of a prescription-medicine overdose, she publicly mourned for an appropriate amount of time, and she never again visited the hospital due to an accidental fall.

Twiz changed the subject. "How's that grandson of yours?"

"Bless his heart, but sometimes I think Dickie's dumber than a sack of rocks," Flo said. "I swear he'll be the death of me. If he wasn't blood, I would've cut him loose a long time ago."

"Men," Charlene said with a weary shake of her head. "They're all the same."

"I tried to explain that to my daughter," Flo said, "but she was boy crazy just like we were when we were young."

"So how is your daughter?"

"Older and wiser," Flo said, "and I'm stuck taking care of her life lesson."

"Who needs a man?" Dee asked. "If I want something to clean up after, I'll get a dog."

They all laughed.

"We'll never need another man," Twiz said. Over the years each had lost a spouse or a significant male figure, though *lost* might not be the appropriate term. They knew where the bodies were. "As long as we have each other, we have everything we'll ever need."

They all raised their glasses.

Mid-morning the next day, Richard "Little Dickie" Rhodes worried his red bandanna between his fingers as he stepped into his grandmother's office. With his hawk nose and weak chin, he resembled his father's side of the family more than his mother's, but he had none of his father's swagger. "I was wondering if I could get an advance on my—"

Flo stopped petting Veronica and looked up from the seed catalog open on her desk. "What now?"

"I owe a guy some money."

"I've already advanced your pay into the middle of next month." Veronica jumped from her lap and climbed onto one of the filing cabinets with Betty and Kevin.

"Yeah, but—"

"Isn't it about time you learned how to manage your money?"

"Just a couple of hundred, Nana," Little Dickie said. "That's all I need."

"That's all you ever need," she said. "You planning to bleed me dry a couple of hundred at a time?"

"No, I—"

"Well, that's what you're doing, and it's time to put an end to this," Flo said. "I promised your mother I would look after you, but there's a limit to my generosity."

"But, Nana—"

"Take your 'but' out of my office and go help Hector load the Johnsons' compost order."

Little Dickie opened his mouth to protest yet again but withered under his grandmother's gaze.

A few hours later, Dee brought Flo lunch from the Piney Woods

Café. After leaving Hector in charge of the cash register, they brushed cats off Flo's desk and opened Styrofoam containers overflowing with chicken-fried steak, mashed potatoes, and purple-hull peas, all smothered in white gravy.

"I didn't want to say anything in front of the others," Dee said after she closed the office door, "but that tattoo on your visitor the other night is a problem."

"How's that?"

"He's Confederate Mafia." The Confederate Mafia controlled much of the illegal activity in East Texas and West Louisiana. "I probably put that man's pappy or grandpappy in Huntsville. Why would they be interested in you?"

"There's no reason they should be," Flo said before she scooped potatoes and gravy into her mouth.

"I ran your description past a retired cop I know," Dee continued. She reached into her oversized purse and pulled out a stenographer's notepad upon which she had made notes. "She said he sounds like Jace Parker, a top lieutenant for Caden Black. Black was in my court a few times, but never convicted. Apparently, he's moved up the food chain these past few years."

"I still don't know what this has to do with me."

Kevin jumped into Dee's lap and tried to stick his nose into her plate. She gently pushed him away. "Whatever Jace wanted, you'd best be ready for him to come back for it."

Little Dickie did not show up for work Friday morning, and it wasn't the first time he'd proven unreliable. Flo called his cellphone several times throughout the day, leaving messages to remind her grandson of the tenuousness of his continued employment, but he never showed up and he never returned her calls. Luckily, foot traffic remained slow, so Flo and Hector were able to meet the needs of their few customers that day.

That evening, after Flo sent Hector home and she shut off the lights, she stepped outside. While searching her ring for the correct key to set the deadbolt, a deep male voice behind her said, "I think you have a problem."

Startled, Flo dropped everything. She turned to see the man who had visited her two nights earlier. She asked, "Change your mind about the petunias, Jace?"

He ignored her question. "Your grandson owes my boss a good bit of money."

"And what's that to me?"

"He says you'll make good."

"He does, does he? Why would he think that?"

"You've got a good thing going here," he said. "Hate for anything to happen to your side business, or to Little Dickie."

"Are you threatening me?"

"If you ever want to see your grandson again, you'll meet with my boss tomorrow afternoon." He told her a time and gave her an address. "And don't be late."

He turned, and she watched as he climbed into a black Ford F-150 and drove away.

After she collected her key ring from the ground and locked the deadbolt, Flo used her cellphone to call Dee.

Despite glaucoma's impact on her peripheral vision, Dee drove Saturday afternoon, following directions from the GPS system on Flo's phone, to a home deep in the Piney Woods an hour north of Theodore. She parked in front of a single-wide mobile home next to a creek that ultimately fed into the Sabine River. No other homes were nearby, and in the side yard lay a twelve-foot-long alligator, a steel collar padlocked around its neck. A thick chain affixed the collar to a steel post driven deep into the ground, and a great length of chain allowed the alligator to soak in the creek if it so desired.

The front door opened at Flo's knock and Flo led the way into the mobile home to find two men—the man who had twice visited her and a heavyset man with a bulbous nose and a Confederate flag tattooed on his left forearm—standing on either side of Flo's grandson, holding him upright by gripping his arms. Little Dickie had his hands zip-tied behind his back, and bruises on his face made it clear he had gotten the worst of whatever had happened since Flo had last seen him.

"You're late," the heavyset man said. He nodded at the window overlooking the side yard. "We were just about to feed Burt Reynolds. It's past his lunch time."

Dee stepped around Flo. "Hello, Caden."

"Good afternoon, Judge," the heavyset man said. He turned to Flo and asked, "Why's she here?"

"To help me negotiate."

"Negotiate? I don't negotiate." He shook Little Dickie. "I get a piece of your business and you get this piece of shit back."

Dee rummaged through her oversized purse. She pulled out a snub-nosed .38, pressed it against Caden's crotch, and cocked the hammer.

His eyes widened. "What the hell do you think you're doing?"

Dee smiled. "Now we're negotiating."

The heavyset man stared into the judge's eyes and swallowed hard.

"Boss?"

"Step back, Jace."

Without taking her eyes off the heavyset man, Dee instructed Flo to take Jace's truck keys and leave with Little Dickie.

Flo asked, "What about you?"

Dee winked at Caden. "I'll be fine."

Two hours later, Dee walked into Flo's Flowers & More.

Surprised, Flo asked, "How'd you get away?"

"I shot him."

"Caden's dead?"

"I just shot him in the thigh. A flesh wound. He'll be fine."

"But what if the police get involved?"

"He won't call the police. He can't afford to. Then they'll start looking at him." Dee glanced around. "Where's your grandson?"

"I sent him to his mother's in New Mexico. He's her problem now."

"He's the one who told them about your special sachets, isn't he?"

"He said as much when I threatened to give him a few more bruises before I let him go."

Flo's Flowers & More was closed on Sundays but Flo often spent her afternoon in the office catching up on bookkeeping. When she arrived, she discovered that someone had turned her greenhouse into a veritable killing field. All the potted plants had been overturned and dumped on the pea gravel walkways, bits of shattered statuary were scattered throughout the mess, and Veronica, Betty and Kevin were nowhere to be found.

Flo phoned Dee, Twiz, and Charlene and the three women arrived within half an hour. They lined their purses up on the front counter before Flo led them into the greenhouse. As they inspected the destruction, Dee told Twiz and Charlene what had happened.

"No man is going to threaten us and get away with it," Charlene said.

"Well, then, let's clean this up."

They'd been at it for almost an hour before Veronica, Betty and Kevin finally surfaced, and all three cats watched from a safe distance as the women worked. By early evening the women had the greenhouse in some semblance of order, and Flo stepped into the building housing the sales floor to call for a pizza delivery.

She reappeared a moment later with a gun pointed at her head.

Jace eyed the women and said, "Looks like you brought the whole gang this time."

He made Flo call her friends into the building, where Caden Black waited. As the women filed in, followed by all three of the inquisitive cats, Caden warned Jace, "Keep them away from their purses."

Jaden directed them away from the front counter.

"We only expected two of you," Caden said, "but it don't matter. We're going to make an example of you ladies. Nobody pushes dope around these parts without my permission, and"— he waved his gun at the judge—"nobody shoots me and gets away with it."

Twiz stepped forward. "You can't—"

Jace backhanded her.

Twiz had lived through worse. She rope-a-doped the slap and stood her ground.

Kevin leapt on Jace's head, digging his claws into the man's cheeks. Jace spun around and tried to bat the cat away.

Taking advantage of the distraction, Charlene grabbed an aerosol can of bug killer from the shelf and sprayed it into Caden's eyes.

Dee grabbed a three-pronged cultivator, swung it like a ping-pong paddle, and buried the prongs into Caden's neck.

Jace finally knocked Kevin free, but as he did, he stumbled backward, squeezed the trigger of his pistol as he fell, and died when the bullet ricocheted off a shovel and buried itself between his eyes.

Caden tried to remove the cultivator from his neck with his free hand while drawing down on Dee. Before he could squeeze the trigger, Flo drove a pitchfork through his lower back.

When the four women caught their breath, Twiz looked at the mess and asked, "What do we do now?"

Flo smiled. "I know where there's a hungry gator."

Jen Conley's best stories unfold the dark recesses of her characters' hearts. She excels at atmospheric tales of betrayal and spent emotions. Here she presses our buttons as we experience Paul's despair while he tries to avoid disappointing his family once again. As Jen tells us in the story, "He just wanted to drink a bottle of water and watch the Mets lose." But there was something he had to do first...

Demon Dogs

Jen Conley

When Paul limped out to the backyard, he neither heard nor saw the little demons. There were traces of them—a ripped up tennis ball they'd been fighting over, pieces of his tomato plants strewn around, several piles of brown poop they'd produced, flies buzzing over the clumps, and a big hole in the crabgrass where they had been digging down to their maker, Satan himself.

"Rory! Brody!" he called.

Nothing.

Paul felt his gut tighten, his heart take up speed. *Shit.* He carefully climbed down his rickety deck, limped around the small yard to the side of the house and noticed another hole he hadn't seen before: they'd dug under the stockade fence. They'd escaped. Like inmates.

Shit.

He fumbled with the gate lock, yanking it open, and hobbled out to the front. The late summer sun was setting and the evening was loud with crickets and the whirring of air conditioners.

"Rory! Brody!"

He was sweating.

Shit.

A boy on a bike rolled by.

"You seen two puppies?" Paul said. "One's brown and white, the other black and white."

The kid nodded and pointed. "Down the street."

"Shit," Paul muttered.

"I'll get them," the kid said, taking off on his bike.

Paul turned back to his house, limped as fast as he could up the cracked front porch to the door, jerked it open, reached inside and snatched two leashes, one red, one black, from the inside hook. Then he moved quickly back down the porch, across the yard, along the street, the boy just turning the corner heading back towards him.

"They're nowhere," the kid said.

"Fuck," Paul snapped. Then he looked at the boy, who was about eleven. "Sorry for my language."

The boy shrugged. "Not offended."

"They're my daughter's pups," Paul explained, gripping the leashes. "She's in St. Martin." He shook his head—he was confused. "No, St. Lucia." Paul and his ex-wife had once talked about going to St. Martin. His daughter was actually in St. Lucia, with her husband. "She left the dogs with me."

The boy raised his eyebrows which were thick and fuzzy like weird caterpillars from the tropics. "Well, you're in friggin' trouble, aren't you?" the kid quipped.

Paul snorted. *Little punk.* "Yeah, I am. So can you help? Get your friends? I've got this limp."

"How'd you get that limp?"

A car flew by them—teenage driver. Paul's stomach lurched. Puppies were always getting hit by cars.

"What happened to your leg?" the kid asked again.

Paul stared at the boy. "I tripped over the dogs." Brody had gotten under his feet, sending him flying to the kitchen floor. This was all true but there was more to the story. "I have a weak ankle," Paul added.

The boy blinked at him. He wanted more.

"Years ago," Paul said, waving it off. "I fell down a flight of stairs." Actually, Paul had fallen off a balcony onto a flight of stairs, then tumbled down to an obscure corner, snapping his ankle almost in half. Nobody had found him until dawn. Those were the Drinking Days. Took another four years after the fall before he became a regular at AA. He was five years sober now.

"You should call the police," the kid said. "The puppies probably have a chip in them."

"Chip?"

"Yeah. With their contact information. They'll call your daughter."

Paul felt the color go out of him. "No, no, don't call my daughter. Let's find them. Come on."

The boy yanked out his cell phone, hit a button, and spoke to it. "Yo! Outside!" and took off. Paul hobbled down the street, leashes gripped in hand, calling out to the little shits. "Rory! Brody!" The kid returned in ten minutes with friends—three other boys on bikes and Razors, swirling around like dragonflies. They were a pack of oddballs: long sloppy shorts, T-shirts with stains, some wearing Nike slides with old socks, one with eyeglasses that made his eyes bulge, all pale with dark circles under their eyes. They were probably in the house all summer long playing that computer game he'd heard one of his AA friends complaining about. Fortnite.

Paul ordered the boys to get on the task—"Go find them!" He, himself, limped some more, shouting desperately to his daughter's dogs. "Rory! Brody!" The demons were four months old, the apples of Katelyn's eyes. Years ago, when she was small, before the divorce, he'd come home with a tiny mutt puppy someone at the bar was getting rid of. His wife was furious because they didn't have the money to keep a pet. But Katelyn fell in love with the puppy and five days later, the little guy died. The vet said that he'd been ill all along. His wife hated him for bringing the dog home. "You're useless! You can't even bring home a healthy puppy we can't afford!"

"Rory! Brody!" the boys called out. They were swirling around Paul again. The streetlights were on.

"You should call the police," the one boy said.

"Not yet," Paul said.

"They could get hit by a car," another warned.

"Or eaten by a pit bull. They're puppies, right?"

"Or kidnapped for fighting. What kind are they?"

"Miniature Australian shepherds," Paul answered.

"Then they'll be kidnapped for bait." That was the one with glasses. His bug eyes gleamed under the streetlights.

Paul let out a heavy breath. "Thanks for your help. I got it now." He shooed the pale knuckleheads home and hobbled back to his house, the leashes still in hand, his ankle probably swollen and bloated into an official sprain. He got in his car with an air conditioner that was shot to hell. He drove around the streets of the neighborhood. It was dark now.

He'd been a terrible father, of course. Years of drinking, before and after the divorce. He'd missed birthdays, her high school graduation, all that. Yet when he sobered up, Katelyn wanted to know him again: "It's important to me." And later, before she left for her delayed honeymoon, she chose him to watch her puppies. "I trust you, Dad. They'll be fine. Besides, Mom hates dogs. You love them."

Not so true. He'd never been an animal person. He'd just been drunk that day he brought the sick puppy home.

"It's just five days," Katelyn said. "It will be fine." But it wasn't fine. His house was small, rented and broken down, and these puppies were wicked little devils. Surely sent from Satan to torment Paul, a demented payback for all the harm he'd caused. Rory barked every morning at 5 a.m., bashing against the inside of his crate like a feral monster in a horror movie. The other one, the black and white one, Brody, chewed anything he could get his mouth on—tissues, Paul's sneakers, electrical cords. Brody was also the smarter of the two—he'd gotten out of his crate the night before, possibly because Paul hadn't latched it properly. Paul woke up to Brody sitting on his chest, breathing hot air onto his face, like that old Poe story with the evil cat. Paul was betting that this escape was Brody's idea. Everything was his idea. He started the trouble, the fights, the wildness where they raced around the house, outside, back in the house, and bit each other until they cried, then collapsed on top of each other for a quick nap. They were exhausting. Which is why he shoved them outside. He needed a rest. His ankle hurt. He just wanted to drink a bottle of water and watch the Mets lose.

He drove around and around, until it was eleven o'clock, the moon high in the sky. The kid was right. He needed to call the police.

Inside his house, he sat on his secondhand couch, cell in hand, trying to figure out if this was an emergency or a non-emergency. In his old life he'd had enough run-ins with the cops to know that it was important to not piss them off, make the wrong call, irritate even the dispatcher.

Then, like a death knell from hell, his cell rang. It was Katelyn. His heart throbbed and hammered. His gut pulled. She was calling late. Something was wrong.

Shit.

He answered.

"Hey Dad!"

Paul could hear muffled music in the background. She and her husband were probably at some island nightclub, drinking cocktails. For a quick second, he felt a pang for his old life.

"How are my puppies?" she asked.

Like a tick from his drinking days, he lied like a champ. "All good. Right here with me." He began to babble. "They ate, played nicely, and then fell asleep. Rory just lifted his head when you called but his eyes are closed now. They're really nice pups. But they miss you. Dogs always miss their owners. Glad you're having a nice time."

"We are, Dad. Thank you so much," Katelyn said. "I'm glad

my dogs are safe and sound. I was worried about them and then Ryan said, 'Call your, Dad. It will make you feel better.' I'm going to be a mess when I have kids, right?"

"Yeah, maybe."

She chattered a bit more, but he said nothing. His heart was heavy as he gazed at the empty dog bed, the right side torn up from Brody chewing the hell out of it.

Suddenly, his daughter stopped talking and a heavy pause followed.

"Dad…" Katelyn finally said, her voice stern, deep, and dripping with irritation, just like her mother. "You can stop now."

"Huh?"

"The police called me. They have my puppies. Alive. So go get them."

There's a mystery in the small town of Cooper, New Hampshire, and Carl Barrington rides in, determined to solve it. But who is Sally Ford? For that matter, who is Carl Barrington? And what are the officials of the town really hiding, simmering beneath their seeming respectability? Brendan DuBois carries us along in this tale of grift and greed in the rural northeast...

The Strangers in Town
Brendan DuBois

In the rural town of Cooper, New Hampshire, word quickly spread when the stranger arrived and rented a room at the Exit 45 Motel, about a two-minute drive away from I-89, the interstate that barreled its way northeast through this part of the state and into Vermont and southern Canada.

Gail Stevens, owner of the motel, quickly phoned Mack Gellar after the stranger had checked in. The man's name was Carl Barrington with a home address of Reston, Virginia, and she told Mack Gellar—the town's head selectmen—all she knew of him: male, mid-thirties, one small black carry-on bag, and that was it. He was driving a plain white Buick sedan with New Hampshire plates and didn't seem to care what kind of room he was going to get.

Gail was instantly suspicious of the stranger and told Mack what she thought.

"You know how it is," she said. "We rent to families that don't want to pay the prices for being near the lake resorts, or for losers on their way to get lost somewhere. This fella don't look like no loser. I don't like it."

Mack Gellar, sole owner and proprietor of Gellar Plumbing

and Heating, said thanks to Gail, and then called Jim Portford, the town's chief of police, and passed on the license plates to him.

But Chief Portford was having none of it.

"Sorry, Mack, I told you before," he said. "License plate queries like these get tracked. I run this down and what happens later when...well, you know. I don't like it. I won't do it."

Yet Mack—who'd been head of the three-member board that ran Cooper's affairs—wasn't going to fold over either and said, "You want that new cruiser next year?"

"Shit, Mack, you know I do. My old Crown Vic's been in the shop more times than it's been out on the road."

"Then think of something," Mack said. "Random training exercise. Say the fella crossed over a double-yellow line. Be creative, Chief."

Mack hung up, rubbing his hands with worry. The phone rang again and it was Gail Stephens from the motel.

"That man Carl Barrington just left," she said. "He asked for directions to the Estates Trailer Park. You told me to always reach out to you if somebody asked how to get to that trailer park, and now he's done that."

"Thanks, Gail," he said.

"Can't you tell me what this is all about?"

"Not now, Gail, I'm busy," he said, and he replaced the receiver and looked down at his paperwork. He was prepping a quote for tearing out a failing oil furnace for Pam Morse and putting in something more efficient. Old Pam was whining about the cost and he was scared shitless she was going to back out of it and leave him in the red for this quarter, but he couldn't see how much more he could massage the damn numbers to get her to buy in.

The phone rang.

It was Chief Portford.

"The plates run back to Hertz, up from the Manchester airport."

"It's a rental," Mack said.

"Better than that," the chief said. "My nice Bridget, she works at the airport, she's dating a fella that works at Hertz, and found out more. The man Carl Barrington, he rented it using a Federal credit card."

"Damn," he breathed. "And Gail told me that Carl Barrington is on his way to the Estates Trailer Park."

The chief said, "Must be an investigator. Looking for Hudson Troy and his money."

"I hope so."

"Third time's the charm, eh?"

"Don't ever say that again," Mack said, hanging up the phone, and rubbing at his chin, looked over the paperwork again.

Those new connecting valves, he thought. He could pull what he needed from the scrap pile in his spare barn, give them a good scrub and put them in fresh boxes. Pam Morse wouldn't know the difference.

That'd knock the price down enough so he could make the sale.

Damn her, he thought, getting up from his cluttered desk. Damn her, this small town, and Hudson Troy.

At the Estates Trailer Park on the outskirts of this little town, I drove around the narrow cracked and crumbling roads until I found a double-wide home with the black numeral "12" on the white mailbox. I parked my rental, slung on my dark blue suit jacket that concealed my waist holster and Sig Sauer pistol, and went up the few steps to the front door.

It was hot. I couldn't believe how hot it could be, this close to the Canadian border.

But at least the mountains had trees. Lots and lots of trees. That I liked.

I had spent too many months in places where the mountains were bare and rocky and hid men who wanted to kill me.

I knocked on the door and a short and wide and wrinkled

111

man wearing a soiled white T-shirt and blue slacks answered the door.

"Sorry to bother you, sir," I said. "My name is Carl Barrington. I'm looking into a young man who lived here a couple of years back. Hudson Troy."

The old man shook his head.

"Don't know him."

"I'm sure," I said. "But did you know anything about him? Friends? Relatives?"

"Nope."

"You sure?"

"Damn right I'm sure," he said. "Anything else you want to do to waste my time?"

I said, "I heard he had a woman he was very close to. Sally M. Ford? Does that ring a bell?"

He started closing the door. "About the only damn bell that's ringing are you fools who keep on bugging me about Hudson Troy."

"You mean there's been others?" I asked.

The door was closed.

I turned and went back to the rental.

A weary looking police cruiser drove by, the officer inside looking at me.

I guess there had been others.

Later in the day, Mack Gellar got another phone call from Chief Portford, and the chief said, "Just like we thought, went up to number 12, spent a couple of minutes with Manny Powell."

"I bet Manny told him to go to hell."

"Probably," the chief said. "But there's a problem. He's still there."

Mack swiveled in his office chair. "What? Still at Manny's?"

"No," the chief said. "He's still in the trailer park. Going door to door. This one...he's turning out to be dedicated."

"Shit," Mack said. "That's a problem."

The chief said, "Maybe not. Maybe this one will get the job done. That'd be nice, wouldn't it?"

"You do your job, Chief, okay?"

Mack hung up the phone, rubbed at the back of his neck.

I went through fourteen homes before coming across one that offered a bit of a trail, faint as it was. It was at the far end of the trailer park, near a small convenience store that served the area.

There were cardboard boxes piled up in the driveway and one overwhelmed young woman with a boy and girl—six or seven, it looked like—who were scrambling around and making a cheerful nuisance of themselves. She was late thirties, pudgy, wearing black yoga pants and a Montreal Canadiens T-shirt that had sweated through in interesting places. She wore black-rimmed glasses and when I introduced myself, gave me a wide smile with perfect white teeth.

"Marty Harrison," she said.

"Glad to meet you," I said. "Sorry to bother you on moving day, but I'm looking for information about a man named Hudson Troy. I understand he lived in this park a couple of years back."

She spared a moment to yell at the boy and girl—"Bill, Jay, stop that right now!"—and she said, "Maybe."

A flash of optimism.

"Maybe? How firm a maybe?"

She ran a hand through her short blonde hair. "My ex-husband Jerry, a more worthless piece of shit you'd never meet—excuse my French—hung out with him back then. Hudson was an ex-soldier, right, served in Afghanistan?"

Close, oh so close, I thought. "No. He was a civilian contractor."

"Unh-hunh," she said. "Okay. Now I remember. And why are you looking for him?"

I said, "Because he was a thieving civilian contractor. Where's your ex-husband Jerry now?"

She struggled to pick up a box. I helped her, and followed her into the empty double-wide. More boxes were piled up in the living room.

"Freezing his ass and balls out in the Bering Sea, I hope," she said, bending down, offering me a nice view of her cleavage. "Jerry got caught up in watching those reality TV shows about crab fishermen, decided to dump me and his kids, go out there and make his fortune. If he's made anything, he hasn't sent any of it back."

She got up and her two kids burst in, laughing and chasing each other around, and I said, "I also heard that Hudson had a friend named Sally M. Ford. Does that mean anything?"

The young girl and boy were on either side of their mother, each tugging at the hem of her T-shirt.

"Mom! Mom! The store over there sells ice cream! Can we have some, please, can we?"

"Shhh," she said. "Can't you see I'm talking to this nice man here? Let me think. I swear, I can't think with the two of you screaming like that."

I retrieved my wallet, took out a ten-dollar bill. "Here. My treat. Go get some ice cream."

They both looked to their mom for permission, and a quick nod from her meant the ten-dollar bill was snapped from my hand, and in a second Marty and I were alone in her near-empty house.

"Well," she said. "Some time to ourselves. Okay. Sally...what?"

"Sally M. Ford. All I know is that Hudson was supposedly in love with her. And utterly devoted."

Marty nodded. "Sounds about right. I remember Jerry telling me a couple of times—when he was just half drunk—that he was going with Hudson to see Sally. And that Hudson was so excited."

Now I was excited. "Did he say where Sally lived?"

Marty said, "Not exactly. Only that she was up over at Perkins Flats. About ten minutes away."

"Thanks," I said.

"But I don't think that's helpful."

"Why?"

Marty said, "Because Perkins Flats is just a stretch of little businesses, right where the train used to stop. There's no houses in Perkins Flats. Just some run down places."

"Oh."

I was stuck there for a moment, and then Marty smiled. She said, "I bet my kids don't come back for a while."

I smiled back at her. "That's good to know. Need help getting your bedroom rearranged?"

Marty said, "Thought you'd never ask."

Mack Gellar was with Chief Jim Portford having a late morning cup of coffee at Polly's Diner when Lucinda Week, president of the Cooper Savings and Loan, came in to join them.

"Hey," she said, sliding into the booth. "What can you tell me about the stranger?"

"He's still here," the chief said. "Spent a lot of time over at the Estates Trailer Park, then I lost track of him."

"Did he go right to Manny Powell's place?"

"Of course," Mack said, looking around at the empty booths and tables. Years back, when Cooper Mills was running full-bore and making leather uppers for L.L. Bean, this place and two other restaurants in Cooper were always busy, filled with happy men and women making good money and willing to spend local.

Now the mill was gone, the other two places were gone, and Polly's Diner barely held on, month after month.

The chief said, "For Christ's sake, I wish Hudson Troy had left some paperwork behind. Fool. All these years, going around and around in circles."

Lucinda looked around for someone to take an order, shook her head. Polly's Diner was now run by Polly, her daughter Cassie, and her son-in-law Bruce, who never quite learned how to cook bacon.

She said, "But the stranger's still here. I wonder where he is, if he's going to find anything."

The door went *jingle-jangle*.

The chief said quietly, "He's right here."

Following the charming and enthusiastic Marty Harrison's directions, I drove over to Perkins Flats to see what was there, and the distressing answer was, not very much. It was a two-way intersection of state roads, with a convenience store, two service stations, a set of self-storage units, an empty four-business strip mall, and a Dollar Store.

No homes, no apartment buildings, nothing that could provide me with a lead for Hudson Troy or his one true love, Sally M. Ford.

I turned around, headed back to the town of Cooper, and stopped at the only eating establishment it apparently had—Polly's Diner. I went into the diner, thinking of who I could speak with next, and as I walked in carrying my soft leather briefcase, the door *jingle-jangling*, I felt like a scratch-off lottery ticket I had purchased on a whim was paying off.

The next few minutes would determine if I had won a dollar, or a thousand.

Mack Gellar saw the confidence and bearing of Carl Barrington approaching them, and there was the look in his eyes and the way he held himself that said he was an experienced man, one who knew his away around weapons. Mack had seen that look a lot decades back, when he was just nineteen and making the run into Kuwait City with his Marine platoon.

The stranger caught the attention of Chief Portford and said, "Chief, may I have a moment?"

"Sure," he said, and Carl pulled a chair away from one of the score of nearby empty tables and sat down with the rest of the group. Mack heard an intake of breath from Lucinda and hoped the stranger didn't notice it.

Carl said, "I'll get right to it. I'm looking into the background of someone who lived here for about six months, a couple of years back. Hudson Troy. Sound familiar?"

The chief cautiously said, "Yes. He lived over at the Estates Trailer Park. Who are you, may I ask. Friend? Relative?"

Carl had bright hard blue eyes, short dark brown hair. "Oh, not hardly." He reached into his coat pocket, brought out a slim wallet, and displayed a tiny badge and a photo identification.

"I'm with the U.S. Army's Criminal Investigation Command," he said with confidence. "Quantico, Virginia."

I had thought earlier about being cautious and kind about my investigation into Hudson Troy, but I saw a chance right before me in this diner, and as the old Tammany Hall pol George W. Plunkitt once said, "I seen my opportunities and I took 'em."

And these three locals were mine.

Mack felt his legs and hands go cold.

This was the third time, and it was definitely different.

"Go on," he said.

The Army agent said, "Excuse me, I didn't catch your name."

"Mack Gellar," he said. "I own Gellar Plumbing and Heating. I'm also one of the selectmen."

"Select what?"

"Selectmen," Lucinda Week said. "Town as small as this, we have a three-person elected board that runs town affairs. I'm the second selectman as well. Lucinda Weeks. And I'm president of

Cooper Savings and Loan."

The stranger said, "And there's a third, then?"

"Next election," Mack said. "Porter Franks got himself a job down in Manchester."

"Fascinating," Carl said. "Well, Hudson Troy is who I'm looking for."

The chief said, "But he's been dead for two years."

"Yes," the Army agent said. "Drowning accident on Lake Winna...Winni..."

Lucinda said, "Winnipesaukee."

"Thanks," the man said. "Drunken boating accident at three a.m., according to official reports. Which was unfortunate, because he couldn't be questioned later about what he did in Kabul."

"In Afghanistan?" the chief asked. "Was he in the Army?"

The visitor shook his head. "No, he was a civilian contractor with extremely sticky fingers."

"How sticky?" Mack asked, although he already knew the answer.

"Just over two million dollars," the man said. "In cash."

I checked the expressions on each of their faces—the lean hard-tanned plumber, the soft lumpy police chief, and the middle-aged woman wearing a sensible dark blue suit—and said, "Did you know that?"

All three said no.

All three were lying. Perfect.

I said, "I went by where he lived earlier, and the gentleman there was no help. Earlier I visited the lake, and found out that during that summer he was there most times, raising hell and spending money, and that the double-wide in the trailer park was where he went to sleep off his fun. His belongings went back to a stepdad, and nothing was there. But we know he stole two million dollars, and we're still looking for it."

The plumber said, "It's been a few years."

"The Army is like an elephant," I said. "A long memory. Now, I also found out that he apparently had a girlfriend in the area. One Sally Ford. Sally M. Ford. You folks...you know this town, know it well. Does that name mean anything to you?"

All three said no, and I was disappointed to sense that they were all telling the truth.

Damn.

Well, I had one last thing to try, and I really didn't want to do so, but I was running out of options.

I went into my soft leather case, pulled out a file folder. I said, "Ma'am, you're the head of the Savings and Loan, correct?"

Her face went the color of the paper napkins on the table. "Yes."

I pulled out a slip of paper. "This is a court order, authorizing you to release the contents of safety deposit box number one-one-nine, said box being rented in the name of Hudson Troy, late resident of Cooper, New Hampshire."

The woman took the slip of paper like it was contaminated by plutonium.

I said, "How does the next fifteen minutes sound?"

When the Army agent left Mack Gellar said, "Damn it, Lucinda, he knows about the safety deposit box!"

The chief said, "It should be empty. I told you that you should have destroyed that slip of paper."

Lucinda looked at the court order, folded it in half, her face flushed. "And suppose some long-lost relative came out of the woodwork and asked to take a look inside the box? And he or she had evidence that the paper was in there and now it was gone? The Savings and Loan is one missed loan payment from having the Feds seize it and put it out of business. You think I need publicity like that, somebody's box being robbed?"

She got out of the booth. "Besides, it's a phone number. On

a slip of paper. What can he do about it?"

Mack called out after her, "You find out, you let us know!"

When she was gone Chief Portford said, "That money...think what we could do with it."

"I know."

"You think he'll puzzle out that phone number? I mean, we called it scores of times, looking for that damn Sally Ford. Backwards and forwards, no luck."

Mack said, "He's the Army. Maybe he will. But in the meantime, dump your cruiser, get in your truck, park near the Savings and Loan. I gotta go home, get something. Then I'll park up the street at Bobbi's hair salon. If he finds out something, we'll follow him."

"Then what?"

"Then we get what rightfully belongs to us."

The woman from the bank, Lucinda Weeks, was crisply professional and took notes, and made photocopies of my identification, and a few minutes after I had entered the very small Cooper Savings and Loan, I was in a tiny office with a slim safety deposit box before me.

Hardly enough room to hold two-hundred dollars, not to mention two-million.

I opened it up wondering what secret Hudson Troy had placed within, and out came a white slip of paper with a series of numbers written underneath a name: SALLY.

There were seven numbers.

A phone number?

I took out my cellphone, dialed.

The number bleep-bleeped back at me, and a voice said it was disconnected.

There you go.

"Shit," I said.

I slipped out of the bank and went to the parking lot, saw

my rental Buick, saw someone's old Jag—definitely not a local—
and two Fords and a Chevrolet.

"I'll be damned," I thought.

I got into my rental and started to retrace my steps.

For times like this, Mack and the chief had burner cellphones,
picked up at the Super Walmart in West Lebanon. The chief
called and said, "He's headed your way."

"Okay."

And yes, there was the rental white Buick. Mack started up
his pickup truck—the spare that ran rough, because he didn't
want to be following the Army man in his work truck—and slid
in right behind him.

Mack said, "On him."

"Okay," the chief said. "I'm seeing you both. Where the hell
do you think he's going?"

"Maybe someone finally answered that phone number."

"Maybe."

Mack focused on his driving, not wanting to let his mind
drift, think back about the previous two times he and Lucinda
and the chief thought they had the two million dollars within
grasp.

"Mack?"

"Still here. He's heading up to Perkins Flats. And
there...well, you know how it is. Five more miles and then he's
in Leah."

The chief said, "Just so you know, Lucinda pulled out of the
Savings and Loan. She's right behind me."

Shit, he thought. He was about to say something else to the
chief when the Army agent's rental Buick started slowing down,
with a turn indicator.

"He's turning left."

"Where?"

"At Perkins Flat."

"Gassing up?" the chief asked.

"No, he's...Oh shit, that's where he's going!"

The self-storage facility was true to its name. Nobody kept office here. There were just a series of signs indicating a 1-800 number to call if one had a problem.

I was hoping I didn't have a problem, only a solution.

I parked the Buick and looked down at the slip of paper I had liberated from Hudson Troy's safety deposit box. Being seven numerals, I thought it had been a phone number.

I had thought wrong.

The first three numerals were one, zero, two.

I walked up to unit one-zero-two.

Hanging from a clasp was a thick combination lock, a strip of rubber over it, protecting it from the elements.

The other four numerals were seven, one, two, seven.

I worked the combination lock with those numerals and after a hefty pull, the lock popped free.

I slid out a retaining bar, reached down to the handle, and tugged the sliding door up.

There.

Light switches.

I flipped them open.

Before me was a wide and deep storage unit, and parked in the middle was a dark blue 1966 Ford Shelby Mustang GT350. I ran the back of my hand along the dusty trunk and whispered, "Hudson Troy, you old thief, you sure had good taste in cars."

There was a small pegboard set next to the light switches. A set of car keys dangled from the top and I took them down, went to the trunk, and opened it up.

"Well, well, well," I said.

Two bulging black zippered duffel bags.

I opened the near one, revealing plastic-wrapped packages of American currency, with Ben Franklin's face smiling up at me.

I heard cars pull up nearby.

I turned and my diner companions from earlier were walking over to me: Mack Gellar, Lucinda Weeks, and police chief Jim Portford. Their faces were a mixture of surprise, awe, and...regret?

They stopped in a line in front of the open storage unit.

Mack Gellar said, "You found it."

"Yep," I said, smiling. "Sally M. Ford. A funny little code and reminder. 'Mustang Sally.' A song about a woman who wanted a Mustang. I guess old Hudson Troy was a Wilson Pickett fan."

"What now?" the woman asked.

"Now?" I said. "I take the cash, go back to my office at Quantico, write up a report and pass the money over to someone at the U.S. Treasury."

The police chief shook his head. "Sorry, sir, we're not going to allow that to happen."

Mack Gellar looked closely at the Army agent, wondering what Carl Barrington would do or say in reply, and was surprised when he said, "That's nice, Chief. But it is going to happen."

Mack said, "No, sir, it isn't."

The agent took one duffel bag out, and then the other, and slammed the Mustang trunk shut.

"What, is this some kind of small-town humor?"

Mack said, "Nothing funny about it, sir. You see, Lucinda and the chief and me, we're sort of an ad hoc committee looking to improve and save this little town. That stolen money is going to do just that."

The agent's face widened in a grin. "You're looking to steal money that's already been stolen?"

Lucinda spoke up. "That's taxpayer money, isn't it? American money. And it was sent overseas to do what? Bribe some warlord? Used to pay off opium farmers? Stolen by the Taliban so they could buy more weapons?"

Barrington shrugged. "Not my circus, not my monkey."

Chief Portford said, "That's our money, and it belongs here, where it can be used for our benefit. Not wasted halfway across the world."

The agent picked up a duffel bag in each hand. "Like I said, not going to happen. Now, if you'll excuse me."

Mack stood still, and so did Lucinda and the chief.

With duffel bags in hand, he stopped, quickly laughed. "What, are you going to stop me?"

Mack said, "Yes."

"How? Shoot me?"

Mack said, "That's the general idea. We've done it before."

I gently lowered the duffel bags to the ground.

This was going very weird.

I felt like I'd been dropped into a Shirley Jackson story.

"Say again?" I asked.

"Twice before we had young men come into town, claiming to be friends of Hudson Troy. They made a nuisance of them-selves, poking around, asking questions. Both said that they would go to the newspapers and Channel 9, to get publicity. We couldn't allow that."

"And?"

"And we didn't let them do it," Mack said. "Do I have to go any further?"

"You could," I said.

Mack said, "Me and the chief, we're Marine vets. First Gulf War. Lucinda Weeks, she's the best hunter in this part of New Hampshire, has a Boone and Crockett record for bagging the best trophy buck. Guns and shooting don't bother us none."

He paused.

Mack said, "That far enough for you?"

I looked carefully at each one of them, and saw a similarity in their eyes.

Something cold nestled right in my chest.

My 9 mm Sig Sauer was safe in its holster, and I said, "That's a hell of a threat."

Mack said, "We want that money. We need that money. And we don't make threats."

"If I pick up these bags then, there'll be shooting, is that right?"

Chief Portford said, "That's right."

"You got a cover story?"

The bank woman said, "Easy enough. Small town. We're trustworthy folks. The chief knows the local state police, the county attorney. We could make up a believable story about how a stranger came into town, fell into some misadventure."

I laughed and in that moment, my pistol was in my hand.

Mack felt his legs go stock still. "That's one against three."

"Sure," the man said. "I'll end up dead, and at least two of you, if not all three, will either be dead or wounded. I've seen men wounded. It's not like the movies. Hurts like hell, maybe you lose a kidney, maybe you end up in a wheelchair. So get out of the way."

The chief had his pistol out, and Lucinda dropped her large purse, her own pistol in her grasp.

"No," the chief and Lucinda said together.

"No," Mack repeated, slowly removing his own 9 mm Smith & Wesson from a hip holster.

More seconds passed.

Mack said, "That's the chance we're prepared to take. That money...you can't imagine the difference it would make for our little town. So why don't we all lower our pistols, you walk out and go back to Quantico, and tell your boss that you found Hudson Troy's Mustang, but the trunk was empty."

* * *

I quickly took in everyone's hard stares, saw the weapons in hand, and slowly lowered my pistol.

"I can't leave here empty-handed," I said. "My unit, my boss, we're invested in recovering these stolen funds, and closing out this case with a recovery would be a good thing for my record, my career."

The heating and plumbing man said, "Excuse me for being blunt, but we don't give a shit about your career."

Three against one.

I had planned, researched, and prepped a lot for this case, but having three armed locals get in the way was never anything I had considered.

"Understood," I said. "Then let's compromise."

The woman banker was instantly suspicious. "Compromise?"

"Yes, compromise," I said. "You need money, I need money. There's over two million dollars here. Let's split it, and we'll all go our separate ways."

The police chief said, "Won't your boss be suspicious?"

I shrugged. "Better to get fifty percent of something than go back with nothing. I'm sure I could make the case to my boss that Hudson Troy had spent half his stolen funds before he drowned. And you folks...I'm sure you could fill a lot of potholes with a million dollars. What do you say?"

Glances back and forth. The man named Mack said, "Suppose we say no?"

"Then you'll kill me and I'll do my best to return the favor before I hit the ground."

More glances, half-nods, and then Mack said, "Mister, you got yourself a deal."

Hours later Mack was in the crowded and cluttered basement of his plumbing and heating store. Wooden shelves were stuffed with cardboard boxes filled with a variety of spare parts from valves to washers. On a stained wooden desk, the stacks of hundred-dollar bills had been separated into three piles. All of the piles save one were made of plastic-wrapped money.

Lucinda Wells nodded in satisfaction. "There. Three hundred and sixty-five thousand dollars apiece."

Mack said, "Never seen so much cash in all my life."

Chief Portford frowned. "I still think we got screwed."

"And that's why you never got what you requested at budget time," Mack said. "You don't know how to negotiate. Remember what that Army guy said? Better to have half of something than nothing. This is a nice haul without a single shot being fired."

Lucinda said, "What now?"

"Now?" Mack put his arm around his share and pulled it near him. "Gellar Plumbing and Heating goes out of business. With the sale of my parts and equipment, plus this, I'm off to Florida. Or South Carolina. Haven't made up my mind. Any place where there's no more snow. You?"

Lucinda started putting her share into her purse. "California. Always wanted to learn to surf. Chief?"

"Any place where people don't think they can boss me around just because they pay taxes," the chief said with quiet satisfaction. "To hell with them all."

Mack stared some more at the cash. Finally, *finally*, they had gotten what they deserved, even if it meant lying, cheating, and killing those two idiots who thought the money belonged to them.

Lucinda said quietly, "Do you think that Army agent will ever check in with us? To see what we actually did with the money?"

Mack said, "At this point, what difference would it make?"

After I dropped off my rental car at the Manchester airport, I got a taxi cab to Manchester Motors, a used car dealership only a couple of miles away. After some haggling and cash passing hands, I got a nice sturdy used Toyota, and started driving west.

No particular destination.

Just west.

At some point, I was on a two-lane state road that passed over a deep and wide river. I pulled over my Toyota and when I was sure I was alone, I dumped my fake Army ID, along with other papers. A long time, a very long time it was, chasing down Hudson Troy and planning how I was going to get our—*mine!*—money back. It had been a joint venture back there in the 'stan, and I had taken my time to get what was owed me. And stupid Hudson Troy had done me a favor, getting his drunken ass drowned.

Otherwise I might have gotten blood on my hands, never a nice thing to consider.

Still, I only got half the funds, but what the hell. It would support me well for a long time.

As for the good residents of Cooper, I wondered how they would spend their money, and if they would ever someday check out the Army agent who had come into their town and found the missing cash.

I walked back to my car, shrugged.

At this point, what difference would it make?

Charlaine Harris's book series have translated well onto the screen, including True Blood, The Aurora Teagarden Mysteries, *and* Midnight, Texas. *Here she brings us to a small town in Texas with a local police officer and a family secret. The officer's trouble starts when he inherits a house and most of its belongings, including what's in the basement...*

Aunt Tally

Charlaine Harris

Getting a house for free is no small thing.

Officer Bob Westmore put the key in the front door of the restored Victorian—wrap-around porch, old stable in back—situated in the oldest neighborhood of Gethsemane, Texas. It was a big moment. He took a deep breath and turned the key. With a smooth click and a turn of the knob, the heavy oak door opened into a familiar hallway lined with photographs, old and new.

Bob squared his shoulders and took a deep breath before he stepped inside and shut the door behind him. Having a place of his own at all, on a policeman's salary, had been something he'd only dreamed of. Taking possession of Aunt Tally's home was beyond those modest dreams.

Bob was not an outwardly emotional guy, but he felt a stew of feelings bubbling up inside him.

There was grief, for sure. Natalie Spencer, known to everyone in Gethsemane as Tally, had been buried yesterday. His mother, Tally's best friend, had been in shock. Everyone who worked at the police station had been in the little Catholic church, in uniform, to honor one of their own.

Bob had talked with Don Carmody after the funeral. When

the lawyer had told him he'd been left something in Aunt Tally's will, Bob had hoped she'd maybe left him her rifles and her personal weapon, a Sig Sauer. To find he'd gotten the house...it had been almost more than he could take in.

Then today, Bob had reported for his shift right on time. He hadn't told anyone about the house. He had to get used to the idea before he could share it with anyone but his mother, who'd gone to the lawyer with him since she was also a legatee. Aunt Tally had left her a pair of diamond earrings she'd inherited from her mother and her own vanity table "since Bob sure won't need it." Everything else was Bob's.

So mixed with the grief was excitement. When you've been living in a cheap apartment, like Bob had been for years, having your own home—a very nice home—for free...well, that was a big thing.

"I can't believe it," his mom had said, delighted for her son. Annabeth had been been Tally Spencer's best friend from childhood, so all Annabeth's kids called Tally their aunt. Annabeth had offered, right away, to go to Tally's house and go through the refrigerator and so on: but Bob had said no. Bob had always liked to do things in an orderly and deliberate way. Bob smiled as he remembered Tally calling him "Judge Bob" when he was little. He'd kind of liked the nickname. He did like to weigh every factor deliberately before he made up his mind. He'd been debating about Sarah Jane Causey for a year now, much to Annabeth's exasperation.

Now, Bob took off his Stetson and hung it on the old-fashioned hall rack. His padded jacket, too. It was January. Even in Texas, January can be cold. But Bob could hear the familiar whoosh of the furnace through the vents. The house was warm.

Bob looked at the pictures he'd seen a thousand times: Tally on her horse, Loose Change, during her barrel riding days; Tally as the 1973 Hollister County Rodeo Queen; Tally in her bridesmaid's dress at the wedding of Bob's parents; Tally in her police uniform. Tally with her marksmanship trophies. Pictures of Tally's parents, too, and Tally's deceased brother, much older than Tally.

Bob felt that at any moment Tally herself would come down the stairs, her hair (which had only gotten gray in the past two years) in its ponytail, her tanned face smiling. She'd be wearing a sweater and jeans, or shorts and a blouse. Tally had liked her comfort, and she'd had the knack of making other people comfortable, too. That had made her a good police officer, equally effective on patrol her first twenty years with the force and later, when she'd moved to a desk job in Dispatch.

Bob already missed her, even as he looked around the ground floor rooms with the new eyes of ownership. He'd been in and out of this house his whole life; his parents' house was only one street over and a block down. Aunt Tally's had been a frequent stop on his childhood perambulations.

Aunt Tally had always had lemonade and cookies, or hot chocolate and snack mix, and she'd always been glad to see him. Aunt Tally had always been on the mercurial side, and she'd delighted in Bob's deliberate nature. She'd really seemed to enjoy his company. Now that Bob was a cop, he'd had some less than happy dealing with boys of all ages, so he kind of marveled at that.

There was a living/family room through a big doorway to his left, and the dining room was to his right. As he moved down the hall, he switched on lights. The kitchen, with its breakfast nook, extended the whole back of the house. It had absorbed the smaller family room during a remodel fifteen years ago.

The hall stairs led up to the three second floor bedrooms, plus a bathroom. There was what Annabeth called a "powder room" downstairs. And in the kitchen were the stairs that led down to the small cellar, a novelty in Texas.

Bob looked around the kitchen, the room in which he'd spent the most time. Tally's presence was very strong here. He could see her strong back, bent over the dishwasher. He could see her capable hands blending and stirring and chopping food as she cooked. Looking out the back window, he could see the small stable where Tally had kept a horse until ten years before. On one wall, Tally had hung a corkboard. Pushpins held a miscellany of items in place. And one was an envelope with "Bob" written on the outside.

Bob had been a cop for eight years, and though Gethsemane was as law-abiding as most small towns, he'd seen some very unpleasant things. Bob was not a jumpy guy, or easily rattled; anyone on the force would have vouched for that. But at that moment, in the silent kitchen, he felt an unpleasant jolt at the sight of his name printed in straggling script on the back of the white envelope.

Bob unpinned it from the corkboard. He sat heavily in the straight chair pulled up to the table to open it.

Bob heard Marlon McGowan's big pickup pull in at the next house. And he heard McGowan calling to his dog in greeting. After some excited barking and the slam of a door, there was silence again. And Bob tore open the envelope.

Inside was a series of numbers. The first one, he recognized: the combination to the gun safe. The second was a social security number, presumably Tally's. The third one she'd designated as her lock-box number at Gethsemane Bank and Trust. And she'd listed phone numbers for her lawyer, the funeral home she'd favored, and the bank. No personal note.

Bob was relieved.

Now, in Tally's kitchen—his kitchen—Bob put his head in his hands and grieved all over again. When that was done, he sighed and stood up, ready to turn to practical things.

The landline rang. Bob jumped a mile, and then laughed a little, glad no one had seen him. He went to the little desk in the living room to answer. "Hello?" he said.

"Hey, honey, I figured you'd be over there," his mother said. Annabeth Westmore was the opposite of her friend: where Tally had been sturdy, Annabeth was wispy. While Annabeth was still fair and sweet-looking, Tally had been olive-skinned and blunt.

"You could have called my cell," Bob said. His heart was still beating a bit fast.

"I guess I'm just so used to picking up the phone and calling Tally," Annabeth said, and Bob could tell she was trying to hold back tears. "It's about the time she'd be getting home from her shift on Dispatch."

Bob glanced at the clock on the microwave. "Well, I'm here. Everything's fine, nobody's broken in or nothing like that."

"So what are you doing?" Annabeth asked more brightly, and Bob realized she was hoping he'd ask her to come over. And Bob almost did that...but then he reconsidered. This was *his* time, *his* house, and he wanted to keep it that way.

"I'm looking things over," he said. "I'm just trying to get used to owning something this big."

"Well, when you decide you're ready to move, let me know," Annabeth said. "I'll help. I know she left it clean, but if you need me to come scrub, I'll be more than glad. Or to gather up her clothes to take to the thrift store."

"I'll let you know, Mom," Bob said, trying to suppress his impatience. "Thanks. Maybe I'll see you later." They said goodbye and he hung up with some relief. Stuffing the numbers into his pocket, Bob went up the stairs.

As a child, Bob had always stayed in the bedroom to the right, in the double bed with the paisley pattern bedspread. But now the biggest bedroom would be his. Bob had a bad moment when he'd stepped in the room, seeing the covers of the big bed thrown back, the pillows piled up to prop up Aunt Tally so she could breathe. That was where Tally been when Annabeth had called the ambulance.

The television remote was on Tally's bedside table, along with a thriller she'd been reading and a bottle of cough syrup. A wastebasket was full of used tissues and an empty bottle of cough syrup. The woman who had used these things would not ever be here again. With a pang, Bob thought of Aunt Tally telling him that he should enjoy every minute of his life. He hoped she had enjoyed hers.

Bob remembered his mother had said something about Tally's clothes. He opened the closet. The garments were hanging neatly, her shoes and cowboy boots arrayed on the floor.

Bob suddenly remembered he should search for Tally's personal firearm, the Sig Sauer. It should be in her night table drawer, where any person of sense kept her weapon. Instead, he found a note, addressed to him just like the one downstairs had been. But this one was not in an envelope. It was on a folded sheet of stationery, and his name was written on the blank side. The stationery was sprinkled with flowers.

Bob was sure his mother had given the stationery to Tally, because it was much more Annabeth-like. He wondered if there were any more communications scattered around the house, and he prayed there were not. This was hard on the few nerves Bob had. When he unfolded the sheet, he saw there was no opening, and the handwriting was wobbly and slanted. Nonetheless, it was Aunt Tally's.

Bob, they keep telling me I'm going to be fine, but I don't know that they're right. I hope you're glad when you find out I left you the house and everything else. Your mom has been my best friend my whole life. You're my favorite kid of hers, Judge Bob.

Bob grinned at the nickname. His little sister Cissy had always been too silly to suit Aunt Tally. Cissy, fresh out of her first marriage, was only waiting for the right man to take her out of this town forever. His older brother Mark was career Army. Mark would never come back to Gethsemane.

Anyway, when you come see me in the hospital—or after I get home!—I'll tell you everything you need to know. The important stuff is: I replaced the furnace two years ago, and I got the roof redone after the ice storm in 2008. It should be fine for another ten years. The paperwork on both is in a file marked "House." Filing cabinet is in the upstairs hall closet. There's a cluster of poison ivy come up in the back yard around the west corner fence post. I remember you're allergic. The refrigerator may last another couple years, but it's old. Just get that freezer in the cellar hauled to the dump right after you unplug it. It's no good. Better not open, there's mold. But...

And Tally's last message to Bob ended with something unsaid. Maybe it had been interrupted when Annabeth arrived, calling up the stairs to let Tally know she was there.

Annabeth had become alarmed when she'd found Tally running a high temperature and gasping for breath. Annabeth had called an ambulance, over Tally's objections. By the time Bob had finished his shift and driven to the hospital, Tally had been unconscious. The next day, she had died.

Bob had been stunned. He hadn't known people could die of pneumonia unless they were homeless and couldn't get medical treatment. It had never occurred to Bob that Aunt Tally was not going to make it, even though he'd been concerned about the coughing fits she'd had at the police station.

Bob searched deeper in the bedside table drawer for Tally's Sig Sauer. No luck. Where could it be? That's where everyone kept a personal firearm. Maybe she'd put it in the gun safe when she'd felt so bad, knowing other people might be coming into her home. Thanks to Tally, he had the combination in his pocket, and he hurried downstairs to check.

Sure enough, Tally's gun was in the safe with the rifles that had belonged to her father, and the ones she'd bought herself for skeet shooting and hunting. He was relieved to scratch that worry off his list. She'd thought of everything.

But it made Bob wonder even more about the things Aunt Tally had not said. She'd lived in this fine house, inherited some money, and she'd possessed so many skills and interests. Why had his honorary aunt never married?

Later that night at his mother's house, Bob asked her. Now that Annabeth was a widow, she seemed especially delighted when he stopped by and said he was hungry. As Bob ate meat loaf and macaroni, he made a point of listening to his mother as she talked about what people had said to her after the funeral, who had ordered flowers for Tally at the shop where Annabeth worked part-time, and the flaws of his sister's newest boyfriend, who had made an excuse to skip Tally's service. "Cissy's going to let it slide," Annabeth told him, shaking her head. "That girl is just hoping he'll be the one. But who should think of marrying a man who won't honor his wife's dear ones?"

Bob didn't want to talk about Cissy, who was incomprehensible to him, always had been. "Mom, how come Aunt Tally always lived alone? She never even got a pet, unless you count the horse."

Annabeth bent to pat her little Yorkie, Toto. "Who wouldn't want one of you little guys?" Annabeth said to the dog. She looked at Bob. "I asked her over and over, 'Tally, you want me to call the breeder, see when Sunshine's having another litter?' But she always said no. 'What about a cat?' I asked her, though I can't stand 'em myself, but she said no to that, too." Annabeth shrugged, widening her eyes to show Bob how amazing she found this. "Me, I like to come home to something living. Tally, she didn't mind the empty house. I think she never found a man who suited her. They came around, for sure."

"I know you guys were best friends," Bob said. "It was like she was my real aunt. Did she have any other good friends?"

"Oh, sure," Annabeth said, sitting across from him. "Peggy who works at Clip N Curl, Shelley who's married to Jeff Cranston. The gals on the bowling team. And all the people she knew through work." Annabeth smiled. "Tally spent a lot of time working in her yard. You remember going over to help her in the spring? She said Mark would just climb trees when he came, but you were a real little helper. And you know how she loved birdwatching! She tried taking Cissy one time, and Cissy started crying and Tally had to bring her home."

Bob realized he might owe the Victorian to an ability to plant petunias where Aunt Tally wanted them, and his talent for sitting still when Aunt Tally was birdwatching.

"But what about men friends, that's what I'm asking. She

was a good-looking lady." Seeing the pictures of Tally as a young woman had reminded Bob of that.

Annabeth's lips pursed. After a second, she said, "Tally dated when she was in her teens and twenties. She was real thick with Tom Boling for a year or two, so I had hopes. But she decided he drank too much. And Peter Satterthwait, him she dated for a good long time. But in the end, she said he was a mama's boy."

"No one else serious?"

"Tally was just real picky. There was one guy. I don't know what happened. After that, she kind of shut down the dating."

"What guy was that?"

"His name was Cliff Howard. He was from out of town." Annabeth seemed uncomfortable, and Bob couldn't figure out why.

"Okay...so this Cliff, he and Aunt Tally were really into each other?" Maybe Annabeth was uneasy because the two had been sleeping together. His mom was old-fashioned about some things.

"For a little while." Annabeth shook her head, got suspiciously busy putting away the leftovers. But Bob had always been persistent, and he was curious, now.

"Did you like him?" Bob said.

"Did *I* like him? I never knew him that well."

"So what happened, if she was so crazy about him?"

"One day, he just left town. And that was it. Went back to Dallas, I guess. It hurt her feelings bad." Annabeth glanced at him. She said quickly, "When do you think you'll move in? That's what you want to do, right?"

"It's a great house. I'll move in as soon as the lawyer says I can."

"Great," Annabeth said, with a more genuine smile. She turned away to put the dishes in the sink.

"Do you remember putting a letter for me in the kitchen? At Aunt Tally's?"

"No, son. Maybe she asked one of the ambulance people? They made me leave the room while they were working on her and getting her ready to go." Annabeth's back was still to him, and her hands had quit moving. After a moment, she said, "What did the letter say?"

"Just stuff about the furnace," Bob said slowly. "House stuff."

When Annabeth turned to ask him if he wanted more meat loaf, her usual smile was back on her face. "Well, I'm glad the lawyer let you have the keys right away," she said. "Not wait all that time, for probate. It only makes sense."

The next week, when Bob wasn't at work he was making phone calls, getting everything switched over to his name. Going by the post office to get a change of address card. Ordering new checks with the new address. Changing his magazine subscriptions. All the hundred niggly details of moving. He began packing up his apartment, which wouldn't take long. He didn't need any of the furniture any more.

Bob found he was excited. So was the woman he'd been dating, Sarah Jane Causey, Bob could tell. But Sarah Jane was careful not to ask to tour the house, not to ask if he needed any help painting or redecorating, not to ask if he wanted her to help him move. She was so careful about not asking it felt almost painful. He wasn't sure how he felt about that. Relieved, maybe.

The next time Bob had a chance to go to the house was a Sunday. His mom, and almost everyone else he knew, including Sarah Jane, would be at church.

It was peaceful, knowing he wouldn't be interrupted.

After Bob stripped the bed in the biggest bedroom—he was making an effort not to think of it as "Aunt Tally's room"—he flipped the mattress and washed the mattress pad. He remade the bed with clean sheets from the linen closet. He'd bought a new bedspread, a red and brown and gold southwestern pattern, to replace Aunt Tally's quilted flowery comforter. The lamps were a bit too frilly for Bob, and he replaced them with some from his apartment. Then he considered the bedroom redecorated.

Bob had brought boxes for the clothes and shoes, and it was easy enough to dump them in. Goodwill would be glad to get them, he hoped.

After he carried the vanity table, the one Aunt Tally had left Annabeth, down the stairs, he sat down to rest for a minute. He hadn't been in the attic yet, but he didn't feel like letting down the stairs and looking. It would undoubtedly be full of junk from years gone by. As the heat came on with the usual gust of air from the vents and a dull whoosh from below, Bob realized he also hadn't been in the cellar, which he thought of primarily as the home of the furnace. The cellar was only half below ground since the house was raised, like most Victorians.

The original cellar had a dirt floor. He distinctly remembered Aunt Tally telling him that when he was a little boy, because young Bob had found that spooky. But for years now, maybe Tally's lifetime, in fact, the floor had been concrete.

The wooden stairs were sturdy, and there was a rail. The lighting was a bare bulb hanging from the ceiling in the middle of the crowded room.

The walls were lined with deep metal shelves from Sam's Club. One held tools, another items Tally had bought in bulk (detergent, toilet paper, tissues). Another shelf was full of Christmas decorations, and the artificial tree was covered with a plastic tent in a corner. Tally's birdwatching equipment took up some wall space, too. She had a camo stadium chair, a big ice chest, a tripod, fancy binoculars and camera equipment. Bob wondered what he would do with all that.

The furnace, which Aunt Tally had assured him was only half the size of the original, squatted in another corner. And the ancient chest-style freezer was along the east wall, under one of the narrow windows. It was almost as tall as Bob's waist. *It probably weighs a million pounds,* he thought.

"How the hell did they get that thing down here?" Bob said out loud. He looked at the width of the stairs, looked at the chest freezer, and shook his head. The stairs must have been rebuilt at some point after the freezer had been deposited in the cellar.

Aunt Tally had told him he should get rid of it. Bob agreed. He remembered, vaguely, that when he was very small, Tally's brother (now many years gone) had come by with two ice chests full of packages: a deer he'd killed and had processed. He'd asked Tally if he could store the deer in her big freezer, since his was full of game.

Bob could almost see her face as she'd laughed and told him he'd have to pay her rent in deer meat.

Well, that deer would be long gone, but there might be food in the damn thing. His aunt had mentioned mold in her letter. But now that Bob considered it, he found it hard to picture Tally letting the freezer sit unused down in her cellar, all filthy. That wasn't her way.

Bob shrugged and lifted the lid. The cold came pouring out, and then a slight but unpleasant smell. Tally had been right about the mold. He leaned over to look in its depths. At first, he thought *It's night in the freezer,* because all he saw was black. Then he realized he was looking down at black plastic. There seemed to be nothing else in the freezer but that. Bob looked at the outside of the freezer, then back at the inside. Something had to be under it. Maybe it was some kind of moisture barrier. Without further ado, Bob grabbed a corner of the plastic in his big hand and yanked it away.

Then Bob was yelling and jumping back, a collision with his head setting the bare bulb to swinging, so that the light careened around the room in a lunatic way.

The dead man in the freezer didn't care.

Bob collected his nerves, reminding himself he was a police officer. He found a flashlight on one of the shelves so he could have a good look. *I've seen worse,* he decided. But not recently, and not in a house he owned.

Five minutes later, Bob looked in Aunt Tally's refrigerator for beer. He slumped at the kitchen table with a Lone Star. He downed the first one in two long gulps. Now he was nursing the second one. And he was thinking grim thoughts.

Bob called his mother's cell phone.

"Hey, honey, I just walked out of church," Annabeth said. "I'm glad to hear from you. What are you up to?"

"Mom," Bob said heavily. "I opened the freezer."

There was dead silence on the other end.

"Well, shit," Annabeth said.

Bob had never heard his mother say that.

He heard her take a deep breath.

"I don't know what-all you found in there," Annabeth said, trying to resume sounding bright and careless. "But I'm sure if Tally told you the freezer needs to go to the dump, *that's where it should go.*"

"I think you better get over here," Bob said.

"Oh, honey, I promised Cissy I'd—"

"Now, Mom."

Bob was watching out the front window as his mother pulled into the driveway, went across to the porch and climbed the steps. There wasn't any spring to her walk. Bob wasn't in any mood to feel sorry for her, though.

Annabeth opened the door, called "Bob!" and then saw him standing in the family room.

"There you are," she said, and plodded over to hug him.

"Mom, I'm a police officer," Bob said. That was the most important thing to him. "Aunt Tally was a police officer. How could this happen? You tell me, because I'm sure you know."

"Bob, it was so long ago."

"That really doesn't make a difference," he said, trying not to sound as harsh as he felt. "As you are well aware."

Annabeth sighed, sat on the couch. Bob sat by her. He was fighting to be calm about this, fighting the urge to yell at her or handcuff her or call someone at the station. This was his mother, and she'd been a good mother to him and Cissy and Mark. He was telling himself that over and over.

"It was a long time ago," Annabeth said again. "Mark was already in the Army, and you and Cissy were out on dates. It was fall, you two were still in high school. You were a senior that year, so we hardly ever saw you. Tally was complaining about that. She called me on a Saturday afternoon. You two were out doing something. Your dad was out of town at one of his conferences." Her mouth twisted a little.

Bob's dad had been a farm implement salesman. Bob had always suspected his dad went mildly wild at these conferences, because sometimes his laundry smelled like liquor when he unpacked.

"Tally had been seeing this Cliff Howard, and she asked me to drop by on this particular Saturday to meet him," Annabeth said.

"So you went."

"Yeah, I did. I was at loose ends. And Tally being so excited about this man, I was curious."

Annabeth was silent for so long that Bob made an impatient gesture. She sighed again. "Well, Judge Bob—remember how she called you that?"

Bob nodded grimly.

"When I got there, they were sitting in the back yard with beers, and I joined them. The man seemed nice enough. Nothing...jumped out at me about Cliff.

"We talked about everything under the sun. All the traveling he had to do for his job. Cliff felt sorry for his brother, a deputy over in Erath County, because a law enforcement job does tie you down. As you know, son." Annabeth gave Bob a quick smile. "Cliff said he was trying to talk Tally into getting into sales, too, and maybe she'd move closer to his home base in Dallas."

"She was a good cop," Bob said, indignant about anyone trying to lure his aunt away, no matter how long ago. "She loved her job." Same way he loved it. They'd spoken the same language.

Annabeth smiled at him. "She was, and she did. But that

day, I could tell Tally wasn't brushing off the idea. She was nuts about this man. He wasn't handsome. He was small, not much taller than her. Just wore jeans and western shirts and cowboy boots, like everyone else around here. But Cliff had charm, yessirree, he did. He'd been everywhere and done everything, to hear him tell it."

Bob bit the inside of his mouth to keep from urging her to speed up. He thought of the face he'd seen in the freezer. It hadn't looked much better than that Ice Man they'd dug up in the Alps.

"The trouble started when we moved inside. I was having such a good time till then." Annabeth still looked upset about that, and for the first time Bob realized that his mother had not had a lot of good times, in those days. "I wasn't drinking much, because I just...never have. There was enough drinking in my family, with my dad..." Annabeth's face looked bleak, just for a second.

"Cliff thought I should have another beer. I said I didn't want one. I guess he'd had a lot more than I realized, because he got more and more...insistent. At first, Tally was laughing about it, and so was I—or trying to—but then it got past that. I didn't want to—I didn't want to be the cause of Tally getting mad at him, so finally I let him open another one for me, but when he went to the bathroom I poured most of it down the sink."

"How was Tally doing?" Bob asked, keeping his voice smooth and quiet so he wouldn't disrupt her narrative.

"She'd had a few," Annabeth said. "Tally could put down some beer. Never drank hard liquor. But she was navigating okay. When Cliff came back, he checked my beer can. It was like he'd had a personality change while he was gone. Instead of being funny but annoying, he was just annoying. And mean." Annabeth's thin hands clenched in her lap. Bob saw that she was beginning to tremble.

"He went off like a firecracker. He said I'd disrespected the hospitality he'd offered me—which I guess meant he'd bought the beer—and he could tell I'd poured it out because of the suds in the sink, and how dare I. He went on and on. We just waited for him to finish. He'd crossed the line, going a hundred miles an hour."

Bob had seen this before on the job. Alcohol could make the hidden things in anyone pop out, and over the most trivial of incidents. Only if you were used to the person who was drunk, only if you'd seen them change before when that internal switch got flipped, could you believe it. "What happened then?" he said, still quiet and careful.

"Went from bad to worse. Cliff started telling us we had to both get in bed with him together to pay him back for the wasted beer."

Bob felt a firecracker going off in his brain. This Cliff had suggested that to *his mother?* And *his aunt?* "I would have bounced him off the walls," he said, meaning every word.

"I wish someone had been there to do that. Tally was mortified. I knew just how she felt, and I told her not to mind, she couldn't have known he was an asshole before that moment. I would never have guessed it if I hadn't seen it. Since that night I've thought about it every day of my life, and here's what I think.

"I believe Cliff was an alcoholic. I believe he hadn't been drinking for a while, and he fell off the wagon that night. They always believe that this time they'll be able to handle it, stick to just a few. But he didn't, of course, just like my dad. It made him crazy." Annabeth shrugged. "If I hadn't come over, I bet Tally could have handled him and bid him adieu the next day. For good. But I was there, and that set him off somehow, and Tally could see I was disgusted, and she was just horrified by the whole incident."

"Did you think of calling the police? Like, the people Tally worked with every day? People who could have taken this Cliff away till he sobered up enough to get out of town?" Bob couldn't temper the edge to his voice.

"Tally was too humiliated. Everyone at the department had

met him while he was working on the system, and everyone knew he and Tally had been seeing each other. She was sure she—we—could handle it by ourselves."

"How'd he end up dead? That an example of how you two handled it?"

"Don't you be an asshole like him," Annabeth snapped.

And Bob, feeling like he'd seen into a cave inside his mother he'd never known was there, said, "Yes, ma'am. I'm sorry. Finish up."

"Tally took him by surprise and handcuffed him."

"That was good," Bob said, nodding.

"But she'd had a few beers, too, so maybe her judgment was a little off. She decided to shut him in the basement and lock the door. There's a deadbolt on it, you know."

Bob remembered seeing it. There was indeed a sturdy deadbolt up high on the doorframe. "Put there when the kids were little," he guessed. "Something to keep them out of the basement, high up so they couldn't reach."

"I don't know which kids, which generation," Annabeth said. "But that's why it was there. And it seemed like a good idea, keeping him put away while he sobered up. So she shoved him through the door. And he turned to argue, and he was just yelling and yelling, and we were scared the neighbors would hear and come find him all handcuffed and drunk. Then he came charging out, and Tally and I were shoving at him so she could close and lock the door. And down the stairs he went."

"And he couldn't catch himself because of the handcuffs."

Annabeth nodded.

"He die straightaway?" Bob felt he'd been sitting on the couch with his mother for a week. He was ready for this to be over.

"No," she said.

"Of course not," Bob said.

"He was groaning down there. I guess those stairs aren't long enough to...anyway, he wasn't dead. Talley talked about calling an ambulance."

"You think?"

"But then we figured it was too late to...remedy the situation."
Bob's mouth dropped open, and he snapped it shut.

"So Tally and I went down there, and after a minute he quit
making noise."

Bob couldn't even look at his mother any more. He stared
down at his hands. "What did she do?"

"I don't know," Annabeth said, in the voice of someone trying
to convince herself. "Maybe she held his nose shut. I'm sure he
would have died anyway."

"And then?" Home stretch, it had to be.

"I left."

"You left Tally alone with the dead man."

"That's what she told me to do."

"You left her alone with the body of the man she'd killed,
and you went home."

"Well, it was late."

"It was late," Bob repeated. He shook his head in wonder.

"So I didn't know what she did with the body. I kind of
thought he *might* be in the freezer, but I didn't know for sure."

"You and Tally didn't talk about it?"

"Only once. When they found his car about a hundred
miles away, close to Dallas. All his stuff was inside, including
his wallet."

"It got there by magic, huh?"

"Well, I told you he wasn't tall or big. Tally put on his
clothes and his hat and drove out of town after dark. She knew
someone would see the car, see the hat, think Cliff had left
town. She said someone *always* sees you, in a town this size.
That's why she didn't put him in the trunk and get rid of him.
Even if she'd dragged him outside at three in the morning, a
raccoon would see her and tell a possum, she said. Tally had
some story ready, if she got stopped in his car. But no story
could explain away a body."

"Mom. You say you don't know about anything that happened

after he fell."

Annabeth's jaw tightened and she stared into a dark corner of the kitchen. "Yes. I don't know, exactly."

"Who drove Tally back, then? Don't tell me she tethered her horse to car and let it trot behind her for a hundred miles and then rode the horse back."

Annabeth turned a dull red. "I don't want to talk about this anymore."

"Mom." Bob looked up at his mother, bewildered. "What am I supposed to do?"

Annabeth stood up. "Well, she called you Judge Bob. I guess you're going to have to do some judging."

After an almost sleepless night, Bob went down to the cellar and looked up at the top of the stairs. He'd gone over his mother's account of the...well, the murder...twenty times during the hours after her departure.

There was Tally, steady and experienced and tough. There was Annabeth, completely distraught and loaded down with bad memories from her childhood. Which woman was more likely to run at someone threatening and give him a shove, get him *away*? And then make sure the *away* was permanent?

Bob made his judgment.

For a while after Officer Bob Westmore inherited his Aunt Tally's house, he took up her hobby of birdwatching. All the other police thought this was the funniest thing ever. He would load his car with her camera gear in waterproof bags and her big ice chest. He'd drive out of town real fast, like he couldn't wait to look at those nuthatches, or warblers, or vultures. He seemed real fascinated with black vultures, and could tell you more about them than anyone wanted to know. He visited every colony he heard of.

Every time he did, Bob left something behind.

After a year of what seemed to his buddies to be an inexplicable obsession, Bob asked a bunch of them to come over for beer and pizza. It was a freezer removal party, he warned them.

It was a challenge to get the damn thing up the short flight of steps. The stair railing had to come down. Once the policemen maneuvered the bulky appliance into the kitchen, the back door had to come off so they could squeeze it through. The biggest pickup available, the sheriff's own new Ford F-150, backed up to the porch with a trailer attached.

All hands assisted with getting the freezer onto the trailer. All the cops followed the F-150 out to the dump and cheered as the ancient appliance became part of the landfill. Bob had a big party that night. Sarah Jane Causey was his hostess.

By the time they were married, the cellar had been cleaned out rigorously. Sarah Jane did ask that they get another freezer.

Bob insisted on an upright.

Edgar-winning author David Housewright gives us a wicked little tale of a love triangle gone askew. Sometimes, as he shows us, the best man in a wedding isn't always the better man...

Best Man

David Housewright

The sheriff and his deputies found Michael exactly where he said they would, sitting with his back against a tree just off the old logging road near Iris Pond, his shotgun lying by his side. They had told him not to move, not to touch anything, and he hadn't except to stroke the fur of the golden Labrador retriever that rested its head in his lap.

The shotgun made them nervous and they approached cautiously. He watched them. It was clear that he had been weeping, yet now his eyes were empty and his face was without expression. A deputy carefully picked up the shotgun. He smelled it like they do in bad TV cop shows. It hadn't been fired. He said so, but the sheriff wasn't listening. Instead, his attention was riveted to the body sprawled across the forest floor near where Michael was sitting, half of its head missing.

"Lenny can't see him like this," Michael said.

"Lenny?"

"Lenore. His fiancée."

The sheriff nodded as if he understood perfectly. He didn't move to the body. There was nothing he could do for Peter, anyway. He circled the corpse from a distance. The radio attached to his uniform didn't work that deep in the woods but his cell phone, like Michael's, had good coverage. He called the medical examiner and his crime scene specialist. He told them both the

149

same thing: "It's bad."

He moved to Michael's side. Both Michael and the Labrador looked up at him. He squatted down, resting a hand first on Michael's shoulder and then the dog's head.

"Nice dog," he said.

"It's Peter's. I gave it to him on his birthday three years ago."

"Tell me what happened."

Michael spoke in complete paragraphs:

Peter had been tired and a little hung over from his bachelor party the night before. Michael had thrown the party; he was Michael's best man. They had been friends since they'd been seated next to each other in elementary school, taking turns shooting spitballs into Lenore's long blonde hair. Today Michael had suggested they blow off the hunt. Yet Peter insisted. It would be his last outing as a free man, he'd said. Besides, he had a grouse recipe that he said would "unroll Lenny's pantyhose."

Peter had said women learn the way to a man's heart is through his stomach, only with him and Lenore it had been reversed. "She loves me because I can cook," Peter had said. "You should learn to cook."

Michael told the sheriff that they had been working the woods near the pond for a couple of hours without any luck. It was Peter's idea to take a break when he rested his shotgun against a tree stump...

Michael pointed at the stump directly behind Peter's body in case there was any confusion.

Peter sat next to the stump and the Lab lay down next to Peter, as was his habit. He rarely left his master's side. Lenore once joked that she had to sleep with the damn dog before she could sleep with Peter.

Peter pulled out his canteen and took a sip and smiled brightly.

Michael was intrigued and asked, "What's in that?"

Peter sealed the canteen and tossed it over to Michael.

The Lab jumped to its feet at the gesture as if the canteen

had been a bird he was supposed to catch. When he did, he knocked the shotgun over. It hit the ground and bounced up and went off and Peter's face disappeared.

Michael continued to stroke the dog's head.

"It was an accident," he said.

Both the ME and the CSI man arrived and examined the body and crime scene carefully. This sort of thing rarely happened in the county and they wanted to make sure no mistakes were made. Later, at the inquest, they both testified that none of the evidence they had gathered contradicted Michael's story. Peter's demise was classified as "death by accident" and condolences were offered to his family.

The sheriff was satisfied with the ruling at the time, but later he began to wonder. It wasn't a densely populated county and he was able to keep track of Michael without too much effort.

He discovered that Peter's fiancée had become so distraught by his death that her family feared for her health. Fortunately, Michael remained almost constantly by her side and eventually brought both joy and laughter back into her life. Eighteen months after the accident, they were married. Lenore's father happily paid $50,000 for the wedding, helped them buy a house, and promoted Michael to the position of executive vice president in his company, a job he had previously promised to Peter.

The sheriff eventually caught up with Michael at a sporting goods store. It was the first time they had been together since the county inquest.

"I feel bad I've let so much time pass without saying how sorry I am about your friend," the sheriff said.

"Thank you."

"Still, it worked out pretty well for you, didn't it? You got the girl, the job..." The sheriff bent down to pet the golden Labrador retriever that stood loyally by his new master's side. "The dog. How lucky can a guy get?"

"Luck had nothing to do with it, Sheriff. I was always the better man."

You can see Kasey perform one of her own songs in the TV series Hap and Leonard *(based on her father's series of novels) or you can listen to one of her albums or you can read some of her short stories or—the list goes on. She's a tremendous talent and entertainer and her story here is a nod to the earlier times of paperback originals and hardbitten PIs. Possibly best read with a fedora...*

Bitter Follies

Kasey Lansdale

It was gray out, not unlike it had been every other morning this fall. I was rested, fed, and carrying around the promise of enough money that I wouldn't have to worry for at least six months about anything.

The home was hidden behind a well-placed fence, covered in strategic greenery like a naked woman with long, convenient hair. I rang the buzzer at the front gate of Raymond Avenue, stared into the camera until I was greeted by the buzzing sound of the electric door latch. Even with the gloom that overhung the city, heat permeated my skin, that smoldering kind of heat that made you wanna confess to things you hadn't done.

The squirrels darted across the lawn, rushing up and down the tall, manicured palm trees, chittering and taunting one another. I walked up the small set of concrete steps and stared up at the six floors of building that stood before me littered with wide, thick windows. I checked my reflection in the one closest, took my pointer finger and smoothed down my brows. I knocked, as I'd been instructed to do, and was greeted by a tall, slender man in his mid-sixties. Tufts of white hair clung to his sweaty forehead as he pushed the door back.

"Miss Daniela is expecting you. Come with me, Mrs. Mara."

"It's Ms."

I slipped through the large wooden double doors and into the palatial lobby where only a grand piano stood on a slick concrete floor. It was no smaller than Madison Square Garden. To my left was a winding, carpeted staircase set in front of a row of large glass windows that overlooked the emerald grass of the backyard. In the driveway I could see a two-door white sedan. There may have been a drought in LA, but it hadn't reached here.

Large wingback chairs were pushed into the corners of the room, though they appeared unused by the state of their pristine cushions. To my right, at the top of the staircase was an oversized oil painting of a middle-aged man with a prissy brown dog perched gingerly in his lap. The painting was stiff, yellowed, and I placed it at about a hundred years old based on the clothing he wore. I walked down the long carpeted corridor to the end of the hall and stopped at the door furthest on my left. We went through the doorway and into another long hallway that was lined with the same tall windows as downstairs, and covered with wall-to-wall carpeting.

A damp, earthy aroma arose from the forest of plants that bordered the room. For the first time since I'd arrived the house smelled of something alive.

In the center of the jungle was a seating area for two on broad, white tiles. In one of the chairs was a gaunt woman staring up at me. I feared if I exhaled she might blow away. Edward led me across the hard surface to my chair, his shoes squeaking in rhythm with each step on the pristine, glossy floor. When the woman shifted, her rose-pink dress draped loosely on her petite frame. Her chestnut hair lay slicked back and clipped over to one side.

"Miss Daniela," the man said, "Mrs. Mara here to see you."

"It's Ms.," I said again.

I pulled the empty chair back and sat down, placed my

pocketbook on the table between us. She stared at me, took a drink from her glass, said nothing. I knew of Daniela Paige; it was hard not to.

"Can we skip the pleasantries?" I asked.

"We may," she said.

"This husband got a record?" I asked.

"Nothing. Never been in trouble." She paused to emphasize her point and continued, "Not so much as a speeding ticket, or a harshly worded letter."

"Those aren't usually the type of guys that go missing."

"It's true," she said.

I could hear it now. Her accent said European—Albania maybe? Bulgaria? She inhaled, her neck muscles tightening across her smooth pale skin as she swallowed. Purple veins danced with every breath.

"He is a good man. I don't know what to do. Where he could be."

She cocked her head to one side, her wet eyes round like saucers, her lips pushed out far enough they looked like bounce house slides. Her breath grew shaky.

I was getting tired of the theatrics. "Every moment that passes is another moment wasted."

Her labored breathing continued. I started to push out of my chair when I remembered that the rent was due in nine days and her promise of funds had yet to be fulfilled.

"Let's try again," I said, fighting for patience.

She stared up at me through her damp, lowered lashes. "He was away on business the morning he—"

She trailed off and her body seemed to shrink into itself. She cast her coal black eyes downward and smoothed out the imaginary wrinkles in her dress, took in a deep breath.

I leaned across the large oak table, cupped my hand beneath my chin and waited for the next ice age to occur.

"He went there on business, set to return that night," she hesitated, "but he never came back."

"What sort of business is he in?"

"Investments."

"Of course he is."

"He was staying at a hotel around Santa Barbara, one of his. I wanted to go with him, but something came up."

"What sort of something comes up that you can't take time away to go on vacation in wine country? Looks to me a girl like you lives for that sort of thing."

"I would have been there, but Aunt May had a..." She paused, choosing her words carefully: "A situation."

I nodded. Aunt May, or Fat Aunt May as most people called her, was rumored to run a small-scale gambling ring just outside the city limits. It was also reputed she'd been the one to call the police about the accident with my folks all those years ago.

"Your aunt is why I'm here," I said. Money didn't hurt either. "She called me, begged me to help her niece. I do wonder though, why wouldn't you just call the sheriff's office? Surely this is a matter for them. Sheriff Rhodes is a friend. I could call him if you want."

Daniela glanced at Edward who was still standing watch at the door.

"You may go."

Edward nodded and disappeared the way we'd entered. Once she was sure Edward was out of earshot, Daniela said, "I'm not proud of it, but I was having an affair." She began to breathe faster and before I could say anything the tears breached the rims of her eyes and big drops fell like rain. She covered her delicate face with her small, spindly hands.

"Sheriff doesn't care about that sort of thing."

"But they might care about some other things."

"I see," I said. "Your lover? Would he do this?"

"Oh no, absolutely not. It's common knowledge the family is well off. It could be anyone. I just can't afford to rock the boat by calling in the police." I wasn't following. I gave her a look that said so. "The affair could disqualify me from getting my green card for citizenship."

She was more worried about her status than her husband, it seemed. Even a woman like her could only get so far. She still had to play by the government rules.

"Maybe the whole thing was an investment gone sour," I said, not even convincing myself.

"If you don't want to help me..." she said.

"I didn't say I wouldn't help you." I could see her nostrils flare. "Do you have the fee we discussed on hand?"

She reached into a purse that had been tucked beneath her chair, shuffled things around until she pulled out a white envelope packed so full it could have doubled as a brick for the downtown streets. She worried with it for a moment before pushing it across the table towards me.

"This should cover it," she said. I untucked the triangle flap, peeked inside to find all hundreds staring back at me. "Please," she said, "find him."

I let myself out of the gate and headed back towards the car I'd left parked on Colorado Avenue. The chittering squeaks of a squirrel fight echoed off in the distance as another made clicking sounds with its mouth from an overhead branch. The fog had dissipated and now the sun shone brightly in the sky. I started the car and drove west until I hit the 134 freeway.

I replayed the conversation with Daniela Paige in my head. Something wasn't sitting right with me. I drove on for about twenty minutes before I exited towards Forest Lawn Drive. I passed the Forest Lawn Cemetery on my left, Warner Bros. Studios on my right. It was ironic that many of the same stars who had made the studio what it was now lay buried just across the street, many of them long forgotten.

I hit the end of the road and made a left onto Barham Boulevard which connected itself to the 101 south. I eased the car into the four lane stretch of road, honking the horn as an old black Buick tried to switch lanes and into my shirt pocket. It didn't take long before I reached Vine and Sunset, and not long after that, the Hollywood Public Library. I parked my car and weaved through the homeless bodies perched on the stone steps. Inside I was greeted by a portly blonde woman behind a circular wooden desk. I could see a name tag pinned to her pink sweater that read *Nancy*.

"Where do you keep your microfilms?"

Nancy led me down a narrow hallway of books and into a back corner where about fifteen microfilm machines were spaced out on individual desks. Behind them, a large catalogue cabinet stood with manila labels and overstuffed drawers.

"Are you looking for anything in particular?" Nancy asked. I told her I was doing research for a real estate firm and was particularly interested in a recent transaction by a Mr. William Paige.

She pointed me towards a metal drawer labeled *N-Q*, then turned and headed back to her perch at the front door. After some searching, I uncovered the box which contained a reel for southern California from the week before when William Paige had gone missing. I slid the canister onto the metal rod and laced the film under the roller and in between the glass. I clipped it inside and turned the knob forward as I searched through the plethora of articles.

A few hours had passed and I was about to give up when I passed a photo that caught my attention. I turned the knob backwards until I reached it once more, then slid the lever to the left so the picture was the only thing on the screen.

On the front page of the *LA Times* above what would have been the fold, was Daniela Paige's husband in a suit and hard hat, standing in front of a building shaking hands with another suit and hard hat.

Attorney Ray Nieto shown here with investor William Paige at the opening of restored villa,

Delle Stelle in Santa Barbara

I looked up to see Nancy lazily pass by.

"Excuse me," I said. "Any way I can get a copy of this?"

She nodded and disappeared into a different room down another hall of books.

Ray Nieto's office was a shiny restored building with pristine glass windows in the heart of Hollywood. I stepped closer to peer inside but was met only by my own worn face. The entrance door was also glass, but it was frosted. I could barely make out a figure seated at a desk. I pushed the lighted button on the wall and waited. The smell of the office lingered in the alcove. It was the same smell I remembered as a child, the same musty odor of every lawyer's office I was dragged into while the state was divvying up my parent's things—namely me.

"May I help you?" A woman's voice asked through the mesh speaker.

"Here for Ray." I tugged at the door but was met with resistance.

"He's on with a client, would you like to leave a message?"

"No, I'd like to come in."

"I'm sorry, but without an appointment you'll have to leave a message." She had too much power here. I pressed my face closer towards the glass.

"Do I know you?" I asked.

"I don't think so." Her voice hung there, familiar, and all at once I realized who it was.

"Lara Jane—is that you? It's me, Mara," I said. Silence. "That's right," I continued. "The same Mara from P.S. 213. And unless you want a repeat of third grade recess, I suggest you let me in."

I was pretty sure I could hear the lone marble roll from one side of her head to the other before the sound of a chair came skidding across the floor as she stood. She approached cautiously. As she neared I could make out the details of her face through the glass.

"What is your problem?" she asked, her nose almost touching the hard surface.

"You want a list?" I asked. "Let's just say the highlight was when you told everyone in our school that my parents had killed themselves because they didn't want to have to raise me anymore. That's the long of it. The short of it is that your boss, Mr. Ray Nieto, is the last person to see someone alive, and I need to know why."

That might have been a stretch.

"You a cop now?"

"PI," I said, and reached into my back pocket to pull out my badge wallet. She studied it for a moment like it was a strange and fascinating piece of art. If she had known what to look for, she would have seen it was worth no more than the funny pages in the Sunday papers.

"Step back," she said. She curled into herself, eyes pointed towards the ground. She was still attractive, trim, dark-haired, with a little too much makeup. She wore a black and white checkered pencil skirt that caused her to take tiny steps as she moved. Her white tank top was tucked inside and her black bra shone through. She seemed slightly underdressed for work, but this was California after all. She had that same, mean smirk she'd carried with her when we were kids, and it was oddly comforting to see that it hadn't left her after all this time.

I closed the door behind me and followed her as she shuffled back to her desk. The room was filled with a mishmash of art and furniture. It seemed like the decor theme was "curbside chic."

"Have a seat. It may be a while. Like I told you," she stopped, made a face that said she'd rather be anywhere but here, "he's on with a client."

Just as I took my seat in the dining room-style chair, the phone at her desk started to ring. She disappeared behind a large lamp as she took the call. I looked around to see the photographs hung against the wall. Every framed picture was of Ray Nieto and some celebrity or another. Based on the background in the photos, they must have been taken in this office. There were no family photos to be found. I continued scanning the walls. There, near a potted plant in the corner was another framed photo. In this photo stood Ray, William and Daniela. Lara put down the phone and began typing furiously.

"Does Ray have any children?"

Lara nodded her head left and right and continued typing. Another twenty or so minutes had passed when the phone rang again. Lara reached for it, said something I couldn't hear, then hung up.

"He'll see you now," she said, and pointed towards the door. Her voice was relaxed, but her eyes said otherwise. I stood and made my way to where Lara was pointing. I reached for the door handle and let myself inside.

"You've got quite the decor scheme going on out there," I said as I entered Nieto's office.

"Oh yes," he said, laughing. "I have a habit of perusing the estate sales that my firm handles. My wife won't let me bring most of it home, so it stays here." I stayed quiet, waiting to see if he would go on. "It's a hobby really. I have the money, it helps my clients, so why not."

"No offense, Mr. Nieto, but I have to side with your wife on this one."

He laughed. "What can I do for you?" He idled over to his desk as he spoke.

Ray Nieto was a tan-skinned man with slicked black hair, a sharp widow's peak, and a sprinkling of grey forming at his temples and brows. He was average height, solidly built, and stood in a way that said his youth hadn't always consisted of suits and ties. He came across as amiable but I had no doubt he could be fierce when necessary. Good traits for a law man. He looked more handsome in person than he had in the black and white photo I'd studied just a few hours ago at the library.

"Miss Turner said you were quite adamant about seeing me. So tell me: what brings you to Nieto & Son on this fine day?"

He gestured for me to sit, and so we did.

"Lara told me you didn't have any children."

"I don't. I am the son in this particular arrangement."

"Understood. Mr. Nieto, the problem is this," I said. "For William Paige, today is not so fine." I pulled out the newspaper copy and handed it to him across the desk. He looked down at the clipping. "William Paige is missing. And as far as I know, you're the last person who saw him."

I watched as he let the information sink in.

"I don't understand," Nieto said.

"That's you in the picture, right? You were with him that night, yes?"

"Sure," he said, "and so were three hundred other people. It was a hotel opening." His eyebrows furrowed.

"Sure, sure," I said. "But it says in the article you were equal investors in that property."

I watched as he seemed to be putting together my line of questioning.

"Has something happened to William?"

"That wouldn't be the worst thing for you, would it?" His eyes grew wide as his face twisted tighter.

"That's a bit of a stretch. I own dozens of properties. I have a thriving practice. I certainly don't need money. Especially from him."

"What do you mean by that?" I asked.

"It's no secret that William liked the tables. Poker, specifically. He liked playing against the tourists, not the house."

"You ever go with him?"

"To Vegas? Oh no. We weren't travel buddies, we worked together. But he would talk about his trips between meetings and such."

"You don't gamble?" I asked.

"We all have our vices, Mrs. Mara. Gambling is not one of mine."

I looked around the room at the degrees and newspaper clippings hung about the office wall. "It's Ms. Mara. And if you say so."

"Is there anything else?" he asked.

"Can you remember if anything strange happened that night? Or anything in the weeks prior?" I watched him, waited for any mannerism that might seem out of place.

"Nothing that I can recall." He tilted his head to the side as he thought. "We shook hands, cut the ribbon, posed for photos, and that was that."

"How is your relationship with your wife?" I asked.

This seemed to give him pause. "Not that it's any of your business," he said, "but things are just fine."

"Why no pictures then? Happy people usually hang pictures of their loved ones."

He pushed out of his chair. I could see the anger beginning to form. He took a deep breath, composed himself before he spoke.

"The reason," he said, "that there are no photos of my wife, is because this is in part, a criminal law office. We do much more than estate sales here. The scum of the earth sits in that very chair." He pointed to where I sat. "And I don't need every one of them to have a full visual of my loved ones. Now if that's all, I am very busy and need to prepare for my next meeting."

He reached toward the phone and hit a button. I heard a noise from behind me and in a moment Lara was standing at the door.

"This way," she said.

I drove in silence as I thought about what Ray Nieto had told me. Had this been a debt collection? The wife hadn't mentioned any financial troubles, and from the looks of things, there weren't any. Maybe William did have gambling debts, and Daniela had cut him off. If he liked the tables, he might have gotten in over his head. That's not too far a stretch. It wouldn't be the first loan shark job I'd found myself a part of.

I logged it away as a possibility to check into at a later time. The traffic on the 101 was clogged as usual. That was the thing about LA. It didn't matter if it was one in the morning or one in the afternoon, there was always traffic, and lots of it.

I decided to head home and start again the next day. I took the exit off Vineland Avenue to Studio City and moved over to the left-hand turn lane. I was only about a block or so from my studio apartment on Aqua Vista but the construction on my street would cause me to go all the way around the block and up the other side to get to my place. I could see the residents' gate was open as I turned into my drive. It was a quiet enough place, and I liked the convenience of Hollywood without the same abundance of people.

The neighborhood had changed since I'd first arrived, become more gentrified, but I stayed because moving now would be impossible on my income. I parked in my designated spot next to my neighbor's dark blue Mustang and closed the gate behind me. It dragged shut with a thunderous rattle, then I walked up the stairs to the second floor. It wasn't much, but it was home.

Once in bed I glanced over at the framed photo of my mother on the nightstand. She had been so beautiful. I was so young when she and my father had died. On nights like these, I longed for her. I got in bed and pulled up the sheets and thought about what I had planned for my life, and how those plans hadn't worked out. I hoped I could sleep. In my dreams things always turned out better, and I was sweeter and owned my own home, and had a cat. I liked cats.

It was about 1 p.m. when I heard the familiar rattle of the gate being opened below. I looked out the window to the grey clouds that threatened to burst and saw my neighbor's car disappearing up the street.

I had made a list of all the facts in the case—though there weren't many—and studied them all morning, but I was no further along now than I had been yesterday. I decided that tomorrow I would make the trek up to Santa Barbara and look around myself. Today though, I would reach out to Petey, have him do some checking for me. Petey was a small time PI who I called on occasion to do some of the grunt work I didn't always have the time or want to do.

"Hey Petey." I could hear him breathing into the receiver, so I continued. "It's me, Mara."

"Oh hey, Mara. I wasn't sure."

"You in some kind of trouble?" I asked.

"You know better than to ask that," he said, a smile behind his voice.

"Fair enough," I said. "Listen, I need you to sit on somebody for me. You free tomorrow?"

"Nah, tomorrow's no good for me. I got business to handle. Personal. I can go now, though. Who ya looking at?"

"I'm not sure I'm looking at anybody, really. But I just need to know if you see anything that strikes you. Today is fine, no problem."

"Full rate?" Petey asked.

"For a half day?"

"I got debts too."

"Alright, Petey. Yeah. Full rate."

I gave him the details and hung up the phone. I'd always liked Petey. Had a soft spot for him since he'd lost his folks at a young age too, and had always fancied myself a bit of a sister figure.

I wasn't sure where to go from here. It was too late to head north now and be back before traffic, and too early to wait for tomorrow. I picked up the phone and dialed Daniela. I was greeted on the other end of the line by a formal voice I recognized.

"Paige residence."

"Yeah, Eddy boy," I said. "Is Daniela around?"

"Not at the moment. Shall I take a message?"

"That'd be great. Just tell her that Mara called. She might remember me as the woman she gave an envelope full of money to."

"I'll let her know," he said, his voice more detached than before.

I hung up the phone without another word and began pacing the floor. I went to the kitchen, grabbed a cup of coffee and sat back down on the couch. I pulled out the newspaper from the day before. I'd asked Nancy at the library to make a copy of the whole thing, just in case. I read the article again, and again and tried to catch up on my thumb twiddling when the phone rang.

"Hello."

"Yeah, it's me." Petey spoke as though he had a hand over his mouth.

"You OK?"

"Yeah, fine."

"Where are you?" I asked.

"I'm tailing your guy. He left the office a half hour ago. I'm at a pay phone down the street in some suburb and—"

"Just stay with him," I said. "And Petey..."

"Yeah?"

"You don't have to whisper. I don't think he can hear you."

I sat back down, ready to start the whole process over when the phone rang again.

"Petey, just—"

"They have him."

"What?" I asked. "Who is this?"

"They have my husband."

"Daniela? Is that you?"

I could hear sobbing on the other end of the line.

"I'll be right there."

***

The gate was open and Edward was waiting for me by the time I reached the front door. "Where is she?"

"This way," he said, pointing past the grand piano. The carpet pattern was as ugly now as it had been the first time I'd come. I followed the howling sounds coming from the end of the hall until I reached what I assumed to be the master bedroom. I rapped slightly on the door, then pushed my way inside. With her head in her hands Daniela sat, shaking and sniffling.

"No time for that," I said. "Tell me exactly what happened."

Her head shot up, a calm seemed to envelope her.

"They told me—"

"Wait," I said. "Who told you? Start from the beginning."

She paused, took a deep breath and began again.

"I was out earlier, running errands. I had just gotten home, walked into the bedroom. I'd barely had time to set down my things when the phone rang." I gestured for her to continue.

"I answered the phone—"

"Why didn't Edward answer it?"

"I don't know. I was closer. What does it matter?"

"It doesn't. Go on."

"I answered the phone and I heard a man's voice on the other end of the line."

By now Edward was standing in the doorway.

"Where were you?" I asked him.

"I was tending to a delivery around back. It came just moments after you rang."

"What did the man say?" I asked, turning back to Daniela. "What did he say, exactly?"

"He said, we have your husband. If you want to see him alive you'll pay. I started crying and he told me to shut up. Then he said they wanted cash."

"How did he say it?"

"He said, we want $10,000 by this time tomorrow. No cops."

I whistled aloud, reflexively. Daniela cut her eyes towards me.

"Sorry," I said. That was quite an ask. I'd had two husbands, and I wouldn't have paid ten cents for either of them. Or combined. "What did he tell you about the drop."

"He said he would call back in one hour with instructions."

"One hour?"

"That's what he said."

"Are you sure you don't want to call the police?" I asked.

"No! No police. They said no cops or they'd kill him."

I mulled this over for a moment. I'd already spent some of the money she'd paid me, money I had accepted on the condition that no police would be involved. But that was back when it was a green card issue. No. A deal was a deal.

"Okay," I said again. "Well it sounds like he's working with partners, so that's something."

Daniela looked over at Edward, who stepped inside the room.

"Can I make you a tea, madam?" Daniela nodded, and with that Edward was gone again.

"I'm fine," I shouted after him. "Thanks for asking."

I looked back to Daniela. She was shaking, curled up into herself, rocking her body in a soothing back and forth motion on the bed. All the while, the tears continued. Within the hour the phone rang and a man on the other end of the line supplied me with instructions. He didn't seem to notice I wasn't Daniela. I scribbled down the address of where to bring the cash.

Already dressed in all black, I was now in my car with a bag of unmarked bills in the seat beside me. Daniela hadn't put up much of a fight on the matter. She figured she was paying me enough, and I figured she was right. Getting the money had been no problem for her. She'd merely sent Edward out and by the time she'd finished her tea, he'd returned with a sack full of cash.

I followed the gravel drive past a sodden patch of grass that housed the remains of a rusted-out Plymouth. The property was as bare as a birch in winter. The shiny rubber of the tires squealed as I turned left and headed further up the path. Everything here had been left to die. The house at the end hadn't fared much better. Dusk had fallen and the clouds had gathered as I drove around to the side of the house away from view and onto another patch of grass. I put the car in park and left the motor running and the headlights on. I didn't plan to stay long.

The purr of the car rumbled in the distance as I climbed up the dilapidated steps of the old building. I knocked, but there was no sound inside. The door was held up by a single hinge and I pushed it back with my fingertips. I let it swing shut on its own as I walked softly, looking for any indication of someone here. I went on through the living room and past the kitchen, keeping the lights clicked off. I could hear rain begin beating on the flat roof as I made my way about the house. Then the sound of a car pulling up out front. I was to drop the money and go, something I had failed to do. I ducked and inched over to what was left of a doorframe and squatted with my back against the wall, waiting and listening. Then I slid like a cat into the bedroom, blackness cutting the air as I clutched the bag of money tight to my chest. Thunder clapped, almost concealing the crunching of gravel outside.

The front door opened and closed quietly, followed by the sound of footsteps. A light shined in through the living room which revealed a closet door behind me. I could hide there. It wasn't original, but it's what I had.

I turned the handle of the door, pulled it open and peered into the dark. As my eyes adjusted, I was met by the dim shape of a man hunched inside. The air around me grew thick, and clogged, as the smell hit all at once. I shut the door, certain I didn't want to hide in there. I turned just as the butt of a gun struck hard against my right temple. An aching white light flashed behind my eyelids as I dropped to the ground. The bag of money fell with me. My grip stayed wrapped around the fabric, my brain unable to send the signal for my hand to let go.

It hurt as much as you'd expect it to. I laid there on the floor as the room spun in sickening circles. I had to give it to him, he had gotten to me faster than I'd anticipated. I watched from the floor as the man dressed in all black rummaged through the desk in the corner.

"What are you looking for?" I asked. "I have the money."

I tried to sit up but the axis of the earth had shifted. I began to crawl towards the chair, something to help me get my footing, leaving the bag of money behind. I felt like my guts had been pulled from my body and spread onto the floor like chicken feed. I looked over to the man who was still busy searching through papers. I had one arm propped onto the seat of the chair, the other pressed against the floor as I tried to find my footing. The man turned, saw me, and in one long stride knocked the chair out from under me with a swift kick. He straddled me, pinning my arms to my sides. I lunged forward, trying to leverage him from my body but to no avail. He leaned his face closer to mine and laughed. A sickly-sweet smell wafted from his mouth and lingered between us.

I lunged again, this time tucking my chin and slinging my head towards his. The crown of my skull made contact with his nose and I felt the waterfall of blood rush down over me like the breaking of a dam. I laid there, stunned, the weight of him bearing down. He was dazed, bleeding through his face mask and gripping my wrists so tight I thought they might fall off then and there. I wanted to yell, to call for help, but I couldn't. There was no breath left inside me. I watched as the soft moonlight through the window dissipated, the sounds around me vanished, and the whole world faded into black.

The man in the room was not the same one as before. His silhouette was smaller, more boyish. He was propped up against the wall, and I was still wadded up on the floor. It hurt to breathe, to think. Every light in the place seemed to be on, shining directly into my brain. My head was throbbing and I felt nauseous as I rolled over to my side then sat up. A long while passed before I tried to open my eyes again. I could hear the sounds of rain falling against the roof, and through my lashes I could see the fuzzy outline of the man with slicked-back dark brown hair.

"Whoo-whee," he said. "That's gotta hurt."

The voice was gruff, like he'd taken a bite of gravel and washed it down with a smoke.

"Oh this, this was licked on by kittens." I reached up and dampness met my fingertips, the smell of blood hung in the air. I was unsure which was my blood and which was that of my attacker.

"In the closet," I said.

"Already on it."

I felt his hand take mine and pull me to my feet. I steadied myself, opened my eyes fully, and was met with the lake-blue gaze of Petey staring back at me.

"I guess it's a good thing I was following your guy, huh? You feel okay?"

"Oh yeah, never better," I said.

"I think I spooked him when he heard me pull up. By the time I made it inside, he'd slipped out the back and was outta here."

I looked around the room, taking time now to study my surroundings. There wasn't much to see. The bag of money was gone, of course. The carpet in the bedroom was brown shag, worn from the doorway to an area where a bed would have been. The paneling on the walls had begun to peel, and the window where the light had shone through had a snaking crack that started in the upper left-hand corner, making its way down and across.

Petey seemed to read my thoughts, said, "It's one of his estate projects. I guess no one was in a hurry to buy."

"Well, the dead body and fresh blood stains ought to punch up the offers a bit."

"Come on," he said, "let's get you out of here."

* * *

171

Back at my place, Petey and I sat on the couch as I gulped down a handful of aspirin and used a damp rag to dab at the swollen bits of my face.

"It's your call," Petey said. "However you want to play it, I'm in."

"You got your piece?" I asked. Petey nodded. "Let's get to it, then."

I grabbed my pistol from the countertop and dropped it inside my handbag.

"You're sure you're up to it right now? We can always go—"

"The longer we wait, the more we'll have to clean up later."

It was Sunday, and the rain had finally stopped. Traffic was light and the parking was easy. We found a spot outside of Ray Nieto's office and made our way up the sidewalk to the front door. The birds echoed out, riled up after all the rain. Everything looked cleaner than it had before, the deluge having washed away the dirt and the transients that had lingered on the sidewalk only days before.

We reached the front door just as a flash of solid white light poured out of the building, accompanied by the harsh ringing boom of a gunshot. A thud reverberated through my toes and into my already throbbing brain. It was a sickening sound.

Petey and I looked at one another. He signaled he would go around back. I nodded and off he went, disappearing behind jade-green bushes. I tried the front door, but was met with no relief. I tried to kick it in, but realized quickly this was halfwitted. Still with my handbag over my shoulder, I reached inside for my gun, placed it in the waistband of my trousers and dumped the remaining contents on the ground. I stuck my hand inside the bag and used it like a glove to punch through the glass of the French door. I knocked away loose shards and reached through to the latch. I pushed it upwards and withdrew my hand. I scooped my items back into my purse and opened the door with the handle. None of this had gone down quietly.

Once inside, gun drawn, I noticed immediately that several

of the framed photos were missing. Large gaps stood out throughout the decor. The big carved lamp was still perched upon Lara's desk, and the slick back dining chair was more or less where it had been. The odor of gunpowder hung in the room. I slipped past the desk toward Ray's office, stopping just shy of the entrance. I could hear the soft breath of someone through the door, followed by the high-pitched sound of shoes squeaking rapidly across the tile floor. I moved to the wall, pressed my back against it, waited. I heard the sound of a screen door slam, then silence. I inched inward, my pistol leading the way, my body snug against the corridor.

Slumped over his broad wooden desk was Ray Nieto. Behind him was a statue of a bird I hadn't noticed before, of an eagle or a hawk. Nieto was still wearing black pants and a black long-sleeved shirt, but his face was exposed. His mouth hung slack and his lips were a strong shade of violet. There was a nasty cut across the bridge of his nose. That was likely my contribution.

The roar of a muffler rumbled through the room and faded just as quickly as my eyes traced over the desk. A coagulated pool of maroon fluid seeped from Nieto's stiff face, across a smattering of papers on the desk.

His eyes were still open, looking up at me. At a glance, it seemed like he'd taken one to the back of the skull. That would match what we'd heard outside. I scanned the room, only to be met with an open back door and Petey standing beneath its frame.

"Did you see anything?" I asked.

"Someone running, getting into a white sedan."

"Which way did they go?"

"East." Petey nodded, looked over at Ray. "Got what he deserved, ya ask me."

I didn't disagree.

"Call it in for me, would you? Ask for Sheriff Rhodes. Tell him I'll come by the station tomorrow to give my statement. Make sure he knows about the husband, too."

"Do you want to go to the hospital first, get checked out?

That lump on your eyebrow, you're starting to make Igor look like a pretty boy."

Daniela's man, Edward, greeted me at the door with a level gaze. He looked tired and worn, the creases in his forehead deep like valleys. Once inside, I followed him down the carpeted hall and towards the master bedroom. Daniela was there, same place I had left her.

She looked to me as I entered the room.

"Is my husband OK? Where is he?"

"I'm sure you're real torn up by his absence," I said.

"What happened to your face?"

"I slipped. Tell me, did you intend for Ray to kill me, or just beat me up? You should think twice about falling for a man who'd hit a woman like that."

This brought her to her feet.

"What do you mean?"

"Don't play dumb with me, though you are convincing. Your little plan had a flaw."

She looked at me, enraged, confused.

"I don't under—"

"Want to know where your husband is? Why don't you ask him?" I said, and pointed towards Edward who still hung in the doorway. I glanced over at him; he seemed to be examining the wallpaper for flaws. "I bet you're wondering why you haven't heard from Ray either," I said. "Well, I can tell you why."

This got Edward's attention.

"That's enough," he said sternly, stepping further into the room. It was the most personality I had seen from him. Daniela's eyes grew to the size of silver dollars. Edward's jaw clenched, turning his face an even paler shade of white. Daniela took a step back, seemingly surprised by his behavior.

"Oh," I said, laughing. "You mean she doesn't know?"

"Know what?" Daniela asked, puzzled. Her face signaled a

slight recognition, then her eyes glazed.

"What did you do?" Daniela yelled, full of rage. Her body began to shake and quiver.

"I was trying to help you!" Edward yelled.

At that moment, Edward slid towards me like a squirrel on fresh ice. I reached into the waistband at the small of my back, withdrew my pistol and aimed it in his direction. This neither startled nor slowed him.

I fired three, swift shots into his chest. Edward hollered out. The yell turned into a groan, and then a wet gurgling sound as he collapsed on the floor in front of me holding his chest. I watched his eyes turn glassy, then roll to the back side of his skull. Blood oozed out of him and across the floor.

"What have you done?" Daniela was screaming. I was unsure if she was yelling at me or was still directing at Edward. She lunged for the telephone across the room, scooped it into one hand.

"Who will you call?" I asked. "The cops? I think it's a little late for that." Daniela studied me a moment, slowly put down the phone.

There was silence. She grew stiff, moving as though she was made of wood. She sat down on the edge of the bed, buried her face in her hands. Her voice was muffled as she spoke and she seemed to be talking more to herself than to me.

"It wasn't supposed to go like this. It was supposed to be easy. No one would get hurt, but then...then things got out of hand." She kept her face hidden, her whole body moving in time with her sobs.

I believed her, though I didn't care. Because of her at least three people were dead. Not to mention this shiner I had was one for the books.

Sheriff Rhodes' office was on the backside of a whitewashed building downtown. The barred third-floor windows offered a striped view of the city. Rhodes sat behind his big oak desk with one foot resting on the edge. He stared across at me, an unlit cigar dangling from his mouth.

"Here we are again," Sheriff Rhodes said, as he fumbled through his shirt pocket to reveal a book of matches.

"That's true," I said, almost laughing. "Sorry it took me so long to get down here. As you can see," I pointed to my face, "I needed more time than I thought."

"The lawyer gave you that, huh?" The wound on my brow had started to heal, but would leave a noticeable scar. "Shooting the butler was clearly self-defense, even the widow said as much. But you seem to be orbiting a lot of bodies on this one. I know you, but surely you can appreciate how this might look to an outsider. The fact that you didn't come to us from the start, some might even say you were in on it."

"Well," I said, "some are assholes."

Rhodes tilted his head backwards and took a puff off his cigar, then let the smoke escape slowly from his thin lips. His eyes never left my own.

"That may also be true," he said. "So tell me, who do you think killed the husband?"

"It's hard to say. Could have been the butler. He could have gone out to the house when no one was there and finished him off. Maybe he was a disgruntled employee who saw this as his chance to give as good as he got. Maybe he loved Daniela. Maybe a bit of both." Rhodes nodded, still puffing his cigar. "I guess we'll never know. As far as I understood from the widow," I continued, "the husband was supposed to be a distraction. She and Ray were going to clear out the accounts, take the money and run. I was supposed to find the husband alive, and she and Ray would be long gone with $10,000 in seed money."

"Lord help us. It's always about the money."

"Or jealousy," I said. "Maybe Ray got jealous, decided to off the husband when he had the chance, but my guess is that he found the husband already dead and he panicked. He told Daniela it was his gun that had been used. That must have been what he was searching for in the desk."

"If it wasn't Ray, how would the butler get his hands on the gun?" Rhodes asked.

"I'm not sure. Maybe Ray brought it with him on one of his sleepovers. Edward could have come across it and hatched up this little plan, thought to frame Ray. With both Ray and William out of the way maybe he thought Daniela would love whoever had the money."

"Maybe," Rhodes said. "And speaking of..." He dropped his voice to an almost inaudible volume. "You don't happen to know where that money ended up, do you?" He lowered his eyes, looked directly into my soul, and waited.

"I don't. It was there, I got whacked, then it was gone."

"And Edward isn't talking."

Sheriff Rhodes stared out at the view, seemed to be thinking this over. There were a lot of ifs and no real answers. He pursed his lips and twisted his mouth, causing them to lose their already faint coloring. He didn't look a day over eighty-nine. When he spoke again, the blood returned to his face, giving him a slight pink coloring.

"I believe you're telling the truth. I don't think anyone would take a hit like that—" he paused, gestured towards my brow— "just to make it look real. I also know you well enough to know that even though your temper used to land you on the other side of the bars as a youngin,' you've always been honest. Honest as you see things, at least."

"I imagine that's as close as I'm going to get to you giving me a compliment in this situation, so thank you."

"But that don't mean I'm buying this whole story. I just figure it's as good a story as any, and with that we can wrap up this case and move forward." He arched his brow, took in a deep breath. "All of us." He placed his foot back on the floor, pushed his chair and stood behind his desk. "If there's more to it, it'll come out eventually. It always does."

I nodded. I hoped that was true.

"Go on now. You can relax. You and your man Petey did good. Speaking of which, he was supposed to drop by today and see me too, tie up a few loose ends. You talk to him, you let him know I'd like to have that chat."

"Sure thing, Sheriff," I said. "Mind if I use your phone?"

Sheriff Rhodes pointed at his desk. "Go ahead, I was just about to grab myself a cup of joe. Interested?"

I shook my head as Rhodes slipped out of the room and into the hallway. I heard the plodding of feet disappear down the hall. I reached for the telephone and dialed Petey's number. I let a minute pass before placing the receiver back down on its base. It struck me as odd that I hadn't heard from him. It wasn't like him to let a payment linger, nor was it like him to neglect giving an in-person statement.

The conversation with Sheriff Rhodes swirled in my brain: *If there's more to it, it will come out in the end...*

I walked down the marble stairs, past reception and out the front door.

Outside I made my way across the lawn towards my car as the sun began to dip behind the San Gabriel Mountains. I watched the red and pink hues blend together in the sky. It was over, for now. Petey was long gone, and Sheriff Rhodes had known. Edward would go to prison, and I would return home to my own sort of prison. I would crawl into my bed, pull the covers up tight to my neck and let the warmth of laziness lull me to sleep. I would dream the same dream as I always did, and for just a while, I would be unbothered by the things of this earth.

Politics and murder come together as the residents of Rosetown try to figure out how to deal with a new economic opportunity. In the end, commerce wins out, but not in the way the city council imagined—sometimes the old ways are best. Here's Angela's own tribute to her dad...

High Time for Murder

Angela Crider Neary

Thwack, thwack, thwack! The burnished gavel fell heavily on the dais, its dull thud reverberating throughout the room and quieting the din of conversation.

"I hereby call to order this session of the Rosetown City Council," the mayor said, her voice broadcast across the chamber through the mini-microphone before her. "The singular item on tonight's agenda is to consider allowing commercial cannabis activities within the city limits."

"Woo-hoo!" someone yelled from the packed throng of citizens. They had converged in force to address this topic of concern to a majority of residents since California had voted to make recreational marijuana use lawful. Some participants added whistling and clapping to the outburst, while others frowned and shook their heads, arms crossed.

The mayor pounded on the platform again. *Whack!* "Order! I won't have this assembly turned into a three-ring circus." She addressed the woo-hoo'er specifically: "George."

"Sorry, ma'am." George stared down at his well-worn sneakers like a chastised youngster. Mayor Jackie Peters had that effect on individuals who attempted to cross her, especially during her sacred committee meetings.

"I know this is a sensitive issue for our municipality, and spirits are running high," Peters said. "But everyone will get their chance to speak, and anyone who disrupts or doesn't follow the rules will be escorted out by Deputy Williams. Is that understood?"

The gathering silently nodded in unison.

"Good. Since the state's new law was enacted, we have been contemplating whether to endorse a local dispensary, or to solely permit medical deliveries. Tonight we will hear public comment on this matter.

"If you want to voice your opinion, please approach the podium in an orderly fashion. There's no reason to rush or cut in front of anybody. You will receive no more than three minutes to state your position as timed by the device fastened to the top of the rostrum. This is not a debate, so please, no remarks, interruptions, or arguments while someone else is talking. Everybody got that?"

The group provided another collective nod.

"Okay, then. Let's begin."

A swarm of individuals stood up. The mayor, accustomed to at most one or two orators, suppressed a sigh.

George happened to be the closest to the front, so he quickly hopped into the aisle and sidled up to the podium.

"May it please the Honorable Mayor Jackie and the esteemed representatives of the assembly," he said, with a flourish of his arm.

"Get on with it, George." Peters waved at the clock. "Time's a'wastin'."

"Okay, okay. I'm George Stilton and I've lived in this community going on sixty years now. The great state of California chose to approve the recreational use of cannabis almost a year ago, and we have yet to create measures to adopt and regulate commercial sales. It's a disgrace! As taxpayers, we deserve to benefit from the state's law. Many of our sick and elderly residents depend on this medicinal herb to cure what ails 'em, or at least make what ails 'em more tolerable. But with no nearby access, they find themselves deteriorating in pain and without hope."

"That's what medical deliveries within the township would be for, you old hippie," a congregant said.

Wham! went the mayor's hammer. "I said no interruptions. And please, be respectful to each other."

Another denizen took the lectern. "I'm Miguel Reyes, and I'm against a cooperative inside the city limits. The traffic situation here would make it reckless to plop a pot shop right downtown."

"Traffic is what you're worried about?" came a voice from the audience. "Ever been to San Francisco? That'll show you traffic."

Whump! The mayor's gavel was getting a workout. "I'm warning you," she said, gesturing in the general direction from where the utterance originated.

"Something like this will clog up the roadways for miles with people coming in from neighboring areas," Miguel continued, undeterred. "That's why a lot of us don't live in a big metropolis like San Francisco—we don't want to deal with the transit and parking nightmares. I'm not against access to marijuana for those who need it or even want it purely for enjoyment. So we should come to an agreement with the county to set up a clinic close by, but not in the city itself."

Next up was a distinguished older gentleman wearing a three-piece suit. He sported a long handlebar mustache, shiny with wax, that he twirled for a second or two before clearing his throat and beginning.

"I'm Steve Keller, and it's my position that a weed outlet would benefit individuals and businesses alike. Since its use has been legalized, we shouldn't make it difficult for our citizens to exercise their rights under the law. We need progress here! We could expand and thrive by instituting this type of industry in the proper fashion. Think of the tourism it would attract!"

"We all know about you, Steve," said a person from the crowd. "You've been in the grass trade since before it was authorized, and your statements are a hundred percent self-serving."

Thwack, thwack, thwack... "Oh, to hell with it," the mayor said under her breath, tossing the gavel onto the dais.

"Hmph." Steve gave his 'stache a final twist, then stalked away from the platform.

An ancient woman moved with a strong and purposeful stride toward the rostrum.

"My name's Peggy Burle. Most of you know me from my delicious and renowned pies that I sell at the weekly farmers market." She turned and cast a beaming smile at the assemblage.

"We all appreciate that," Peters said, "but this isn't a forum to advertise you wares."

"I'll get to the point at hand. Ganja commerce in our fair city will bring heaps of problems, like drifters from all parts of the region coming and going. Do we really want exposure to mind-altering dope corrupting our youth? What will they think when they're walking to school past a reefer store and smell that awful, skunky stench?" She wrinkled her nose, waving her hand in front of it.

"Buffer zones between distribution centers and educational facilities would solve that problem," somebody from the gallery piped in. The mayor didn't bother to pick up her gavel.

"Neutral sectors won't deter gun-wielding criminals from invading our beloved hamlet," Peggy said. "Our city and valley are known for our cultivated world-class wines. We shouldn't become known for depraved pot use." She relinquished the stand to the next resident.

"I'm Eddie Sutter and I think stinkweed dissemination in town would be disastrous! Remember that man caught running around in nothin' but his birthday suit and a pair of tennis shoes, half out of his mind after smoking grass?"

"That wouldn't have had anything to do with the methamphetamine he also took, would it?" someone said.

Eddie ignored the comment. "And why was he nekked, for

goodness sakes? It was fifty-five degrees outside. I'll tell you why. 'Cuz folks under the influence of stimulants get elevated body temperatures. He had to shed his clothes to cool off. Then he raced across the baseball field in the middle of a night game, nekked as a jaybird, right in front of women and children. Ol' Ralph, the snack concessioner, had to tackle him on third base and hold him down, armed with nothing but a pair of hotdog tongs, until the police arrived. That's just the sort of thing we don't want here, and dispensaries would make it commonplace."

"I agree that the meth had more to do with it than the ganja," someone else from the crowd said.

"It was pretty funny when the baseball announcer started playing the 'Bad Boys' theme from *Cops* while the guy ran the bases," an audience member said, eliciting hoots from the congregation.

Eddie left the lectern with a scowl for those who didn't take this sort of dope-fueled public streaking incident seriously.

As the night wore on, citizen after citizen took the opportunity to express opinions for and against the proposition. Finally, the last one sat down and no one followed.

Peters, hopeful, raised her hammer and said, "Seeing no one rise and approach the podium..."

"Wait a minute!" A slight young man wearing a T-shirt emblazoned with the slogan, "Vote Smart, Vote for Art—for Rosetown City Council" in bright red and blue lettering, dashed into the gathering toward the stand, out of breath.

Peters hung her head and dropped her mallet yet again.

"My name is Art Ferguson, and I apologize for my late arrival. I encourage the committee to put aside its personal biases and vote to initiate recreational cannabis sales. Some people require this herb for a decent quality of life. Medical deliveries are costly, and we don't know how many places are willing to provide this service. I'm running for the board in next week's election. When I'm elected the governing officials will move from a conservative to a progressive majority, and we can institute local dispensaries!"

Many of the participants applauded. Art left the pulpit and a hush descended over the room.

Peters hastily lifted her gavel and said, "Seeing no one approach the podium, I will close the public session." *Thump.* "Do any of our officers have opinions on this proposal?"

"We need further investigation, studies, and time to weigh comments before we can establish a distribution facility," delegate Bruce O'Malley said. "Therefore, I move to introduce an interim ordinance that prohibits the commercial trade of cannabis in the city but allows for deliveries for medicinal purposes where the company has secured the appropriate license."

"I second the motion," representative Walter Goldman said.

"Let's take a roll call," Peters said. "What say the council?"

"Aye."

"Aye."

"Nay."

"Nay."

"And I say, 'Aye.' I'm not yet convinced that a retail marijuana facility is a good idea for our town. With three 'ayes' and two 'nays,' the temporary ordinance to forbid cannabis co-ops but to permit medical deliveries passes. This session is adjourned." The mayor gave a final halfhearted plunk on the bench with her gavel.

The gallery rose. Some residents cheered while others jeered, but all were ready to return to their families and cozy domiciles after completing their civic duty for the evening.

As everyone filed out, Art Ferguson shouted over the hubbub, "Remember, when I'm elected, there'll be a plurality of progressives in power. So, if you care about your community, get out to the polls next week!"

Art sauntered out into the crisp night air, slipping a fleece jacket over his campaign T-shirt. He hesitated, proudly regarding the motto across his chest. He was loath to cover up his advertising even for the brief trip to his house, but the chill that came with the nightly fog rolling into the valley made it practical, if not completely necessary. Besides, he liked to take the bike path and then cut through the vineyard that led him directly to his back-yard, so he wasn't likely to bump into any potential voters whom he could influence with his snappy slogan.

The meeting had gone well, he thought, as he walked with a spring in his step. He was lucky to have just made it to the last cabinet assemblage before the election. What were some of these people thinking, he wondered, trying to block the implementation of the state's recreational marijuana use law? They wouldn't get far with that kind of backward mentality. It really didn't matter, though, since the pendulum would swing toward the left when he was elected.

He smiled with self-satisfaction as he bounced down the murky lane, the dusky light cast by the crescent moon, intermittently covered by hazy fog, the only thing illuminating his way. He looked forward to becoming one of the youngest members of the Rosetown legislative body and infusing new life into the place's antiquated policies. He hoped to replace one of the conservative commissioners who was retiring and not competing for an additional term. He inhaled the fresh and invigorating scents of the damp gray pines, Douglas firs and coast redwoods that lined the trail, then made a sharp left, angling along a row of grapevines to complete his short trek home.

As he neared his deck, he heard a noise behind him, like the slight whispering of leaves. He thought maybe Henry, his orange tabby, had seen him coming and had hightailed it over to beg for his nightly meal. Henry had his own cat door and could go and come as he pleased. Art turned, ready to greet his furry friend, but saw nothing.

"Henry?" he said, peering into the blackness and remaining motionless. He didn't hear anymore rustling, so headed back toward his residence. His heart leapt out of his mouth when he nearly ran into a dim shape standing in his path.

"Oh my gosh!" he said, catching his breath, then chuckling

with recognition. "You scared the wits out of me, lurking out here in the dark. Out for an evening stroll? I was planning to heat up the kettle if you'd like to join me for a cup of tea." He pointed toward his cottage where the warm halo of his porch lamp beckoned.

The silhouette didn't respond. Was that a slight smirk crossing its lips? He couldn't tell. In the shadowy glow he could barely make out the outline of something in its hand. The last thing that registered was an arm rising up, then swiftly and decisively speeding toward his temple. Art crumpled to the ground in a heap. *Thwack, wham, whack.*

"Looks like we've got our murder weapon," Deputy Sheriff Maxwell Williams said, holding up a clear plastic bag containing a blood- and hair-encrusted ceremonial mallet. "The perp dropped it next to the body. We'll check it for prints, of course, but I suspect it's been wiped clean."

"Thanks, Max," Sheriff Carrie Evans said, circling the remains of Art Ferguson. "A judge's gavel? Now that's original."

"Yep. Appears to me that somebody advanced directly from the front and clobbered him."

Evans crouched down and scrutinized the left half of Art's face since the opposite side was mostly mush due to its close encounter with the auctioneer's club. Art's lifeless gaze failed to provide her with insight into who had done this to him or why. She shook her head at the senselessness of a young life in its prime being snatched away so suddenly and permanently.

She had been with the Rose County Sheriff's Office for over five years now, but had only recently taken commanding office after surviving the first contested election in nearly a quarter of a century. Various popular sheriffs had run unchallenged during the previous decades, and when the last one retired, there was a void into which several aspiring chief law enforcement officers attempted to leap. Evans had come out on top and was now the first female sheriff to take the oath in the county, although she'd had to work twice as hard as her predecessors to earn the respect of her mostly male colleagues.

But some days she wondered whether she had been victorious or else handed a booby prize, and this was one of those days. She couldn't believe anyone would do this to Art, a popular teacher at the high school who had caused a bit of controversy when he began dipping his toe into local politics.

When she had first hung up her lieutenant's hat in San Francisco to pursue a career further north, her uncle Dan, who was a sheriff in Texas and whose advice she'd always welcomed, counseled her that handling law enforcement for a rural township was grimmer than one might expect. In a large urban area, for example, it was much easier to ignore the darker side of human nature than it was in a small municipality where you often knew the perpetrators personally. Her experience confirmed that Uncle Dan had hit the nail on the head. She winced at her own expression, considering what had been done to Art.

Max interrupted her reverie. "I hate to say it, but this looks an awful lot like the gavel Jackie Peters uses at commission assemblies. I was at the one last night and it was pretty lively."

The mayor would request the presence of an off-duty officer if she thought things might get rowdy, which was infrequent. Although the cabinet regularly addressed important points, they were usually not as intriguing to the population as the topic of social drug use.

"The weed dispensary dispute, I take it?"

"Yep," Max said. "And Mr. Ferguson here was the last one to speak. He was clear that if he were elected next week, he would make sure there was a marijuana mart here."

"I've heard the mayor's against it, although I can't imagine her doing something like this. Especially with her own gavel. But I'll talk to her."

"If you interrogate everyone who's against a cannabis clinic, that'll be a lot of interviews."

"Let's focus on the folks at the meeting, for a start," Evans said. "Somebody may have been upset by what Art said and followed him home. There's also the gavel connection. You'll have to get me up to speed on what happened."

"Will do. Although it could be something completely unrelated."

"It could indeed."

"Is this yours?" Evans slid a photograph of the bagged and tagged evidence across Jackie Peters's desk.

"Ugh," the mayor said, cringing and averting her gaze after a quick peek at the image of the gore-coated bludgeon. "Could be. I haven't been able to find mine since the meeting. I didn't kill him, you know. I'm not a murderer."

"But it does look like your gavel was used as the weapon so I have to ask. What did you do after the meeting?"

"I was here in my office for at least an hour with some of the officers, having a cup of coffee and talking about the night's events. After that, I went home. Look, Sheriff, I can see why you're here, but why would I kill someone with my own gavel? Anyone could've easily picked it up after the session. It was chaotic in there."

"Deputy Williams briefed me on the forum. He let me know that you were in favor of the interim ordinance, which might have been overturned if Art won a seat on the council next week. And he could have made things difficult for those with traditional views, like yourself."

"That's exactly what it is—an *interim* ordinance that gives us time to explore all of the concerns associated with a dispensary. I can assure you that I had nothing to do with Art's death. It's my job to work with the administration, whatever their political leanings are. But I'm happy to assist with your investigation in any way I can. I'm sure Deputy Williams let you know that there are quite a few citizens vehemently opposed to pot distribution who might have had motive to want Art out of the way. Bruce O'Malley and Walter Goldman supported the temporary rule, too, so I assume you'll be talking to them."

"Don't worry. I'm always thorough. Did you have anything personal against Art Ferguson? Or the idea of a sales outlet, for that matter?"

"No. I'm only interested in what's best for the community."

"All right. Thank you for your time and willingness to assist."

The sheriff's next stop was Eddie Sutter's 1920s bungalow. Evans thought the property had probably been in the man's family since it was originally erected. She didn't know if he had ever updated it, but he kept it nice and tidy, at least if you were viewing it from the street. She had never been inside.

She pulled the department's Ford Explorer up to the curb in front of the house, and spotted her target energetically raking his lawn. This struck her as odd. Aside from the fact that most people used leaf blowers these days, Sutter had already made neat piles at the edge of his drive from the foliage that had fallen from the Japanese maple trees framing the dwelling, and there were no more leaves in the yard itself. Yet he continued to sweep away.

Evans approached the wiry senior and said, "Can I talk to you for a few minutes?"

Sutter, who had been so busy gardening that he hadn't noticed the sheriff, looked up with a start and said, "I didn't do it!" then peeked over each shoulder as if somebody might nab him from behind.

"Do what?"

"Did that Peggy Burle rat me out?" He brandished his rake. "She always was a little tattletale, ever since our grade school days. I swear, I thought it was a free sample!"

The sheriff peered into his eyes, which were bloodshot and dilated.

"Are you under the influence of drugs or alcohol, Mr. Sutter?"

"How dare you! All I've had today is a piece of Peggy Burle's dessert that she's selling over at the market. And I've never touched a drop of booze or taken any drugs in my life!"

"So, you took something from Ms. Burle without paying for it?"

"I already told you, I thought it was a free sample." Sutter glanced left and right.

"Okay. I'll verify that. Where were you after the town council meeting?"

"I came straight here, why do you ask?"

"Can anyone corroborate that?"

"My wife, Sheila, can vouch for me."

"Did you see Art Ferguson after the assembly?" Evans asked.

"No, but if I had, I'd have given him a piece of my mind. He wants a weed store right downtown. Drugs will be the demise of our society. If they open that facility, it will be complete mayhem, with folks runnin' around nekked all over the place!"

"I'm not convinced that allowing the sale of pot will convert Rosetown into a nudist colony." Evans regretted her unprofessional sarcasm, but had been unable to resist in the face of her suspect's bizarre theory.

"You mark my words." Sutter nodded, all knowing.

Evans excused herself and went to the house to talk to Sheila. She didn't ask about the leaves.

"Deputy Williams to Sheriff Evans," came the radio call.

"Evans."

"What's your 20?"

"En route to the farmers market."

"I'll meet you there and update you on my interviews."

"10-4."

The sheriff pulled into the parking lot where the weekly market was in full swing with a hodgepodge of vendors, food trucks, and even an acoustic guitar player to entertain the shopping crowd. She exited the SUV and scanned the area until she identified the booth where Peggy Burle was hawking her county-famous sweets. Evans had never tried one of the baked goodies, but had heard rave reviews about them. Peggy was a local institution. In fact, a handful of women shared the stall with her, all proffering doughy treats, but she was the only one with a line of patrons stretched out in front of her.

Evans leaned against her truck and waited for Max. She noticed that Peggy had numerous blue ribbons fastened to the counter before her and on the awning above. She watched as the woman sold pie after pie and slice after slice while her colleagues stood by, mostly idle.

"Hi, Sheriff." Max joined her at the Explorer.

"Hi, Max. How did your inquiries go?"

"I talked to Miguel Reyes. He denied having anything to do with Art's death, and his wife confirmed his whereabouts when he got to his residence. Although there's the same problem with everyone at the assembly—unless they left with somebody else, they don't have alibis for the time between departing and arriving home, which is probably when the attack occurred."

"Do you like Reyes as a suspect?" Evans said.

"Well, aside from disagreeing with drug sales here because they might increase traffic, his family owns several wineries and has for decades. He's a winemaker at one of them. A popular theory hereabouts is that marijuana ventures will steal profits from the wine industry. There's also an attitude that wine is sophisticated, and some would rather be known for that than what they think of as low-class drug use.

"So, he had a motive and could be our guy. Except one store in a little town like ours probably won't be much competition for his wine businesses. And he let me know that Jackie Peters is a partner in a couple of his family's companies."

"Interesting," Evans said. "She didn't mention that to me when I interviewed her. That gives her a financial motive. Did you question anyone else?"

"I talked to Steve Keller. He spoke in favor of the dispensary, and it's common knowledge that he was in the pot trade long before it was legal. But he may want to stick with his illegal operation and not have to compete with a legitimate business."

"Makes sense."

"Yeah, but he left with friends to have drinks at a local bar, so he may not fit within our timeline of when Art was killed."

Evans filled Max in on her conversations. "Peters held back important information, and Sutter is enough of a loose cannon that he might've lost his temper and followed Art home. Representatives O'Malley and Goldman voted in favor of the interim ordinance, so we should chat with them, too."

"And now we need to talk to Peggy Burle who spoke out against a pot shop," Max said.

"I've been watching her pie tent. Most of her desserts are on the table behind her, and when a customer orders, she picks out an item and exchanges it for payment. She also offers tarts by the slice—see the ones lined up on the counter?"

"That might explain how Sutter swiped one of them without paying."

"Possibly. And every once in a while she selects a pie or a wedge from that big cooler at her feet."

"Maybe those have to be kept cold."

"Let's find out." Evans pushed herself off the vehicle and made a beeline toward Peggy's stand.

They waited in line so as not to interfere with the baker's business. Evans used the time to make a few additional observations about Peggy and her merchandise, like the manner in which she handed out her products and recorded her transactions in a small notebook.

When they arrived at the head of the queue, Evans extended her left hand toward Peggy, who accepted it with a strong grip. Must be all of that mixing, whipping, and beating of baking ingredients, Evans thought.

"Hi, Sheriff. You interested in my award-winning pies?"

"They sure look good. What kinds are there?"

Peggy grinned and motioned toward her display of delicacies, ever the spokesmodel for her goods. "Today, there's pumpkin, pecan, and for my fruit choice, apple. They're available by the slice, too, if you're interested in just a nibble."

"Mmm, mmm, those sound great." Max salivated. "I missed lunch, so I'm hungry. What about these here in the cooler?"

"Uh, those are the same flavors. I keep them there to replenish the ones on the table when I run out."

"But I've seen you take them directly from below and hand them to customers," Evans said.

Peggy hesitated. "Well, those are my regular clients. They've been supporting me for a long time so I like to give them the fresher ones." She winked.

"Is Eddie Sutter a routine buyer?"

"Is that why you're here? That old coot stole one of my slices this morning! But I won't press charges against him, bless his heart. He's a little touched in the head."

"We'd like to try one of the pieces that Mr. Sutter had," Evans said.

"Comin' right up."

Peggy pivoted toward the rear table, and Max took the opportunity to reach down and grab one of the 'special' slices out of the cooler. He snagged a plastic fork from a cup on the stand and dug into the pie. As he raised a bite to his mouth, Peggy turned and her smile transformed into an expression of horror.

"Don't eat that!" she yelled, thrusting her palm across the bar and smashing the entire confection into Max's face. She packed such a wallop that he staggered backward and sat down hard on the pavement.

For a split second everything went deathly quiet as the three of them gaped at each other in surprise. Peggy spun on her heel, preparing to take off, but crashed over the buffet of baked goods and fell to the pavement. Her fellow bakers watched, eyes wide and mouths covered, although it wasn't clear whether they were hiding attitudes of dismay or of satisfaction at her misfortune. Her constant bragging and overwhelming sales could tweak the nerves of even the most righteous amateur pastry chef.

As Max licked at his face and wiped sugary goo out of his nose and eyes, the sheriff hustled over and clasped Peggy's arms behind her back.

"Ms. Burle, what did you do after the town council meeting?"

"I walked straight home, of course. What do you think I did?"

"I think you killed Art Ferguson."

"That's preposterous!" Peggy struggled to get up, and the sheriff found it difficult to restrain the hardy elder woman.

"You're left-handed, aren't you?"

"What's that got to do with anything?"

"The person who murdered Art was left-handed."

"So what? There're plenty of us lefties around here."

"Not who had a motive to kill Art Ferguson. You're also pretty strong, as I bet Deputy Williams can confirm."

"Now why in the world would I hurt Art Ferguson?" Peggy wriggled about, but the sheriff held her steady.

"Because his plans to institute regulated marijuana dissemination would interfere with your unlicensed sale of cannabis-infused pies."

The nearby merchants gasped. Max sputtered and brushed the offending substance off his face more frantically than he had before.

"And I'm sure that if we review your ledger, we'll see how certain products brought in much bigger sums than others."

Peggy sighed and stopped squirming, the fight gone out of her. "That troublemaker would've ruined my business! How could somebody like me compete with commercial distribution? I'm an elderly woman on a fixed income that barely pays the bills. He couldn't leave well enough alone. Besides, he was a teacher at the high school and shouldn't have been influencing young minds with his immoral politics."

"Says the person dealing drugs disguised as pastries."

"I didn't sell them to children, and I wasn't hurting anyone."

"You hurt Art Ferguson." Evans clamped handcuffs on Peggy's wrists, placed her under arrest, and guided her into the back seat of her SUV.

Max met her at the vehicle, still rubbing at his face and dusting crumbs out of his hair. "I thought that filling tasted a little off. I hope I don't fail a drug test." Although marijuana consumption had become legal in the state, it was against law enforcement agency policy for employees to partake.

"I'm sure it won't be a problem," Evans said, "and I bet they'd make an exception in a case like this."

"I hope so. I guess we'll be learning a lot about this stuff since it's been legalized."

"It's high time that we do," Evans said. "And I doubt you ingested any of that pie, did you?"

"I think I spit it all out," Max said, then smiled. "But I swear it wasn't my pot."

"Sure, Max." Evans laughed. "That's what they all say."

"Crime and comedy, eh?"

Evans nodded. "Better than dope."

James Reasoner is a professional's professional for whom writing over a million words a year is something of an annual tradition, a truly awesome feat that seems like it will go on forever. In this story, Brodie doesn't know if Clate Shively is an incorrigible punk or a reformed criminal. After Clate breaks out of jail on Brodie's watch, Brodie's determined to pay him back—one way or the other...

Hunting Down Clate Shively

James Reasoner

I've been told that I'm too soft-hearted, and as I lay there on the cement floor of the Comingor County jail, bleeding from the cut on my head caused by the wallop Clate Shively gave me, I told myself there was probably some truth to that.

But the way I see it, you've still got to have some compassion for your fellow man, even when you're a jailer and find yourself around sorry, no-account fellas most of the time.

Compassion or not, I had a set of brass knuckles in my desk that I figured on introducing to Clate Shively the next time I ran into him. Which was going to be soon, I hoped. First, though, I had to get up.

The open cell door was within reach. I was in the part of the jail where the drunk tank was located. The individual cells were down a nearby hallway. I closed a trembling hand around one of the vertical iron bars in the drunk tank door.

Hanging on to it steadied me enough so I was able to reach the bars with my other hand, too, and slowly but surely I got my knees under me and then stood up. The world lurched and started spinning the wrong direction for a couple of seconds as I hung on for dear life, but then it righted itself.

Clate had been the only one left in the big, open cell. I'd already shooed out all the other overnight guests after giving them coffee and toast for breakfast. One man was too hung over for food, but all four of them guzzled down the java.

Clate wasn't in for public intoxication. He'd been facing a more serious charge, disturbing the peace, because he'd got into a fight at the Flambeau Lounge, a mighty fancy name for a place made of cinder block and plaster. So he didn't get kicked out with the drunks who'd slept it off.

Now he'd have even more serious charges hanging over his head, for example breaking out of jail and assaulting a deputy sheriff.

I clung to the bars and worked my way along the front of the cell. By the time I reached the door that led into the office area, I was feeling steady enough on my feet to let go. As jailer, my office was the closest to the cell block. I stumbled in there, leaned on the desk, picked up the phone receiver, and rotated the dial for the three numbers of the sheriff's direct extension.

"This is Sheriff Dameron," he said in my ear. That was enough to make me wince. Right then, my head didn't like loud noises, such as my heart beating and the blood rushing in my veins. The sheriff sounded like he was yelling at me through a megaphone.

"Sheriff, this is Brodie down in the jail." I'm not sure why I added that last part. I was the only Brodie who worked for the department. "We got trouble."

"Clate Shively didn't hang himself, did he?" The question came fast from the sheriff.

"What? Hang himself? No, sir. That son of a buck done broke outta jail."

Sheriff Dameron was always the calm sort. It took a lot to rattle him. But he sounded rattled just then as he said, "Are you hurt, Howard?"

"Well, I'm bleedin' a little, I suppose," I said. "How'd you know that?"

"Because I knew you wouldn't let a prisoner escape without putting up a fight."

That made me feel good and bad at the same time—good because of the confidence the sheriff had in me, bad because I'd let him down.

"Are you in your office? Sit down and rest. I'll get some help to you right away."

"Better put the word out on Clate first," I said. "He's probably still pretty close."

"Don't worry about that, just take care of yourself." The phone banged down on the other end.

But I did worry about Clate, for a couple of reasons. I wanted him caught as soon as possible, because while Clate had never been as bad as some others who'd come through the jail, when you've got a prisoner on the loose, you just can't tell what's going to happen. Innocent folks could get hurt.

But at the same time, I didn't want the other deputies to catch him. I wanted to do that myself. I opened my desk drawer, took out those brass knucks, slipped them on, and flexed my fingers a couple of times before forming a fist.

Yeah, I'd teach Clate Shively a lesson if I caught up to him first.

Doc Yantis turned off the little light he'd been shining in my eyes, annoying the heck out of me, and straightened up to say, "Pupils look all right. There's a good chance you don't have a concussion, Deputy. You should go home and get some rest. But don't go to sleep. That's important. Sit up and stay awake. Have someone stay with you to make sure of that."

That was going to be a problem, since I lived alone in a rented room over the hardware store and didn't have any family in these parts since my folks passed away. I sometimes went out with Josette Dobbs—you know, to eat Mexican food or take in a picture show—but she was checking at the Handi-Mart and they didn't like it if she took off work. It wasn't like we were all that serious about each other, anyway.

But Doc sounded like he meant what he said, so I just nodded and said, "Yes, sir, I'll do that." When you're fixing to do something you know somebody won't like, I've found that it's usually better to go ahead with it and try to explain later.

Sheriff Jeff Dameron came into the office then. He'd been the sheriff of Comingor County for going on twenty years, but he still looked more like a fella who taught algebra in high school than a lawman. He looked at the bandage on my head and asked, "Is he going to live, Doc?" His tone was light but I could see the worry in his eyes.

"Yeah, I think so. That cut looked bad, but head wounds always do. I cleaned it up and closed it with a couple of stitches. I'm pretty sure there's no concussion. What'd he hit you with, son? A piece of metal he'd pulled off a bunk or something like that?"

"No, sir," I said. "He walloped me with his fist. I think I hit my head on the cell door on my way down, and that's what caused the cut."

Doc grunted and looked at the sheriff. "I think you can still call it assault with a deadly weapon."

"That's not up to me," Sheriff Dameron said. "The district attorney will decide about any new charges. My only concern right now, other than Deputy Brodie's health, is capturing Clate Shively before he hurts anybody else."

"Good luck with that. You know how hard it can be to run these old country boys to ground. It's like chasing a wild animal."

I thought it was a mite unkind for Doc to say that, considering how many of his patients were old country boys, but I didn't comment on it.

"I told Brodie to go home and take it easy," Doc went on. "I'll go by there and check on him tomorrow."

"I'll see that he gets home," the sheriff promised.

Doc picked up his medical bag and left. Sheriff Dameron looked at me and went on, "Come on, Howard. I'll take you home."

"You don't have to do that, Sheriff. It's a three-block walk, that's all. I can make it just fine by myself."

He frowned. "I'm not sure Doc would want that."

"Doc's an ol' worry-wart, you know that. And you got better things to do, like huntin' down Clate."

The sheriff perched a hip on the corner of my desk and said, "I've already put out an all-points bulletin. Tell me about him. You know him better than I do." He paused. "That is, if you feel up to it."

"I don't feel too bad, just a little headache, that's all." By now, that was true. My mother always said I was hard-headed, and she was right. "I'm not sure I know Clate any better than you do, though, Sheriff."

"You went to school with him, didn't you?"

I shrugged and said, "He was two years behind me. We were on the football team at the same time when I was a senior and he was a sophomore. But he was an end and I was a lineman, so we didn't have a whole lot to do with one another."

"He got in trouble a lot even then, didn't he?"

"Mostly for things like drinkin' and hot-roddin'. He always had the fastest car and was the slickest driver you ever saw. Might've been able to make something of himself with the kind of talent he had. He ran with a rough crowd, though."

"Seems like I arrested him once for fighting."

"Yeah, he tangled with Scooter McIlhenny under the bleachers at the football stadium and busted his nose. Might not've amounted to much if Scooter's dad hadn't been Leroy McIlhenny."

Sheriff Dameron nodded slowly and said, "Mayor McIlhenny at the time, as I recall."

"Yep. And Clate had just turned eighteen the week before, so he got tried as an adult and did six months in lock-up."

"Which didn't exactly rehabilitate him."

Why I stood up then for a fella I intended to work over with brass knucks when I found him I couldn't tell you, but I said, "Clate's not that bad. He's never been convicted of anything that'd get him sent to prison."

"Suspected of such," the sheriff pointed out. "Burglary, grand theft auto, larceny, as I recall."

"Yeah, but he's cleaned up a lot since he married Linda."

"Preacher's daughter, right?"

"Yeah." Linda Clarkson's father was Albert Clarkson, pastor of the First Baptist Church of Comingor. Everybody had been surprised when she up and married Clate Shively, who was widely regarded as a no-account, and rightly so for the most part. But what I'd just told the sheriff was true: Clate hadn't been in any trouble that I knew of since marrying Linda, until that fight at the Flambeau Lounge the night before.

"Well, I sent a couple of men out to their place to check and see if he's there. Not that I expect him to be. Often, though, criminals don't really have a lot of sense."

Considering some of the things I'd seen while working at the jail, I had to agree with him about that.

He stood up and motioned for me to follow him. "Come on. I'll see that you get home. Should we take a car?"

"It's only three blocks," I said again. "Why don't we just walk, Sheriff, if you're bound and determined to come along?"

He smiled. "All right, but if you start feeling woozy, you let me know."

Comingor is the only good-sized town in Comingor County, both of which are named for Major George Washington Comingor, a veteran of the Texas Revolution who served under General Sam Houston and was also one of the early pioneers in the area. And when I call it a good-sized town, that's only relatively speaking. The last census put the population at just over six thousand people. But that's big enough to have a business district that takes in several blocks in all directions from the courthouse square. The jail isn't in the courthouse itself. It's in a separate two-story building a couple of blocks off the square, constructed in 1901 out of tan sandstone blocks. In old photos I've seen, it has a partial third story that looks like it served as a watchtower, but that part had been demolished and removed by the time I came along. When I was a kid, the jail always reminded me a little of the Alamo, but nobody ever made a last stand there, as far as I know.

As Sheriff Dameron and I walked along the street on that pleasant spring day, he stuck his hands in the pockets of his uniform trousers and asked me, "How did Shively manage to knock you out, Howard?"

If I hadn't been walking, I would have shuffled my feet in embarrassment. "It was mighty stupid of me, Sheriff. He claimed he was sick, and when I opened the door to check on him, he jumped me. I thought it could've been true. I mean, he was in that fight last night, and when you get roughed up, sometimes you don't really know how bad you're hurt until the next day."

"You should remember that, since you're the one who got roughed up today." He paused, then after a moment went on. "Shively took advantage of your soft heart, in other words."

"Soft heart, soft head," I muttered. "Reckon they go hand in hand with me."

"Now, don't feel like that," the sheriff said. "Why do you think I asked you to run the jail?"

"I don't know. Some of the other fellas claimed it was because you didn't think I was smart enough to be out on patrol."

"That's not it at all," he said, and he sounded a little mad. "They shouldn't have ragged on you like that."

"I didn't take any offense," I said, although actually, at the time I sort of had.

"I wanted you to run the jail because I knew you'd look out for the prisoners' welfare. In a little town and a mostly agricultural county like this, most of the time they're not really bad sorts. Not hardened criminals, if you know what I mean."

"Yeah, I suppose I do."

"So, while they have to answer to the law for their crimes, I don't want them coming to any harm, either from themselves or other prisoners, while they're in our custody. That make sense to you, Howard?"

"Yes, sir, it does."

"So, the truth of the matter is that I figured you're tough enough to crack down on those who need it and kind enough to look out a little for those who don't." The sheriff paused. "That tells me you didn't consider Clate Shively one who needed to be cracked down on."

"No, I suppose I didn't," I said. I touched my pocket where I'd slipped that set of brass knuckles. "I sure turned out to be wrong. I won't make that mistake again, after we've got him locked up."

"You won't have to worry about that for a few days," Sheriff Dameron said as we paused by the bottom of the stairs leading up the side of the red brick hardware store building. At the top of those stairs was a landing and a door leading into the second floor, which was cut up into four rooms the owner rented out. "You need to take some time off to recuperate."

"Yeah, it'd probably do me good."

"You've got a phone up there, don't you?"

He ought to have known that, since I was a deputy and had to be on call when I wasn't on duty. But I said, "Yes, sir, I sure do."

"You let somebody know, then, if you need anything. Anything at all."

"You bet." I smiled and nodded, waiting for him to leave.

He didn't show any signs of doing that, so I had to go on up the stairs, pausing on the landing to smile down at him again before I opened the door and stepped into the upstairs hall. I closed the door behind me.

Then opened it again after I'd counted to thirty. By that time, I could see the sheriff walking along the street toward the jail. I waited until he'd turned the corner and was out of sight before I went back down the stairs.

When I got to the bottom, I turned around and went up again. I was supposed to be off duty, and I didn't want to do anything wrong by wearing my uniform. So I went in my room and changed to jeans and a lightweight flannel shirt. I put the brass knucks in the right front pocket of my pants.

I keep my pickup parked on a side street in front of a small appliance repair shop that had closed down a few years earlier. The store was still sitting there vacant, so I wasn't interfering with anybody's business. I got in and drove off, heading west out of Comingor on the Prescott Highway.

Clate and Linda Shively lived in an old farm house on one of the county roads, several miles off the highway. When I was a kid, all of those roads were dirt. Some of them had been paved over the years, but not this one, so my pickup trailed a cloud of dust after it. Anybody looking in this direction would know somebody was coming but there wasn't a thing I could do about it.

Clate had grown up in that house and had inherited it when his father dropped dead of a heart attack and his mother passed away in a nursing home in Prescott a few years later. He had a couple of older sisters, but they had gotten married and moved away from this part of the country a long time ago.

The house was a white frame with dark brown shingles on the roof. The paint was faded and peeling. The flowerbeds along the cement front porch were overgrown with weeds. Clate wasn't much on keeping a place up. A separate one-car garage, built at the same time to look like the house, sat to the left and back a little ways, at the end of the driveway. Mostly behind the house but still visible was a stone well house with an old cistern on top of it. Farther back was an unpainted frame barn with a pen to the left that held a couple of milk cows. To the right of the barn was a muddy hog pen with about a dozen black and white and pink hogs rooting around in it. Layers of dried mud mostly covered up those colors.

I tried not to shudder when I thought about hogs. I hated them and had ever since I was a kid and one of my chores had been slopping the hogs on my family's farm. I had to climb on the fence and lean over to pour the buckets of slop into the feeding trough, and my brother liked to tell me that if I slipped and fell over the fence into the pen, the hogs would eat *me*. I believed him, of course; he was my big brother.

I recalled, too, that the sheriff in the next county over had had several mighty dangerous encounters with feral hogs. I don't know if they would have eaten him, but they came all too close to killing him. Anyway, I've never cared for hogs, even the ones like those Clate and Linda raised that weren't feral.

An old car was parked in the garage. I didn't know if Linda had a job, but it looked like somebody was home. Trying not to think about the hogs, I went up on the porch and knocked on the door facing.

Enough time for somebody to walk from the kitchen through the living room went by, and then the wooden door opened. Linda Shively looked through the screen door at me and said, "Yes? Can I—" Then she stopped as she recognized me. "Howard Brodie? My goodness, is that you?"

"Yes, ma'am, it is."

She laughed. "Oh, for heaven's sake, don't call me ma'am. You're older than me."

It's true, I was. She was the same age as Clate, which had put her two years behind me in school. We'd been acquainted with each other, but only in a sort of glancing off fashion. I'd dated a good friend of hers for about a month. Linda had always looked at me like she disapproved of me and thought I wasn't good enough for her friend, but I'd figured that was because she was a preacher's kid and those seemed to come in only two varieties, the disapproving kind and the ones who were wild as hell.

"It's a warm day," she went on as she pushed the screen door open. "Come on inside. Can I get you something to drink?"

I tried not to look at her belly under the cotton print housedress, but it was hard not to notice it. She was in the family way, not ready to pop, but definitely visible. Maybe four or five months along. Not being a married man, it's not easy for me to judge such things.

Clate hadn't said anything to me about how he was going to be a daddy. Not that the subject comes up that much in jail.

I stepped inside and Linda asked, "How about a glass of iced tea?"

No self-respecting Texan is going to turn that down, so I said, "Thank you. That'd be nice."

She waved a hand at the sofa and said, "Sit down. I'll be right back."

She went off to the kitchen, and I sat down and wondered why she hadn't asked me what I was doing there. She came back with a couple of jelly jars that had been washed and turned into tea glasses. As she handed mine to me, I saw tears shining in her eyes.

"You've come to tell me something bad, haven't you?"

"Uh...what makes you think that?"

"You work for the sheriff's department," she said as she sat down in an armchair across from me. "You've come to tell me that Clate's been hurt or...or worse. Was it a car wreck?"

Now I was getting confused, sure enough. Sheriff Dameron had said that he'd send a couple of men out to question Linda and take a look around for Clate. But here she was acting like she didn't have any idea he'd even been in jail, let alone busted out.

Something had happened to delay those other two deputies, I realized. That was the only explanation that made any sense.

Which meant that I got to talk to her before she knew what was going on. I felt kind of bad about keeping the news from her, but if she could tell me what I needed to know, I supposed I could get over it.

"Take it easy, Linda," I said. "As far as I know, Clate's fine, and there haven't been any wrecks in the county for several days. I was just looking for him, is all. He's not here?"

She sighed and pushed back some blonde hair that had swung forward in front of her face. She'd always been a pretty girl and still was, but time and circumstance had put some hard lines in her face, the same as they do to all of us.

"I haven't seen him since yesterday evening, Howard," she said, "and I'm starting to be worried sick about him."

She'd be more worried if she found out he was a fugitive. Or maybe she already knew, I thought. It occurred to me that maybe Clate *had* been here, and he'd given Linda a story to tell, to throw off anybody who came looking for him. Like me.

I'm generally pretty good about knowing when somebody's lying to me, and I didn't think she was. I didn't know how good of an actress she was, but I didn't remember her being in any school plays or anything like that.

"I don't think you need to worry," I told her. "That can't be good for you, in your condition."

She turned pink and put a hand on her mounded belly. "You noticed, huh?"

Would've had to be blind not to, but I didn't say that. Instead I said, "I'll bet ol' Clate's pleased as punch, isn't he?"

"Of course. I mean...he's a little concerned...about the money and all. But he told me that everything's going to be all right, and I believe him."

"You said the last time you saw him was yesterday evening?"

"That's right. After he talked to Teddy Keller."

Teddy Keller. That was a name I hadn't heard in a long time. I hadn't missed it a dang bit, either. Teddy was a year younger than me, which put him between me and Clate in age. He'd been one of that bad crowd Clate ran with.

I remembered a time when Teddy had come swaggering up to me in the Rexall Drugstore while I was looking at the paperbacks on the store's spinner rack. A couple of his friends were with him, hanging back to give him an audience. Like I said, he was younger than me, and a couple of inches shorter, but that didn't stop him from planting himself right in front of me. He was all red hair, freckles, and smirk as he said, "You want to fight?"

"What?" I'd said.

"I asked if you wanted to fight. We'll go, right here, right now. You just say the word."

"No, I don't want to fight."

"Scared of me, aren't you, fat boy?"

Now, I wasn't really fat, just husky. Which is why I made a good lineman when it came time to play football. I didn't like the way Teddy was talking to me, and I might've taken him up on that offer, but right then my mother walked up with the prescription she'd gotten filled and said, "Come on, Howard, we still have to go to the grocery store."

"Yeah, run along with your mama," Teddy said. My mother gave him a quizzical look and he wandered off with his buddies.

"Was that boy bothering you?" she asked me.

"Nah." I didn't offer any explanations.

"Well, I didn't like the look of him."

Neither did I, and that held true the rest of the way through school. Teddy Keller was one of those kids who always had cigarettes and seemed able to put his hands on a six-pack of beer whenever he wanted to. He got in fights, got sent to juvie for breaking into stores, and while he may not have been the biggest thug in Comingor High School, he was one of the top five.

I'd heard that he had done at least one more stretch behind bars, this time at the state pen in Huntsville, but I'd never bothered to check on the details. Mostly I just never thought about Teddy Keller.

Now I had to, since Linda had said he had been here the day before. Trying to sound like I didn't think much about it, I said, "So Teddy stopped by, did he?"

"That's right. He and Clate were good friends in school, you know, but Clate hadn't seen him for years. It was a good reunion. They sat in here and talked and laughed for quite a while before Teddy said he had to go."

"When was that? Right before Clate went out?"

"No, it was yesterday afternoon, and Clate didn't go out until after supper. He said he was just going out for a spell, but he'd be home early." She frowned at me, cocked her head a little to the side, and asked, "Why are you looking for him, Howard?"

"Oh, I thought I'd talk to him about rebuilding an engine for me," I said, coming up with that off the top of my head. But it was a good answer, because Clate was a heck of a mechanic, a skill he'd picked up back in his hot-roddin' days. He had worked for several garages in Comingor and picked up some shade tree mechanic work, as well. As far as I knew, that was mainly how he earned a living for him and Linda.

And for the little one on the way, I added to myself. *If* Clate could manage to stay out from behind bars, which considering what he'd done today was looking less and less likely.

"I'm sure he'd be willing to do that," she said in response to my fib. "If you can find him." She rubbed at her forehead. "I just can't think where he might be. He *never* does this. He's never stayed out all night since we've been married, and he always calls me if he's going to be even a little bit late."

"I reckon something must've come up. If you see him, tell him to give me a call, okay?" I didn't expect Clate to call me, but it seemed like that's what I would have said if I'd been telling the truth about getting an engine rebuilt.

"Of course." She looked at the jelly jar in her hand. "We got to talking and didn't drink our tea."

"Oh, I can take care of that." I drank the whole thing down. It was good, too. Maybe a little too sweet.

Sort of like Linda, who'd taken a chance on Clate Shively. And I hoped it wasn't going to backfire too badly on her.

The Flambeau Lounge had been around for as far back as I could remember, but when I was a kid it was called the Palomino

Lounge and had a statue of a golden horse on the roof. I don't know if the horse was made of plaster or plastic or what, but it had been a local landmark for a good number of years, until one spring a tornado came along, tore it off the roof and deposited it mostly intact on the fifty-yard line of the high school football field in the next town to the east. The lounge's owner didn't want to pay to have it hauled back and put on the roof again, so he changed the name of the place to Baxter's (which was his name). The business had changed hands several times since then, and gotten a new name each time, until a fella from Dallas named Gordon Harrington bought it and dubbed it the Flambeau. I'd talked to him a few times but never thought to ask him why he picked that name.

There's twenty miles and a county line between Comingor and Prescott, and the lounge was about five miles past the city limits on the Prescott Highway, still well within Comingor County and the jurisdiction of the sheriff's department. Which is why we got called when the fight broke out between Clate Shively and Dan Pollard. Pollard was just a name to me; I didn't know anything about the man or why Clate would want to fight him. I thought maybe Gordon Harrington could tell me.

The Flambeau was open when I parked in the gravel lot beside it. Maybe not open for business, but the front door stood wide open as if to air out the place. Considering the atmosphere in most beer joints, it could probably use it.

I went inside and found Gordon sitting at a table with an adding machine in front of him, along with some scattered papers. In the sunshine coming in through the door, the place looked shabbier than it did with the lights dimmed of an evening. Not that it was the Ritz to start with, you understand.

Without looking up, Gordon said, "We're not open yet." Then his eyes flicked toward me and he recognized me. "Deputy Brodie. Are you here about the fight last night? I already told everything to the deputies who arrested Clate Shively."

"I'm here about Clate, all right, but I'm off duty." I pulled a chair from another table, turned it around, and straddled it. "You mind if I ask you a few questions? You don't have to answer." I wanted to do this proper-like and make sure he knew this was just two fellas talking, not him being questioned by a deputy.

He shrugged and said, "Sure, go ahead. But first tell me what happened to your head."

Gordon was a decent guy, short and stocky, with a neatly clipped brown beard. He sounded genuinely concerned, and I believed he was.

"I got bunged up a little when a prisoner escaped this morning." I gestured toward the bandage Doc had put over the stitches he'd taken. "Clate Shively."

Gordon stared at me. "Clate broke out of jail? Really? I didn't think there were such actual things as jailbreaks anymore."

"Oh, yeah, it happens now and then. Not in Comingor County since I've been the jailer. Not until today."

"Are you all right? Were you badly hurt?"

"Naw, just a scratch and a bruise. About that fight...?"

"You want me just to tell you what happened?"

"Yeah, if you don't mind."

He shook his head and said, "Of course not. But I don't really *know* what happened, or what caused it, anyway. Clate came in about eight o'clock, ordered a beer, and sat there for a while drinking it." He nodded toward the bar with its empty stools lined up along it. "He finished it and ordered another one, but he hadn't drank much of it when he got up, walked over to one of the booths, and called Dan Pollard a name. Dan was with his wife, so he didn't want to just sit there and take it, of course. He stood up and told Clate to leave them alone. That's when Clate swung on him and the fight started."

"So Clate threw the first punch."

"Oh, yeah, no doubt about that. I saw the whole thing, and so did at least a dozen other people. Dan was just defending himself. That's why the deputies didn't arrest him last night."

"Tell me about Pollard."

Before responding to that, Gordon gestured toward the bar and asked, "You want a beer? Since you're not on duty." He smiled. "Despite the fact that you're clearly interrogating me."

"I may not be on duty but I want to find Clate, sure enough. And I'll pass on the beer, thanks. Still a mite early in the day for me."

"It's after noon," Gordon said as he glanced at a clock on the wall with a beer company logo on it. "I'll be opening up in another hour or so."

"What about Pollard?" I asked, to drag him back onto the subject.

"If you're looking for Clate Shively, I don't think Dan can help you. I don't believe they even knew each other."

"Who came in first, Clate or Pollard?"

"Clate was here first. Pollard and his wife came in about twenty minutes later, I'd say."

"They speak to each other when Pollard came in?"

Gordon shook his head. "Clate never turned around. He was just looking at that beer he was nursing along."

"Did anybody *else* talk to Clate while he was here?"

"Just me, when I served him the beers. I asked him how he was doing. Just making small talk, you know. He said fine, but he seemed worried about something. That was probably why nobody else spoke to him. He didn't seem like he was in any mood for conversation."

"What business is Pollard in?"

"He works for the peanut company. Does something in the office, I don't know exactly what."

Gordon didn't have to say which peanut company, because there was only one and it was one of the county's largest employers. This was peanut country, along with cotton and sorghum. It didn't seem likely that there would be any sort of business connection between Pollard and Clate Shively.

I sat there and mulled over everything Gordon Harrington had told me. To make sure I had it straight in my mind, I said,

"So Clate comes in, gets a beer, and sits there brooding over it for a while. Then he goes over to a booth, picks a fight with a fella he doesn't even know, and gets himself arrested."

"Yeah, that pretty much sums it up," Gordon said. "Before he stood up, though, he sort of turned on the stool so he could look around the room."

"Like he was hunting for somebody in particular?"

"Maybe. He looked like he was trying to make up his mind."

"Picking out who to fight," I said. "He was on the hunt for trouble."

"Yeah. That's what it was like, all right. But why did he pick Dan Pollard? Dan's a good-sized guy, and even though he works in an office, he seems like he can handle himself."

"You said he had his wife with him. Clate must have figured that if he walked over and insulted Pollard, Pollard was bound to take offense because he wouldn't want to back down in front of her. He wouldn't have known she was Pollard's wife, but that didn't matter. She was a woman and he wouldn't want to look bad in front of her."

Gordon laughed and said, "You make it sound like Clate *wanted* to get arrested."

"Yeah, it does kind of seem that way, doesn't it?"

"Why in the world would anybody want that?"

I could think of a reason, but I kept it to myself for the time being, at least until I could dig into things just a little more.

It was getting on toward three o'clock in the afternoon by the time I walked along the sidewalk toward the big red brick Comingor State Bank on the southwest corner of the courthouse square. I hadn't taken the time to eat lunch, and my stomach was letting me know it. I mean, there were more important things going on, sure, but try telling that to your stomach.

There was one step down from the sidewalk to the parking spaces along the street. I went down it, moved around the back of a car, and came up alongside the open driver's window. I'd watched the car pull into this parking space a minute earlier.

Resting my right hand on the window sill, I said to the driver, "Howdy, Clate. If you got a gun in there, I sure hope you got enough sense not to reach for it."

He took a deep breath. Both hands were on the steering wheel, and I saw them clench tighter on it. But he kept them there, so I knew he wasn't going for a weapon. He turned his head and looked up at me, his face rawboned and sweating under the short blond hair.

"Howard, I'm so sorry," he said. "I never wanted to hit you—"

"Like you didn't want to hit Dan Pollard. You just decided he was the mostly likely fella in the room to pick a fight with, and getting arrested and stuck in jail was all you cared about."

"You don't know—"

I interrupted him again. "Yeah, I do. Leastways, I think I've got it figured out. What did Teddy do? Threaten to hurt Linda...and the baby?"

Clate swallowed hard. "He never really said what he'd do, just that I'd be sorry for the rest of my life if I didn't help him. There was nothing I could do except tell him I'd go along with what he wanted. And...and pretend to Linda that nothing was wrong..."

His voice broke a little then. Clate was a big, rugged guy, but at that moment he looked and sounded like a scared little boy.

I glanced at the bank, where the tellers would be getting ready to close up for the day. Since nothing was going on just yet, I said to Clate, "Then you figured out that if you were in jail, Teddy couldn't hold it against you for not helping him. Only you had second thoughts, like maybe he'd hurt Linda anyway, and by this morning, you knew you had to get back out and go through with it."

"You remember how he is, Howard. He's crazy. He's never changed."

"Oh, I know that," I said. "I looked up his record since he

left Comingor. Convicted of two bank robberies and suspected of more than half a dozen others. When Linda told me he was back in town, I figured it couldn't be for any good reason."

He looked at the steering wheel, not wanting to meet my eyes.

"I'm supposed to be off duty for medical reasons, you know. But the sheriff wasn't too upset with me for coming back in," I went on, "once I told him I had a pretty good idea there was gonna be a bank robbery this afternoon, and that Teddy Keller was making you be his getaway driver. You always were the fastest man behind a wheel in these parts. That's how it all shakes out, isn't it?"

He hesitated, then nodded without saying anything.

"Can't really blame you for not knowing what the best thing was to do in a situation like that. You were mighty scared for your wife and your unborn baby, after all." I shook my head. "Slugging me wasn't it, though."

He made his right hand into a fist and tapped it lightly against the steering wheel. "Just when I think I've got it all figured out, I realize I've done the wrong thing. Always. That ever happen to you, Howard?"

"All the dang time," I said, then I turned fast toward the bank because I'd heard the door slam open and footsteps slapping on the sidewalk. Teddy Keller was running toward us, wild-eyed, and behind him from the bank where they'd been waiting for him, out of sight, came the sheriff and a couple of deputies. Teddy skidded to a stop when he saw me, but he was already close enough that a long, fast step brought me within arm's length.

He had a gun in his hand, but I didn't give him a chance to raise it. I'd already decided that I wasn't going to use those brass knucks on Clate after all. Seemed more fitting to introduce them to Teddy. Anybody who'd threaten a pregnant woman like that had it coming.

But I guess I really am soft-hearted, and soft-headed, because I left the brass knucks in my pocket and hit Teddy Keller with a plain ol' right fist instead. Broke his jaw even without them, and unfortunately, one of my own knuckles to boot.

It sure felt good, though, and as I looked down at Teddy sprawled on the sidewalk, moaning and gobbling with that busted jaw, I couldn't help but remember that day in the drugstore when he'd got right up in my face.

"Yeah," I told him, "I reckon I *do* want to fight."

Just for the record, once Dan Pollard found out what had been going on, he didn't press charges against Clate, and neither did I. The district attorney wouldn't hear of not charging him for the jailbreak, though. He did three months in the county jail and was out in time to be on hand for his son's birth.

I hired him to rebuild my pickup's engine. It needed it.

Poet, critic, writer, essayist, translator—Jim Sallis is a true man of words. With "Big Day at Little Bit" the protagonist acts on behalf of an old friend of his. Named Bill. Who is a writer and a college professor, among other things. No last names are given and the circumstances surrounding their friendship in the story are somewhat mysterious...

Big Day in Little Bit

James Sallis

A gentleman, I thought the first day we met, his soft-spoken greeting and hushed Southern drawl flowing across the table to where I stood in my new yellow work boots. Soon I'd discover he was a writer as well, but never held that against him. In this world we make our living as we can.

Thinking this could not possibly be the man for whom I was there, I offered apologies and made to withdraw, whereupon he remarked that I appeared to be new in town and perhaps might take a moment to sit, have coffee, talk a spell?

Why not? I never had a clock to punch, only jobs to do.

And this, I'd learn, was Bill's habitude. He served as Little Bit's sheriff (I never held that against him either) and regularly haunted the bus station, the Sinclair station on the edge of town or Millie's Good Eats watching who came and went. Some of those who went did so at Bill's urging.

So we sat and drank coffee sweetened with Bill's jokes, chewing on nuggets of downhome philosophy till our talk turned to books, which quickly proved what we had most in common. This began, as I recall, with some mention he made of Peter Rabe, how slippery the bad guys were in his work, how hard to get hold of,

219

in *Kill the Boss Good-by* for instance. I saw his bet with Vin Packer's *Come Destroy Me* and raised him Charles Williams.

The thing is, people listened when Bill spoke, just like I did. I remember how once, waiting for some small repair on his truck, he regaled six mechanics with the story from Günter Grass's *The Flounder.* They were spellbound, and I have to wonder if this wasn't due to Bill's telling more than to the story itself, or to their all being themselves fishermen.

In his spare time, I should mention, Bill taught at the local college. The question to be asked here is how the hell he *had* free time. I figure that's what? five, six jobs? Writer, sheriff, town greeter, family man, professor...Oh, and all those reviews and columns he wrote about smelly old paperback books, the kind that sold off wire racks in drugstores for thirty-five cents. Just thinking about all that made you need to sit down and rest up.

What it made me do, after sitting there with Bill for better than an hour that first time, was get up, head back to the Motel 6 out by the Sinclair, and use the phone in my room to cancel my contract in Little Bit, the first and only time I ever did that. No way I was going to bring trouble to Bill's town. I went back to Little Bit again and again after that, but never for work. I'd have a job in Chicago, Portland, New Hampshire, I'd set it up so's to fly back through nearby Serenade, rent a car, and layover a few days in Little Bit, sitting around the bus station, the Sinclair, or Good Eats with Bill. It's the only town I ever felt a part of, the only place I ever felt welcome.

My third or fourth visit—I can't be sure, but I think I'd just done a double up in Minnesota, which would make it number six—Bill said if it weren't too much trouble, he could use a favor.

"Absolutely."

We were walking alongside one of the town's many dried-up creek beds. White heads of dandelions made it look like a gathering of old men down in there. On the bank, someone (a child? a rogue artist?) had sculpted dirt and stone into a tiny version of Native American cliff dwellings.

"Thought I might get your professional opinion," Bill said.
"Professional?"

The smile told me he knew. Which actually didn't come as much of a surprise.

"I've had information that one of your fellow travelers is here in Little Bit. Working. As the two of you share a profession, I thought it possible you might know him."

"There's a good chance."

"A man everyone calls simply Wilson."

"We've not met. I know *of* him, of course."

"What I'm wondering is how concerned I should be over this—assuming it to be true."

"Do you know why he is here? For whom?"

"I have my suspicions."

It was early afternoon, dwarf shadows walking beside us, horizon ashimmer. "Give me some time," I said. "Let me look around, ask a question or two."

I was waiting in his room at Sunrise Motel the next town over when Wilson got back that night. Earlier I'd dogged him long enough to assure myself of his reason for being here, then gone out for an unhurried dinner of basic comfort food. The meatloaf, mashed potatoes and gravy were still with me. The room smelled faintly of spicy aftershave, no doubt from its former tenant. We pass through rooms and this world leaving brief imprints of ourselves behind.

He came in and shut the door. I was sitting in the corner. He remained where he was, shadowy in dim light from the curtained window.

"Here you are," he said. "I half expected you to come over and say hello this afternoon."

"That seemed hardly necessary."

"Professional courtesy aside. Of course. And by the way, that politician in Minnesota last year?"

"Hronka."

"Nice touch, the fuzzy dice on the bathroom mirror."

"By special request."

"Forever interesting, isn't it, all the messages out there. But those dice, that's the kind of thing that gets talked about."

"Exactly the point."

"When so seldom we can tell what the point is. Of our actions."

From habit he'd begun to edge closer, then stopped himself. Car doors slammed outside, a perfect triplet. I waited for voices to fade.

"Having covered epistemology, maybe in our next class we might move on to a discussion of ethics."

"I'm afraid neither of us would find that to be a strong point."

"I suppose not. The question being, do we need to have the rest of this conversation."

He held out his hand, palm flat, moving it in small circles as though balancing...what?

"Had I known the circumstances, your involvement—"

"And now?"

"Ah. I'm certain to be needed elsewhere."

"Your current sponsors won't be pleased."

"Assuredly. But we're not good men to be angry with, are we? And who knows, maybe someday others will talk of this meeting as they have your fuzzy dice."

I'd planned to call and let Bill know the matter was taken care of, but when I pulled in at the motel there he was, sprawled in one of the rusty metal chairs lined up under the overhang. Legs everywhere. *A gentleman from sole to crown, clean favored and imperially slim,* as some old poem or other has it. To this day I don't know exactly how much he knew—always hard to tell with Sheriff Bill—just as I wondered then if, having had two failed contracts, they'd send a third.

"Care for a walk?" he asked and, with dark clouds to the east promising rain, Bill's spidery legs and my bandy legs stepped out together onto the parched fields adjacent. I had to think about what all those fields had witnessed. Nations, battles, families, crops, blood. Once you poke at history, pry up the floorboards, it won't stop coming. There's too much of it. Nationally, personally.

"Appreciate your help, my friend," Bill said.

"I did nothing but exchange a few words."

"Words can turn away storms."

"Or just as easily bring them on."

"True enough." A crow large as an alley cat dipped over our heads, quickly judged us uninteresting, and flew on. "When will I see you again?" Bill asked.

"Difficult to say. Rest assured I'll be keeping an eye on things."

"History repeating itself as it does, you mean."

"Yes."

"All things considered, it's a good place, Little Bit. A good life." Bill came to a stop, gesturing ahead. "We'd best start back."

And so we did, turning around, the rain behind us, where it stayed.

Terry writes a mystery series featuring a laid-back Texan named Samuel Craddock but here she gives us a story of a different hero. Mama knows best in Terry's story of domestic disturbance, love triangles and deadly violence. Doesn't matter what the sheriff of Yoakum County has to say, Mama will handle things...

Double Exposure
Terry Shames

"Aunt Annabelle, I can't be running over there every time you and Aunt Betty have a fight," I said. I watched the fly that had been annoying me for the last twenty minutes settle on the edge of my desk. Be patient, I told myself. Let him get complacent...I tightened my grip on the rolled up real estate magazine I was using as a fly swatter.

"Why not?" Her voice could peel paint.

"Because I'm busy. Why don't you call Mama and get her over there? She'll sort things out."

Mama would kill me if she knew I was siccing Aunt Annabelle on her, but as sheriff of Yoakum County, Texas, I had better things to do than sort out squabbles between my two aunts. They've been living together in the house they grew up in for sixty years, and there hasn't been a day when they haven't argued with each other. You'd think as they got older they would mellow out, but you'd think wrong.

The fly moseyed closer. Somebody had told me the time to go for them was when they started washing themselves with their wings. The wings fluttered but then settled back down. *Patience.*

"Not this time, she won't."

Something in Annabelle's voice distracted me from the fly. "What's different about this time?"

The silence went on for so long that I said, "Annabelle? You still there?"

"I'm still here. Trying to decide whether I should tell you or if you should see for yourself."

There. The fly was washing itself, the little wings flashing iridescent in the sunlight from the window. Slowly, slowly I eased my arm away from my lap. Slowly, slowly, I sneaked the magazine up over the edge. *Wham!* "Got it."

"What in the world was that?" Annabelle asked. "It sounded like a gunshot."

"Nothing. Now why don't you go make up with Betty and you two go to a picture show or something."

"A picture show at ten o'clock in the morning?"

"You know what I mean. Go somewhere fun. Go to a matinee."

"That's not going to be possible."

"Well, whatever. I have to go now."

"Travis, you need to get over here. I am not kidding around." I recognized that tone of voice. It still had the power to freeze me in my tracks.

Billy Kindle's pickup careened into the parking lot, spraying gravel everywhere. I'd told him a hundred times not to do that, but so far he hadn't paid any attention. I guess when you have a twenty-three-year-old deputy you have to expect some showing off.

"I'll come over in a little while."

"Now would be better, or it might be too late."

I sighed. "Aunt Annabelle, I'll be there in a half hour." I hung up before she could say any more.

Billy climbed out of his truck, stuck his baseball cap on his head, and brought out a paper sack and a coffee cup holder with two cups. I hustled over to open the door. I'd trade the sprayed gravel for him picking up breakfast.

"Hey, Billy, what you got there?"

"Jolene made jelly donuts today. Raspberry."

He opened the sack on my desk and I snatched up one of the donuts. Having plenty of prior experience with her jelly donuts, I spread a napkin onto the desk and leaned over as I bit into it. Sure enough a dollop of bright red jelly fell onto the napkin. Better there than on my white shirt.

Billy ate half a donut in one bite. He has the biggest mouth I've ever seen this side of a gator. It stretches wide into his cheeks. My wife calls him "Froggy."

"What's up this morning?" he asked. Apparently his mama never taught him not to talk with his mouth full. I got a glimpse of teeth and tongue, as red as if he'd just murdered something with his teeth.

"Nothing. Annabelle and Betty at it again."

"One of these days one of them is going to go too far." He snickered and shook his head.

My phone rang again. It was my mama's number.

"Did Annabelle call you?" I said when I answered.

"Yes, and Travis, I don't see why you don't go on over there and settle things down. It's only five minutes away."

"I'm busy."

"Doing what? You and Billy are at the donuts, aren't you? You're going to get fatter than your daddy." That was her theme song with me.

"Daddy's not fat. He's just husky."

"Don't change the subject. Seriously, Travis, Annabelle sounded funny. Do you think maybe she's getting senile?"

"Been senile." I licked jelly off my fingers.

"Oh, she has not. She just wants attention."

"Should of gotten married then. All she needs is a little rumpty-tump."

Mama laughed. "Now stop that. I didn't raise you to have a mouth like that."

"Okay, I'll go on over there. I know you won't give me any

peace until I do."

I hung up, grinning. I get along well with Mama. And the crazy thing is, she and my wife Karen are thick as thieves. They love to egg each other on. Makes for a good life. Karen's folks are another matter, but they live way up in Dallas and we don't have to see them too often.

"You are so henpecked," Billy said as I got up, stuffing the last of the donut in my mouth.

"Yep, that's me." I put my cowboy hat on. "Don't let things go all to hell while I'm gone," I said.

Aunt Annabelle and Aunt Betty are Mama's older sisters—Annabelle three years older, and Betty two years. Annabelle is a robust woman who took after their daddy, while Betty was more slender and smaller, like their mama. I never knew my mama's daddy, Pete. He died in a tractor accident before I was born but Grandma Ida was around most of my life. A little bitty woman, she lived to be almost ninety years old and never met an ailment she didn't think she had. And after a while, she was right. But she never had to go into a home because Annabelle and Betty lived with her and took care of her until she died, unlike their two brothers who got out of town as fast as they could.

The two-story house had started out small, but every time Ida and Pete had another child, they added another room until it sprawled out every which way. Still, it had been kept up over the years, the white paint and Kelly-green trim always sparkling. I had put in my time doing maintenance the same as all the family men.

I figured the two women would be in the kitchen, so I walked around to the back of the house. "Aunt Annabelle?" I banged on the screen door.

"Come on in." Sure enough she was sitting at their big family-size wooden trestle table. It was hardly suitable for just two people but Annabelle and Betty didn't want to change anything about the house after their mama died.

"Took you long enough. Get yourself some coffee if you want," she said. Her voice was harsh, like she was mad at me. I got one of the big mugs out of the cabinet and poured myself a cup.

"I got here as fast as I could," I said.

"Doesn't matter. You're here now."

"Betty around?"

She tossed her head. "In the other room."

"Okay." I pulled out a chair and sat down across from her. Annabelle had a photo on the table in front of her. I knew it well. It was the spooky one of her that looked like a man was standing in the shadows behind her. I had been afraid of the picture when I was a kid because Annabelle told me it wasn't a real picture of a man, that it was the ghost of her dead fiancé, Bradley Beyers. Usually she kept the photo in a gold frame with hearts around the border, but now it was lying bare on the table, surrounded by shards of glass. "What are you doing with that?"

"Studying it." She picked it up and tossed it toward me. "Take a close look."

I picked it up. She had been pretty when she was younger, with long soft curls, big blue eyes and a sweet smile. She wasn't much of a smiler in her old age. In the photo she was at the kitchen table, pretty much where she was sitting now. Behind her, standing in the hallway just beyond the kitchen, was a tall man dressed in a short-sleeved shirt and jeans. His face was blurred, but you could see that he had dark hair and was grinning.

"Interesting," I said. Not a brilliant comment, but I couldn't think of anything better to say. "Why did you take it out of the frame? And why is the glass broken?"

"Do you think it looks real?"

"I'm not sure what you mean."

"It's the ghost of my fiancé. Do you think it looks real?"

I wanted to give her an answer that would satisfy her. It was a photo she treasured because she didn't have any other photos of Bradley. After he died, his mama wouldn't give Annabelle any pictures of him. She blamed Annabelle for his death, because he was on his way to see her when he had a wreck and was killed.

"I never met him," I said, "so I don't know if it looks like him or not."

"That's not what I mean," she said. "I mean, does it look like he's a real person?"

"You mean instead of a…a ghost?" It seemed silly to think it was a ghost. How could anybody take a picture of a ghost, even if her sister said she had?

"Yes, that's exactly what I mean."

This was heavy slogging. "Okay, I guess it looks like a real person."

"It is a real person."

I felt a headache coming on. I'm not prone to headaches, except when I have to talk to Annabelle and Betty. I pinched the bridge of my nose between my thumb and forefinger. "Okay. Is that what you and Betty are fighting about?"

Annabelle glared at me. "She always told me it was the ghost of Bradley."

Such tricky ground. Should I tell her she was acting ridiculous, or should I humor her like everybody else had been doing for decades? A brilliant thought struck me: when in doubt, sidestep the question. "Well, she should know. She took the picture, didn't she?"

"Now she tells me it was a lie."

"What do you mean. She didn't take the picture?"

"Travis, sometimes I think you are one of the stupidest people I know. If you weren't my nephew, I'd think you'd been hatched." Her voice was a fierce hiss.

I froze. I had heard Aunt Annabelle's sharp tongue my whole life but as far as I could recall, she had never been downright nasty to me. I felt my face getting warm. What could I possibly say in response? I refused to be petty and answer in kind, but I didn't want to give her the impression that I was a pushover, either. I stood up. "Maybe it's best if I come back later."

"Where do you think you're going? Sit down!" Her voice was so commanding that I flopped back down into my chair without thinking about it.

"Aunt Annabelle," I said, hunching forward to catch her eye, "it seems like you're in a bad mood. I'll come back when you're feeling better."

"That won't be necessary. We can deal with this now." She slapped the table for emphasis.

I'd really had enough. "Just tell me what you want to know about the damn picture."

"There's no need to curse. I was just telling you that Betty said she lied about that being the ghost of Bradley."

"Who is it then?"

This time she slammed her fist down on the table. "That isn't the point. The point is, she's been lying to me for forty years."

I was beginning to wish that Betty would come in and take the brunt of Annabelle's temper. At least she was used to it. "Where did you say Betty was?"

"She's in the living room. We'll get to that in a minute."

Get to what? The living room was close by. As far as I knew there was nothing wrong with Betty's hearing, so why hadn't she come in when she heard Annabelle yelling?

"I'll go get her," I said.

"No! Don't do that. I said we'd take care of her in a minute. I just want your opinion about whether it's all right for someone to lie to her sister for forty years."

I ran my hand through my hair. I wish I had told Billy to call me and pretend something urgent was going on, so I'd have an excuse to beat it out of there. "It depends on why she told you something that wasn't true. Did you ask her?"

She picked up the picture again and looked hard at it. "It does look like him."

I heard a noise like a thump from somewhere in the house. Maybe Betty was coming to the kitchen now. Annabelle sat up at attention, glowering at the kitchen door leading into the hallway. "No, I didn't ask. I don't care why she lied. I'm just tired of her pretending to be so sweet and kind. Pulling the wool over everybody's eyes. Nobody knows what I have to put up with. When it's just the two of us she can be mean as a rattlesnake."

"Well, you two have been at it for a long time now."

"No more. It's over. I'm done with her."

Another thump. "What do you mean, 'no more?' Are you going somewhere?"

"No, but she is."

This time the thump was frantic. "What is that sound?"

"Don't worry about it."

I got up, and this time I had no intention of sitting back down. "Aunt Annabelle, you're making me nervous." I walked toward the door. "Betty? Betty, is that you?"

Annabelle lurched out of her chair with such violence that it tipped over backwards and fell to the floor with a clatter. "Don't you go in there," she yelled.

She rushed over and caught me at the door, grabbing my arm and pulling me so hard I almost lost my balance. "I'm warning you," she said, her eyes narrowed to little slits.

"Get off!" I snatched my arm away and strode down the hallway. "Betty?" I opened the door to the living room, but before I could step inside I heard a sound I recognized and it chilled my blood and stopped me in my tracks. I turned and saw that Annabelle had picked up the ancient shotgun that always stood in the kitchen corner, and was pointing it at me. The sound I had heard was her cocking it.

"What the hell do you think you're doing?" I hollered. I was mad and scared in equal measure. "Do you want to end up in an insane asylum?"

"She aggravated me one time too many, and now you're doing the same thing."

I rarely have occasion to move fast, but this seemed like the right time. I sprang at her and grabbed the shotgun and pushed the barrel up just as she pulled the trigger. The sound was thunderous in the narrow hallway, and I heard the light fixture shatter. I wrenched the gun out of her hand. She screamed like she was being murdered. At the sound, the thumping started up again from the next room.

"Annabelle, get in the kitchen. Right now." I was shouting. I don't get mad often, and it's usually teenaged boys that are up to no good who get the benefit of it, but as Mama has often said, if I'm pushed too far, look out.

Annabelle glared at me, but moved back toward the kitchen.

I plunged into the living room and couldn't believe what I saw. Betty was trussed up in a straight chair, arms and legs tied tight, tape around her mouth and a scarf around her eyes. As I approached, she reared up so the chair tipped back and came down with a thump. She moaned, too, but the sound was so muffled that I figured that's why I hadn't heard her.

"Annabelle, get in here," I yelled.

"No. You deal with her yourself," she yelled back.

I snatched the scarf off and untied the gag. Betty's eyes were wild. "Water," she croaked.

I started for the kitchen, but it occurred to me that maybe it was best not to go in there with a crazy woman. In the bathroom, I found a cup and filled it with water and took it back. When Betty had taken a few sips, I said, "I'm going to cut you loose. Sit still." I took out my pocketknife and sawed through the ropes while Betty wailed.

As soon as she was free she leaped to her feet. "I'm about to wet my pants. She's had me there for three hours." She ran toward the bathroom.

I took out my phone and called Mama. "You need to get over here," I said. "Annabelle has lost her mind."

"Oh, you know how they…"

"No! I mean really. This times it's bad."

"Well, I have a cake in the oven. I'll be over there as soon as I can."

"Get somebody else to watch it. Annabelle tied up Betty and half-killed her."

"She'll be fine," Annabelle's voice came from the doorway.

"She's too evil to die." She went over to stand near the bathroom door, waiting for Betty.

"Oh, my Lord, I'll be right there," Mama's voice said from the phone.

I heard the toilet flush in the hallway bathroom. "What in the hell were you thinking?" I asked Annabelle.

"How to kill her," she said. "That's what I was thinking. The only thing that saved her was that I couldn't decide whether to stick her with a knife, shoot her with my shotgun, or set the house on fire with her in it."

Betty came out of the bathroom, behind Annabelle. "Get out of my way," she said.

"Make me."

As small as she was, Betty put all her strength in to shoving her, hard, and Annabelle hit the door frame. Betty scooted past her. She marched over and stood in front of me, hands on her hips. "You heard what she said. She was going to kill me. That's attempted murder. I want you to put her in jail." I'd seen infuriated goats that looked calmer than she did.

"You want to press charges?" I said. I had to stall until Mama got there and calmed things down.

"I sure do. I'm tired of her pushing me around."

"And I'm tired of you pretending to be so goody-good that everybody thinks you are sweet as pie when all you are is just plain mean." Annabelle was inching into the room.

"You can't stand the truth, that's all."

I sighed. "What truth?"

"That picture," Betty said.

"Damn you," Annabelle muttered.

"Annabelle, get back," I said. She retreated a few steps.

"What about the picture?"

"I got tired of her always mooning over it. I decided it was time to tell her the truth. That wasn't her old boyfriend's ghost. It was nothing more than a trick of the camera. The camera had a double exposure." There was a malicious gleam in her eye.

At that Annabelle let out a fresh howl that raised the hair on the back of my neck.

"A double what?" I asked.

"You wouldn't know anything about it," Betty said. "Sometimes in old cameras the film would stick and not go forward. When I had the roll on the camera developed, I saw that's what had happened. I had taken a picture of Bradley, and then later a picture of Annabelle sitting at the table, but the camera didn't advance so both images were printed on the same photo."

"Just plain mean, that's what," Annabelle said. "You didn't have to tell me that. You could have just let me..." Her voice broke and for a second I felt sorry for her.

"Annabelle, what difference does it make?" I asked. It's still a picture of your fiancé, and that's what matters."

"Not really," Betty said.

"Not really what?" I asked. I was getting confused again.

"Her fiancé."

"Did you hear that?" Annabelle screeched. She rushed toward Betty, who yelped and ran over and picked up the chair she'd been tied to and held it in front of her.

"Calm down!" I grabbed Annabelle's arm and pulled her away. "What is wrong with you?"

"Did you hear what she said? She said Bradley wasn't my fiancé, when he most certainly was." She tried to get free, but I held on. For once I was afraid they were going to come to actual blows.

"Was not," Betty said. "I'm sick and tired of keeping the secret. I'm tired of you always lording it over me that he was your boyfriend and that I didn't have one." She was pointing the chair this way and that, like a demented orchestra conductor. She advanced on the two of us. I stepped back, pulling Annabelle with me.

Betty's eyes were narrow slits. "You always said you didn't know he was coming to see you that night he was killed and you're right, he wasn't. It was *me* he was coming to see. We were going to talk about how he was going to break up with you."

"That's not true," Annabelle screeched.

"After the accident, everybody made such a fuss over you. Poor, pitiful you losing your boyfriend. I told Mama it was me he loved and she made me keep quiet about it. She said it was wrong for me to sneak around behind your back and that with Bradley dead it would only be worse if you knew."

Annabelle was trying to wriggle away from me, and I had to hold tight. I was beginning to understand why she was so mad, but I couldn't let her at Betty.

"Aunt Betty, you ought to leave the house for a while," I said. "You need to give Annabelle time to settle down."

"I don't have to leave if I don't want to," she said. "It's my house too. And like I said, you should take her to jail. She tried to kill me."

"Yoo-hoo! Where is everybody?" Mama's voice rang out from the back door.

"In the living room," I hollered. My voice sounded as desperate as I felt.

Mama bustled in like she always did, looking like she was ready to take charge. She was the youngest of the family but had always been the boss among her siblings. "What's going on here? Why is everybody standing around?"

"Annabelle, you sit over there," I said, pointing at one of the easy chairs. "And Betty, you sit on the sofa."

"You can't tell me what to do," both of them said at once.

I threw up my hands. "Then stand there! I don't care what you do, but keep your hands off each other."

"Who is going to tell me what's going on?" Mama said.

"I am," I said. I gave her the short version, or as short as it could be with Annabelle and Betty interrupting every few sentences. I love Mama. I could see her little brain just twirling with ideas. When it comes to family, she's the best at sorting everybody out.

"Ha!" She snorted, when I was done. She looked from one to the other of the two of them. "Sit down. I have something to say about this."

They wouldn't sit for me, but they both obeyed Mama. When they were seated, she stood where she could see them both. I stayed back, but ready to act if they got at each other.

"You're both fools," Mama said. "Bradley was two-timing the both of you."

My heart sank. Surely she wasn't going to tell them she had been seeing him, too? That would stretch things a little too far.

"What do you mean?" Betty asked. Her voice sounded like she'd swallowed a handful of gravel.

"It's true, he was coming over here to see you that night, Betty. But he was also coming to see Annabelle. He was going to tell both of you that he had taken up with the homecoming queen, Laura Bell, and was fixing to marry her. You remember what a beauty that girl was?"

"I don't remember her being all that pretty," Betty said. "How do you know he was going to marry her?"

"I ran into him that afternoon and he told me. He said he'd been trying to decide between the two of you, but when he met Laura, he knew he'd been waiting for her his whole life."

"Laura Bell! Why that two-faced little witch," Betty said.

"How could he think she was cuter than Betty?" Annabelle asked.

"Or cuter than Annabelle, for that matter," Betty said.

"She only got to be homecoming queen because she had messed around with half the football team," Annabelle said.

"All I know is what he told me," Mama said. "It was a shame what happened to him, but I don't think it was much of a loss for either of you. Who needs somebody who's no better than a two-timing cad?"

Five minutes later, with Annabelle and Betty on speaking terms and squabbling over the light fixture that got shot out, Mama said, "I have to go. My cake is about done."

"I have to go, too," I said. I scooted out with her, hoping Betty wouldn't call me back to tell me she still wanted Annabelle locked up.

I opened Mama's car door for her. She got in grinned up at me. And that's when I knew.

"Did Bradley really tell you he was going out with Laura Bell?"

"Heck no. I never spoke to that boy in my life. But I had to figure out a way to get those two not to kill each other, and that was the most efficient way I could think of."

"Suppose they find out you were wrong?"

"How are they going to find out? Laura Bell got pregnant and ran off with her English teacher a year later. She hasn't been back since."

"So, what was the truth?"

"How should I know? All I know is that Annabelle and Betty have lived together too long to break up over a boy they both dated forty years ago."

I watched her drive away and then climbed into my pickup and headed back to the station. Sometimes I think she'd be a better sheriff than I am, but we don't always have that much excitement around here. Her talents would be wasted.

Suzanne writes some of the most powerful short stories in the genre. Here she offers a tale of small-town bizarre and Florida weird that Bill Crider fans appreciate so well. She writes about the sights, sounds and feel of the state like a beat reporter, including gamblers, developers and con men. Much like the place itself, "Gelding Season" hypnotizes with its depiction of the strange and macabre...

Gelding Season

S.A. Solomon

Investigator Miri Berger of the Collier County Special Crimes Bureau walked the perimeter of the pasture, looking for anything out of the ordinary. Clods of manure dotted a flat field that was more dust than grass. The crime scene unit had already scoured the area, photographing the scene and bagging and tagging any items of interest. The medical examiner had come and gone, taking the body with him—if you could call it that.

It was actually parts of a male body, contained in an alligator's stomach. The veterinary pathologist had been here too, to remove the animal's corpse after the Fish and Wildlife folks trapped and euthanized the ten-foot creature. Miri wondered how the two pathologists divided up the labor. It was an interesting puzzle, although not hers to solve: she was a special crimes detective, dealing with sexual crimes, domestic violence, child neglect and abuse. This case involved an abducted (and living, thank God) child.

Collier County was located in southwest Florida on the Gulf side of the state. East Naples was the county seat, the nesting ground of snowbirds and retirees. There were beautiful beaches that reminded her of home. But there was plenty of wild territory too, the Big Cypress swamp and the Everglades and the piney pasture lands in between.

Home, for Miri, was Netanya, Israel, where she was born.

After her parents divorced, her mother, an American, brought her and her brother to live in North Miami Beach. Miri took every opportunity she had to go back to Israel, most recently to fulfill her two years of army service. A lot of her expat friends hadn't served, but filed for an exemption on religious or other grounds. They had caught the American disease: they were soft, reliant on others to protect them. One day, when all hell broke loose—and history had proven, time and again, that it would—they would be useless, clogging the roads in their SUVs, trying to get to Whole Foods for supplies, frantically checking Facebook to see what their friends were doing.

She hadn't planned to stay in Florida, but her military intelligence background had made it easy for her to advance in law enforcement. She was recruited by a number of departments and chose the west coast, where it wasn't as crowded. She liked her job. Usually. Today the heat and humidity were off the charts, although the ground was surprisingly dry for the rainy season. She felt a sharp bite and slapped at the skin below the short sleeve of her department polo shirt. The drought hadn't managed to tame the ferocious mosquito population.

In Israel, they didn't wait on the seasons or the forecasters' predictions: they made their own weather, planting trees, making the desert bloom using sustainable water management practices. Here in South Florida, they'd made a bollocks of it, giving farmers and the sugar industry free rein to cause droughts, floods, and a red tide that was like something out of the biblical plagues. There was no communal sense of ownership or responsibility, just the wild west code of taking what you could get.

And that code was apparently what had led to the crime she was investigating.

The kidnapping victim was a nine-year-old girl who'd been

living with her mother's boyfriend in a ramshackle house on the property just vacated by the crime scene unit. The boyfriend went by Jack Trevally. He wasn't believed to have hurt the girl, but he didn't have lawful custody of her either. She was a ward of the state, made so after her mother died in a car accident caused by her father, who was now serving time for vehicular homicide.

Trevally had actually been a suitable candidate to serve as her legal guardian. According to social workers, he'd fed and clothed the girl appropriately and made sure she went to school. They had seen no evidence of drug or alcohol use at the home. But he hadn't appeared at the guardianship hearing, probably because he wasn't using his real name. When child welfare agents showed up at the address, Trevally and the girl were gone.

The place was abandoned. Nobody could locate the owner, an elderly man named Wilbur Small. The ME would determine whether it was Mr. Small's remains in the gator's belly or someone else's. Miri wouldn't have been surprised to learn that somebody had wanted him out of the way. He had a substantial life insurance policy in his name. And something else: this dilapidated ranch was the last parcel of land that hadn't been cleared and sold for a nearby housing development. Small had grown children, who were the beneficiaries of both the life insurance policy and his will. Again, a lead for the homicide detectives to run down. But it affected her investigation too, since Trevally and the child were the only tenants on the property.

Her cases were always affected by other people's crimes, since the perpetrators were often convinced, despite all evidence to the contrary, that they were fit parents. Most of them were not. Of course, she encountered the extremes in her line of work, horrifying things that most law-abiding people didn't have the slightest notion of. They had the luxury of ignorance, which was just as well. If they knew what she knew, they would never let their kids out of their sight.

Miri looked at the photograph she'd collected at the house. The girl was small for her age, thin and dark, like Miri herself had been as a child. She sat on a black pony with a white blaze on its face and a braided mane. She was half rising out of her seat, looking back at the camera as the animal broke into a canter. There was a wild joy in the frame that the shot managed to capture, despite the blur of motion.

There hadn't been much else of interest in the place. Along with cheap furniture, there were dishes, pots and pans, bedding and towels—things you'd find in a furnished rental. But all the personal items were gone. She saw that a lot, families carting only what they could carry, their possessions dwindling as they moved from place to place—motel rooms, campgrounds, cars—in order of descending affordability.

Her mobile buzzed and she felt a strip of anxiety across her chest, loosening when she heard a child's voice repeat *mama, mama, mama,* until she laughingly answered.

"Yes, darling?"

"Mama, where you?"

"Right here, darling."

"Where, mama?"

"I'm coming home now," she said.

The voice of her two-year-old son was one reason she couldn't just pick up and go back to Israel for good. Well, there were two reasons, she thought, as another, deeper, voice came on the line. Her husband Roland's family had escaped Castro's Cuba and consequently, he was allergic to the idea of communal life. But she'd taken him to Netanya on their honeymoon and he had fallen in love with it. She was sure he could be persuaded to move. It's not like they'd be living on a kibbutz (not that she'd mind: she had wonderful memories of vacations spent at her grandparents' kibbutz in the north).

"Sorry, babe, I forgot to pick up groceries," Roland was saying. "Would you mind stopping on the way home?" He sounded tired. He was an ER doctor; they'd met on the job.

"Not at all, sweet, what do you want for dinner?" She was tired too, but he worked nights, which allowed them to split the child care.

"Whatever you want, as long as there's ice cream." He had a sweet tooth that she had to keep a lid on. They both had one, but she at least went to the gym. Anyway, too much sugar was bad for the child.

"Okay, I'll text you from the store," she said, and disconnected the call, distracted by the sight of buzzards—here they called them turkey vultures—circling overhead. She looked around before approaching the barn: no sense in startling a predator over its prey. Especially if the gators here had developed a taste for humans. She checked her sidearm, a department issued Glock 17 9x19mm, which probably wouldn't even put a dent in that prehistoric hide.

The smell hit her before she saw it: blowflies like an iridescent beaded curtain on a clump of decomposing flesh. Probably just animal remains, but she took pictures for the CSU folks in case they wanted to loop in the pathologists.

Back in the car, she switched on the air and sat cooling off for a bit before putting it in gear and bumping along the pot-holed track to the gate. That Ram truck she'd noticed on the way in was still there, parked on the dusty strip. She took a picture of the plate and texted it in along with the others, checked her email and messages ("suspect still at large"), and headed to the grocery store. It was going to be a long night.

Jack Trevally had won the pony in a poker game and knew he shouldn't have collected. He'd done it for the girl, though—she was horse crazy. The animal had been trained for the circus. If you knew the hand signals, you could get it to count, shake hands, curtsey, even play dead. But it wouldn't perform in front of large crowds. It was too spooky. That was its name, Spooky. It was a delicate creature: tiny and well-proportioned, all black except for a white blaze on the forehead and white markings on the legs, like ankle socks. The silky mane and tail were perfect for braiding. The girl took more of an interest in that pony than in anything since her mother died. She was up at dawn, currying the smooth coat until it shone, examining the hooves for rocks, mucking out the stall. It was difficult to get her away from the barn when the school bus came, but at least she went, knowing Spooky would be there waiting when she got home. After school, she would leap onto the pony like an acrobat, riding bareback with just a side pull halter. He didn't let her go outside of the pasture. It was too dangerous, with the traffic and all.

Now they had to leave town, fast, and once again, he ignored his better judgment. The girl had begged him to let her take the pony. It was a mistake, but she had bonded with the animal. Sometimes it seemed to him that they were actually communicating, even though he knew it was just a circus trick. The girl had thrown her arms around him, the first sign of affection she'd shown since the day in the hospital when she learned her mother hadn't survived the wreck that had flung the two of them out of the car and into the canal. That was how she lost her hearing. The doctors said it was probably reversible and the tests were encouraging, but so far it hadn't come back.

She had acted out when it came time to return to school. She was bullied, fought back, was punished for it. He'd been planning to ease her into the idea of a foster family. It would have been better for them both. Maybe one of those couples who drove to the farms for U-pick. They'd take her home, make her pancakes with strawberries and whipped cream. She'd have a pretty room, a bed with crisp sheets, and a quilt that didn't smell musty (like hers did, no matter how many times he put it through the coin wash). Maybe even a dog. She loved animals.

Or maybe, like he had, she would end up in a house with people who took in kids for the government check.

It was his fault: in the rush to leave, he failed to inspect the trailer, just walked the pony in and tied its lead. The animal was skittish, ears back. He considered leaving it, but the girl would have a meltdown and delay their departure. He couldn't chance it. He closed the tailgate. The latch was sticking and he had to bang it shut. He loaded the tack and a bin of oats into the pickup and wondered briefly how he was going to board and feed the animal on the run. Well, he'd cross that bridge when they came to it. He could always sell it. It was a trick pony, after all.

He remembered once when he couldn't find the girl at the stables and was about to call the cops, despite the risk. She came riding in around dusk with a rare smile on her face. She told him that a man had driven by and stopped when he saw her putting the pony through its act. He said he'd pay her to come to his kid's birthday party. He lived in one of the new subdivisions down the road. The pony was a hit, not spooky at all, and all the kids asked if she would come to their parties too. The man gave her fifty dollars and his wife gave her ice cream cake and a goody bag.

She was so proud of herself and the pony that he almost didn't have the heart to punish her. He did, though, because you couldn't just trust people like that. Especially not men. Also, she knew she wasn't supposed to leave the pasture. No riding for a week. She cried and raged, refused to talk to him, pulled out her hearing aids. He gave in after a couple of days, when he thought she'd gotten the point. And really, it wasn't such a bad idea, as long as he was around to supervise her. Fifty bucks a party. He was sure he could get more.

They hadn't even reached the highway when he heard banging coming from the trailer. He nearly fishtailed into oncoming traffic but managed to pull over on the grassy shoulder. He told the girl to stay put and went around back to see what had happened. The pony's front legs had punched through the wooden floor. Its liquid black eyes were wild with pain. The girl had followed him and now wouldn't leave its side, even though he yanked her roughly away. He was afraid she'd be hurt by the animal tossing its head in agony. Rubberneckers glared at him from stopped cars, blaming him for the sobbing child, the bloodied horse, the splintered wood of the cheap trailer.

He spent his last hundred bucks on the vet who came to put the animal down.

Someone had called 911 and when the officer thought to check his plates and ID, it was over. He watched from behind tinted windows in the squad car as a woman cop tried to comfort the inconsolable girl.

It would serve him right, he knew, if they locked him up and threw away the key.

Jack Trevally.

Ray knew he'd found an in when he saw Trevally at work in the casino. He'd watched him win steadily at the Omaha Hi/Lo table. Ray wasn't a poker player, but he'd observed that there was a certain type who won at these tables. Hi/Lo wasn't a bluffer's game. It was more about calculating odds. The casino was a handy recruiting ground for people looking for work off the books. Sure, there were the busloads of retirees for the slots and bingo. But there were also the transients and cash-only types. People who needed to feed their gambling habit. Guys with fake IDs and names like Jack Trevally.

Ray was a fisherman, so he knew "Jack Trevally" was the name of a sport fish.

"Jack Trevally" didn't drink alcohol, at the card table or afterwards. He was pleasant to the dealers and servers, generous but not flashy with his tips. He didn't wear a wedding band and didn't appear to use a cell phone. Physically, he didn't stick out in any way: short dark hair, tanned skin, clean-shaven, wore jeans and T-shirts, drove an old Ford pickup. Ray sat at the table next to him in the restaurant and struck up a conversation. Trevally didn't talk much either.

Here was a man who didn't want to attract attention, exactly what Ray needed for this job.

Ray worked for a real estate developer. That was enough of a gamble for him in an industry and state that was perennially boom and bust. Right now, southwest Florida was on the upswing. Buyers were snapping up properties west of Miami and the agricultural industry—sugar, tomatoes, berries, beans, peppers, corn, and so forth—had a firm upper hand on the politicians, who in turn kept a thumb on the environmental do-gooders. The economy, along with the real estate market, had recovered, and people flush with cash needed a big house to advertise it.

That's where Ray came in. The area he was working for the new subdivision was nearly cleared, except for the odd property owned by holdouts, the rare family farmer or rancher descended from the old Florida crackers. Not that he didn't have some sympathy for these individualistic types, but their day was done.

Jack Trevally had come into the picture when the last holdout, an old man with cured skin like the rawhide whips the crackers had used and were named for, let him board his girl's pony on the property. This after Ray had nearly gotten the old geezer to the finish line. He had children, and Ray had already worked on them. The price for the parcel had gone up considerably due to the old man's mulishness, and the kids had families and mortgages and dollar signs in their eyes. It wasn't like they'd grown up on the property. The old man was operating it as a hobby ranch. In fact, the last time Ray was there, the old man had a vet over for gelding season. This was like neutering your dog or cat, except you had to deal with a thousand pounds of horseflesh, so it was a bit more labor intensive. He'd come in the aftermath, when the animals' testicles were strewn around the dusty pasture, roosters spearing them like hors d'oeuvres at an open house.

Anyway, he'd managed to get rid of most of the boarders with a letter saying the property was being rezoned and they would be fined if they continued to keep their animals there. He'd had to take more drastic steps with the others. One left after her horse somehow got loose and had a close call with a speeding vehicle on the access road. Another lost his dog to the ubiquitous gators patrolling the network of canals. There was only this one guy left. Jack Trevally, who didn't seem to respond to the usual motivations of greed and fear.

And that was because he used them himself in his line of work. He had a game going. Ray just didn't know what it was yet.

Ray wasn't heartless. He wasn't going to do anything to hurt a deaf girl's pony. He'd seen her work with the animal when his wife asked him to pick up their daughters at the neighbor kid's birthday party. He'd have to go at it another way.

But, as he'd found happened with most opportunities in life, it came to him that what seemed to be an obstacle was in fact an advantage.

The one thing Ray had been able to learn, through a gal he knew, a dealer at the Seminole Casino in Immokalee, was that Jack Trevally had won once too often at the blackjack tables. They said he was counting cards and banned him. He'd moved on to the cash poker tables at another casino, in Hialeah. They didn't offer live blackjack since the Seminole Tribe had that exclusive concession. You could play the ponies, after a fashion—they threw a few nags on the track and called it racing, as state law required for them to keep their gaming license. It was a far cry from the glamor days when Triple Crown winners like War Admiral and Seabiscuit tore up the turf.

"Haven't I seen you…?"

Trevally glanced over at him and back at his plate. He sprinkled hot sauce on his eggs and forked them into his mouth.

"Yep." Ray snapped his fingers. "Gas station on Osceola Drive, am I right?"

Trevally shrugged. "Maybe." He buttered his toast, ate that, drank his orange juice, and called for the check. It was crowded, so he had to wait.

"Best gas prices around because it's tribal land. They own the oil rights."

"That so?"

"Yup. I grew up around there. Ray's the name, real estate's my game."

"So what are you doing here?"

"Meeting a client. You?"

"You're looking at it."

"You work here?"

Trevally chuckled. "Let's just say I win here."

"Why not go to the Seminole Casino? It's closer. If you live down by Osceola?"

"What's it to you?"

"Just wondering. What brings you to Florida?"

"Who says I was brought here?"

"*Habla español?*"

"Nope."

"You a fisherman?" At this, Trevally's eyes hardened, but he kept his cool.

"Look, buddy, I don't know what your deal is, but I'm not interested."

"My deal is, I'm looking for a guy who knows a good deal when he sees one, that's all. If you like it down here and plan to stick around, I've got a lead on some undervalued property in the southwest. It's about to explode out there and I have an exclusive relationship with the developer. People who get in on the ground floor can double their investment."

Trevally grinned. "I've heard that before."

"No, this is the real thing." Ray reached for a battered leather portfolio. "I got the plat map right here." He noticed Trevally twitch a little and filed it away. Ray was carrying, of course. You had to be an idiot not to, this being Florida.

He unrolled the map, then looked around him, hesitating, like he was having second thoughts.

"Maybe I'd better not, unless I know you're serious. This deal isn't for amateurs."

"Have it your way," Trevally said, but Ray noticed his eyes

stray to the map. There was a bold outline around the old man's parcel.

With that, Ray learned two things: one, Jack Trevally could read a plat map sideways, and two, he recognized the marked property. The man nodded slightly at Ray, who rolled up the map. In a show of good will, he signaled the waitress and paid both of their checks, leaving a generous tip. The older woman— or middle-aged? when they hit forty, it was all the same to him— smiled her thanks, sun-creased lips framing crooked teeth. You could always tell someone's financial situation by their dental work, he thought. His wife and girls all had their teeth straightened and whitened. He'd insisted on it. Ray himself was blessed with perfect teeth and a brilliant, confident smile. There was something about a showroom smile that worked on people like a fishing lure. He wasn't book smart, not into pop psychology or any of that crap, but he knew what played and what didn't. And he thought Jack Trevally did too. He dropped another five on the table and turned to go.

Jack Trevally observed this without comment. They stepped out into the parking lot, the bright sun bouncing off car windshields like spears aimed at the eyes. Ray put on his aviators. Trevally squinted under his ball cap and said, "Thanks, but I pay my own way."

Ray shrugged as Trevally counted out crisp new bills. "It's on my expense account," he said.

"More for you," Trevally said. "Why don't you tell me what's on your mind?"

They climbed into the air-conditioned cab of Ray's Ram 1500 Laramie. The heat rippling off the asphalt receded in the cool leather-scented retreat, windows tinted against the glare. It was his mobile man cave, his wife joked to her friends. She was right, he had to give her that.

After Ray explained what he wanted, Trevally said he had two conditions.

"I do it my way."

That was fine with Ray. The less he knew, the less exposure he had.

"No guns," gesturing at Ray's Smith & Wesson M&P 45 in its concealed carry holster.

"You'd want one too if you ever came within ten yards of a gator," Ray said. "They're faster than they look."

"I don't need a gun to scare off an old man," Trevally said.

When the pony came, something in her came back to life too.

They were alike, she and this animal that had been taught to perform for its food and board. She was a child, but she'd seen enough to know that was her future too. She set herself to learning how to communicate with Spooky. She understood that the signals were all part of the animal's training, but this contact was more real to her than what people did. They'd say one thing and mean another. Her father had said he was sorry so many times she'd lost count. She had stopped believing him long before her mother had.

She met Holly at one of the birthday parties. She'd already gone to a few by the time Jack found out and punished her. She didn't blame him—he was only warning her about something she'd known for a long time. In her experience, one where parents who couldn't afford daycare had to work anyway, stranger danger was beside the point: the people you knew had already done their worst.

That was why she kept going back with Spooky to the kids' parties. Not for the limp bills slipped to her in the fathers' damp palms or the gift bags and fake sympathy of the mothers. No, it was to make a list of all the things to look for—or not—in a forever family.

She knew Jack was going to leave when she found the ripped-up court papers in the trash. Also when he kept asking wouldn't she like to have a family with brothers and sisters and her own pretty room?

He meant well, but all he was doing was looking for an exit. Men were expected to do that, and women to make deals to get them to stay.

So anyway, this Holly had told her that her father was rich, that he worked in real estate. She flashed a toothpaste-white smile, her arm stacked with those popular bracelets that meant the dad could afford fifty bucks for each charm. Her own mother had explained, when she'd pestered her for one like it for her last birthday, that it was a day's work for her, for just one charm, not even the whole bracelet. She was ashamed to remember screaming that all the girls at school had mothers who loved them but no, not her. And how her mother had managed to save enough to buy her a bracelet but it wasn't the same one the other girls had so she threw it on the floor. And then seeing her mother cry, this woman who had faced the hard fists of her father without tears.

Holly wanted to ride Spooky and learn the tricks. She said she'd pay, but it had to be soon because she'd heard from her dad that the owner, Mr. Small, was selling the ranch and they'd have to leave. Holly's dad would get a lot of money in commissions and he told her he would buy her a pony. She wanted Spooky. You can't afford to keep her anyway, but I'll let you ride her whenever you want, Holly said, her eyes darting sideways so they both knew she was lying.

She said okay because she'd just remembered something. The other day the vet had come out to the barn. She asked one of the boys who worked there what was the matter. He made a snipping motion with his fingers, which she figured out when she saw what the vet was doing. She got upset, cried even, wondering if it hurt the horses, and the boys taunted her, saying you couldn't have stallions running around the place because of the mares, and they rocked their hips back and forth, grunting and laughing.

The cut bits were still on the ground and the owner got after the boys to clean them up because the carrion attracted vultures. The old man was having trouble with the people who paid to board their horses. They'd complained about their animals running loose or getting into the feed bins, which could kill them from colic. By the end of the week, they'd all loaded their trailers and left and it was just her and Spooky.

One of the boys wanted to buy her a coke and chips with money he said he got to open the gate after hours. She wouldn't have to pay him back, he told her, just be nice, and made that grunting noise.

If the old man knew Holly's dad was behind it, maybe he wouldn't sell.

Okay, she told Holly, but you have to do me a favor.

Holly's nose wrinkled like she smelled something bad and she whined, *But I already am.*

The girl cut her off. Can you keep a secret?

At this, Holly's head swiveled and her eyes got shiny like a bird's.

I need money to get back to my mother's family. Jack's—here she paused for effect—he's not my real father.

Holly's eyes were practically pinwheeling.

You can't tell your dad that—your mom either. Not anyone, the girl said.

But you'll let me have her, the pony? Holly asked.

Tell your dad to meet me at the ranch tomorrow night at six o'clock. But he has to bring the money.

That was when the old man did his last rounds, making sure things were locked up because of all the trouble he'd had. The boys would be gone.

How much? Holly asked.

Four hundred. She'd picked a number out of the air.

Holly hesitated.

Do you want Spooky or not?

At this the pony snorted, flaring her nostrils. Don't worry, friend, the girl thought. I'd never give you up.

I can't be there tomorrow, Holly said. I have dance class.

Just tell your dad to come with the money.

The next day at six she told Mr. Small that she'd seen a strange man hanging around the pasture. She knew he was fired up about the boarders leaving. He got his shotgun down and said stay here, girl, enunciating like people do when they think you're stupid because you're deaf. She had hearing aids and could lip read just fine. She was a quick study, Jack liked to say.

Holly's dad was right on time. The old man saw him and called out, but he didn't look up. From where she was hiding (Spooky safe in her stall) the girl could see what the old man couldn't make out in the dusk.

There was a gator bellying up to the open gate, attracted by the bits of flesh the boys had left to rot there. Holly's dad panicked and he whipped out his pistol. Mr. Small saw that all right. He pulled the trigger and even she could hear the shotgun's blast echoing painfully in the thick air.

Holly's dad went down to his knees and the gator charged.

That night, Jack said they had to get out of town before the police came. Not because of anything she did, he made sure to say. The old man had found her in the barn and marched her into the house. He called Jack and they talked in low voices so she couldn't hear.

She didn't care whose fault it was, as long as she could keep Spooky. She knew Jack couldn't stand her tears and would give in. He bought the trailer off the old man and loaded the pony as she hurriedly packed her small suitcase.

She'd won, she thought, although it was unclear to her what game they were playing.

She only knew it was the one adults had taught her, and if you wanted to survive you had to keep up.

Miri passed on the sad-looking produce and was eyeing the prepared foods at the deli when she got a text message. State police had picked up Trevally and the girl heading out of town. He would've gotten away if it hadn't been for a gruesome accident: the pony he was transporting had kicked though the wooden slats of the trailer. Poor creature, her forelegs were sheared clean down to the bone where they had scraped the pavement. Any man who treated an animal like that deserved to be jailed. But that wasn't why he was in custody. In addition to kidnapping, the man who called himself Jack Trevally had warrants out on him in three different states under three different names. Identity theft, insurance fraud, passing bad checks—all property crimes, nothing violent or drug-related, but not victimless. Those kinds of crimes hurt people too, and the targets of the scams were usually those who could least afford it.

That poor child had already had enough tragedy for a lifetime. Her parents were divorced and her mother had gotten a restraining order against her father. He violated it, showing up at the house and forcing them into his car. He was speeding on the turnpike, headed God knows where, and flipped the vehicle. The mother was killed and the girl sustained a head injury that cost her her hearing—possibly permanently, the doctors couldn't say for sure.

And even though Trevally appeared to have treated her well, and no one had reported him, anonymously or otherwise, that wasn't the end of it. She'd have to look into him too, since women in domestic violence situations, like the girl's mother, often repeated the pattern. In fact, when they were picked up, a witness at the scene said she'd seen Trevally pulling on the girl's arm. The girl was with a caseworker now and would be placed into foster care.

Sometimes these cases worked out for the best. Then she recalled the girl's wild joy in the photograph and amended the thought.

Sometimes they worked out without more unnecessary violence and death.

And sometimes that was all you could hope for in this world.

Her phone buzzed again—no message, just a picture of her two guys waiting for her at home. Maybe a move wasn't what they needed right now. She decided to call the social worker and ask if she could arrange for a visit with the girl. She'd talk to Roland and they'd see.

At the deli counter, she picked up a roast chicken and sides of mashed potatoes and green beans.

She didn't forget the ice cream.

Sara is a true legend and pioneer, not only for her creation of the seminal private investigator V.I. Warshawski but for her role as the "founding mother" of the Sisters in Crime organization. In "Storm Warning" Sara shows us how nature not only brings its own drama but conceals the doings of something else entirely...

Storm Warning

Sara Paretsky

1

As soon as the sirens sounded, Big Arnie and Junior went down to the cellar. Kelly Anne listened to Junior's cast thumping on the stairwell, listened to him taking the Lord's name in vain, but she refused to follow him. She went to the kitchen stoop, watching the storm thicken and drop fingers along the northwest horizon.

Myra hollered at her from the kitchen, "Get a move on now, you useless girl, I don't want to pay for your funeral." And, "A wife belongs with her husband, get your sorry ass down with your husband, although what he ever saw in you I'll never know."

The basement had a dirt floor and smelled like mold. Myra had taken Kelly Anne down there when she and Junior first arrived at the farm, to show her where all her canned vegetables were stored. As Kelly was pretending to be interested in row upon row of tomatoes, green beans and pickled beets, she'd seen a spider bigger than her hand saunter behind the shelves. She'd screamed and fled up the stairs, catching her shoe on an exposed nail, and landing hard on her shoulders.

Myra said, "Nobody ever teach you how to climb stairs?"

"It was that spider," Kelly Anne cried. "Didn't you see it?"

Myra snorted. "You're not a city girl, you must have seen a wolf spider before. Come back down here."

When Kelly Anne refused, Myra clomped up the stairs and grabbed her legs, pulling her down on her belly. Myra was eighty-something but still had all the strength that comes from a life spent milking cows.

The next day, looking at her purple stomach and thighs, Kelly Anne had the mordant thought that at least she had bruises that hadn't come from her husband.

Out on the Schapen farm, she felt as though she were remote from any world that she knew. No, she felt as though she were remote from herself. The farmhouse was old and rundown, with one bathroom for the whole family, and a tiny mirror just big enough for Kelly Anne to see her face if she stood on tiptoe—it was mounted at the right height for Junior and his father to see to shave.

Myra took for granted that Kelly Anne was there to do housework, and it was back-breaking work, without even a modern washing machine, just an old mangle unit that Myra had brought to the marriage from her own mother. She forced Kelly Anne down to the cellar to bring up jars of tomatoes, or odd items from a junk room—a length of twine—*No, not the brown, you silly girl, the medium-thick white, how did Junior choose someone so useless?* Kelly Anne learned that in addition to spiders the basement had a healthy supply of snakes.

"What were you thinking?" Kelly Anne whispered to her face in the mornings. "Why was marrying him such a hot idea?"

Junior had been a football star at Tonganoxie Bible College, where Kelly Anne had gone to study language arts. She was planning to be a first- or second-grade teacher when the athletic department hired her to tutor Junior in Bible History so he could keep his scholarship.

He became unexpectedly famous when his family's dairy farm was in the news. The pro scouts, who would never have heard of a boy from a small Bible college, saw clips of his games and started showing up in person. The Cowboys and the Falcons both invited him to summer tryout camps. It looked like he was going to be rich, famous, and Kelly Anne could see herself living in Dallas or Atlanta, never having to work. They got married in May, and then in July, at the Dallas camp, Junior tripped over his own feet and broke his left leg.

They came to his family farm for Myra—his Nana, whose pet he was—to nurse him back to health. He couldn't ride his Harley or shoot at birds, so he picked on Kelly Anne. *Picked on* meaning slugged her when he felt especially frustrated at his slow rehab.

Myra kept the keys to Kelly Anne's car, doling them out like an allowance when it was time to drive to church or take Junior into the nearby town of Lawrence, Kansas for his physical therapy sessions.

Even now, with the sky a greeny purple-black, and the wind so fierce Kelly Anne had to cling to the door jamb, Myra made sure she had Kelly Anne's car keys tucked into her brassiere.

2

The storm had flattened barns and houses all over the county. The Fremantle house, a showpiece for a century and a half, had been spared, but the land itself was a wreck. Bur oaks, cottonwoods, hickory, that had stood for almost two hundred years, lay with their roots exposed to the sky.

A giant cottonwood blocked the Fremantle driveway. Cady parked her squad car on the shoulder. She stopped to stroke the tree's rough, overlapping bark. "What noble roots are here o'erthrown," she murmured to it, and then blushed: she wasn't a social studies teacher any more, she was a sheriff's deputy—a small one at that, who couldn't afford to act strange in public.

She squared her shoulders and strode around the cottonwood, only to stumble on a cast iron skillet. She picked it up and continued to weave around the fallen trees, following the sound of chain saws. In a moment she came on a group starting the business of cutting up the trees—all men except for Hayleigh Fremantle, who was holding her end of a tree saw, her bright hair pulled up under a cap, eyes shielded with goggles. She saw Cady and shouted something at the children who were carrying small branches to a pile at the north end of the drive.

One of the Fremantle boys trotted over to Cady. "Have you come to help?"

She smiled down at him. "Came to make sure everyone here is safe."

"We're fine but fifty-two trees got tore up. Me and Dad counted them this morning."

"Torn up. Dad and I," Cady said, but softly, under her breath. Let Hayleigh's children speak ungrammatically—damned near everyone did these days.

Hayleigh and her sawing partner finished their cut and laid down their saw. "What a mess," she said, but cheerfully—when was she ever not cheerful? "We got off easy—can you believe, not a single window broken? But the Grellier place—every greenhouse was flattened. There's glass everywhere, and they can't stay in that house."

"Yeah, there's no roof," the boy said. "No one can sleep without a roof."

"They could put a tent up," piped up another child. "You and me, we sleep in tents all the time."

"Coffee, Cady?" Hayleigh offered.

Cady took a cup. "I'm heading there next. Lara Grellier called me from the Seattle airport this morning—she's on her way home but she says they've got a big crew in place already—everyone who isn't here, I guess. They'll be okay—physically, I mean, but the loss!"

All the adults nodded, or made solemn clicking noises. Crop insurance, homeowners, it would cover some of the damage, but for a working farm to be demolished mid-summer was an economic disaster.

"We've been blessed," Hayleigh said. "They can sleep here while they sort things out, right, Rope?"

Roper Fremantle, her husband, grunted agreement. "Hayleigh, you go on over now, make sure Jim and Susan know. Make sure they *come*—they're the only two people in the county more stubborn than you are. Janey, Mikey, Alex—you go set your tents up in the attic, like you do for sleepovers. Jim and Susan can have your beds—make sure you change the sheets—got it?"

The Fremantle children might not know the difference between subject and object, but they shared their parents' boundless energy and good will. They raced to the house, carefully removed their boots, and disappeared through the porch doors.

"We'll keep sawing here. I heard on the news they're saying it was an EF-4 storm but might have been a five. What are they saying at the sheriff's office?"

"Same as they're saying on the Weather Channel," Cady said. "The worst damage is in this sector. Seems like the west part of the county hardly got touched. Hayleigh, you want to drive over to Grellier's with me, until the crew gets enough of the trees moved that you can drive out of the yard?"

"So—how you like chasing crooks instead of hormone-crazed teens?" Hayleigh asked Cady as they drove west to Grellier's.

"Most of our county crooks are the same hormone-crazed kids whose illiterate essays I used to correct," Cady said. "Seriously, though, I bet I taught half the people in the county in the eight years I was at Central—it's a big plus on the job that they know me and like me. Or mostly like me—there's the handful I had to fail."

"Were the Schapen boys ever in your class?"

Cady made a face. "Both of them. Robbie was a good kid, but Junior! And you know he's back at the farm after breaking his leg at that tryout camp."

"Myra says someone broke it deliberately because the pro

players were jealous of his talent," Hayleigh said. "Rope says he was such a mean SOB that the starters for the Cowboys tripped him up to make him look bad. You been over to their place?"

"Not yet—I've been putting it off, but I'd better do it before I have to cough up a lame excuse to the sheriff." She made a hacking sound. "'Uh, boss, uh, Grelliers and Fremantles needed extra hands on board so I couldn't get to Schapens.' *Perec, don't fuck with me—I know as well as you that everyone in the county is looking after those two families. Get your sweet behind over to Schapens before I come out and drive you there personal.* And of course, I can't say, 'Uh, boss, it's 'personally'.'"

Both women laughed.

"You see that woman Junior persuaded to marry him?" Hayleigh said. "She must be dumber than my eggplants to see anything valuable in him."

"I saw her with Myra at the drugstore one afternoon," Cady said. "She had a black eye the size of a saucer—really, a yellow and purple eye—and I tried to give her a card with links and numbers to domestic violence services in the county. Myra snatched it out of my hand and yanked the girl away."

When Cady pulled into the Grellier yard, both women became quiet. For once, Hayleigh couldn't find anything cheerful to say. She gripped Cady's hand—this could have been her and Rope's home, lying in pieces of wood and stone. You couldn't tell these twisted lengths of metal, those glass shards and boards, had ever made up a home, a barn, a greenhouse.

Cady got out to see whether she could send someone out with water or food, but Jim and Susan waved her off. "Everyone's pitching in," Susan said. "We've got casseroles to live on until Labor Day, just need a refrigerator to keep 'em in."

The Grelliers' organic market was popular throughout the county. A dozen people were collecting scrap into the big farm wagons that someone had lent Jim. Another handful were going through the wreckage to salvage clothes or hardware—anything the storm had left intact. Other volunteers were picking through the remains of the greenhouses, pulling the seedlings free from the glass that had rained on them.

The sheriff phoned Cady, demanding an update. She wandered to the side of the road where she could hear him over the noise. As she filled him in, she saw a giant grandfather clock in the ditch. It was famous among the farm families. Back in the 1850's, when Schapens, Grelliers, and Fremantles had come together from Boston as anti-slavery emigrants, Arnie's ever so great-grandmother had carried the clock with her. When Arnie's younger son Robbie was in Cady's class at the junior high, he'd created a photo-essay about it, one of the most original student papers ever produced for Cady's classes.

As Cady talked to the sheriff, she bent down. She was half listening to Sheriff Drysdale's instructions, half inspecting the clock's works. The case was intact—one of those tornado oddities you always hear about—and while the weight chains were tangled up and one of the counterweights missing, nothing seemed broken. The pendulum was twisted but that could be straightened. She was looking around for the pendulum when a noise she'd only half heard registered: cows were bawling in the distance. Cady wasn't a farm girl, but the bellowing didn't sound good.

"Uh, boss, uh, I think I need to see what's bothering some cows."

She went back to the crowd and got Jim Grellier's attention. He walked with her to the road and then cried out in dismay.

"That's coming from Schapens'. Those cows sound like they need milking. Which means Arnie or Myra or both can't get to them. I'd better drive over, I guess."

He ran hands through his dirt-crusted hair. His face was streaked where sweat had run through the dirt covering it; his eyes were so red Cady wondered how he could see anything.

"No. It's my job, they're on my route," Cady assured him. "You've got more than you can handle right here."

She got back in her SUV and drove up the county road to the

dirt track leading to Schapens'. She'd flunked Junior Schapen when he was in her 9th grade language arts class. The football coach had bellowed at her—Junior was the best defensive end he'd coached in years, she needed to get over her uppity attitude and give Junior a passing grade. D-plus would do. He even tried to change her grade sheet in the computer.

Pressure from the coach and the principal had been unpleasant, but not nearly as horrific as the assault by Myra and Arnie. Myra had threatened Cady with eternal damnation, then backed it up in the here-and-now with threats of legal action. Even worse, she'd devoted her Twitter feed to trolling Cady, including publishing Cady's phone number.

Cady tried changing phone numbers, but the trolls found them easily and her service broke down under the onslaught of calls. Pickets waited for her every day coming into the junior high. Things died down at the end of the school year. The principal himself altered Cady's grade sheet so that Junior could leave 9th grade for high school. Her fury over the principal's intervention was tempered by relief—Junior was another school's problem. The summer break sent the trolls looking for fresher meat, but Cady began planning for a career outside teaching.

When she finally took the entrance exam for the sheriff's police, she'd fantasized about patrolling the county and shooting Myra and Arnie "accidentally." The Schapen dairy herd was famous; in her fantasy, she'd be following a lead to cattle rustling.

In reality, she tried to avoid the Schapen place when she was on patrol in the east sector of the county, but now their milk cows were forcing her onto the farm.

Their lowing grew louder, more disturbing as the SUV bumped down the lane to the house. When she parked in the yard, every muscle in her body was so tight that if Arnie punched her in the stomach, he'd break his fist.

The tornado had been through here, not as savagely as at the Grelliers'—the milking barn was intact, and the house damaged but still standing. The house had been built in the 1870's and hadn't been renovated since, except to add electricity and indoor plumbing. Even before the storm it had looked forbidding: the siding and window frames needed paint, and the doors and windows were askew from the way the house had subsided. Now, with the kitchen door gone and most of the windows shattered, it looked like the setting for childhood nightmares.

Cady climbed down from the SUV. Except for the cows, the farm was quiet. No one had come to help put the Schapens back together. *Serve them right,* she thought. *What you sow you shall reap.* She was the law, though; she had to serve and protect even God-awful taxpayers like Arnie and Myra. She texted her location and her worries to the sheriff before heading to the kitchen.

Her boot caught on a piece of rope. When she stopped to disentangle herself, she realized it was a clothesline, complete with pins. She'd heard Myra liked to do everything the hard way—no modern conveniences at the Schapen farm; they only encouraged laziness and invited people to do the devil's work for him.

No one wondered Big Arnie's wife had run away, although Cady couldn't understand how she could leave her two little boys—even Junior had been a little boy once—to be raised by Myra. And now Myra had a new captive, Junior's unfortunate young wife.

Cady stepped over the wood splinters on the stoop into the kitchen. Typical of the Schapens to be so bare-bones—no entryways or porches.

The damage inside was worse than outside. The kitchen ceiling had collapsed. Some of the wood joists had fallen. Others hung at crazy angles, jagged slabs of plaster dangling from them. More plaster filled the sink. Plaster dust covered the floor and the old cooktop. It lay so thick on the kitchen table that you couldn't see the chips in the enamel.

It wasn't until she'd gone back to the squad car for a hard hat and flashlight that Cady realized the lump slumped at the

Sara Paretsky

table was human. One of the joists had fallen on the figure's head, pushing it down to the table. A shower of plaster had landed on top of the board, making it look like something from a low-budget horror movie, maybe a mummy about to shed its wrappings and rise from the table.

A bubble of frightened laughter rose in Cady's mouth. She fought it down, but inhaled enough plaster dust to start choking.

"You're a sheriff's deputy now, Cady Perec. Pull yourself together. Go see if it's—if it's Myra or Arnie. See if they're alive. Call it in." She spoke out loud to re-enforce her lecture, coughing again on the dust she stirred up.

She moved gingerly to the table and was about to remove the joist from the body when she remembered one of her lessons at the academy. Sgt. Oliphant on evidence: *Take a picture. Once you've touched something you've tampered with the crime scene. It can never be reconstructed to what it was before you altered it.*

Cady took out her phone and snapped the scene from a dozen vantage points. Not that this was a crime scene, unless you were going to arrest Mother Nature for sending an EF-4 tornado through Douglas County last night, but still—better safe than sorry.

She lifted the board, exposing the head. Myra. Her cast-iron hair had been stained red-brown. Cady stuck out a tentative finger, squeamish at the thought of touching blood or brain, but forcing herself to pat the hair. It was still damp, probably because the board had kept the blood from drying.

Cady texted the sheriff, including the pictures she'd taken before she'd removed the joist. *I'm looking for Arnie,* she added. *The cows are going crazy. I'll see if any of the volunteers over at Grelliers' know how to milk them.*

When she'd hung up, she heard a faint thumping and shouting underneath her feet.

***

3

Myra was still alive, the EMT crew told Cady. "Amazing. She's eighty-whatever, took a blow to the head, and is still breathing."

"I did feel for a pulse when I first saw her," Cady said.

"Isn't much of one," the tech assured her. "Not something you'd find beneath the plaster and so on. We'll take her into town and come back if you need us after your team gets that basement door open."

Cady had found someone at Grelliers' to look after the cows, but the sheriff had told her to stay around in case there were any additional casualties.

It took four hours to bring Arnie and Junior out of the basement. The collapsed ceiling blocked the door, and when Cady and a trio of civilian volunteers cleared that away, they found the stairs were partly buried under an avalanche of plaster and dirt.

By the time the Schapen men were rescued, they'd been buried for close to twenty-four hours. They'd broken into some of the canned vegetables, but they hadn't had water; they were covered in dirt from trying to claw through the basement walls and they were angry, ready to blame anyone for their time underground. When Big Arnie realized Cady had been the sheriff's deputy on the case, he spewed venom at her in a hoarse caw: she hadn't been able to end Junior's football career when she taught at the junior high, so now she'd tried to kill him by leaving him buried alive in his own home.

"Mr. Schapen," she interrupted. "We didn't find Junior's wife. Wasn't she down there with you? I searched the house and the grounds and didn't see her."

"You searched the house? My house? Without my permission?"

Cady stood very straight and spoke in a toneless voice. "Under exigent circumstances it is permissible or essential for law officers to enter a residence without a warrant. We rescued you and your son by coming into your home without a warrant. Your mother is still alive because I came into your home this morning and got her immediate medical help, without a warrant. I got someone into your dairy barn to milk your cows without a warrant. I believe a court will agree that these all constituted exigent circumstances, but you are free to lodge a protest."

Arnie glared at her, thought of speaking, but stomped out to the yard to an old hand pump. He worked the handle until water gushed out. He knelt to rinse his head, and drank deeply, then lumbered off to the cow barn.

"Was your wife in the basement with you?" Cady asked.

"Stupid bitch wouldn't come down to the basement," Junior said. "She was afraid of spiders and snakes. If Nana dies it'll be because of her, stupid cunt."

"I see you cherish your wife, just as you swore you would when you made your wedding vows," Cady said.

Junior raised a crutch to take a swing at her, but Cady ducked under it, then caught the crutch with her free hand. One of the civilian trio grinned broadly and applauded, which made Junior darken with fury.

Cady turned her back on him and spoke to the civilian aides. "We need to hunt for Junior Schapen's wife. I know everyone is beat—I am, too—but if she didn't go down to the basement, she could be in the yard some place where I didn't spot her."

"Storm could have carried her away," one of the volunteers said softly.

"I know," Cady agreed, "but we still have to look."

On her way out to the yard, Cady stopped at her SUV. She carried a cooler with Dr Pepper in it, along with peanut butter, crackers and apples. She'd been so busy rescuing Schapens that she hadn't stopped to eat. When the sugar in the soft drink hit her body, the rush almost knocked her out. She wobbled as she went out to join the search, taking the sector north of the dairy barn, beyond the perimeter she'd searched earlier.

Just beyond the pasture fence she lost her footing, landing

hard in the high grass there. When she pulled herself together, looking around furtively to make sure Arnie hadn't seen her fall, she found she'd tripped on a metal cylinder. It was old, but hadn't been in the yard long—it hadn't rusted, it wasn't covered with dirt. It was shaped like a cow bell but was solid inside.

She tucked it into her vest, on the side opposite her gun and flashlight, trying to balance the load. Her low back often ached when she got off duty and this iron cylinder gave her a stab that made her take it off and place it along the edge of the drainage ditch, marking it with a red board that had come loose from one of the barns.

Sunlight glinted on it when she put it on the board. Something like blood had dried on it. She stuck it back into a pocket on her vest despite the pain the added weight pushed into her neck and shoulders.

4

Myra called her a useless girl and her husband said she was a stupid cunt, but Kelly Anne came from a small Kansas town. She knew if you're caught outside in a tornado, you don't try to outrun it, you lie down in the lowest place you see and wait it out.

Rain had been so heavy all spring that the drainage ditches still had standing water in them. The high wild grasses were rank with the smell, but Kelly Anne lay down in it, feeling the dank water soak into her jeans and T-shirt. She watched the clouds turn the same color as the slime she was lying in. All at once, the storm was right over her head.

The sound was louder than anything she'd ever heard, louder than a hundred thousand Harleys all revving their engines at once. She tried to cover her ears, but she couldn't take her eyes from the swirling clouds. A finger came down, as if it were the hand of God. She could hear Pastor Nabo's voice at Myra's church: *confess your sins, confess your sins, confess your sins.*

Kneel before the Lord and confess your sins.

She couldn't suppress a nervous giggle. *I'm kneeling, maybe that's good enough. If the Lord takes me now at least I'm on my knees.*

The biggest finger came down a quarter mile away. Grellier's farm. Jim and Susan were such good, kind people. Why couldn't I have been part of their family?

The giant finger went back into the cloud, came down, rose again, moved on to the east. All around her pieces of wood and glass rained down, and then the rains themselves came, hard, merciless, pounding into her exposed head.

5

At nine they were having a wrap-up meeting in the sheriff's office. No one had been killed in the storm; that was the good news. The hard news was that damage had been severe throughout the northeast sector of the county, wreaking wanton destruction as it moved toward Kansas City.

The deputies were exhausted. They'd helped dig people like the Schapens out of their rubble, Deputy Kellogg had delivered a human baby while Deputy Junger had helped old Mrs. Kanopolis's pig farrow. She'd tried to offer him a piglet in thanks.

"Should have taken it, Jung, bacon for all of us in the fall," another deputy teased—Junger was a committed vegetarian.

"Kelly Anne Schapen is still missing," Sheriff Drysdale said after everyone had spoken. "We've pulled photos from her Facebook and Instagram pages, and we'll circulate those tomorrow. For now, everyone get some rest."

Cady took off her tactical vest and felt for the weight she'd retrieved. She was looking at it, wondering whether those were really blood stains on it, wondering if she should show it to the sheriff when all she wanted was a hot bath and a proper meal.

Before she could speak, though, the sheriff told her to stay behind. "I've had Arnie Schapen on the phone. He has a long catalog of complaints about the job you did at his farm today."

Cady felt the blood leave her face. She clutched the back of a chair to keep from falling.

"I saved him and his son, along with his mother. I don't know what he can be complaining about, boss." Her voice was coming from far away, so far away that she wasn't sure she'd spoken loudly enough for Drysdale to hear.

"He says you've had it in for Arnie, Junior ever since he was in your class at the junior high, and that you hoped they would die in the basement. He also says you tried to bury his mother when she was still alive."

Cady didn't say anything.

"I talked to the EMT crew. They said you thought Myra Schapen was dead when you called."

"Yes, boss." She remembered the pictures she'd taken and pulled out her phone to show Drysdale. "I felt her neck for a pulse and didn't find one, but, as the tech told me when they were taking her away, she was so covered in dirt and plaster it was hard to find an artery. I moved her out from under that big beam—" She pointed to it on her screen. "It wasn't quite touching her head, but I was afraid if I waited for help the rest of the ceiling would come down, not just on her but on me, as well."

She scrolled through the pictures of the civilians digging out the cellar. Someone had airdropped pictures of her working as hard as the big men who'd been volunteering.

Drysdale nodded and handed her phone back. "Still, you're on administrative duty until I know how serious these charges are going to be."

You will not cry in front of the sheriff, Cady ordered herself. *You will stand at attention until you are dismissed. You will salute and say 'yes, sir.'* Her light-hearted banter with Hayleigh Fremantle, about correcting the sheriff's grammar, came back to her. That had happened a long time ago, maybe as far back as when the Schapens and Fremantles had come west with the

Grelliers to loose the bonds of the oppressed.

The sheriff said some more things but the words buzzed in her head from that remote place; she couldn't make sense of them, until he said sharply, "I told you, dismissed."

"Yes, boss." She paused in the doorway. "Sir, did Arnie—Mr. Schapen—say anything about Junior's wife? Why she wasn't in the cellar?"

"He said his mother tried to make her go down but the silly girl was afraid of the spiders. He says his mother was struggling with her when the storm hit."

"He's not worried about her safety, boss?"

The sheriff looked at her sharply. "You go home and don't get involved in anything to do with the Schapens. Not even trying to find Arnie's daughter-in-law. That's an order, Perec. You could get in deeper legal hot water if Arnie thinks you're meddling."

She saluted, almost hitting herself in the head with the weight she'd been carrying. "Got it, boss."

"What's that you're holding?" the sheriff asked.

Cady looked down at the weight, at the rust-colored stains on the end. "Just a souvenir from the storm, sir."

6

Cady was the only officer in the duty room the next morning when Phyllis Dortmunder called from the hospital. She was an administrator with the hospital surgical unit, but Cady knew her because Phyllis attended her grandmother's church.

The surgeon who'd operated on Myra Schapen wanted to talk to the sheriff but Phyllis figured it was okay to pass a message on through Cady.

"They say they found a bruise on her left temple. They figure the roof beam must have struck her there, knocked her off her feet, because there wasn't any injury to the back of the head."

"Could be," Cady agreed.

She pictured Myra slumped at the kitchen table. She'd been seated when she'd been hit, Cady would stake what was left of her badge on it; the beam hadn't come all the way down, so Myra had been struck before the ceiling collapsed.

Phyllis chatted with her for a few minutes, wanting details on what Cady had seen when she'd been out at Grelliers'—like everyone in the county, she shopped at their produce stand.

"Terrible thing to happen to Jim and Sue," Phyllis said. "But trust Myra to survive being hit by a support beam."

Cady hesitated, remembering the sheriff's warning to stay away from anything to do with Arnie, but finally asked if Kelly Anne had checked into the hospital. Someone might have picked her up along the road and brought her in.

Phyllis called back half an hour later. "The emergency room had a gal that could have been her—twenty-something blonde who said she'd been caught in the storm and lost everything, car, wallet, and gave her name as Lara Grellier. The charge nurse is new to the area, didn't know the Grellier family, didn't know Lara was staying over to Fremantles, besides not being a bottle blonde. The ER treated this gal for shock and exposure—winds had torn some of the skin clean off her arms and hands when she covered her face with them. They say when they discharged her, they gave her the address of the community shelter."

When it was time for her lunch break, Cady left her badge and her vest in the duty room and drove out to the shelter. Most people in town knew her from her teaching days, or because her grandmother—the woman who'd raised her—was active in so many volunteer organizations. The shelter director was no exception.

Leon Hartfeld came out from behind his desk to hug her. "So, you're a detective now. From the kid who used to raise hell in Sunday school to the one on the other side of the badge. How's it feel?"

Cady smiled. "I wouldn't have put up with me the way you

did, that's for sure. I'm here privately, though, not part of the posse. We wore ourselves out yesterday digging people out of basements and what-not, and the sheriff is letting us rest for about four hours.

"Junior Schapen's wife has come up missing. I heard from the hospital they might have sent her to you—she may have amnesia from the storm."

Cady had downloaded a couple of photos of Kelly Anne from her social media pages and showed those to Hartfeld.

The director frowned at her. "If she's here, and that's only *if*, Deputy Perec, she needs quiet and healing from a lot more than the skin burns the storm gave her."

"If she's here, I only want to talk to her privately, woman to woman," Cady said steadily. "This is on my own time. The sheriff doesn't know I'm here. Not even Gran knows I'm here."

Hartfeld laughed with her: most people in the county would agree that Gertrude Perec was a more formidable presence than Sheriff Drysdale. He led Cady to the shelter kitchen, where she recognized Kelly Anne at once, the same pretty, nervous face she'd encountered with Myra in the drugstore a few months ago. She was stirring a big pot of something on the stove, Sloppy Joe mix from the smell, and didn't look up until Hartfeld went to her side.

Cady watched as he spoke to Kelly Anne, pointed at Cady, smiled winningly. Kelly Anne looked at Cady with so much fear that she joined the pair, despite Hartfeld's forbidding head shake.

"Kelly Anne? I'm Cady Perec, I'm the woman who gave you a card for shelters in the county at the drugstore, and I'm here just to talk. I'm not here as a sheriff's deputy or anyone but a woman who knows you've been through a whole lot more than most of us can stand up to."

The muscles in Kelly Anne's throat worked, looking like a snake swallowing a rabbit, except that she was the fearful rabbit. She tried to say something but couldn't get any words out.

"Do you know I was Junior's junior high teacher before I

joined the sheriff's police? I don't want to put you on the spot with your husband, but when I failed him in 9th grade social sciences, Big Arnie and Myra were so vicious to me that I started thinking I'd leave teaching.

"And then, yesterday, I was assigned to go to the Schapen place. Junior and Big Arnie were trapped in the basement, beneath a ton or so of plaster and wood and dirt, God knows what else. It took the better part of the day to dig them out. Meanwhile, Myra, she was at the kitchen table, unconscious: she'd taken a blow to the head that the docs at the medical center think came from a big kitchen beam when it fell down.

"You'd think Arnie would be grateful—I saved his bullying ass, saved your husband, saved his mother. But grateful isn't how he sounded when he called the sheriff and lodged a report against me."

She stopped speaking. Kelly Anne's throat worked a few more times until she managed to blurt out, "Myra didn't die?"

"No, ma'am. Seems like there's enough poison in her system that it's pickled her so she can survive blows that might flatten you or me."

"You're not lying?" Kelly Anne demanded.

"No, ma'am. You can call over to the hospital and check. Or get Mr. Hartfeld here to do it."

"I'll do that for you," Leon Hartfeld said, and moved away so the women could talk alone.

For a brief moment, Kelly Anne seemed relieved, seemed to relax, but then her shoulders hunched up around her ears. "And Junior?"

"He's alive, too, unhurt." Cady paused for a beat. "No one knows you're here, Kelly Anne. I can't live your life for you, but you don't have to go back to Junior."

"He'll find me," Kelly Anne said listlessly. "He doesn't love me, but he hates to lose."

"You can let your life be ruled by fear, Kelly Anne, or you can let it be ruled by freedom. If you decide to leave Junior, you'll need a lawyer, you'll need an order of protection, you'll need a way to support yourself and to protect yourself. People at the shelter can help you find those resources, but you have to decide whether you want them."

Kelly Anne stared at the floor, not moving, not even trying to speak.

Cady pulled the weight from her backpack and held it out to the other woman. "I found this on the farm when I was looking for you yesterday. I was going to put it in our evidence locker, but when big Arnie called with his complaints against me for saving him and Myra, I thought maybe I should give it back to you. It's from the big old clock that Schapens brought west with them in 1858, isn't it?"

Kelly Anne nodded fractionally.

"You take it, you keep it as a reminder that you can stand up for yourself. Keep it as a reminder that I know how you did it and I won't let it slide a second time."

Kelly Anne smiled tremulously. She blurted out some disjointed thanks. Cady brushed them aside and turned to leave, but the younger woman tapped her shoulder.

"What did you do when Arnie and Myra threatened you over Junior's 'F'?"

"It wasn't just them, but the football coaches at the junior high and high school and nearly half the school board. I told them America needed thinkers more than she needed offensive linemen and I wouldn't lower my standards for them. They huffed and puffed, one of the coaches even tried to sneak into the computer system to change Junior's grade, but the school finally decided to let him graduate and move on to high school.

"My lunch break is over; I'm going to be in more trouble with the sheriff if I don't hustle back downtown to the office. You be well, call 911 if you need the sheriff's help or protection."

Leon Hartfeld stopped Cady as she left the room to say the hospital confirmed her report on Myra's condition. "But that isn't Lara Grellier. I don't know who she thinks she's fooling."

"Let it be, Leon. No crime in calling yourself any name in the phone books as long as you aren't committing fraud with it."

7

Over the next week, Cady kept looking at missing persons reports, wondering if Junior would start looking for his wife. She finally called Hayleigh Fremantle, to ask if Kelly Anne had returned to Schapens'. Of course Hayleigh and everyone else in the county knew Cady was on administrative duty, with orders to stay away from Schapens.

"No one's seen any sign of her. Junior's going around telling everyone he threw her out on account of her disrespecting Myra. He says she'll come crawling back and he'll decide then whether to let her. You think she's dead?"

"If she'd died in the storm, someone would have found her by now," Cady said.

When she hung up, she looked up with a guilty start to see the sheriff next to her desk. "You talking about Junior's wife?"

Cady nodded, too embarrassed to speak.

"You really don't know where she is?"

"No, boss. I really don't." Not a lie: she had no way of knowing if Kelly Anne was at the homeless shelter, the women's shelter or on the road to California.

"Junior Schapen just called in a car theft—the Honda he and his wife own. If I send you out there, you promise not to touch him or Arnie?"

"I'm on administrative duty, boss," Cady reminded him weakly. "Shouldn't Kellogg or Junger go?"

"Giving you a chance to step up, Perec. Take it or leave it."

She went out to the Schapen farm, took a statement from the surly Junior. His cast was off but he was limping badly. His football days were gone; he'd have to stay on to look after the cows. Cady kept her face and voice expressionless while she wrote down the make, model, license plate number, day the car was last seen.

That night at dinner, as she and her grandmother recounted the details of their days, Gertrude Perec said, "Today was our clothing drive day at the church. Phyllis Dortmunder was there. Of course, she shouldn't tell us about the condition of patients at the hospital, but we all wanted to know how Myra Schapen was doing."

"Dead?" Cady asked hopefully.

"Elizabeth Cady Stanton Perec, don't you—oh, never mind. Jesus doesn't want her yet. She's making an amazing recovering. But she says one of the candy-stripers came in and took her car keys from her yesterday. Phyllis says Myra tried to ring for the nurse, but the candy-striper had disconnected the call button. What do you think?"

Cady said, "I think if Myra wants to file a report, it will have to be with the Lawrence police. Sheriff can't be involved in Lawrence crime, so it's not my problem. But, honestly, Gram, Myra must have some kind of brain damage to dream that up about a candy-striper."

Gertrude grunted agreement. "There's apple pie left over from our working lunch. You go get yourself a piece, bring me one, too. And don't do that wild dance on your way back in with the plates or you'll trip and fall. My own great-grandmother brought those out from Boston with her; I'm not having you throwing them around the dining room."

From Sara: This is my homage to Bill Crider's Sheriff Dan Rhodes books, which I loved. My protagonist, Cady Perec, is a new-minted sheriff's deputy in Douglas County, Kansas, where I grew up. As a nod to Sheriff Rhodes, Cady carries Dr Pepper and peanut butter and crackers in her cooler, although Sheriff Rhodes liked those peanut-butter filled Ritz crackers you used to get in vending machines. I loved those crackers, too—they sometimes were my lunch when I worked downtown. This story also brings in characters from my own novels set in Kansas, Bleeding Kansas *and* Fallout. *There's a particular pleasure in revisiting characters from previous books and seeing them in a new light. I'm glad to take part in this project, but wish instead we still had Bill with us to give us more of his own lovely, quirky novels.*

Bob Randisi has written more books and stories than many people have read. He's also the founder of the Private Eye Writers of America, the group that gives us the industry's annual Shamus Awards. Like Bill Crider and many of the writers in this collection, he has written across many genres and continues to invent and shine with both his novels and short stories. Here we need to find out just...

Who Killed Mr. Peepers?
A 70s Rock 'n' Roll Mystery
Robert J. Randisi

1

I stopped in front of the DeMille Theater to look at the lobby card for *Cleopatra Jones*. Tamara Dobson was something else. On the other side of the box office was another card touting William Marshall and Pam Grier in *Scream Blacula Scream*.

It was early 1974 and Black exploitation movies were exploding. All the theaters knew what side of the bread their butter was on, so you could walk down a street in Manhattan and see Richard Roundtree on a *Shaft in Africa* poster, or Jim Brown on a *Slaughter's Big Rip-Off* lobby card, Ron O'Neal for *Super Fly T.N.T.*, Fred Williamson as *Black Caesar*, or the hot Pam Grier again, this time as *Coffy*.

I enjoyed the good ones, skipped what I presumed to be trash, and sometimes took one in just to stare at Pam and Tamara.

I was heading from W. 47th Street where my shoebox office was, to meet a client at his office in the famed Brill Building. According to the phone call I'd received that morning, he was in the music business and heard that I had been involved in the case of Reuben Massey just over a year ago. Massey had become a member of the 27 Club when he was killed, dying at that age along with Jim Morrison, Jimi Hendrix, Janis Joplin, and Brian Jones of the Rolling Stones. Just by coincidence, I had also been 27 during that case. I was happy to say I had made it to 28 and would be staring 29 in the face, soon.

Since that incident my business had picked up. 1974 had been a good year, as I seemed to have become the go-to guy for cases that involved rock'n'roll. Bill Graham, who was managing the band Santana, flew me to San Francisco because some black magic woman with evil ways was threatening Carlos Santana, who seemed to believe in it; The O'Jays management group came to me because some backstabber had gotten on their love train and wouldn't get off; right in Manhattan, Carly Simon came to me because some vain guy thought one of her songs was about him and was harassing her; and the highlight of the year was having the Rolling Stones fly me to London because some poser thought he had the moves like Jagger and was trying to rip Mick off.

My bank account had become pretty healthy, but I maintained my 47th Street office rather than blow bucks on an expensive Madison Avenue address.

This time the caller, a man named Lyle Tomlin, said he needed somebody familiar with the business to solve a problem. I told him I'd meet him and listen to what he had to say.

The Brill Building was located at Broadway and 49th Street, just north of Times Square, so I was able to walk there. It had been considered the center of the music industry since the 60s, and many hit songs had been written there, but the building actually dated back to the big band era.

The building had eleven floors. I took the elevator to his floor and almost swallowed my teeth when Lesley Gore got on as I got off. She was an adorable little thing and I was struck dumb as the doors closed. Walking down the hall I could hear music, as songwriters were working on their craft and the sounds all mixed together. I walked past the offices of Red Bird Records, and Paul Simon Music.

As I entered the office I stopped short. I hadn't been expecting Mr. Peepers. In fact I was kind of shocked, because Wally Cox—who had played Mr. Peepers from 1952 to 1955—had just died earlier that year, at forty-eight years of age. But here I was, looking at him.

"Mr. Tomlin?"

"That's right." He put his hand out and I shook it. "It's a pleasure to meet you." He was about five-and-a-half feet tall. For a small man he had a firm grip.

"So this is your office?"

"No, I'm in the Alden Building at 1650, down the street." Brill was at 1619 Broadway. "This office is used by Neil Sedaka. I'm tryin' to steal him from his reps, but he's not here today."

Damn, I thought.

"Please, let's sit," he said.

He didn't sit behind the desk in the room, so we sat in front of it, facing each other. Across the hall someone was singing.

"Is that—"

"David Gates," Tomlin said. "He's working on songs for a new album Bread is gonna release next year."

I nodded, impressed. As eventful as 1974 had been for me, I had never been in the Brill Building. If I happened to see Laura Nyro I was going to shit a brick.

"I have a problem," he said.

"So you said," I replied. "What's goin' on?"

"Well, first let me tell you that people stare at me."

"Do you know why they stare?" I asked.

He waved a hand.

"I'm aware of my resemblance to Mr. Peepers. In fact, I'm taking steps to change that." He pointed to his wire-framed glasses, which did not match the black rims that Peepers wore. "New glasses."

"Ah," I said. "So what's the problem?"

"This is different than being stared at," he said. "I believe you call it a shadow?"

"Shadow?"

Tomlin leaned forward.

"When somebody's following you?" he whispered.

"Oh," I said, "and why do you think someone is followin' you?"

"I think they plan to kill me."

2

"Can you be specific?" I asked. "First. What is it you actually do?"

"I manage singer-songwriters," he said. "People like Carole King, Jim Croce, Joni Mitchell—"

"Joni Mitchell?" I asked. I loved Joni Mitchell. I'd been waiting for her next album after *For The Roses* in '72.

"No, I don't represent *them*," he said, "but artists like them."

"Anyone I would've heard on the radio?" I asked.

"Not yet," Tomlin said, "but we're getting there."

"Okay, go on. You manage singer-songwriters, none of whom have made it yet. Why is somebody trying to kill you?"

"I don't know."

"What makes you think someone is followin' you?"

"I see things," Tomlin said, "in the shadows, mainly."

"The shadows?"

"Yeah," he said.

"What shadows?"

"Come on, man," he said. "The shadows are everywhere. They're all around us."

"And there is somebody in the shadows followin' you?"

"That's what I'm saying."

"Do you think you were followed here?" I asked.

"No," he said. "No shadows. But tonight, when the sun's going down, I'll be followed."

"Yeah, you will," I said. "By me."

"So you'll help me?" he asked.

"I'll try," I said.

"I can pay you."

"That's good," I said. "I like gettin' paid."

I wasn't sure he was in his right mind, but I was willing to find out. After all, he said he *was* going to pay me.

3

Before I left I asked Tomlin, "What are you gonna do now?"

"I have some calls to make, so I'll go back to my own office."

"When will you be done?"

"I'll probably be leaving around five," he said, "but I have an appointment tonight."

"Where?"

"CBGB."

"Really?" CBGB stood for "country, bluegrass and blues." "You're goin' there and you handle singer-songwriters?"

"The Magic Tramps are playing," he said, with a shrug. "I like them. Plus the artist I'm meeting wanted to meet there."

"All right, then," I said. "I'll be around, but whatever you do, don't look for me."

"I'll try not to," he said.

CBGB was located at 315 Bowery, right on the border but still considered part of the East Village.

I picked Tomlin up outside his building, spent some time getting a minor thrill by watching the Brill artists and songwriters going in and out—spotted Neil Sedaka going in, and Carole King coming out. Carole King had hit it real big a few years ago with her *Tapestry* album, but she was still writing songs for other artists as well. She and Gerry Goffin had written tons of hits for others while they were married, but since their divorce in 1968 she seemed to have taken off as a solo act.

When Tomlin came out and got a cab I followed him to CBGB, waited for him to go in, then checked the street to see if anyone had followed him before I entered.

It had opened in December of '73. It was doing okay its first few months, but I had the feeling it was going to explode with big name groups, and those who would *become* big names.

As Tomlin had said, there was a group called Magic Tramps headlining that night, but opening for them were three girls who were on stage now. The one in the center was stunning with extremely photogenic features.

"Hey!" I grabbed the arm of a passing waiter. "Who are they?"

"The Stilettos," he said. "That's Elda Gentile and Amanda Jones, and that doll in the middle is named Debbie Harry." I could tell from his time and the way he was looking at her that he was gone on Debbie.

"They're not that good," I said, "but she sure is."

"You mark my words," the young man said, "that girl's gonna hit it big someday soon."

He moved off and I started to look around for Lyle Tomlin. The floor was a sea of bodies and I was starting to think I should've stayed glued to his back when he entered. But he and his Mr. Peepers appearance turned out to be easy to pick out among the crowd of mostly young people. Even at my age I was feeling old.

Now that I had him spotted I realized how vulnerable he was in that crowd if somebody really was out to kill him. A slight bump from behind with a knife or a needle and he'd be done. And with the music as loud as it was, even a gunshot might go unnoticed.

I moved in closer to him. At the moment he seemed to be

alone, just watching the stage and moving to the music. When I saw somebody approaching him I almost intercepted them, but I waited because it was a woman. She was holding two bottles of beer and when she reached him she gave him one. He showed no surprise, and accepted it. Then they stood there together, bopping to the music of the Stilettos, and probably waiting for the Magic Tramps to come out.

I had no choice but to wait with them.

As much as I liked the singer-songwriters of the day, and was still a fan of the Beatles and the Rolling Stones, I wasn't particularly fond of what the Magic Tramps represented, which was "glam rock." It had as much to do with what they were wearing as what they were playing. There were times when they not only dressed flamboyantly, but performed in white face—and this was one of those nights.

The Stilettos took their leave to a smattering of applause, and the Magic Tramps took their place. As the music started I saw Tomlin and the woman he was with slipping away. I thought that was odd since he had told me he was going to CBGB to hear the Magic Tramps. Now that didn't seem the case. I hurried to stay behind then, not too close, but within sight. They went towards the toilets and I wondered if this was going to lead to sex in one of the bathrooms. And if it did, was this something I wanted to interrupt?

I held back, to give them time to commit to whatever it was they were going to do, and then I moved in to discover what it was. If it *was* sex, I was going to leave them alone and go back to the music.

When I got to the restrooms I realized I didn't know which one they were in, men's or women's. The music was kind of muffled back there, so I thought pressing my ear to the doors would tell me what I needed to know. I was wrong.

What I got was a scream.

* * *

4

I burst through the door of the Ladies' Room and saw the woman on her knees in the center of the room, with Tomlin lying next to her. She stared at me with a shocked look on her face, her bloody hands held out in front of her.

"Take it easy," I said. Outside the bathroom the music was still playing, and nobody else had come running in. It seemed as if I was the only one who'd heard the scream.

"Is he dead?" I asked.

"I—I—I—" she stammered.

"All right," I said, "stay right there. Let me check him."

I leaned over Tomlin, across from the woman, and pressed my fingers to his throat. I couldn't detect a pulse.

"Is he—" she asked, but her voice caught in her throat before she could finish.

"He's dead," I said. "What happened?"

She stared at me with wide blue eyes that, under other circumstances, would have been pretty. Now they were frightened and shocked.

"I—I—don't know," she said. "I went into one of the stalls. I heard something, and when I came out to see what it was, he was like...this."

Tomlin's chest was covered with blood.

"What did you do?"

"I saw the blood and tried to stop it," she said, waving her hands.

"What's your name?"

"Beverly."

"Beverly," I said, "I'm sorry, but I think you have to stay right there while I call the police."

"Of course," she said. "Where would I go like...this?" She shook her hands again, and this time drops of blood flew off.

I got up and backed toward the door, telling her, "Just stay still, don't move. I'll be right back. There's a phone down the hall."

"A-are you a policeman?" she asked.

"No, I'm a private detective," I said. "Tomlin actually hired me today."

"For what?"

"To keep this very thing from happenin'," I said, "and obviously, I didn't do such a good job. Just stay put."

"All right," she said, "but could you hurry, please?"

"As fast as I can."

Right outside I stopped a guy who was coming out of the men's room.

"Hey, man, do you know who the manager of this place is?" I asked.

"No idea," he said. He waved me away without slowing down.

As he rushed away from me, I spotted blood on the leg of his trousers.

"Hey, hold it!" I shouted.

And he started running.

Of course he started to run.

The floor of the CBGB was even more crowded now that the Magic Tramps were playing.

He was young, and fast. Chasing him made me feel a lot older and slower than I was. He zigged and zagged around the dancing crowd, while I bounced off several people, leaving them furious.

"Stop that guy!" I shouted, as we got near the front entrance.

I was hoping one of the bouncers would hear me. They not only heard me, they saw me. Next thing I knew a bouncer in a tight black T-shirt planted a shoulder right in my midsection, taking me off my feet and driving most of the air out of my lungs. Then he stood there proudly, dumb smile on his face, looking down at me.

"Wrong guy," I gasped.

* * *

5

"Okay, Mister Private Eye," the detective said, "let's try again."

I was in a Manhattan South interrogation room with Detective Mike Weston. His partner, Detective Jim Leland, was outside the room at the moment.

"I told you," I said. "Tomlin said somebody was following him, keeping to the shadows. He thought they might be planning to kill him."

"Did he say why he thought that?" Weston asked.

"No."

Weston was the senior partner, in his fifties, with over twenty-five years on the job. If I was any judge, Leland was in his thirties, probably had a dozen years in.

"So you just bought it?"

"He was my client," I said, "he was paying me. And I thought by following him myself, I'd be able to prove or disprove what he was sayin'."

"Well, you proved it," he said. "Somebody wanted him dead, and he's dead. Helluva job, P.I."

"Knock it off," I said. "I feel bad enough."

"Why? Because you didn't get paid?"

I pointed my forefinger at him and said, "Well, that's one reason."

"Don't get smart!"

"You brought it up."

"Okay, look, I don't think you killed your client…"

"Thanks."

"…but I think you're keepin' somethin' from us."

"Why would I do that?"

"Because you're a fuckin' P.I.," Weston said. "Ain't that what you do?"

"That's a terrible cliché, Weston," I said. "I'm just tryin' to help."

"Okay, then tell me somethin' helpful."

"Oh," I said, "you mean you're ready to listen?"

"I'm ready," he said, waving a hand. "The floor's all yours."

"When I came out of the restroom to call you," I said, "there was a man comin' out of the men's room. I didn't think nothin' of it, until I saw the blood on the leg of his pants."

That got his attention.

"You sure it was blood?"

"I know blood when I see it."

"So what happened?"

"I tried to talk to him, but he ran. I lost him in the crowd."

"Damn it!" Weston said. "Why didn't you just shoot him?"

"I don't carry," I said.

"Why not?"

"I wasn't created by Mickey Spillane."

The door opened at that point and his partner, Leland, entered.

"There's nothin' on this guy," he said. "He's clean."

"How can he be clean?" Weston asked. "He's a keyhole peeper."

"Ouch," I said, "enough with the clichés already."

"Okay," Weston said, "tell us what the guy in the club looked like and you can go."

I gave him the best description I could, considering I only got a fleeting look at him before he started running. Weston took it all down, and then Leland opened the door.

"You can go."

"What about the girl? Beverly?"

"Beverly Halliday," Weston said. "We're still questioning her. She was in that bathroom when Tomlin was killed."

"We still don't know she didn't do it," Leland said. "We can hold her as a material witness."

"Why don't you let her go," I suggested, "and let me see what I can get out of her. You guys are probably scarin' her."

Weston and Leland exchanged a look.

"If she thinks I got her out, she'll think she owes me," I went on, hoping I had them.

"She is shakin' like a leaf," Leland said to Weston. "Maybe…"

"This guy?" Weston asked.

"Why not? What've we got?"

"We can sweat her for forty-eight more hours," Weston said.

"Jerry, I don't think she's gonna get any better," Leland said. "Not in here."

"And what if she killed him?"

"If she did," I said, "I'll find out. I promise."

"Why?" Weston asked. "Tomlin wasn't even your client. He hadn't paid you."

"He *was* my client," I said. "I just hadn't billed him yet. I want to find out who killed him as much as you do."

Weston looked at Leland.

"Whataya say, partner?" the younger man asked.

"Jesus," Weston said. "Yeah, okay." He looked at me. "We'll tell her we're releasing her in your custody."

"No," I said, "just tell her I got you to release her. I don't want her to feel trapped."

"Yeah, okay," Weston said. He looked at his partner. "You take care of it."

"Right."

Leland left the room and Weston turned on me.

"If you fuck us on this—"

"Why would I do that?" I asked. "I'm just tryin' to be helpful."

"If you think I buy that," he said, "I got a bridge I wanna sell ya."

6

It was morning as I waited out front for Beverly Halliday to come out.

"They told me you got me released," she said. "Are you a policeman?"

"Private detective," I said. "I don't have that power, but I did speak for you."

"You don't think I did it?"

"I don't know," I said. "Did you?"

"No!" she said. "I told you the truth at the club."

"Okay, then," I said, "you must be pretty tired. Can I see you home?"

"This is gonna sound odd," she said, "but I'm hungry. How about breakfast?"

"Let me get a cab."

She said she lived on the east side, so we got a cab to take us to the Lexington Avenue Diner.

Over bacon and eggs we reviewed the facts again.

"I'm a songwriter, I was looking for representation. I called Mr. Tomlin and he said he'd see me if I met him at CBGB."

"So you had never seen him before?"

"No, last night was the first time."

"How did you know him?"

"He told me what he looked like," she said. "You know, the whole Peepers thing."

I studied her while she ate. I wondered if she always did it so voraciously, or if this was a one-time thing? I guessed her age at thirty or so, but at the moment she could have been a tired and bedraggled thirty-five. A good night's sleep and the lines in her face might disappear.

"Then what?"

"He wanted to listen to the band, but I tried to talk to him at the same time and it didn't work. So then we decided to go into the restroom."

"The ladies' room."

"It was the first one we came to," she told me. "I checked it to see if it was empty, and then we went in, But before we started to talk, I had to, uh, use the facilities."

"So you went into a stall."

"Right," she said. "I tried talking to him from there, but he didn't answer. Then I heard something."

"What, exactly?"

"I don't know. Shuffling feet, grunting, sounded like...a struggle."

"And you didn't stick your head out to look right away?" I asked.

"Not right away," she said. "I was...you know...seated. So I pulled up my pants, opened the door and...there he was. I tried to help him, you know, pressure on the wound? I learned that from TV. But—" She shrugged. "It didn't do much good, I guess. Then you came in and saw me—like that."

She looked down at her plate, as if she was recalling the blood on her hands and it was ruining her appetite. But they had let her wash it off at the station, and now she went back to her eggs.

"Why don't you think I did it?" she asked me. "I mean, there I was alone in the bathroom with him, his blood all over me."

"The weapon," I said.

"What?"

"Where was the weapon, if you did it?" I asked. "Did you flush it?"

"A weapon?" she asked. "You mean, flush a knife down the toilet?"

"Exactly."

"Why don't the police think like that?"

"Because then," I said, "that would mean they'd be thinkin' like normal people."

7

"Why were you there?" she asked.

"He hired me," I said. "He thought somebody was following

him, and they were gonna hurt him."

"Jesus," she said, "he was right."

"I saw a man come out of the men's room," I told her.

"So?"

"I think he might've killed Tomlin, then went into the men's room to wash the mess off himself. I saw blood on his pant leg."

"Why didn't you grab him?"

"I tried, but he disappeared into the crowd."

"Why didn't you just shoot him?"

"I don't carry a gun."

"Why not?"

"Because I'm not Race Williams," I said.

"What?"

"He's a pulp character—Never mind," I said. "I didn't shoot him, and he got away. He was wearing grey pants, and a blue shirt. Did you see anyone dressed like that anywhere near Tomlin?"

"No," she said. "He was alone when I approached him, and then it was just him and me."

I paid the check and we went out to the street.

"I live a couple of blocks from here," she said.

She didn't say anything else. Was she inviting me up?

"Look, here's my card," I said. "I'm gonna be tryin' to find out who killed Tomlin. That means I'm also workin' to clear you."

"Do I need a lawyer?" she asked. "They didn't tell me."

"No, you don't need a lawyer," I said, "but give me a dollar."

She took it out of her purse and handed it to me.

"Now I'm workin' for you."

"Is that legal?"

"I work cheap," I said. "And if it comes to that, I'll see that you have a lawyer."

"Why?"

"To defend you."

"No, I mean, why are you doing this?" she asked. "It's not

because of my looks. You haven't even tried anything."

"Give me time," I said. "Look, I was supposed to look out for Tomlin. Instead, he gets killed on my watch. I've got to find out who did it, and why."

She leaned in and kissed my cheek.

"What's that for?"

"I don't know," she said. "Maybe to encourage you not to take too much time."

"I'll call you," I said. "Go home, wash the stink of the police station off you and get some rest."

"Where are you going?"

"The Brill Building."

8

I didn't actually go back to the Brill but to the building where Tomlin had his office. In the lobby I found the Tomlin Talent Agency on the directory, fourth floor. The door was open and I could hear a woman talking. When I entered I saw her sitting at a desk, speaking into the phone. She held up one finger at me.

"I don't know where he is, but I'm sure he'll be here soon," she said. "Yes, I'll have him call you. Yes, I swear!" She hung up, slamming the receiver down. "Wolfman Jack!" she said, and took a deep breath. "Can I help you?"

She was in her thirties, with large framed eyeglasses on a chain, and her brown hair rolled in a bun.

"If you're looking for Mr. Tomlin he's not here," she said. "Fact is, I don't know where the hell he is. He's supposed to be here."

"Are you his secretary?"

"I'm his temp," she said. "This is my second day on the job. Would you like me to give him a message?"

"No," I said, "Look, I met him last night at CBGB."

"Are you the songwriter? I thought it was a girl."

296

"She is a girl," I said. "She met him there, too, but he came to me yesterday and hired me. I'm a private investigator."

"A private eye? Why did he need you?"

"He thought somebody was followin' him."

"And was there?"

"Yes," I said. "Look, there's no easy way to say this...he was killed last night."

She stared at me, blinking rapidly. "What?"

"I'm sorry, but he was killed last night."

"How? Where?"

Somebody stabbed him in the...bathroom at the club."

She looked down at her desk, then back at me.

"What do I do now?" she asked.

I saw the file cabinets and wanted to get a look at them without her around.

"I guess you might as well go back to your agency and tell them you need another placing."

She nodded, slowly stood up, picked up her sweater from the back of her chair, and her purse. She took uncertain steps towards the door, then turned.

"I guess I don't need to file these canceled contracts, but...what about...locking this place up?"

"I'll take care of that," I promised. "You go ahead."

She nodded again, moved slowly toward the door, then suddenly sped up and almost ran out.

Once she was gone I went past her desk and into what had to have been Tomlin's office. Where her desk had been clean, his was a mess. There were file cabinets around the room, some with papers sticking out from partially open drawers, others with stacks of paper on top. I sat down at his desk and got started.

I was hoping that notes about recent appointments would be right on top, but his calendar was blank. I went through his desk drawers, found old contracts, some of which had a huge "X" drawn through them. It appeared that many of Tomlin's artists either canceled, or broke their contracts with him. But why would one of them kill him? It was more likely he was killed by somebody *he'd* dropped.

I went to the file cabinets, which were a mess. I couldn't go through all of them. but there was a bottom one labeled "canceled contracts."

I opened the drawer, found one folder filled with papers. I took it out and over to his desk, where I started to go through them. On the ninth one I came to, I thought I had found something. But then I went to the outer office and remembered the temp said she was filing canceled contracts. I sat at her desk and went through the documents and headshots, and *then* I thought I had something...

9

When she opened the door she smiled. I wasn't even sure it was the same woman. This one was very pretty, her hair hanging down past her shoulders, and no eyeglasses.

"What took you so long?" she asked. "I've been expecting you."

"Have you?"

"Come on in."

She smelled like she was fresh from the shower, wearing a dress that showed off her figure, and her legs. She was carrying a drink in her hand, and swaying slightly. All in all, she was presenting a different image from the one I had first seen.

"How are you doin'?" I asked.

"Oh, I'm fine," she said. "I showered and had a drink or two to loosen me up." She turned around quickly, making her skirt swirl to show her smooth thighs. "Do I seem looser?"

"You seem a lot looser," I said.

She was holding a highball tumbler, half-filled with brown liquor. She gripped it with four fingers and tapped it with a nail.

"Why didn't you try to come up here with me?" she asked.

"Don't I appeal to you?"

"You're very appealing, Beverly," I said, "but I didn't want to take advantage."

"Oh, you're a gentleman." She said it like it as a bad thing.

"Well, you may not think that for long?"

"Why is that?"

"Because," I said, "I think you had somethin' to do with killin' Tomlin. In fact, you may have done it yourself."

She stared at me, sipped her drink.

"That's silly," she said.

"Is it?"

"I had no time—you came rushing in—"

"I didn't actually rush in," I said. "I just sort of came in, and crashed the party."

"Party?"

"You, Tomlin, and your boyfriend," I said. "The guy I chased. See, I think you lured Tomlin into the ladies' room, and either you killed him or your boyfriend was waiting and did it."

She was not as outraged as I thought an innocent person would be.

"Why would I do that?"

I took a piece of paper from the folder I was holding.

"Because of this," I said. "It's the contract you had with him, which he canceled." I handed it to her, but she didn't bother looking at it, just crumpled it in her hand. "And here's Barry Hiller's contract, which was about to be filed in the canceled drawer." I showed her the folder and the headshot inside. "That's the guy I chased when he came out of the men's room. You gonna tell me you don't know 'im?"

"He's not my boyfriend," she said. "Sure, I've seen him in Tomlin's office. So what?"

"What I don't get," I went on, "is how you got Tomlin to meet you."

"He was a dweeb," she said. "I told him I'd blow him in the ladies' room if he met me and listened to what I had to say. See, when he canceled my contract he said it was because I had no originality. Well, I showed him some originality." She was no longer playing innocent.

"By killin' him? That's not original, Beverly. That's probably the most derivative thing you've ever done. I don't know why, but violence seems to be most people's go to reaction."

"He ruined my career!" she snapped. "That nerdy little dweeb!"

"He gave it a shot with you, didn't he?" I asked. "Did any other manager do that?"

"No," she said, "nobody would sign me."

"So you killed the only one who showed any faith in you?"

She glared at me.

"I didn't kill him," she said. "Barry did. I just got him into the—"

At that moment a door slammed open and the young man whose headshot was in the folder I was holding stepped out of the bedroom. He was also the guy I'd seen in the club with the blood on his pants.

"I told you not to talk to this guy!" he snapped. "Now you're tellin' him I did it?" He looked at me. "It was all her idea. I just helped her."

"Why?" I asked. "You love her that much?"

"Hell, no!" he said. "We ain't together. We just met in the office and found out we wuz both bein' dropped."

He was in his thirties, looked like he spent some time in the gym. His hands were empty, though. No weapon.

"Whose idea was the knife?" I asked.

"Hers!" he snapped. "We couldn't get a gun. She killed him and I was gonna help move the body, but then we realized we couldn't. Not in that crowded club. So I got out of there and she was just gonna play innocent, sayin' she found him like that."

"Barry, shut up!" she ordered.

"Why? He knows we did it," he argued, then looked at me. "You shoulda seen her dip her hands in his blood. She loved it!"

"Well, he knows now!" she yelled back. "Now we have to kill him, too."

"See?" I said. "Violence is the first—"

"Shut up, shut up!" she shouted. "What else was I supposed to do?"

"How about tryin' to write somethin' original?"

"That's what I said," Barry argued. "But she said no, we hadda kill 'im. She got me all...riled up."

She turned and tossed the remainder of her drink into his face.

"Go in the kitchen and get a knife!" she shouted.

"You go get a knife!" he shouted back. "I ain't killin' nobody else for you."

"Nobody's killin' anybody," I said and walked to the door and opened it. Out in the hall were Detectives Weston and Leland. "Did you hear all that?"

"We did." Weston waved and two uniformed cops came into the room. "Cuff 'em," Weston said.

Beverly and Barry were still shouting at each other as the cops led them out.

"How'd you figure it was her?" Leland asked.

I picked up the crumpled contract page from the floor, smoothed it out and handed it to him.

"I didn't *know*," I said, "but I couldn't figure why Tomlin would agree to meet somebody he'd already written off."

"So she promised him somethin' special?" Weston asked.

"I think he just wanted to hear the Magic Tramps and told her he'd be there. Then I found this—" I showed him Barry's folder and head shot "—and it linked them."

"You got lucky," Weston said, and left.

"Don't mind him," Leland said. "I told him you might figure it out."

"Thanks for the vote of confidence."

"What about your client?" Leland asked. "What was all that stuff about somebody in the shadows?"

"I don't know," I said. "Maybe Barry had been followin' him.

I guess you and your partner can find that out. You figured it was her, though, didn't you?"

He nodded. "We just couldn't prove it. We had you outside the bathroom, so it looked like she was the only one in there with him, but then you tossed that guy into the mix."

"He must've just made it from the ladies' room to the men's before I got there," I said.

"Well," Leland said. "We'll get the facts out of 'em now that they'll both probably turn on each other. My partner'll never say it," he said sticking his hand out, "but thanks."

"Yeah, no problem."

"Sorry you're not gonna get paid," he said, walking to the elevator.

"Yeah," I said, "me, too."

SJ is the highly decorated author of the Lydia Chin/Bill Smith series and Bill Crider first suggested she write a story featuring Lydia's mother for Duane Swierczynski's collection of "geezer noir," Damn Near Dead. Of course it's fitting that in this collection honoring Bill, we have another...

Chin Yong-Yun Finds a Kitten

SJ Rozan

I am not the kind of person who approaches stray animals. In my village in China, we did not have strays. Animals were too valuable not to be claimed. Each had an owner, though few stayed home: all of them, dogs, cats, chickens, ducks, pigs, rambled the lanes together. Any vagrant animal that wandered into the village unowned would immediately be taken in by someone. If a chicken or pig, it would eventually become dinner. If a dog, it would help herd the chickens or pigs. If a cat, it would chase the mice away from the chickens', pigs', or dogs' dinner.

In New York things are different. When we first came here many years ago, chickens would sometimes escape from the poultry market on Essex Street, to be found roosting in trees in Sara Roosevelt Park. But now that market is closed. In all the years I have lived here there have never been pigs. People with pets keep their dogs on leashes, their cats indoors. An animal on the street in New York without an owner is not cared for. It may be dirty, with diseases. Even the squirrels, which can be very funny to watch, are best kept at a distance.

However, I am also not a hard-hearted person. The chickens are gone from the park, but I feed the pigeons there. When the squirrels come for food I throw their peanuts across the walkway, but I don't chase them away. So when a tiny gray kitten mewed at me from the alley by the Madison Street pharmacy, I stopped.

Round, fluffy, its tail still short, it bounced on its toes as kittens do. It was adorable. Of course it was. All kittens are adorable. So are puppies. Babies, also, though some are more beautiful than others. I am fortunate that all of my grandchildren were beautiful babies. They are still beautiful as they grow.

Two of my grandchildren, the children of my oldest son, have recently been given a puppy. When I visit, the puppy is very friendly to me. My son has said he thinks the puppy is lonely during the day, when the adults are working, the children in school. I believe he thinks I am lonely, myself, because my daughter spends many hours each day in her detective work. Also, more often now than in the past, she spends the night away from our apartment. She tells me she's working, which I pretend to believe. She pretends to believe that I believe her. This saves face for us both. Of course I know she is with the White Baboon, her detective partner. In my village a mother would have locked a daughter in their home rather than permit an association she didn't approve of. However, such things are not done in America. Here I must allow her to live her own life.

I would rather she had not selected the White Baboon as a partner for that life, but if forced to it I would have to say she has not chosen entirely badly. If she insists on remaining in her dangerous profession it will be a comfort to me to know he is by her side. He is brave, he is steadfast. Three of my four sons like him. The fourth, my youngest, likes no one, so his opinion must be discounted.

Because my daughter is now away more, while I am getting older, all my children have suggested, in their various ways, that I should consider moving to Queens to live in the home of my oldest son. My oldest son has said that if I were to come live with his family in the apartment on the ground floor, the puppy would be very glad for the company. Possibly this is true, but, soft-hearted though I might be, I am not going to plan my living arrangements around the happiness of a dog.

However, the tiny gray kitten mewing in the pharmacy alley presented me with a problem. It could easily trot into the street as it explored its surroundings. Although Madison Street is not a highway, the drivers in New York are too busy looking out for jaywalking pedestrians to be wary of kittens. Or the kitten might eat some poisoned food left in the alley to control the rats. Or even if it just walked on the sidewalk, a person who did not like kittens might throw something at it.

The kitten mewed once more. Turning around, it took two bouncing steps into the alley, then turned to look at me with another mew. I decided to follow it into the alley. Perhaps it had a home. If so I would no longer have to think about it while I went about my day.

Halfway into the alley I was heartened to hear a voice calling from the back. "Yizhi!" the voice whispered. "Yizhi, where are you?"

I continued on to where the alley stopped, blocked by an extension to the building next door. The alley made a turn to the left, where it was hung overhead with washing, though the sun most likely never reached in this far. Smells of food cooking mingled with the aroma of what had been food on previous days. I was reminded of the years I spent with my husband in Hong Kong before we were able to come to America.

The whispering call came again. "Yizhi. Come, Yizhi. Here, Yizhi." The voice was issuing from a door, opened only two inches, where the alley turned left. I could see a young woman sitting on the floor inside the doorway.

"There is a kitten out here," I said. "Is it yours?"

"Shhh! Please!" she whispered. "I'm not allowed to talk to anyone. Do you have my kitten?"

"I don't have it. It's right over there."

The young woman stretched to try to see where I was pointing. The gray kitten was across the alley, pouncing on a scrap of paper.

"Can you give him to me, please?" The young woman stood up.

"Come get him. I don't want to have to pick him up. He might be dirty, with diseases."

"He's not dirty. He keeps himself very clean. His mother taught him before she left him in the alley alone. But I can't come out. I can't open the door. This is as far as it opens."

"Is it broken?"

"No. It's nailed. It's only to get some air. I'm not allowed to leave this room."

I peered through the gap at the young woman. She appeared to be perhaps twenty years old, very thin, her eyes sunken, her hair dull. "Are you ill?" I took a step back, wondering whether she, not the kitten, was the one with diseases.

She shook her head. With a sad smile she said, "No, Auntie. I'm in love."

I frowned. "I was in love with my late husband for many years. Being in love never caused me to get locked in a room. Also I never looked like a piece of straw."

"Did your mother approve of the man you loved?"

"Yes, she did." I narrowed my eyes at her. "Yours doesn't?"

"She doesn't. She doesn't like him at all."

"I see." I glanced across the alley. Little Yizhi was licking a paw. "Why not?"

"For two reasons. He's not Chinese. Also, he's a policeman."

I thought about this. "Is he a good policeman?"

"Yes, of course! But my mother's father was arrested by the police in China years ago, when my mother was a child. He was beaten. My grandmother lost her job. The whole family suffered. They escaped to America but she's never stopped hating the police."

"I see. So she wants you to give up your young man because he's a not-Chinese policeman. But you refuse. Now you are locked in this room until you come to your senses?"

"But I won't!"

"Is she feeding you?" In my village in China, hunger was sometimes used as a weapon to soften the resolve of a locked-in daughter.

She hung her head. "Only some rice. But I don't care!"

"Tell me, what's your name?"

"Lan Li."

"Who is your mother?"

"My mother is Lan Si-Pei. This is the storeroom of her shop."

I thought about the storefronts on Rutgers Street. "Your mother is the owner of Perfect Beauty?" When she nodded I said, "My name is Chin Yong-Yun. Please continue your story. I'm interested."

"My mother will be very angry if she finds me speaking with you."

"I'll say I just happened into the alley chasing a kitten. I'll tell her we weren't actually talking." This was very close to the truth, although according to my daughter a small fib in the course of detective work is not, in any case, considered wrong. Not that anyone had asked me to do any detecting, but I am a person who can tell when she is needed. "The kitten is lying down just now," I added, in case Lan Li had any worries about Yizhi who, finished with his bath, was curled up on a bag of trash. "So please. Continue. You were telling me your mother wants you to give up your young man."

"Worse than that, Auntie. She went to a matchmaker. The matchmaker found a man my mother approves of. But I won't marry him. I won't, no matter how long she keeps me in here!"

"I understand." That was true. I did understand. I have had, myself, an unsatisfactory experience with a matchmaker.

My youngest son, he who likes no one, is a concern to me. He's thirty now, with excellent prospects, a corporate lawyer. My daughter says he's boring, but I think she puts too heavy an emphasis on the value of excitement. Many young women would be pleased to be the wife of a handsome, reliable young man with a good salary. However, my son works very hard at his corporation. He has no time to look for a wife. I've tried to help, introducing him to some lovely girls. Finally, like Lan Li's mother, I even went to the expense of consulting a matchmaker, Min Bi-Ren of East Broadway. This was before I realized that in America that is not a good idea. In China, where villages are isolated one from the other, the matchmaker is a person who knows everyone in the district, who in which village is available, what their situation is. In America, though, everything is crowded together. Young people are much more likely to meet each other on their own. Therefore the matchmaker deals in what my daughter calls 'bargain basement material.' I'm not sure why she uses this phrase, as many of Chinatown's best merchants sell their wares out of basement shops where they do not give you a bargain. Nevertheless her meaning is clear. In America the matchmaker's clients are young people whose ability to find a mate on their own is limited. Thus all the young women the matchmaker suggested for my son were unacceptable to him after only one or two meetings. After the fourth young woman, an unlucky number, I requested my money be returned. Min Bi-Ren declined. She told me that my son was too particular.

We did not part on good terms.

"I see," I said again to Lan Li. "You don't like the young man the matchmaker found for you?"

"No! He's awful. Pompous. An importer of cheap plastic toys. He's not young, either."

"Lan Li, perhaps it's none of my business, but this is America. Mothers are not permitted to lock up their daughters here. It's against the law. I could call the police."

"No! Don't you see how awful that would be for my mother? She'd go to jail! Like what happened to her father. I can't do that to her."

"That's admirably filial of you. But she already has you in jail."

Lan Li hung her head but said only, "I can't do that."

"Tell me, then," I said, "why hasn't your young man come

to rescue you? Your policeman?"

"He doesn't know. He's a cybercrime expert. The Paris police asked the New York police to send him there for a month to train them. My mother waited until he was gone."

Although I don't know what cybercrime is, clearly it's something significant. I shook my head in wonder that a man so important as to get sent to Paris for a month was unacceptable as a son-in-law, but said only, "Doesn't he wonder why you haven't contacted him?"

"Probably. I'm afraid he'll think I don't love him anymore. Auntie, is it possible…"

I sighed. I took out my cell phone.

"Oh, thank you!" She did that dance with her thumbs on the phone that my daughter can do, though I think my daughter does it faster. Handing the phone back to me, she said again, "Thank you. I texted him that I lost my phone. I said I was borrowing a friend's. I said I loved him."

"Why did you do that? Instead of telling him the truth?"

"Because if he knew, he would do what you were going to do. He'd have my mother arrested. But she's my mother. Also, when I marry him, I want them to reconcile. He'd never forgive her if he knew she'd done this to me."

"When will he return?"

"In two more weeks."

"What do you intend to do then?"

She shook her head helplessly. "I don't know. If he sees me here, like this…"

I thought. "All right," I said. "Tell me the name of the matchmaker your mother consulted."

Lan Li looked confused, but said, "She's Min Bi-Ren."

As I thought. "Pah. I know her. I found her services highly unsatisfactory. All right, Lan Li. I would advise you to have patience. I believe your circumstances will change soon."

"I don't think so," Lan Li said, sounding despondent. "But thank you for your wishes. Also for the use of your phone.

Auntie? Before you go could you please bring me Yizhi?"

I looked with distaste at the kitten on his garbage bag.

"He's the only friend I have, locked in here," Lan Li said. "He has no other friends, either."

I sighed once more. I made my way across the alley to pick the kitten up. He did not object. When I held him to my chest so he would not fall, I felt him start to purr. The sensation was surprisingly pleasant. At the door I handed him to Lan Li through the gap. "Lan Li," I said. "If the matchmaker finds you another new young man, I want you to promise to meet him."

"I—"

"You must promise. After the meeting, you must return to your jail as the matchmaker will insist. Also, tell me the name of your policeman."

"He is Nico Amario. But Auntie, what—"

"Lan Li! I have no time for foolishness. Make this promise."

The young woman shrugged. "It will be a waste of the young man's time."

"I think," I said, "that he won't mind."

I walked back up the alley, hearing the door click shut. I went around the corner to Rutgers Street. I hadn't intended to buy a new lipstick today, but perhaps it was time to consider it.

A bell tinkled as I opened the door of Perfect Beauty. Bright fluorescent lights shone on shelves full of cosmetics, perfumes, shampoos, creams, combs, brushes—any product meant to improve the attractiveness of the female person. I made a note to suggest to my daughter that she might find the shop interesting.

On the short walk I had wondered how I would identify Lan Si-Pei, but it turned out to be simple. Perfect Beauty had three saleswomen. Two were young, probably no older than Lan Li. They had the beaten-down appearance of employees whose employer is quick to blame others. The third woman was not only twice their age, but also sour-faced, clearly a woman wrestling with difficulties on her mind. In fact, she appeared so cross that the customers were gravitating to the younger women. This was convenient for me.

"Hello," I said to the older woman. "You are the owner, Lan Si-Pei? Can you recommend a good color of lipstick for me? I asked my daughter to accompany me here to help me choose but she refused."

"Pah, daughters!" the sour woman said. She scrutinized my face. "For your skin tone, I'd suggest these." She took three different sticks from a box behind the counter.

"Thank you," I said, examining them. "Do you have a daughter? If so I hope she's more filial than mine." As I have said, a small fib in the middle of a case is permissible.

Lan Si-Pei snorted. "My daughter, filial? She's head-strong. Self-centered. She has no consideration. Try this one, it's more delicate."

I wiped the first lipstick off my mouth with a tissue, took the Q-tip she offered me, painted on another. "Then you have my sympathy. Those certainly are bad traits in a daughter. Although I have an unmarried son who enjoys the company of headstrong young women." Another small fib, although if my youngest son allowed himself time to enjoy anyone's company, if might turn out to be true, I supposed. "He's a very busy corporate lawyer. I have asked him what good does his excellent salary do him, his beautiful apartment, if he has no one to share them with? But he tells me he's too busy to look for a wife."

Lan Si-Pei's eyes lit up. I pretended not to see, concentrating on the mirror.

"Have you consulted a matchmaker?" she asked me.

"Oh, yes. Min Bi-Ren. But he didn't like the young women she suggested. I think they were too meek for him. Also, too thin. He likes women who are healthy, well-fed."

"Ah!" Lan Si-Pei's heavily-pencilled eyebrows went up. She said, "Min Bi-Ren. I know her. By reputation, of course."

"Of course."

"If you like," she said in an offhand way, "I could talk to the

311

matchmaker. To see if she might consider my daughter a prospect for your son."

"Oh," I said. "An interesting thought. But why not let the young people themselves meet to decide?"

"The situation is...delicate."

I suppressed a snort. Delicate. In other words, if Lan Li were let out of her jail without proper supervision, she might simply run away to her policeman. I kept up my pretense, however. In detecting work it is important to be able to play a part.

"Of course," I said. "The matchmaker must consider the suitability of our families for one another. I approve of your caution, Lan Si-Pei. My name is Chin Yong-Yun. My son is Chin Tien-Hua. I'll hope for a call from the matchmaker."

"I'll contact her immediately. Now, Yong-Yun, which of these lipsticks do you like?"

I shook my head. "None of them seems right to me. Thank you, Si-Pei. Goodbye."

From the sidewalk I called my youngest son.

"Ma! What's wrong?"

"Nothing's wrong, Tien-Hua. I need your help."

"Can it wait? I'm at work."

"When are you not at work? This is also work. It's about a detecting case."

His voice grew suspicious. "Ling Wan-Ju never asked for my help in her life."

"This is not your sister's case. It's mine."

"Oh, no, Ma. Are you—"

"Min Bi-Ran will contact me soon about a young woman by the name of Lan Li."

"That matchmaker? Are you serious? No. Ma, no. I'm not—"

"Tien-Hua, try not to get so excited. I told you, this is a case. Lan Li isn't a match for you, though the matchmaker doesn't know that. The young woman already has a young man. Your part in this will be to help them come together."

"What are you talking about?"

I explained my plan to my son.

"No. Absolutely not. No."

"Tien-Hua," I said, "I understand you're very busy. I am, also. If this case has to be handled some other way I might not have time to make salt-baked prawns for your visit on Sunday."

"Ma! That's extortion."

"Is it really?" I asked with interest. "I thought it was blackmail."

"There's a difference. In blackmail—"

"Never mind. You're much too busy at your corporation to explain legal details to your mother. Just, when the matchmaker calls me, I'll call you. Be prepared to do as I say. Thank you, Tien-Hua."

It was not too much later in the day when the red telephone in my kitchen rang. Quickly rinsing my hands so the telephone would not take on the smell of ginger, I answered it.

"Chin Yong-Yun, this is Min Bi-Ren. I hope you are well."

"As well as a woman can be whose youngest son is still unmarried," I replied rather coldly.

"Ah. Tien-Hua continues in his finicky ways?"

I spoke in a haughty manner. "My son understands he has an obligation not only to his own happiness but to that of his entire family. His 'finicky ways' are appreciated by those whose lives his future wife will share."

"I'm sure. Chin Yong-Yun, I may be able to help."

"Min Bi-Ren, I've wasted enough money on your unsatisfactory services. I'm not interested."

"No, no. This will cost you nothing. The young woman's mother is my client."

"Ah." I pretended to consider. "Who is the young woman? Who is her mother?"

The matchmaker proceeded to give me the details of the Lan family. As I listened I allowed her to believe she was persuading me. In the end I said to her, "All right. I'll tell my son. You may arrange for the young people to meet. I hope this won't be another waste of his time, Min Bi-Ren." I said that, knowing that it would.

I was required to listen to a number of tiresome complaints from my son centering on the time he did not have, with an aside for the dreary nature of the young women Min Bi-Ren had brought him in the past. I added steamed pork buns to Sunday's menu, finally promising to include egg tarts for dessert. After we hung up I wondered who had been extorting whom.

The first date, three days later, proceeded exactly as I envisioned. I wasn't there to witness the entire thing, of course, but I waited across the street from the restaurant where the young people were meeting so that I could see Lan Li arrive. The matchmaker held her arm in a firm grip. I was pleased, though not surprised, to observe that she looked more healthy than when we'd met. My son, after all, did not like girls who were too thin.

Later my son reported to me.

"That snooty matchmaker sat at the next table. I think she listened to every word we said."

"That wouldn't surprise me. Did you like Lan Li?"

"Actually, Ma, she's kind of nice. Skinny, but she has a good appetite. She's smart. Pretty feisty, too."

"Her mother calls her headstrong. I'm glad that you like her. Your next date will be five days from now."

Tien-Hua's objections, though they seemed to me not as full-hearted as before, could only be silenced by the promise of grouper steamed with spring onions for this week's Sunday dinner.

Once again on the evening of their meeting I hid myself to watch Lan Li, who, of course, arrived with the matchmaker. Now her cheeks were full, her hair glossy. Any young man would be pleased to be with her. Even my contrary son.

This date, according to my son, went very well also. The two discovered interests in common: some in music, some in films. I was surprised to hear that my son had any interests.

"Very good," I said. "Now you can ask her on your final date. You will bring her here to Sunday dinner. We'll have claypot rice."

I supposed, as I hung up the red kitchen telephone, that I had been unfair to my son in supposing he had no interests outside his work. He has always been very interested in food.

With a cup of tea, I took my cell phone to the living room sofa. After a few fortifying sips I called Min Bi-Ren. Making my voice sound grudging—in detecting work it is important to be able to act—I said, "My son is enjoying the company of Lan Li."

"So I understand." Min Bi-Ren sounded smug. I don't think she was acting.

"He's invited her to my home for Sunday dinner."

"Has he really?"

"Yes, he has. I'll be glad to welcome her. However, this is a very small apartment. I shall be their chaperone. Your company will not be required."

"I see." I believed I heard Min Bi-Ren suck her breath between her teeth. It was not an attractive sound. "I'll have to ask Lan Li's mother how she feels about that."

"I'm sure she'll have no objection. Have a pleasant day."

I sipped more tea. My next task would be to compose a text message. This was bound to take me quite some time, as my thumbs cannot dance. Also, it had to be in English. My English is not as bad as my children think. However, as it is not a language I often use for writing, I admit to being occasionally unsure of my spelling.

Apparently, however, I made my meaning clear. The reply, coming a few hours later—the delay can be accounted for by the difference of time zones—accepted my invitation to Sunday dinner. "I'll be jetlagged," it warned, "because I'm just getting back the day before," which of course I knew. "But I can't wait to see Li! I wish she'd gotten a new phone so I wouldn't have to bother you. But thank you so much. See you Sunday."

On Sunday, after a leisurely breakfast, I put up the rice to soak. I chopped the Chinese sausage into a bowl with the pork belly. Fortunately I own enough individual casserole dishes that each person would be able to have his, or her, own. That's the way my husband always served his claypot rice. I have never seen a reason to do things differently.

At exactly three p.m. a knock came on the door. I opened it to find, as I expected, my son. He is always very punctual. With him was Lan Li, who looked quite healthy. She stopped on my doorstep, her eyes wide.

"Chin Yong-Yun!" she said. "I didn't expect—are you—"

"Come in," I said. "Please remove your shoes. This is my home. Tien-Hua is my son."

"I—" she said again, hopping around as she took her shoes off.

"Come, sit here." I led her to my husband's chair. "How is Yizhi?"

"Yizhi? Yizhi's fine. He's adorable. Why didn't you tell me—or you?" She turned to my son.

"I—tell you what?" Tien-Hua was clearly confused.

"Here are some seaweed crackers," I said. "Dinner is all ready, we'll sit down to it soon. We're just waiting for—ah, here is our other guest." The buzzer downstairs had rung. I pressed it, then waited at the door. The footsteps of a large man in a hurry came bounding up the four flights.

"Hello," he said as he reached the landing. "Are you Chin Yong-Yun? I'm—"

"NICO!" Lan Li shouted, leaping from her chair. The young man picked her up, swinging her around before I had time to tell him to remove his shoes.

Dinner, when we finally sat down to it, was lovely. The meal was somewhat delayed, though, because at my suggestion Lan Li took Nico Amario into my son's former room, now my sewing room, for a private talk.

"Ma?" Tien-Hua said when they'd disappeared. "What's going on?"

"I told you Li already had a young man."

"That's him?" I thought I heard a wistful note in my son's voice.

"Yes. They've been having some trouble getting together. He has been away. Also, her mother doesn't like him. I decided I would help."

"You took a daughter's side against her mother?" Tien-Hua's eyes were wide with amazement.

"I prefer to think I took the side of love. Now come, Tien-Hua, tell me about your work at your corporation."

My son began a lengthy discourse upon something called an IPO, which I pretended to be interested in—as I said, acting is an important skill—until Lan Li emerged from the sewing room hand-in-hand with Nico Amario. Both appeared glowing.

"We're getting married as soon as we leave here," Li said. "Nico has a cousin upstate who's a judge. We'll go right there. Once we're married my mother will have to accept him."

"I'll wear her down," Nico said. "I'll be unbearably nice to her. She won't be able to resist me."

I met the eyes of Lan Li. She shook her head slightly. So she had not told her young man about being locked in the storeroom.

"Well," I said. "That sounds like an excellent plan. You will, of course, call Lan Si-Pei so she won't worry? Once you are far enough away?"

They looked at each other. "All right," said Li.

"Now. May I suggest we eat before you leave for upstate?" I don't know where upstate is but I believe it's rather far. "Fortunately claypot rice only improves as it waits."

We ate. The three young people conversed in English as I watched, at times unable to follow their rapid conversation but content nevertheless. The entire case, as far as I was concerned, had ended quite satisfactorily.

My son had discovered that not all young women I suggest to him are to be avoided. This in itself is a valuable outcome.

Min Bi-Ren the matchmaker had, to use another of my

daughter's phrases, "ended up with egg on her face." As is usually the case when my daughter says this, there is no egg involved anywhere, but again, the meaning is clear. Min had failed in a way that would be quite embarrassing to her. While I am not the type of person who likes to see another person embarrassed, Min had brought this situation on herself.

Lan Li was now together again with her young man, who still did not know how pitiless his soon-to-be mother-in-law could be. I had no doubt his charm would win Lan Si-Pei over eventually, though possibly that would not happen until the young people started to have babies, which, given the attractiveness of the couple, were sure to be adorable.

I was thinking these pleasant thoughts while we ate the last of the red bean dessert soup. Suddenly Lan Li spoke up. "Yizhi! What will happen to Yizhi? Oh, Chin Yong-Yun, could you—? Do you think—?"

I sighed.

The next morning, leaving my red kitchen telephone to record all the angry messages from Min Bi-Ren, I went to the alley next to the Madison Street Pharmacy. Walking up it, I called, "Yizhi, where are you, Yizhi? Come, Yizhi."

Halfway up the alley the gray kitten bounded out from between two garbage pails and landed at my feet. He mewed. When I picked him up he purred pleasantly. I settled him against me for the walk to the veterinarian, to make sure he had no diseases. After that, I took him home. It would be nice to have his company in the apartment.

In addition to being a filmmaker and scenarist, Eryk has written and produced a fascinating True Crime podcast about the unsolved Valentine's Day killings of a North Carolina couple. His short stories and novels feature a wild and distinctive voice and the story here is no exception. Kurt wants to become a writer and here he is, living the dream...

Los Hermanos Mil Sinto Y El Pinche Mundo

Eryk Pruitt

The flea market, like an old-world bazaar. A patriotic explosion of green, red, and white. Alive with the fricative, cacophonous calls back and forth from the county's many Mexicans manning card tables and beds of pickup trucks and fruit crates, forming aisle after aisle of anything imaginable.

Seriously: *anything.*

Pet lizards, pet snakes, pet hermit crabs. Pet rabbits, or rabbits to eat. Speaking of eating, there were tanks of tilapia, flounder, Florida lobster (the ones without claws), shrimp, and some sea creature which Kurt could not identify. There was fruit both in season and out, leaving him to scratch his head and wonder how the hell someone got their hands on a watermelon in Virginia that late in the year. Tomatoes. Onions. Every leafy green in the book.

Knives. Swords. Guns. Paintings of guns. Paintings of Jesus, Mother Mary, and all twelve disciples, sitting down to dinner. Of Bob Marley, Che Guevera, and Pancho Villa. Velvet Elvis. Velvet bullfighters. Velvet *Planet of the Apes.*

Shoes, lots of shoes. From knockoffs of the top name brands to knockoffs of the shitty generic ones. Everything off-brand. Off-brand toaster pastries. Off-brand boxes of macaroni and cheese. Off-brand spaghetti rings with off-brand meatballs. Off-brand reproductions of retro furniture. Reproductions of antique furniture. Repros of mammy dolls, lawn jockeys, and little dark men running from gators. Campaign buttons: *I Like Ike. Southern Farmers Support Bush/Cheney. Vote Yes for Proposition Nine.*

New tires. Used tires. Sunglasses, any shape, any size, any color. Lanyards. Clothes, both old and new. Commemorative ashtrays. Electronics. Matchbooks. Coins. Bootleg CDs, DVDs, and books.

Lots and lots of books.

Like the ones which spun in the metal rack. Kurt Reynolds, the only white guy for aisles and aisles of dollar store detritus, plucked a book from the rack and ran a finger along the fantastic Technicolor cover. Giant red letters: *"EL CHAPO Y LOS VAMPIROS!"* Three ghouls in nun's habits menaced a stone-faced, mustachioed Latin man in a trucker cap. The book was no bigger than the size of his hand, wrist to fingers. Two dollars.

The lady who ran the booth could have been a ghoul herself. Her face, gaunt and stretched tight against her skull and the three teeth in her head. She looked like she was straight from the countryside, but a countryside far, far away. She pointed a trembling, crooked finger to the book and smiled.

"You know El Chapo?" she asked.

"Yeah, I know El Chapo," said Kurt. He jerked a thumb over his shoulder to Braulio and Frankie, the two Mexicans who'd driven him to the flea market. They stood behind him in the middle of yonder aisle, reenacting the final scene from *Scarface* before a framed, velvet portrait of Al Pacino. "Those guys there told me all about El Chapo. He's their favorite. They like the crime books. The *microsuspensos*. They've got them all. You know, *El Chapo Y El Milenio Cartel* or the one where El Chapo defeats the ragtag band of American expat mercenaries.

What was that one called again? Oh yeah...*El Chapo Y Los Picaros.* Or the one where El Chapo kills an entire squad of dirty CIA agents with a helicopter in Honduras. Cheesy? Sure. The writing style is pure pulp, but it's efficient. Me?" He slapped the cover with the back of his hand. "This is more my speed. I like horror and sci-fi. Those two over there eat it up whenever El Chapo gets a new girl or takes down a nosy *federale,* but I've seen all that before with 007. You know...James Bond? This right here is new. An effortless blending of genre. A cartel boss taking on vampires or aliens or zombies. *El Chapo Y Los Werewolves.* They could never get away with that up here in, you know, American publishing. It's new. It's innovative. Bold."

The old woman showed all three of her teeth.

"Si," she told him. "El Chapo."

Kurt flipped out his billfold and shook loose two crinkled one-dollar bills. He laid them flat on the old lady's card table and held up the book.

"Nobody ever remembers the name of the guy who writes the El Chapo books," he said. "If they even list it anymore, it's in small print on the back cover. Right here: Gustavo de la Paz. What do you want to bet that's not even a real guy? Or maybe he used to be, but I'll bet you all the tamales you can eat that he doesn't even exist. There's probably some poor asshole chained to a wall in a Mexican dungeon, forced to write these things with a gun to his head."

Said the old woman, "El Chapo."

Kurt's debate in favor of further conversation was cut short from a sharp whistle Braulio blew through two fingers to his lips.

"*Guero!*" he hollered across the flea market.

Unlike his brother, there was nothing graceful about Braulio. He moved like a bull. A rhinoceros. He didn't walk; he *charged.* And when he *charged,* he left behind him a wake of broken everything. Broken CDs, chairs, mirrors, cutlery, pens.

Braulio was especially hard on pens. If he needed to write anything—and God forbid he carried his own pen, so he forever borrowed them—he would press down the nib hard on paper and, unable to comprehend why it didn't write as smooth as he'd seen others do, would begin a series of lethal jabs. Then, when unable to take it any longer, would snap the pen in half, or disassemble it, or just plain jettison it to the distance.

Kurt had lost hours contemplating Braulio's stupidity. Those dark, horrible eyes, flat like computer screens. Always in a constant state of incomprehension. Laughter most mean. The man often communicated with his brother in a series of whistles, clicks, and grunts. At times, when Braulio found something new and alien to him, Kurt was fascinated watching him suss out its meaning or use or overall purpose and, falling short of that, would bend said item across his knee to crack it in two.

If anything horrified Kurt more than Braulio's simplicity, it was the cunning of his little brother Francisco. His everything wallowed in deceptiveness, but most so was his smile. That twisted sneer anarchised the otherwise smooth features of his face. Eyes a little more subdued, skin a little brighter, almost to jaundice. Were it not for the mustache, he could have been a child, and may still be, for Kurt could not tell whether the brothers were seventeen, of if they were thirty.

Earlier in the day, while filling up the shitty blue minivan which the boys drove, Francisco had splashed gasoline on Kurt's shoes. He apologized in Spanish, sure, but he also smiled and that smile warned Kurt the flame might soon follow.

So Kurt had no idea which the folks in the flea market should fear more when they found their target. After nearly an hour, they set sights on two fresh-faced Latino boys, both wearing electric green bandannas as do-rags. Neither boy older than high school, both softer, more acclimated to their rural Virginia surroundings. Not so much field workers, or the sons of field workers, but perhaps the grandchildren of field workers. They dressed street, but *clean* street. Their shirts and baggy pants creased sharp enough to cut a man and Kurt thought of them as the funhouse mirrors of Frankie and Braulio.

Braulio spit another high whistle, this time at his brother. Frankie nodded. Braulio went at the two boys fast and hard, a silverback approach awash in low beats and chuffs, tossing aside children and metal folding chairs...tables, anything which came between he and his target, yet still no other vendor— perhaps still reeling from horrors found atop railcars speeding through countryside unforgiving or at the hands of a ruthless coyote—dared look up from their business, as if they'd prefer not to get involved.

The two boys in Day-Glo bandannas were not so fortunate. No sooner had it started, than it had ended, and Braulio filled the frame of both their faces at the same time, despite standing a good three or so inches shorter than the both of them. Neither boy moved. For all their naivete, they still had survival instinct and that told them not to flinch, not to blink, not to fucking move. Keep their collective shit together, it said, while Braulio cocked back his bulging head and stared at them down the length of his nose.

Behind him came Francisco.

"*Que andas, pendejo?*" Francisco hissed as he neared the two boys, then rattled off an explosion of Spanish, too fast for Kurt's rudimentary understanding and perhaps too fast for the boys. Francisco caught wind of their confusion and backed away, the question mark on his face blossoming ever brighter. He asked them, "You no speak Spanish?"

The taller of the two pantomimed an inch between his thumb and forefinger. "*Pequito*," he answered. "I speak it to *mi abuela*."

Braulio clicked his tongue against the roof of his mouth. A disapproving sound—*TCHK*. He muttered something to Francisco, but didn't look away from the two boys. When finally he addressed the two boys, Braulio's Spanish came even quicker. Brusque. The shorter of the two *cholos*, just as lost as Kurt, while his *amigo* used his every inch's worth. Braulio prattled machine-gun fast, as if some passive-aggressive display of supremacy of the mother tongue might shame the boy for losing track of his ancestry. The shorter one caught sight of Kurt and, after putting two and two together, spoke up at him.

"Hey," he hollered over, "why don't you tell these two ass-holes here we don't know nothing about selling no cocaine?"

"I would," Kurt hollered back, "except I don't speak any Spanish either."

For some reason, this gave the taller of the two something resembling confidence. He puffed out his chest and slipped on a pair of knockoff Ray-Bans. He snapped out his arms like he was trying to pop out the creases of his shirt sleeves.

"If none of us can communicate," he, in all his wisdom, said, "then I don't get the point of continuing this conversation."

"You ain't never heard of the Mil Sinto brothers?" Kurt asked them.

"The who?"

"This here is Francisco Mil Sinto. Which makes that one Braulio Mil Sinto."

The two brothers postured appropriately.

Neither *cholo* appeared impressed.

"So what?" one of them asked.

"So you ever heard about the Shootout on I-85?"

The look they exchanged said they hadn't.

"That diner, where all those people got killed?"

"No..."

Kurt shrugged. "You know they never caught the guys that did that."

"Did they really have something to do with it?"

"Yeah," said Kurt. "Sure."

Neither Braulio nor Francisco blinked. The taller of the two *cholos* removed his sunshades. The shorter one found something else to look at.

"If I was you," said Kurt, "I'd find a way to communicate with them. But more important..." Kurt folded the El Chapo paperback and slipped it into his back pocket. "I'd find a way to get them whatever they want."

* * *

Had they been in the Old West, the two brothers might have ridden into town atop a cloud of red dust. But they were not in the Old West, they were in Lawles County, Virginia, and neither did they ride horses, but instead, a blue minivan, much like one a housewife might employ to ferry her children from school to soccer games or to pizza night out with their friends. Only now, the minivan delivered cocaine.

Lots and lots of cocaine.

Behind the wheel: the devilish Francisco Mil Sinto. Don't be fooled by his babyface. Behind those soft features lie cunning and calculation. There were few people in this world he would not kill for so much as a sideways glance.

One of those people would be his brother, Braulio. For Braulio, the matter was brawn. Where Francisco displayed finesse, Braulio made no such claims.

Despite the differences in their approach, one thing remained the same: These two men were killers. Behind them lay a wake of death and destruction, from Jalisco to the Carolinas. Their calling card was bloodshed. Their siren call was the sound of gunfire. All across the hills of—

Kurt ripped the sheet of paper from the yellow tablet, crumpled it to a ball and threw it against the bathroom wall. It bounced without a sound and fell unsatisfactorily to the floor, where it would join the others.

What was he doing wrong?

Kurt rested his head against the bathtub and massaged his temples. He had lain in there for the better part of two hours, yet all he could produce was a waste of paper and ink.

"You're not writing *Gone With the Wind*," he muttered to himself. "What's your damn problem?"

This was supposed to be easy. How much consideration did he actually need in order to shit out a series of pulp novels about two ne'er-do-well Mexican cartel wannabes? What level of perfection would the prose actually require? Hell, he thought, half his good stuff would be lost in the translation to Spanish anyway, so why bother?

Why indeed?

He blamed the brothers. He'd been given little peace, barely a moment for his own thoughts. Their sing-song, back and forth banter was only half as unsettling as their long periods of silence. At least whilst they jabbered, he could divine their demeanor. Not so much what they were saying, but whether or not their mood on him had turned. *Buyer's remorse?* Did they want their money back? Would his body soon be found in a shallow wooded grave?

Would it be found at all?

Kurt tapped his pen against his own forehead a couple of times before finally saying *fuck it* and throwing in the towel for the night. He climbed out of the bathtub, kicked aside the scattered fruits of his labor and mouthed a silent prayer to himself before opening the bathroom door to step into the motel room.

What he found there eased his angst none the slightest.

Braulio sat on one of the rumpled twin beds. Beside him lay a dog-eared copy of *El Chapo Y Los Extraterrestres*. Twin lines of powdered cocaine stretched across the glossy cover art portraying El Chapo rescuing a Mexican village from alien invaders. Between them rested a rusted razor blade and a rolled-up dollar bill. There were several other Franklins and Jacksons and Hamiltons scattered across the bed spread. And in his lap, positioned as a substitute for his cock, Braulio held with both hands the largest automatic rifle Kurt had yet to lay eyes upon.

"What the fuck is that?" he asked them.

This was a genuine question, for he had no idea was it an AK-47 or an Uzi? To him, it could have been any number of weapons from a rap video or gangster movie or first-person shooter game. What he did know was that it was dangerous AF, but that didn't stop Braulio from gesticulating with it, stroking it with both hands. Gyrating. He wore sunglasses and a smile from which a blunt emerged from clenched teeth. He grunted and bucked.

All of this was for the benefit of Francisco, who snapped pictures of his brother from every angle imaginable with his cell phone.

"What the fuck is that?" Kurt repeated.

Neither brother answered. They kept on keeping on.

"I'm serious," said Kurt. "Is that thing real?"

"*Es mi pi pi*," Braulio grunted.

Francisco let fly a high-pitched titter, then snapped another pic.

"Is that...Is that...Is that a fucking *gun?*"

Francisco rolled his eyes. "*Callete, pinche guero.*"

The two brothers: snapping pictures. Laughing. Preening and posing.

"Guys, nobody said anything about fucking *guns*." Kurt's voice rose an octave. He used the motel room wall for support. "Nowhere, at no time, did anybody say anything about *guns*."

"*Guero!*" hissed Braulio. "Shut up!"

Kurt searched the room, as if he might find counsel. Short of that, he laid eyes instead on the half-full bottle of cheap whiskey he'd nursed the night before. He snatched it by the neck and, foregoing the plastic cup which had earlier served him well, he chugged two swigs straight from the bottle. Fuck it: three.

Neither brother gave him any notice. Instead, Braulio sucked one of the lines off the El Chapo book into his nose while knocking the other into the bed sheets.

Once Kurt collected himself, he asked, "Guys, what are you going to do with those?"

Braulio glanced over top of the frames of his cheap sunglasses at Kurt. He laughed out the side of his mouth, then sucked his tooth in that disconcerting way of his. *TCHK!* Moving on, he ran a stubby finger across the front of the book's cover, then licked it clean.

"What do you think you are going to do with that thing?"

Kurt slammed another swallow from the bottle.

"Say hello to my little friend," cackled Francisco.

Kurt collapsed into the corner with the bottle. Too anguished to drink, he rested the whiskey against his forehead.

"You assholes are starting to believe your own press," he sighed. "You do realize you had nothing to do with that shootout on I-85, right? They don't know who did that, which made it easy to write that chapter. But it was *fiction*. It wasn't *real*."

Francisco cooled and cocked his head like a curious dog.

"Yes!" Kurt moaned. "*Fiction!* I no *sabe* how to say it in Spanish, but things either happen, or they didn't happen. *Fiction* is when the things didn't really happen, but you can write about it anyway. I can't help but think you guys manufacture some of these potentially dangerous situations just to make the stories more fantastic, but you don't have to. You see, you don't have to do half the shit you guys are doing because all I have to do is wri—"

Braulio could stand it no more. He snatched the El Chapo book from the bedspread and fired it across the room. It missed Kurt's head by an inch, then struck the wall in a puffy cloud of coke dust and a shower of pages after the cheap glue in the binding gave.

"You no speak, *guero*," Braulio thundered. "You no talk. You say *nada*."

Kurt, unable to close his mouth, stared at the remnants of the paperback scattered at his feet.

Growled Braulio, "You *escribe*."

Write.

Kurt understood.

This was the lot he had cast for himself.

He gathered up what pages he could, licked the nib of his ballpoint, and then returned to his spot in the bathtub.

* * *

Before the sun might purple the horizon, Kurt made his way by foot down the access road to a twenty-four-hour diner he'd spied upon an earlier mission to sell cocaine. He left the boys snoring and murmuring into each other's armpits on one of the motel's twin beds. Braulio, in his sleep, caressed the automatic rifle like a baby, but did not stir as Kurt quietly slipped shut the door.

After his third cup of piping hot coffee, the waitress delivered his breakfast. However, he could not touch it. His appetite, like his sleeping patterns, had gone straight to the toilet. He fiddled with the fork a while, pretended to take interest in the goings-on of the sleep-eyed populace in the diner's other booths, then finally pulled his cell phone from his pocket.

"Jesus Christ, Kurt?" asked the voice on the other end of the phone. "Do you know what time it is?"

"I figured since you New Yorkers are up and at 'em so early..." Kurt didn't bother finishing the sentence. Immediately, he felt like an idiot. He considered his upbringing, his current surroundings, and everything in-between. He saw himself as he feared others might see him.

Particularly his literary agent, a man he only ever heard referred to as *Warner*.

"Look buddy," said Warner, his voice strained by lack of sleep, "I've got a couple plates spinning at the moment, so if we can skip all the prologues and get right to the inciting incidents."

Kurt hopped to it. "Well, yes...of course. It's...Well, it's about that story I was pitching you last week. You know, about the..." Kurt glanced around the room at all the people who paid him absolutely no mind. "Look, there've been a few *developments*..."

The agent sighed. "What story?"

"I told you about those two guys I met? The ones from *down south...?*"

"Hey buddy, I don't have time to Scooby Doo this shit. If you don't feel you can nail this in a ten-second elevator pitch, may I suggest you practice it in front of the mirror a couple of times, then get back—"

"I'm talking about those two Mexican guys. The Mil Sinto brothers? The ones with the kilo?"

"I'm not following you."

Which came as no surprise to Kurt, who honestly felt Warner did very little listening to him at all. But still...

"Remember how I told you I took that job at a restaurant?" Kurt gave no time for an answer. "I never heard back from you on those three novels I've sent you and, well, I gotta pay the bills, so I scored a part-time gig at a seafood joint in town. There's two guys there. Brothers. One of them works the line and his brother washes dishes. Anyway, one of them—don't ask me how—came across some cocaine—a *lot* of cocaine—and, piece by piece, they've been selling it off."

"Wait a second." Warner sounded interested. "You're interviewing two guys in a cartel?"

"Not exactly..." Kurt didn't want to lose him, so he talked faster. "These brothers, they're regular guys, same as you and me. Well...me, anyway. They come *el norte* thinking they might make something of themselves, but ended up instead scrubbing pots and toilets in a restaurant. That's where we met."

"You're scrubbing toilets?"

"No. I'm a waiter." Kurt smiled at the woman refilling his coffee and waited for her to split again. "I mean, I *was* a waiter. These two brothers heard I was a writer—er, I mean, I *am* a writer, so they showed me this stack of pulp novels they've been collecting. El Chapo books."

"They're in with El Chapo, the drug lord?"

"Do you really not read any of the emails I send you?" Kurt shook it off and dove back in. "Not El Chapo, but a *personification* of El Chapo. This whole thing is fascinating, especially from a sociopolitical aspect. The fact that these boys, in their attempt to rise to the next station in life, even inside the cultural vortex of the United States of Am—"

"Hey, buddy..." Warner snapped his fingers on the other end of the line. "Stay with me, you hear? You're telling me you're writing pulp novels about El Chapo to impress a couple of dish-washers. Why is this something you can't put in an email?"

"They're not El Chapo books," said Kurt, "but more *like* El Chapo books. These books are cheap and easy to make. Me and the boys, we got to talking after a shift one night and, well, let's be honest: I can write one standing on my head. Would it be my best work? Not necessarily, but by the time whatever I wrote was translated to Spanish, it'd lose most of its luster anyway. I reckon I could write under a pen name, take their money, and self-publish on Amazon. I hate to say it, but it's a writing job and those have been in short supply as of late."

That was intended to be a dig, and Kurt regretted it the second it left his lips. However, any insult was missed by the agent. Warner instead cleared his throat.

"You said these guys are paying you to write the adventures of two former restaurant workers?" he asked.

"Two former restaurant workers with a *kilo*. These guys aim to make their mark in the drug world and I've positioned myself quite nicely to be there to write about it."

"How much?"

"How much what?"

"How much are they paying you?"

Kurt sipped his coffee. He felt his oats. He sat not in a diner booth, but rather in the catbird seat. Or so he thought.

"Like I told you," he said, "I quit the restaurant job. But that's not what's important. What's important is what we can do with these books after the two brothers get their copies. Best case scenario: I see these two clowns printing up a couple hundred copies to show off to their friends and family back home. There's nothing in writing regarding any rights, but I'm writing them with an eye for cinema, or better yet, serialized televi—"

"Hey, buddy...Don't tell me what is and isn't important. Last I checked, that was my job." Kurt felt the disdain firing from Warner's lips on all cylinders. "So jot this down if needed: what's important are the answers to the questions I ask you, and I asked you what these two dishwashers are paying you."

"The only reason you're interested is because you want fifteen percent off work you didn't bother to get me."

Warner took a deep breath before launching into him. "Of course I do," he said. "Why else do you think I would spend any time on the phone with some guy riding around with Mexican drug dealers in a minivan so he can write comic books for a cartel? I'll give you a hint: it's for the money. There's a reason I haven't gotten back to you about those three documents you turned in, buddy. That's because they sucked. Not just *Star Wars*-prequel sucked, but *Ishtar* sucked. It's taken me this long to break you the news because I couldn't find a positive spin to put on just how bad those books are, which is remarkable considering I have three interns working for me around the clock. I have to tell you though, this is quite a weight off my shoulders. I'm relieved to finally check this box. One less thing on my to-do list. Thank you, buddy. Thank you."

Kurt stared at his phone like he was afraid it might jump from his hand and run from the greasy booth.

"Maybe some of my metaphors were a touch obscure," he reasoned. "Did you not get the underlying message about identity politics and its effect on American drug culture?"

The sound from the other end of the phone could have been Warner choking to death, or it could have been him laughing. Kurt was not sure.

"Metaphors?" Warner asked. "I stretched the limits of my imagination trying to determine what it was you were trying to do, because—believe me—I was certain you were going for something. But now that you've explained what it was I can definitely confide to you that the mark was indeed missed. By. A. Mile. But bravo to you: another straight, white male with a hot take on identity politics for his science fiction novel. Bravo."

Kurt opened his mouth to explain that it wasn't *science fiction* per se, but rather something literary, beyond the genre, perhaps even a melding of genres, straddling something that had yet to be defined, but definitely within the limits of what past masters had claimed. But had he gotten that far, he would have said it to an empty line.

He sat there with the phone to his ear longer than necessary, lest any of the other patrons in the diner see that his agent, along with his dreams, had abandoned him.

He paid his tab and began the long walk back to the motel room.

Kurt had no idea what happened.

Long before the motel came into view over the rise, he saw the sweeping pools of red and blue emergency lights singing across the early breaking dawn.

His first thought: someone saw those two idiots flashing that gun, so they called the police.

His second thought broke him into a mad dash for the motel parking lot.

The small bumpkin county road didn't have much for entertainment at that hour, so nearly every citizen with a police scanner turned out to stand in the early morning's rusty glow. They stared slack-mouthed into the parking lot which had only recently filled with every emergency vehicle possible. Police cars. Fire trucks. Ambulances. Cops in uniforms unrolled crime scene tape across the lot. Two detectives in suits emerged from a shiny, silver Mustang and joined several other cops at the door where, only two hours earlier, Kurt had been living.

The motel room he had shared with Francisco and Braulio.

"What happened?" he asked a woman in a bathrobe and her hair in curlers.

"I'm not sure," she said. "I came as soon as I heard the sirens."

"Just another day," said a black man in a white T-shirt. "Police be shooting everybody."

"I heard it was a pickup truck full of Mexicans with machine guns," said the lady in hair curlers. "I heard they shot up the place and drove away."

"It wasn't a pickup truck," said a man in a trucker hat who stood next to her. "It was a four-by-four."

"Were you here?" asked another woman, this one hoisting a baby on each hip.

"No," said the man. "I heard the gunshots, though."

Kurt watched the motel doorway with growing anticipation. He waited for the uniformed police to escort the two young Mexican boys in handcuffs from the room. He envisioned the mischievous wink Francisco might offer, or the string of brutish curses from Braulio.

"They killed everybody in that room," said the man, as if reading Kurt's mind.

"Who were they?" asked another woman.

The black man shrugged. "Who knows? They're dead, which is all that matters now."

"Dead men tell no tales," said the dude in the trucker hat.

No, Kurt thought. *They sure don't.*

But most certainly, someone else would.

Kurt had no idea what happened in that motel parking lot, but that didn't keep him from guessing.

After all, he thought to himself, *it's fiction.*

BOOKS

On the following pages are a few
more great titles from the
Down & Out Books publishing family.

For a complete list of books and to
sign up for our newsletter,
go to DownAndOutBooks.com.

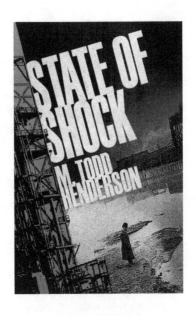

State of Shock
A Royce Johnson Thriller
M. Todd Henderson

Down & Out Books
February 2021
978-1-64396-151-4

The dean of a prominent law school is murdered. Royce Johnson can help. But he doesn't have an investigator's license, much less his old job with the FBI. He's fresh from prison due to his rogue investigation which toppled a Supreme Court justice.

Hero to some, a criminal to others, Johnson finds himself at the intersection of higher education, money, Chicago politics, and murder.

Suicide Squeeze
A Diamond Mystery
TG Wolff

Down & Out Books
February 2021
978-1-64396-177-4

Diamond is a former CIA agent turned widow whose future is sealed. In her darkest hour, the curve fate pitches is a blonde with a situation virtually identical to her own with one exception: Hanna's man might still be alive.

Putting her plans on hold, Diamond dives into the mystery, surfacing in a scavenger hunt for a secret known as Poe's Raven. It takes Diamond's flair for the impossible to capture this bird, only to discover what's in her hand has the potential to take terrorism to a chilling new level. And fate isn't done with Diamond, forcing her to put it all on the line or risk setting the caged bird free.

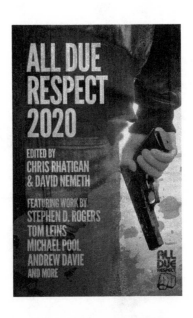

All Due Respect 2020
Chris Rhatigan & David Nemeth, editors

All Due Respect, an imprint of
Down & Out Books
November 2020
978-1-64396-165-1

Twelve short stories from the top writers in crime fiction today.

Featuring the work of Stephen D. Rogers, Tom Leins, Michael Pool, Andrew Davie, Sharon Diane King, Preston Lang, Jay Butkowski, Steven Berry, Craig Francis Coates, Bobby Mathews, Michael Penncavage, and BV Lawson.

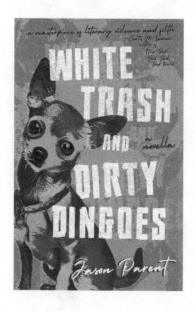

White Trash and Dirty Dingoes
Jason Parent

Shotgun Honey, an imprint of
Down & Out Books
July 2020
978-1-64396-101-9

Gordon thought he'd found the girl of his dreams. But women like Sarah are tough to hang on to.

When she causes the disappearance of a mob boss's priceless Chihuahua, she disappears herself, and the odds Gordon will see his lover again shrivel like nuts in a polar plunge.

With both money and love lost, he's going to have to kill some SOBs to get them back.

CPSIA information can be obtained
at www.ICGtesting.com
Printed in the USA
LVHW021427070621
689574LV00015B/659

9 781643 961781